Caffeine N

THE NO:

# CURIOSITY

~STEAM, SMOKE & MIRRORS~

*Volume 3*

# Colin Edmonds

Further insights and extracts from the secret
journals of
Professor Artemus More PhD (Cantab) FRS

Fiction aimed at the heart
and the head...

Published by Caffeine Nights Publishing 2019

Published in Great Britain by

Caffeine Nights Publishing

4 Eton Close

Walderslade

Chatham

Kent

ME5 9AT

caffeinenight.com

caffeinenightsbooks.com

British Library Cataloguing in Publication Data.

A CIP catalogue record for this book is available from the British Library

ISBN: 978-1-913200-06-0

Cover design by

Rebecacovers

Everything else by

Default, Luck and Accident

## COLIN EDMONDS

From the day he borrowed his first book from Kensal Rise Library, Colin Edmonds knew he wanted to be a novelist. But after selling his first jokes at the age of 16, a 40-year diversion as one of television's most prolific light entertainment scriptwriters began. During that time, in addition to working on hundreds of shows, Colin provided material for most of the U.K.'s leading entertainers including Paul Daniels, Sir Terry Wogan, Chris Tarrant, Des O'Connor and Roland Rat. He was also the principal writer for the award-winning comedian Bob Monkhouse and recently worked as Series Producer of the three-part documentary series 'Bob Monkhouse: The Million Joke Man'.

In 2015, Colin finally got around to achieving his original ambition with the publication of his first novel, a Steampunk comedy murder mystery.

'The Nostradamus Curiosity' is the third book in the 'Steam, Smoke & Mirrors' series.

Also by Colin Edmonds

~Steam, Smoke and Mirrors – Volume 1~
ISBN: 978-1-907565-94-6

~The Lazarus Curiosity~
Steam, Smoke and Mirrors – Volume 2
ISBN: 978-1-910720-83-7

~The Windsor Curiosity~
A Steam, Smoke and Mirrors short story eBook
And paperback novella
ISBN: 978-1973559-30-6

*"In his Steam, Smoke & Mirrors novels Colin Edmonds has created a truly magical world that I love escaping into just as I used to love escaping into the novels of HG Wells when I was at school. Fantastical plots are peopled by a cast of remarkable characters - Michael Magister and Phoebe Le Breton are now personal friends of mine! I become so engrossed in these stories that I feel I can step into the pages to inhabit the Victorian Steampunk Sci-Fi alternative past and future realities so brilliantly brought to life. Gothic darkness is tempered by wonderful humour too, making for the most entertaining, exciting, imaginative and enormously enjoyable ride. Film directors please take note!"*

**Ric Sanders - Fairport Convention**
*(Writing from a dimly lit low carbon footprint cottage somewhere in the Cotswolds!)*

*"It says something when you don't want to put a novel down, because you care so much about what happens next. Colin Edmonds' The Nostradamus Curiosity is precisely that. Conversely though, on at least 3 occasions, I got so wrapped up in the exposition that I did deliberately pause and stopped myself racing on - but only because I wanted to savour the moment. Edmonds' immaculate wordplay, end-of-the-pier puns, X-rated gags and double entendres had me laughing, worried and excited, in rapid rotation. You can't help but get engaged from the outset - which means, while we're waiting for Hollywood to pick up his canon of work and allow us to see what this new author's characters and locations look like, we're left in no doubt - thanks to the brilliantly-constructed plot, storyline and detailed narrative. It was such a joy to read, I can't wait for the next in the series: The Conan Doyle Curiosity.*

**John Orchard – musician, pianist and composer of the 'Steam, Smoke & Mirrors' theme tune.**

# ACKNOWLEDGEMENTS

The book you are now holding was made possible only by the generous help of many highly talented people.

My publisher Darren Laws, along with Natalie Laws at Caffeine Nights, is a paragon of patience whose support for the 'Steam, Smoke and Mirrors Project', right from the start, remains unstinting. But for his faith and enthusiasm, none of this would have happened. And I'd be just sitting here twiddling my thumbs.

Angela Ryder is a classics scholar who, with wry good humour, somehow fashions my garbled grammar and constant misuse of commas and colons into more acceptable English. How she also finds time to assist me *and* administer the SS&M website never fails to astonish. But I'm immensely grateful to be astonished.

Also, the website would be far less comprehensive were it not for the motoring and photographic skills of my old schoolfriend Stephen Smith, as we travel the country in search of the book's locations. His indulgent expression when we make frequent cemetery stops to visit the grave of anyone who appears in the story is a wonder to behold.

Mike Dixon, Ric Sanders and John Orchard are not only three of the country's most gifted musicians, they also form my much-trusted triumvirate of final draft readers, whose friendship and honesty make such a difference.

The diligence of my history researcher and genealogy expert Pat Smith, and the recycling creativity of Steampunk prop-making adviser Barry Down remains a constant source of joy.

Jacky and Charles Balchin in the U.K., and Sherrie and Jim Firn in the rest of the world, continue in the vanguard of SS&M flag-wavers, while the backing of Lorraine Surridge and Jaqueline Bennett at the Gerrards Cross Community Library, along with Susan Goode, is never less than heroic.

The help and advice of Gary Nicholls, photographer, author and creator of the internationally renowned Steampunk epic "The Imaginarium" always goes beyond the bounds of friendship, and the sage wisdom of Steampunk guru John Naylor is never anything but straight and true.

I will always be grateful to producers Geoff Posner and David Tyler, and the author Garry Bushell who, some years ago, were the first to spot the potential of Steam, Smoke & Mirrors – and now also to the actor Karl Jenkinson whose masterful performance this year on the audio version of "Steam, Smoke & Mirrors" drew out even more in the characters and narrative than any of us realised was there.

Once again, during my frequent hours of need, Joan Prichard and Abigail Monkhouse always made available their magnificent research libraries, and shared precious memories of my two much-missed mentors.

Also, Joe Pasquale's bond of kinship continues to know no bounds, especially during those late-into-the-night discussions concerning pace and plot, and the appreciation of horror film heroines.

Finally, it's those I cling to the closest who make the 'Steam, Smoke & Mirrors Project' worthwhile. The cajoling, often exasperated, guidance of Lucy and Mark keeps me apprised of the increasingly ephemeral worlds of technology and popular culture; while the serene, frequently gritted-teeth patience of Kathryn keeps me firmly grounded in reality. As I've said before, they know they have all my love.

And your sympathy.

P.S.

"It's only magic if you don't know how it's done."

Colin Edmonds, 2019

www.steamsmokeandmirrors.com

## 'THE NOSTRADAMUS CURIOSITY' PRIZE WINNER

In November 2018, at the end of my author question and answer presentation at Buckinghamshire's Chesham Library, I announced to everyone who was still awake that I was running a free Steam, Smoke & Mirrors prize raffle. Whichever audience member was the first to have their name drawn out of the top hat would appear as a character in 'The Nostradamus Curiosity'.

The winner was Nigel Donaldson.

Look out for him.

Dedicated to the memories of three special people

Adine Randall 1921 - 2017

Jack Longbon 1983 - 2018

Patricia Edwards 1934 - 2019

in whose company I wish I had spent more time

# ~INTRODUCTION~

I flatter myself in thinking you are not new to these strange curios, these unlikely, but I would say perfectly true memoirs and recollections. But, in truth, as it's more likely you're totally unfamiliar with my ramblings, I wonder if a brief recap might be in order.

I promise not to get too over-zealous in the retelling.

We have two heroes. Victorian Music Hall magicians. Michael Magister, the Industrial Age Illusionist, the handsome, stylish, charismatic conjuror, in his late twenties; and Phoebe Le Breton, the Queen of Steam and Goddess of the Aethyr, his stunning, feisty, upper-crust associate. She is twenty-one. Both had been retained as advisors to Scotland Yard's Special Branch to help them solve crimes which baffle science and defy logic.

And we left it where Michael had died. Yes, Michael Magister, one of the great up-and-coming acts in London and one of our leading characters – dead. And to make matters worse his death was horrible, agonising; from the corrosive effects of the foul chemical Brimstone Gas in Westminster Abbey. I know. Who would have thought? Being allowed to die in such a world-renowned place of worship! Someone 'up there' must have been snoozing on the job. I imagine, in Canterbury Cathedral, that's just the thought which went through the head of dear old Thomas Beckett. Before the knight's sword, that is.

Anyway, Michael gave his life saving the lives of the Prince of Wales, the Prime Minister Lord Salisbury, and other assorted officials who considered themselves dignitaries. Naturally, in these secretive Victorian times the attempted assassination of the heir to the throne and elimination of half the Government was deemed a temerity with which the citizens of the Empire – referred to within Establishment circles as 'The Unwashed' (note: not 'The Great Unwashed', just 'The Unwashed') – need never concern themselves. Everything associated with the horror was promptly swept under the thick-pile Whitehall Axminster: rescinded, redacted and in every other way removed from the anals of history. Yes, it is spelled 'annals', but listen, deep down you know I'm right…

In agonised desperation, Wicko, my splendidly surly dwarfish confederate, along with the aforementioned feisty, gorgeous Miss Phoebe Le Breton, flew Michael across West London to Regent's Park. There they entrusted his cooling corpse into the care of the enigmatic bank robber and outré bio-engineering genius, Dr Phunn and his beautiful, medical pioneering sister Wu Hu.

Are you following much of any of this? Maybe it's better I wind back the clock to where we left off last time…

***

The Metropolitan Theatre of Steam, Smoke and Mirrors had stood dark for three weeks. 'No Further Performances' announced both the sandwich boards and the straplines plastered diagonally across the framed posters front of house.

The Music Hall and ale house scuttlebutt across the metropolis and beyond was awash with rumour. Tales of Magister having been killed while rehearsing an illusion and the accident covered up. Many claimed to have heard screams as he was crushed, smashed, impaled, skewered or, ironically, gassed. Others speculated that the lovely Phoebe Le Breton had, in a lapsed moment, seduced her performance partner on the Guillotine of Deadly Beheading while in the throes of passion, inadvertently elbowing the release lever. Another less unlikely scenario had it that Michael was unmanned by a jealous husband with a smaller and rustier blade. Either suggestion would have met with Michael's approval.

Father Connor O'Connor had never been seen weeping quite so uncontrollably since he was barred for life from The Green Man. Illusionists and conjurors of all cities and stripes, even the great Maskelyńe and Cooke, enquired about purchasing our illusions and offering Phoebe various positions.

But it was agreed this had gone on long enough. The truth had to be admitted. So, an advertisement appeared in the Paddington Mercury, announcing that at seven-thirty this evening at The Metropolitan Theatre of Steam, Smoke and Mirrors, Phoebe, Goddess of the Aethyr and the Queen of Steam would appear on stage to make a heartfelt announcement. Special invitations were sent and, once again, the 'House Full – Of Course It Is!' signs stood outside the doors of the theatre.

Amid fanfare and applause, I cranked the Lift'n'Shift and in a billow of purple smoke, Wicko fired the spotlight, exploding its vivid beam onto the magnificent Phoebe. The shock and the sound stunned the crowd into applause. Somewhere out there in the darkness of the smoky auditorium sat Superintendent William Melville, Inspector Walter Pym and Sir Cumberland Sinclair, bemused and indignant. Father Connor O'Connor sat several rows in front breathing beery fumes over Sir Arthur Conan Doyle and Bram Stoker, with Pamela Colman Smith diplomatically sitting between them, and Sir Hugo de Bathe, who really did not want to be there but was forced to accompany his wife, Lillie Langtry.

As Phoebe took each slow, high-booted step to the centre of the stage, the audience settled. Her demeanour was deliberate and sombre. None of them had ever before seen Phoebe so modestly dressed. Entirely in black. They knew their worst fears were about to be confirmed.

At the centre of the stage the forlorn, lonely figure stopped and turned to face the silent crowd.

"Ladies and gentlemen. Since the beginning of this year, you, and so many others have graciously supported our performances of illusion and magical fantasy, here in this beautiful and very special theatre. Yours was support for which I and, of course, Michael will be eternally grateful. But tonight, it is my duty to inform you, officially, that the rumours you heard, the gossip you shared and the snippets you read, all the wild speculation of Michael Magister's death – have been true."

The audience gasped, some shouted "No!" and began that noisy thrum that you and I have come to know in our time together. Phoebe looked imperious and held up her hands requesting silence. The crowd obliged and the noise finally fell away.

"Almost a month ago, in the strangest of circumstances, while displaying his trademark courage, Michael died."

Phoebe glared at the hierarchy of the Special Branch and those in Government sitting next to them, while the audience gasped again. Women dabbed their eyes. Men removed their hats. Her fury continued.

"But let none of us ever dare to forget. I am Phoebe! Goddess of the Aethyr and the Queen of Steam! And with my power over the Aethyr, I commanded – no, demanded – his restoration to the finest and fullest of health. So now, ladies and gentlemen, I display my miraculous power! And invite you to welcome back to the stage – The Industrial Age Illusionist – Michael Magister!"

In a burst of golden smoke Phoebe was gone and there in her place stood ... well, you know who stood there. Not a mark on him. Affecting modesty and bathing in the applause.

As Phoebe tearfully said four days ago when, at last, Dr Phunn raised the lid of the sarcophagus: "Welcome back!"

***

With you now, I hope, more fully apprised, *finally* let's get on with it...

*"Time is the father of truth"*
*Giordano Bruno 1548 - 1600*
~ PART ONE~

Yes, Michael Magister, the Industrial Age Illusionist, had died. His face, hands and the best part of both his lungs, perished in a caustic cloud of yellow Brimstone, the merciless vapour confected by man purely, although purity had little to do with it, for the sole purpose of destroying his fellow man.

It was in the nave of Westminster Abbey, in an absurdly unexpected display of uncharacteristic courage – motivated perhaps by the chance of a knighthood – that Michael saved the craven lives of almost all the ruling elite, fine upstanding pillars of society who naturally could hardly wait to demonstrate their ingratitude!

Wicko, my brilliant dwarf confederate, was only too aware of the monumental sludge storm flying our way faster than a front carriage full of terrified cattle on the Coney Island roller coaster. You get what I mean. And the fault was mine.

You see, Michael's misguided exhortations to decency and goodness and thwarting such an international outrage was so earnestly convincing, I allowed us to expose ourselves. I let 'altruism' trump our survival watchword of 'all-false-ism'. Yes, I know it is not a proper expression, but needs must – and here is how we were exposed. The existence of 'The Ferrous Dodo', our compact, highly advanced dirigible, a secret we guarded so well and for so long, was revealed.

Despite the dusky gloom, hundreds of witnesses in those streets surrounding Parliament and Westminster Abbey shouted and screamed and tried to tame their rearing horses as they saw our silver-skinned airship sweep right around the clock tower of Big Ben, over the Thames before coming about and descending quickly to a shuddering turf-churning halt on the stretch of green beside the Abbey's north door. The wide-eyed throng then pointed and gasped as a stylish man and a stunning woman jumped down from a side door in the belly of the beast and sprinted across the lawn and, in a burst of distracting fire crackers disappeared through the north door of the great gothic Abbey.

The majority of the stunned crowd pulled horrified faces and maintained a cautious distance, alarmed by the malevolent moan which resonated from the idling propeller at the rear of the monster from the sky. Others, more fascinated and less sober, came for a closer look, daring to poke and scratch the metal skin, although their reward for such curiosity was a blue crackle of arm-jolting static. Then, from within the Abbey came a loud and unholy commotion. The north door was flung open and well-to-do men in morning suits spewed out.

"What's goin' on? Who are they?" wondered aloud a lady in the crowd.

Those around her watched as the toffs in question, with arms a-flailing, howled and fought and fell over one another in their panic for self-preservation.

Without a second thought everyone said, "Politicians."

The hardly great and not so good had barely bundled aboard carriages and made off, when the beautiful woman emerged in great haste from the Abbey followed by a sturdy soul bearing the body of another. The woman supervised the loading of the patient aboard the silver ovoid which promptly lifted from the ground and with an ear-piercing whine, dramatically swung its nose to the west and took to the sky.

Some in the crowd with interest or access to books, knew of powered balloons, dirigibles and airships having thrilled at the aeronautical adventures of 'Robur the Conqueror' aboard his Clipper of the Clouds in the best-seller penned by my old Frankish friend Jules Verne. But Jules' Clipper was a fantasy. This silver streak really existed. The people wouldn't be a problem. But the Government would be. And Wicko knew it.

As soon as he and Phoebe entrusted Dr Phunn and his sister with the care of Michael's corpse, Wicko was keen, no, desperate to get the Dodo back in the sky.

"We need to get underway," he told Phoebe in no uncertain terms. "Miss. Listen to me. We cannot stay here. We need to leave. Now!"

She saw his face. Stern and implacable.

"Then you must go without me." Phoebe's insistence was equally firm.

"No! We have to get to the theatre. You've got to alert the Professor while I conceal the Dodo! I don't have time to do the lot of it myself."

"Wicko, I am staying with Michael."

Dr Phunn could barely believe the fury and frustration on the faces of the dwarf and the woman as they squared up to one another.

"Thank you, Dr Smawl and Miss Le Breton. But I have a solution," announced the Oriental genius. "Mr Spindleshanks."

Spindle, Dr Phunn's painfully thin acrobat associate stepped forward and snapped a sharp bow.

"Thank you, to be kind enough to assist Dr Smawl?"

Manswick Smawl. That was our dwarf's given name, so naturally we called him Wicko.

"Chriiist." Spindle's spavined bodied stiffened. He was not best pleased.

"Spindle!" Dr Phunn's wondrously beautiful sister, Wu Hu hissed her disapproval.

Suitably chastened, the skeletal funambulist whispered: "As you desire, Doctor. And Miss Wu Hu." while bowing so deeply his slender frame resembled a large hairpin.

The urgent problem resolved, Wicko turned without looking at Phoebe and scurried as best he could with small legs, while Spindle somersaulted the short distance to the Dodo. His was a speedy but showy method of reaching a destination. If he'd had the time, Wicko would have smacked Spindle a purler with a spanner, but he had neither. Instead he clambered aboard and up into his Captain's seat, there at the business end of the Dodo's plush Flight Saloon. In a flurry of purpose Wicko fired up the Aethyr generator, turned this and yanked on that to close the access door, all while easing the Dodo from the moist grass of Regent's Park and up into the now dark sky. The diminutive aeronaut spun the helmswheel to the left and began issuing his orders.

"Right, Spindle, this is what needs to be done. Here, never mind any of that looking outside business. Listen to what I'm saying."

Spindle was naturally mesmerised by the panoramic view through the five Windowscreens: the silhouetted skyline ahead, the rows of yellow-dot lamp lights lining the roadways three hundred feet below.

Inside, the eerie green glow from the array of clocks and dials bathing Wicko's face lent him an air of evil menace: "Right. Listen to me. I'm going to dive her down to the roof of the theatre, close as I can, but I won't have time to land. So, I need you to jump down onto the roof. Understand?"

"Chriiist!" said Spindle, his limbs stiffening again.

Wicko took Spindle's complexion turning the colour of curdled milk to be a clear sign that he did. "Then, you need to get inside the theatre. Never mind none of your burgling malarkey, there's a keyboard 'neath a cover flap on the right of the Stage Door."

Wicko frequently shifted his glances between Spindle and the Windowscreen while he spoke. "Using the keyboard, you need to type in the five letter code. That opens the Stage Door. The letters to type are M A G I C." He spelt it out.

"Chriiist!"

"No. Not 'Christ'. 'Magic'. Now tell me you've got that."

Spindle nodded.

"Then, listen, then, I need you to find the Professor. Though I reckon once you've got yourself inside, he'll find you. Then I want you to forget the formalities, just tell him this." Wicko explained what to say.

"Chriiist! What does it mean?"

"He'll know. And Spindle. Spindle! Thank you."

The acrobat nodded.

"Now. Best get yourself ready, me bony old friend. We are coming up on the theatre fairly damn quick."

Spindle began stretching and bending, contorting his limbs into the most unimaginable positions as the Dodo tracked Church Street below, over the Market, then she came upon the junction with the Edgware Road where Wicko helmed a sharp left. At once the airship pitched over to port. The welcome outline of the ornate twin cupolas atop the roof of the Metropolitan Theatre of Steam, Smoke and Mirrors suddenly hove into view. Wicko hauled back on the power, dropping the Dodo like a stomach-churning stone. A tug of the overhead lever slid open the access door. A shrill blast of cold, damp air exploded into the flight deck. Twenty feet. Fifteen. Ten feet. The wet, leaden flat roof swept along below. Spindle needed no prompting. He leapt, landed with a roll, was up on his feet, vaulting the ornate balustrade and scuttling down the back wall into White Horse Alley, all in one endless fluid action. Wicko saw none of it. He had purged the engine and raced the Dodo up and away toward the Marble Arch.

~2~

Almost before the shouting began and the Brimstone billowed, Superintendent William Melville, head of the Metropolitan Police Special Branch, had heaved and hauled the Prince of Wales out of Westminster Abbey into his carriage and commanded the royal coachman to drive! Melville pinned the strewn Royal to the back seat of the coach. A position with which Edward was not unfamiliar, although usually it was Mrs Keppel or Mrs Langtry doing the pinning.

Only when satisfied the coach was well clear of danger did Melville allow The Prince of Wales to restore his dignity.

"Fine work … from young Magister … back there, Melville," shouted the Prince, between deep nerve-settling draws on his cigar which, in the turmoil, he'd somehow managed to light. "My daught… Miss Le Breton? She is safe?"

"So far as I could see, sir." Melville ordered the coachman to steer for the Prince's residence, Marlborough House.

"Belay that," hollered Edward. "Steer to Pont Street!" He looked at Melville. "Mrs Langtry. She knows how to sustain a fellow in trying circumstances."

"That I do not doubt," thought Melville.

With the Prince of Wales safely wrapped in the consoling limbs of Lillie, Melville collared a Hansom to Arlington Place and the Prime Ministerial residence. Lord Salisbury much preferred the palatial luxury of his own Mayfair mansion to the muddle of rooms in that terraced house in Downing Street. Salisbury, too, was puffing furiously on a cigar as he paced up and down his dim-lit living room.

This had been the second outrage in a matter of weeks where the Prime Minister had escaped certain death, he complained, by being bundled without recourse to any decorum into his carriage. Such ignominy. And in public. Worse yet, both assassinations had been foiled thanks not to the police but to Melville's consultants! Those two Music Hall magicians. And making bad matters worse, one was an American and the other a girl! Of all the things! And – and – most recently, Magister and Le Breton thwarted that attempt on the life of Her Majesty the Queen at Windsor Castle. (An account of this particular nail-biter can be found recorded in my paper, "The Windsor Curiosity".)

"How could we not know of such a thing," whined Salisbury, waving his cigar and peppering the air with orange ash. His was a shrill voice, very much at odds with anything you might expect from a man of such great size. What little hair was splayed across his bald head was amply compensated for by the fulsome grey-brown bunch of facial bush dangling to his chest.

"Indeed, Prime Minister," said Melville calmly. "Mercifully His Majesty was unharmed. Nevertheless, the secrecy of the meeting was compromised, and without doubt we are possessed of a traitor in our midst."

"I speak not about the plot to kill myself and His Majesty, Melville. We know there's a traitor among our ranks. I speak of the flying machine, man. Did you see the flying machine?"

Melville took a pause. He knew where this was going. "It could hardly escape my attention, Prime Minister."

"Then you saw, did you not, the manner in which it soared aloft. The ease with which it took to the heavens!"

"Indeed."

"Then, sir, as the head of my Special Branch, should I not ask you this question? How can a pair of tuppenny ha'penny Music Hall conjurers possibly possess such a vehicle when Her Majesty's Government, with all the infinite resources at its disposal, does not?" Salisbury's face was disdainful even at the best of times. And now was most certainly not the best of times.

"There is much in the life of Mr Michael Magister and his menagerie of associates which confounds us, Prime Minister. And now with his airship, it would seem he has surpassed all expectations."

"Ye Gods, man, it would seem he has! As we speak Count von Zeppelin beseeches the Schwarz widow for the patent of her husband's dirigible. The French are long advanced in the industry of mechanised flight. The armies of Europe must not be afforded such aeronautical advantage over Her Majesty's Empire. The nation needs Magister's airship, Melville. And you shall procure that vehicle for me."

"With respect, Prime Minister…"

"Do as I order, Superintendent," growled Salisbury, as best anyone could with a falsetto voice given to the dusty end of the keyboard. But those glaring sag-bag eyes left Melville in no doubt as to the Prime Minister's resolve. "I want that airship, Melville. Even if you must kill to get it."

~3~

Me? I was sitting at the work bench in the Dungeon beneath the stage trying to concentrate on my patent perpetual motion device, which I was now convinced would work if only I could get the damned thing started.

The red warning bulb on the brick wall before me glowed. Much relief. Wicko, Michael and Phoebe had returned safely from their annoying mission of mercy. In time for the late performance. Except that … they would descend from the roof aboard the Lift'n'Shift platform. The red bulb only signalled pedestrian access through the Stage Door. That was disturbing. More so when the bulb began a series of repeated flashes. Someone, other than my magicians, was at the Stage Door tapping away at the entry keyboard and failing with the password not once but twice. We were resigned to the occasional Phoebe worshipper brute-forcing his luck through the door, or to an hormonal Michael follower looking to sate her passion by gaining access to the theatre, but not while the drinking dens were still serving.

Perhaps it was a furious patron demanding to know if the second show would proceed. Then the red light died. Splendid. The stage door Johnny or Jenny had given up and gone. Then the green lamp shone brightly. Ah. That was not quite so splendid. Whoever it was had not given up and gone at all. Instead, they'd happened on the correct entry code – and gained access to the theatre. I ran a gnarled finger along the various blunt, sharp and heavy work precision tools at my disposal. What would Wicko use? He was merciless. But I could be worse. I selected the axe.

Outside, in White Lion Alley, under the Stage Door light, Spindle had squinted at the keyboard and with one finger tapped in M A F U C to no charming effect and then tried M A J I C. Clearly spelling had never been the strongest, nor most necessary skill amongst the acrobatic community. Give Spindle a safe he could crack it in moments. But, you see, that was numbers. He was already jigging and jumping. Mercifully, before he started cursing and Chriiist-ing, Spindle hit success.

M A G I C.

The Stage Door hissed, unclicked, and swung inwards a tad. Spindle nudged it marginally wider with a cautious finger, waited, then slipped easily through the gap, from the airy light of the alley into the eerie darkness of the lobby. Feeling more at ease, the consummate burglar squinted his eyes to penetrate the murk. This was his world. Where he who could see could not be seen. Or something like that. Sadly, his comfort was somewhat short lived when the lamps of the lobby flickered, then warmed the lobby in light. Wicko's desk and chair, and the props trunk, the double swing-doors which lead to the dressing room stairs, all in gentle sepia tones.

Spindle jumped again when the Stage Door hissed and closed behind him, then jumped a darn sight higher when the lid of the props trunk hinged open and I emerged; hunched, wild-eyed and wielding an axe like a psychopathic killer from a tableau in Tussaud's Chamber of Horrors.

"CHRIISST!!"

"Spindle?" Yes, I knew him.

"Professor?! Don't kill me!!" He cringed and protected his head. "Chriiist!! No! I've brought a message! From the dwarf. He said to tell you – it's London Bridge!"

"What did you say?"

"It's London Bridge."

It was always inevitable. Always. Nevertheless, my blood chilled.


~4~


Phoebe peered at Michael's corpse through the porthole atop the Sarcophagus. His eyes were masked with goggles. The strange curative green light bathing his entire naked body. As it had with Lazarus. But this time she realised Dr Phunn's remarkable machine flattered to deceive. For only now she noticed the fluid

24

lines snaking into Michael's arms and legs. Air, or gas, she had no idea what, breezed gently into the heavy metal tomb.

Phoebe felt a comforting hand squeeze her shoulder. "Patience," said Wu Hu.

Michael never saw the two beautiful faces looking down upon him. But in the deep void that is death a single spark of life flashed through his mind. Like a lamp's splutter. Then another flash. And another. The images came. Faster. Brighter. Smashing into his vague and distant thoughts. Becoming clearer. The explosion. The falling. The memories. Swirling clearer and clearer.

Michael's body tensed. Finally – he knew the answers. He knew where he came from and how! He remembered it all!

~5~

At that same time, from his aeronaut's seat aboard the Dodo, Wicko could just about make out the great expanse of Hyde Park over to the right. The needle on the Altitudometer wavered at around a hundred feet. The moon glimpsing out from behind the thick clouds now and then was a blessing.

He had overflown his favourite waypoint of the Marble Arch, then tracked the lines of carriage lamplights juddering along the length of Park Lane before banking the airship to the right. Through the forward Windowscreen it took a few moments of squinted-peering to pick out the Serpentine, that stretch of water dug out by George the Second's Gardener Royal, Charles Bridgeman. Poor devil, thought Wicko. And he thought he'd signed up to plant a few tulips and do a bit of mowing.

The Serp glittered its welcome with a break in the cloud. Wicko eased back the power on the patent Alytheium Generator to slow the Dodo and swoop her down and back over the water's edge, just above that spot where eighty years earlier Percy Shelley's first wife, Harriet, drowned herself. Twenty-one she was. Not much older than Phoebe. Never mind that. Concentrate.

Wicko dropped the dirigible low now, enough to make out the five arches of the Serpentine Bridge. With the gates long closed for the night to the public, anyone in Hyde Park now was either kipping or canoodling. Far too distracted to care about the whining Dodo.

Beyond the bridge, the Kensington Gardens end, it's known as 'The Long Water'. Because it's long, Wicko supposed. And watery. But anyway.

He lined up the Dodo, square with the middle arch. The deepest section. He cut the revs on the propeller, slowing the blades to an easy idle, and lowered the airship gently on to the surface of the lake. In a flurry of lever pulling and stop-wheel spinning Wicko shut down the patent Alytheium Generator. It was a shame no one could have seen that. Especially as his last water landing, on the River Seine, involved bouncing, skimming and cursing like a sailor.

Here and now, everything was quiet. Save for the gentle lapping of the water. Bathed in a green glow from the indicator gauges Wicko clambered down. Beneath his aeronaut's seat was that polished door, twelve inches square. The thick pile carpet cut neatly around it. An access hatch. He prised and hinged open the lid. On the underside were carved the words "IT MUST BE BAD. BUT ARE YOU QUITE CERTAIN?" He was. And this was the planned strategy if ever the existence of the airship was compromised.

Wicko reached down, turned the brass tap two turns to the left, lefty loosy, righty tighty, to the left we're bereft, to the right we're in.... SSSSSH! He immediately heard the gush of the water. Enough to compromise the buoyancy. Then tightened the tap. Amid streams of straight-line bubbles, the Dodo submerged until, with a hollow FLUMPH! she set on the muddy lake bed. The murky depths. Well, seventeen feet. Which gave plenty of clearance between the roof and the surface.

Wicko noticed the silence was different. Hollow and heavy. Broken by the occasional

GLOOP!

as the Dodo made itself more comfortable and sediment clouds settled. More importantly, no worrying drip-drip-drip.

"Good girl. That's the way we like it," said Wicko. We always knew the Dodo was watertight but she had taken a heck of a battering of late.

He shut down the green light glow from the gauges, casting the Flight Saloon into total darkness.

"Bugger. We never really thought this part through."

So, punctuated with the occasional cuss, Wicko had to feel and bump his way into the ante-chamber between the Flight Saloon and the engine room at the rear. Of the many dark wood cupboard doors, yes, they had to be dark, didn't they, he found the least tall, opened it up and stepped inside. This was Wicko's own Escape Diving Bell. Well, Diving Box really, given it was shaped like a coffin, made of soft, light balsa.

The action of closing the door on his Diving Box cranked the chain which squeaked open a red sluice wheel, sliding the hatch on the roof open, allowing the

SPPULLUBLE!

of air to rise, to be replaced by a torrent of ripe Serpentine water.

With Wicko standing dry inside, his musty-smelling box floated free of the submerged airship, before righting itself gently on the surface of the lake. Wicko hinged back the dripping lid and lay looking up at the thick wind driven clouds.

He sat himself up, licked his finger, held it to the breeze, and got his bearings. There was the bridge, there was the bank. Sailing? Ha. With a dozen strokes of the balsa paddle, Wicko canoed his coffin round and made landfall on the northern coast, then dragged his vessel by its rope out of the Serpentine and into a copse of stately bankside trees. Who needs a sextant? Magellan would have been proud.

Admittedly, it was all rather more effort than Wicko would have preferred, so he sat down to catch his breath while he considered the future. The Dodo was now concealed and that was a start.

Revealing the existence of a craft capable of controlled flight would lend Superintendent Melville's Special Branch Barbarians sufficient excuse to storm the gates of the theatre and cart away our secrets. Incredible secrets way in advance of anything they might yet conceive.

Magister, and Phoebe, had the best intentions, saving those high-ranking self-important lives at Westminster Abbey, but at what cost? And no good deed ever goes unpunished.

But now he needed to get himself back to the theatre. What was the best route? Mooch past the solid colonnaded gunpowder magazine building by the end of the bridge, then head north along The Riding, out onto the Bayswater Road via the pedestrian Westbourne Gate and hail a Hansom. It was a bit of a step, and a hell of a fag, but it had to be done. But that plan popped like a Montgolfier balloon as soon as he heard the sound of rattling.

~7~

Wheels. On the cobbles. It was a carriage. No. Not without horses. It had to be a push cart. Up on the bridge. Which was what, twenty yards up ahead.

Wicko held back in the cover of the trees. The parting of the clouds revealed the occasional hint of movement. Yes, up on the bridge. A person. A woman. He could just about make her out. Behind the hip-high parapet. She was dressed all in black with a black bonnet which did not help a great deal in this light. Maybe that was the idea. And was she pushing a hand cart? It was now that Wicko wished he carried an Obsidian Lamp.

"Thisss isss the place," hissed a throaty voice, carried away on the breeze.

"Oh, and quite the perfect spot, my dear," trilled the voice of an old woman.

Wicko could see her. But not her companion.

She leant over the parapet. Looked down at the water slopping against the arches. Wicko was immediately convinced she was going to jump. Then the moonlight beamed down, enough for him to see the old woman lift something up from the cart.

Wicko caught his breath, the back of his hand to his mouth. It was a body. A man's body. A big man's body far too heavy for her to lift. But she was somehow managing – and with ease. Then the clouds closed and the light dimmed.

SPLOSH!

She dropped the body into the Serp? She must have.

"Death to the Aquarian," hissed the hideous voice from nowhere.

"Quite so, my dear. Death to the Aquarian." And that was most definitely the old woman repeating the phrase.

A dead body dump! The poor fellow floated face down while the waves radiated outwards. Then his clothes, sodden and heavy, helped him slip below the surface.

Now, although Wicko didn't know the circumstances, it might be something perfectly plausible. Like relatives of a mariner too mean to give him a burial at sea, or something even far-fetched – but with the best will in world all that talk of 'Death to the Aquarian' did not sound like remorse. No, Wicko had enough on his plate to worry about already.

So, he turned around and headed back along the bankside in the direction of Park Lane. He could shimmy over the fence and hail a Hansom from there.

Blimey, this really was turning out to be a bugger of a night.

~8~

A mile and a half to the north by the Macclesfield Bridge at Regents Park, Phoebe was pacing and agitating in Dr Phunn's elaborate mobile pagoda.

"Thank you, Miss Phoebe Le Breton. Where there is a chance there is always hope," said the doctor. He sat upon his golden throne calmly puffing on the ivory mouthpiece on the end of the golden hose which snaked to the glass-bellied hookah vase. The clear fluid bubbled with every draw. "A little menthol to ease your soul?"

Phoebe politely declined the Chinaman's offer of the spare pipe. Her soul currently felt so drained there was little left to ease.

An hour had passed since Michael was delivered into the best of hands. For years Dok Tor Phunn and his exotic younger sister Wu Hu had waggoned their way across the U.S. and Europe, paying their way by dispensing therapeutic miracles with their unfathomable "Diag-Knows-it" cure-all apparatus. That was before they conceived and crewed their Carnival of Mechanical Miracles, which served as a cover for their high-end bank robberies. And, of course, financed the building and development of the Sarcophagus of Hippocrates: the medical marvel which repaired and restored human cells.

Wu Hu emerged from the Laboratory which lay behind Phunn's extensive bookshelves.

"You did well," said Phunn's sister, wiping green gunk from her hands with a cloth. Wu Hu's accent was as gently American as her brother's was Eastern. "The speed with which you delivered Magister here gives me hope. If he can survive the next two days … then we'll know his respiratory tract can fully repair."

"His lungs are well developed," Phoebe assured her, more desperate to remain positive. "Michael was well-practised at holding his breath."

"That I remember," said Wu Hu.

The ability to avoid breathing for long periods was an indispensable skill when escaping on stage from a trunk submerged in a tank of water. Or when coping with the acrid output of Father Connor O'Connor's wretched digestion.

"There is little you can achieve by remaining here," Wu Hu told her.

"Thank you, Miss Phoebe Le Breton, but my sister speaks with sincerity." Phunn raised a hand before Phoebe could object. "You shall better serve your cause by returning to your Metropolitan Theatre. I imagine Professor Artemus More is expecting circumstances to take a disagreeable turn in the coming days. Your energetic support will prove more effective if directed toward him. I will arrange for Mr Merman to convey you."

Mr F. L. Merman was a joyous Southern States man, born without a lower torso, but rendered mobile, and agile, with the addition of four legs. From my previous volume, you may recall his adage: "Why do I got four legs? Because there wasn't room for six."

Merman was sold at birth to a travelling Carnival where he was displayed as a 'specimen', then spent his formative years with a rubber fishtail strapped to his torso, appearing as 'The Fijian Merman'. Until Phunn happened upon the appalling Carnival, bought all the exhibits and with time and medical skill he and Wu Hu granted them the kind of dignity they had never before experienced.

With Merman at the reins, the buggy ride from the Regent's Park to the Edgware Road was also an experience. Merman assured Phoebe he was mighty familiar with the route to the theatre. Plain thought dictated that by 'keepin' that good ol' the North Star shining bright down on the horse's ass, what in hell's name was gonna go awry?' Well, the cloud cover for one. And mistaking that fleeting glimpse of Venus for the pole star, which knocked his internal compass way out of kilter, was another.

As pressing as the journey was, it was to impossible to take issue with a man whose mobility for the first part of his life was dragging himself about on his hands.

It was only when St John's Wood Road Underground Station came around a second time but from a different direction, Phoebe felt the need, in the politest possible way to take the reins. Mr Merman then promptly showed his gratitude by dozing off.

~9~

By the time Phoebe steered the buggy along Bell Street, she could already see the line of black carriages parked in front of the theatre. Police. Special Branch. She hauled the horse to a stop, turned the buggy about, woke Mr Merman, thanked him for driving her and sent him back on his way. With clear directions.

In the yellow light which always bathed the front of The Metropolitan Theatre of Steam, Smoke and Mirrors", a dozen or so men were rattling, pushing, shouldering and even trying to jemmy their way in through the front doors, all to no avail. Wearing dark long overcoats, bowler hats and most wearing gas masks, theirs was a style of uniform she had seen before. When such coppers were complaining about spiriting the hefty corpse of Cardinal Corvus of Rome from the high-class bordello of Catherine Walters on South Street. Yes, this was a division of the Police pressed into service for sensitive, highly clandestine work.

"Oppn-uh!" muffled the men in the masks and they bashed and crashed on the doors. The scene was farcical.

Detective Inspector Walter Pym was one of the few unmasked officers she recognised. Along with Detective Constables Beatty and Willzen. And there was Superintendent Melville, shaking his head, who eventually ordered use of the Battering Ram.

KRANGG! KRANGG! KRANGG!

The hefty wooden tree trunk was swung with impressive gusto but even then, failed to even dent any of the coloured glass and wood framed doors. At least the noise caused every dog in Paddington to wake up and start yowling.

"So much for stealth and surprise," thought Melville, before ordering: "To the stage door, gentlemen."

"Might it not be simpler to purchase a ticket?" The purring sound was right behind them. Simultaneously, the raiders turned to see Phoebe Le Breton, leaning on a cast iron pillar which supported the ornate glass canopy under which they stood. Her arms were folded, ankles crossed while she watched their manly exertions with barely concealed contempt. "Alternatively, Superintendent, one could always try knocking."

She sashayed past the coppers and rapped a couple of taps on the glass with the back of a gloved hand.

The Special Branchers looked at one another.

There was silence for a moment. Then the theatre foyer flared with light and Wicko strode forward to unlock the door. Poking his face through the gap the dwarf looked up at Melville and the rest of his crew.

"Who's that knocking?" he demanded. "You lot? We're closed."

"Sir, we are in possession of a High Court warrant to search this theatre for an airship," said Pym, without humour or any attempt to produce the aforesaid Court Order.

Wicko shrugged, looked at Phoebe, pulled the door open wide and Melville could have sworn he heard the dwarf whisper: "Air ship you reckon? Good luck with that."

On the stage of the theatre, I adopted my Dickensian swivel-eyed crookback posture and grunted in a plaintive manner. I gestured at the elaborate performance illusions resting malevolently in the gloom of the onstage work lights: the Guillotine of Deadly Beheading, the Iron Monger's Coffin of Death, The Graveyard Spikes of Impalement, and signalled in elaborate cut-throat mime that if touched, any one of these mechanical monsters possessed the potential to maim, dismember or at the very least badly bruise.

"Listen, see. Can't 'ardly understan' a wor' 'ee's utterin'," said Beatty in his Merseyside brogue.

"Myself neither, and I work with him every day," lied Phoebe innocently. Ha. If any of them lost a limb, my conscience was clear.

Melville followed Wicko on stage.

"Mr Smawl," he said, quiet but firm. "The flying machine. And I shall brook no falsehood in this matter. You were witnessed by Inspector Pym at the controls of this craft. Its location if you will."

"Well, there's nothing of that sort down here," said Wicko.

"Indeed." Melville frowned and repeated: "Nothing of that sort down here…" Then it dawned on him. "We might afford access to the roof of this building how?"

~10~

The outwitted dwarf cursed himself, admitting, "All right, all right. You best follow me." Wicko led Melville into the shadows of the prompt side wing and to the foot of a wooden ladder bolted vertically to the black brickwork. Melville's eyes followed Wicko's finger which was pointing upward. The ladder went on and on, its perspective narrowing as the rungs and rails disappeared into the blackness above.

"Bit of a climb, gents," said Wicko.

But not for Melville. "Detective Constables Willzen and Beatty."

The two Special Branch Detective Constables were promptly at Melville's side and just as promptly wished they hadn't been quite so keen. "Kindly investigate the roof."

The policemen removed their overcoats, folded them on the floor, and an 'after you', 'no, listen, see, you first,' exchange, the policemen began their agonising climb, Willzen first, Beatty directly behind him.

"It's a nice view, gents," said Wicko.

"Listen, see, no' from 'ere iss not," grumbled Beatty.

On the other side of the theatre, off the first-floor corridor, Pym was delving around in Michael's dressing room. Small but comfortable and dominated by two mirrors, naturally. There was a chaise, and a row of performance suits hanging from a silver rail. The frock coats revealed linings of golden, garish silks and innumerable hidden pockets.

On the make-up table a neat pile of scented handwritten letters, each ticked and with "replied" pencilled neatly in the top right corner. Pym had a nose through the mail. Much of it gushing and adoring, the rest disgusting and appalling. Who would have thought women could think those things? Clothing and eye make-up. It wasn't right. But there was plenty about that Magister which didn't ring true.

He fiddled with a straight brown stick two feet long. Tabbed either end in two inches of burnished brass. A magic wand. In the middle a sliding ring, concealed by the hand, which operates the mechanism inside the wand. Slide the ring forward, the front-end brass droops. A cue for all sorts of suggestive patter. Slide the ring backwards, the rear end droops. The Inspector refused to appear impressed. Even to himself.

Pym moved to Phoebe's dressing room. The much larger of the two. The drawers, the costume rail, outfits which most often defied imagination, some of which defied propriety. The prospect of a rummage around here was a very pleasing prospect until Phoebe appeared at the door to ask if he'd found what it was he was looking for.

*** 

Up on the roof of the theatre, the hot and panting Willzen and Beatty were grateful to clamber up through the fanlight and into the cool night air following their muscle-burning climb. The flat lead roof was kinked here and there to aid rainwater flow. Willzen and Beatty took a pause to take in the view then peered over the front parapet overlooking the Edgware Road below. Dark buildings were chequered with squares of dull light as more people were rising to face work. It was four a.m. after all.

"Ay. Listen, see," said Beatty, tapping his chest with the palm of his hand which was always his wont when he needed to impart something of what he thought was importance. "Wosh diss 'ere?". Which sounded close enough to "What's this here?" for Willzen to understand. Beatty claimed to be a son of the north west but spoke in an accent totally unfamiliar to the many proud Merseysiders who were fluent in Scouse.

The object of Beatty's bafflement lay in the middle of the roof. An apparatus we could have never adequately disguised, even with the luxury of time and invention. The rig looked akin to the skeleton of a run-aground sailing smack where weather and rot had now left only the metal stanchions of the hull curving upward. These six ribs provided the housing in which The Ferrous Dodo stood secure and high, above the public gaze.

34

"For nought with which I am acquainted, Beatty," said Willzen.

"It's the cradle," admitted Wicko. "For the flying machine."

The dwarf had appeared from nowhere, leaving Beatty temporarily speechless. What was it about this place? That was the second time someone had appeared from nowhere. First that Phoebe woman and now the dwarf!

"How did you arrive here?" demanded Willzen.

"That, gents, is not your concern," said Wicko. Willzen and Beatty watched him with stunned incredulity as he picked his way straight past them and toward the rear of the theatre roof. "But I would have thought – *that* is."

The small chap hefted himself up onto the brick parapet and pointed down, over there. Not far away, on Paddington Green, just beside St Eadie's Church and Sarah Siddons's grave, flames licked and flared, embers glowed and plumes of grey smoke swirled from the cremated remains of a pile of something the Special Branchers could barely make out.

"Ay. Listen, see, woss goin' on?"

"What's going on, gents, is – that's the flying machine you're looking for."

"It is destroyed!" exclaimed Willzen.

"That's what happens when a flying machine hits the ground too hard."

"We must inform the Superintendent. Immediately."

"If you're going to be in that much of a hurry you might just as well come back down with me," said Wicko, leading the way to the door set in a brick-built housing the policemen took to be a decorative cupola.

Moments later, Willzen and Beatty stood on the Lift'n'Shift watching as the rows of brick slid upwards as the elevator took them down. Beatty was unnerved, but Willzen had once ridden an elevator, an 'ascending room' as they called it, at the Grosvenor Hotel near Victoria Station when he and Melville arrived to arrest a one-armed Prussian gun runner who was posing as a dentist from Woking. But I digress.

Both coppers were left wondering how a theatre possessed the wherewithal to install a lift. And how those in the theatre could build an airship? And as Beatty so eloquently put it, while rubbing his chest: "Listen, my small man. Why wasn't we afforded the opportunity to ride aboard this gubbins, 'stead of havin' to scale all the ways up th' rungs o' that death-trap ladder?"

Wicko shrugged. "You never asked."

Out on Paddington Green, the two Special Branch men raked over the embers of the wreckage with tree branches to no avail other than causing showers of red smuts to rise and catch the breeze. Twisted, hissing molten metal was strewn across a distance of easily twenty yards, but nothing was salvageable. Or even recognisable. The debris could have been anything.

Which of course, as you have guessed, is exactly what it was. A pile of wooden off-cuts, metal spars and shattered glass, detritus, stored in the church woodshed in case of a necessary deception such as this.

Beatty tossed his branch into the ash in frustration.

~11~

Back in the theatre, Melville stepped slowly about the Dungeon. I watched him as he worked. His eyes darting everywhere. Under copper-domed work lights the void beneath the stage resembled a bright and busy industrial workshop.

Air claggy with the scent of oil. Surfaces laid out with tools. Lathes, tower drills, sheet metal cutters. Deconstructed mannequins lay in orderly piles of bodies and limbs. There were trunks and chests and cabinets, dark wood and metal all in various states of construction and repair. Two skeletons hung from hooks. Wooden shelves skirted the walls, supporting battered manuals and books, sightless skulls and glaring masks, heads on plates, the ephemera of anything that was far from normal.

Melville traced the runs and right-angles of our elaborate pipework. Occasionally, a joint hissed a squirt of steam. All the time there was the hum of idling machinery.

I offered him the occasional smile and quietly prayed that in the general jumble of the Dungeon Melville's keen attention would not be drawn to the back wall. Well, naturally, my celestial pleas were ignored, because he ran his fingers over the guilty brickwork. Hopefully he would not feel the warmth and the gentle vibration.

"What lies behind here?"

He did.

Quickly I reached out and pulled a blueprint from the shelf of rolled up design sheets, shifted a clutter of tools and flattened the drawing on the surface. I pointed out the relevant boundary wall, the underground services beyond, especially the 'Paddington District Bazelgette low level intercepting sewer'.

"Is that so?" Behind that impassive countenance and bristle of a black moustache loitered deep suspicion. Cheek. But I could feel it.

Then both trap door Lift'n'Shifts cranked down from the stage. Willzen and Beatty squeezed uncomfortably aboard one platform, and Wicko on the other. Wicko gave me the wink.

"Distressing news to say the least, Superintendent," said Willzen.

"Sir, dat flying machine? Burnt to a cinder," said Beatty, rubbing his chest as he said it. "Espied it wid our own eyes we did, sir."

"Entirely destroyed?" queried Melville.

"Nought but a pyre of ash and buckled metal," apologised Willzen, as if it was his fault.

Wicko and I again exchanged knowing looks.

Beatty gawped and gazed his way around the Dungeon. "Ay, listen. What's all dis detritus? Da Chambers of 'orrors?"

"Constables, be so kind as to arm yourselves with heavy work tools," said Melville, coldly. "They lie abundantly hereabouts."

Beatty grabbed the sledgehammer and grinned, very much liking the feel of it. Willzen favoured a hefty wrench. In that moment, for us, the presence of the police had darkened from meddlesome to worryingly menacing.

"Here, gents," said Wicko holding up placatory hand. "There's no call for violence."

"Detective Constable Willzen. Better you find the hammer and cold chisel." All the time Melville's eyes never left me. Had the exasperation of dealing with us all finally twisted the brains of the head of the Special Branch? Turned him into some kind of a callous torturer? I needed to make a decision. What was the expression – flee or fight? Have made my decision I wiggled my toes to make sure the laces on my boots were good and tight.

"This wall appears to be suspicious," said Melville, tapping the black brickwork.

"No, it's not," shouted Wicko. "Gents, there's nothing suspicious about it. Nothing suspicious whatsoever." The dwarf stood with arms folded with indignation.

He and I once again exchanged knowing glances. This time Melville saw us. "Break it down," he ordered.

~12~

With trembling fingers Pym persisted in his delve around Phoebe's dressing room, uncovering all manner of items of interest, but found nothing of what he was looking for, which was anything to do with the flying machine.

"I know you've had a bit of a night of it, Miss," explained Pym, embarrassed. "But know this raid comes on express orders. From the Prime Minister himself."

"I have no doubt it does," said Phoebe, who was lounging with her feet up, eyes closed, on the chaise in her dressing room. This had been the first time she'd actually paused for breath since the outrage in the Abbey. Her adrenalin finally spent; exhaustion started filling the void.

"Where'd you take the body, Miss? Magister's I mean. After you flew off with it." Pym immediately regretted the unsympathetic tone of his enquiry.

"Does it really matter, Walter," sighed Phoebe. "And you would never believe me if I told you."

Pym tried to put together some words, a sentence or two of consolation concerning Michael's passing, but nothing seemed appropriate. Instead he murmured a sound like 'Excuse me' and left the dressing room. It was only when the door was closed that Phoebe allowed herself to bury her face in the damask cushion and deeply sob.

\*\*\*

Pym was still berating his mishandling of that situation as he made his way down the stairs, when he heard the most acrimonious cursing coming from the stage. Through the window of the pass door, he caught sight of the cause of the turmoil.

Detective Constables Willzen and Beatty were waddling awkwardly, still holding their tools, and coated head and chest in sewer-slime: multifarious shades of chestnut, russet and tan. The assault on the nostrils was stomach retching. Ahead of them, Wicko led the way, complaining about not being listened to and demanding greater urgency to get their ripe selves quickly off the stage and outside. The indignant unfortunates tried in vain to wipe their eyes and faces as they followed the dwarf into the gloom of the off-prompt wing, through the lobby, out of the Stage Door and into the fresh dawning air.

Melville and I followed at a judicious distance.

"What…" was all Pym could manage as he stepped back to avoid the progress of the effluent entourage. Melville ordered his Inspector not to ask and to quickly follow on.

"You can't say we never warned you what was behind that wall," called Wicko after the policemen. He shook his fist at them. Once their backs were turned, obviously.

You see, the small chamber which lurked behind the wall contained secrets of which even Michael and Phoebe knew nothing. The entrance was cunningly concealed and Willzen and Beatty had fallen foul of a booby trap we conceived with the architect of the Metropolitan Theatre of Steam, Smoke and Mirrors. Our purpose-built disincentive to further investigation was a glass tank framed against the back wall. A tank containing matter siphoned from the Paddington Green system. If any unsuspecting nosey parker took it upon themselves to try to breach the wall, they would also break the glass tank which in turn would discharge its vile soup through the aperture and onto the perpetrators. As Detective Constables Willzen and Beatty would testify. After they had been hosed down with a stirrup pump…

…and Wicko and I had been arrested!

~13~

Yes, all right, I said Wicko and I were 'arrested', but we were more firmly invited to attend a meeting in Superintendent Melville's office at Scotland Yard. Melville's office, with the painting of the Queen glowering disapproval behind him; it struck me the Superintendent was more a prisoner of his calling and this was his cell.

Regarding our present detention, I must give Melville some credit, no truly I do, he was working under duress from the Prime

Minister. Salisbury wanted the Dodo, but now she was apparently crashed and burned on Paddington Green, Melville's next course of action was to know how we came by such technology. I, of course, had adopted my Richard the Third posture and grunted very little. So it was for Wicko to explain how, during our various European excursions, we met with those 'controlled free-flight pioneers', my dear old associate Arthur Krebs along with his partner, Charles Renard (whom neither of us cared for), who had built and flown their non-rigid airship-shaped balloon called, for some reason, 'La France' back in 1884.

Wicko told Melville that at the time, I often dubbed them 'The Boys in the Blimp', but they remained unamused. 'Les Garcons Dans Le Blimp' doesn't possess the alliterative elegance.

Pym interrupted with a point of order. Annoyingly correct. "How can he have dubbed them 'The Boys in the Blimp' if he doesn't speak?"

"Who? The Professor? Oh, he used talk. Then he lost the ability," said Wicko, looking at me with that evil glint. "Which didn't much matter in the end because most of the time he didn't have much worth saying."

Wicko then continued his narrative embroidery. Which, quite honestly, you can skip if you like –

(about how he offered Arthur and Charles suggestions for improvements, while I sketched a couple of surreptitious copies of their original design.

That was after we had to flee Europe. Well, you see, a Croatian called David Schwartz, again, an old friend, he designed the first rigid airship, a pointy-nosed affair, with a skin fashioned in aluminium. That's the airship not Schwartz by the way. Naturally David's dirigible could not contain the lighter-than-air gas effectively and in desperation he turned to us. Wicko claimed credit for the idea to line the inside with a vast airtight gas bag, which naturally solved his problem. David never lived to see his airship fly. We met him for fine dining in a posh Vienna restaurant where he promptly collapsed and died. It could have been tragic but luckily, he carried a copy of his designs in his attaché case, and we took hold of them for safe keeping. Well, Carl Benz who built the thing, and Ferdy von Zeppelin went potty when they found out, which is why we escaped to England, pursued halfway across

Europe by the German army in pickelhaube helmets and with bayonets fixed. So, we combined the Renard and Krebbs and Schwarz designs to cobble together our own version of an airship!)

Anyway, by now, as you can imagine, Pym was bored to tears with Wicko's flowery history lesson, because unlike yourself, he had to sit through it.

Melville, the cool pragmatist, stated bluntly: "The question is this. Can your flying machine be rebuilt?"

"No," said Wicko firmly. "Cannot be done."

"Indeed. Of course, there is the prospect of a lengthy prison sentence to consider."

Wicko gave it a moment's consideration. "Give me a moment while I confer with my associate."

Huh. Suddenly I was his associate! Anyway, he leaned up and I leaned down to meet him halfway so he could whisper in my ear: "I think they've got us a little bit stymied here."

I had to agree. Although it betrayed everything we agreed when we first sailed to England a decade ago. Maybe there was a way to agree to something, but then not deliver. Salisbury would understand that notion. He was a politician.

So Wicko said yes, we would recreate the plans for an airship. Said nothing about letting those government scientists and engineers try to construct it.

"How long will these designs take to draw up?"

"Two months," said Wicko confidently. That bought us valuable time.

"Indeed." Melville was calm and understood perfectly. Until he said: "However, you have one month. In perfect freedom. In your own facility. Any further time producing the blueprints will be spent as personal guests of the governor of Pentonville Prison."

Wicko and I exchanged looks. "Very good of you to be so reasonable," said Wicko. "A month it is then."

~14~

Melville then found himself distracted by a body found floating by the side of the Serpentine. Ordinarily it would never have crossed his desk, but this man was Sir Milton Grist, a senior economic adviser to Sir Michael Hicks Beach, the Chancellor of the Exchequer.

It's always a worry when someone who predicts the future of the economy commits suicide. But the post-mortem noted that, while drowning was the cause of Sir Milton Grist's demise, his lungs were brim full of clean, well relatively clean, horse trough water, bearing no similarity in terms of colour and content to the water of the Serpentine. "The man drowned. But not where he was found," stated the surgeon's report, with aspirations to sensationalist poetry.

As a consequence, responsibility for a strategic watch on our movements to and from the theatre passed to the local X Division constabulary at Harrow Road Police Station. Which was very good news. It is not that the Paddington Police were more susceptible to skills of our chicanery and deception, but their experience lay in policing the petty crime of West London.

With the theatre dark and no further shows planned, the majority of our surreptitious excursions were to Dr Phunn's encampment, out more to the West of London, to the top corner of an eighty-acre area known as Wormwood Scrubbs. It was audacious and typical of the man. He had orchestrated the recent successful bullion raid on the Bank of England but still circled his circle of elaborate caravans barely half a mile from the site of Her Majesty's newest prison.

Phunn, Wu Hu and their cohorts had benevolently reconsidered their plan to escape to the Continent, given Michael's respiratory damage, deciding a quiet lay-over would be more beneficial to delicate repair. Each day Michael's physical condition was markedly improved. In time, the deep green gloop Wu Hu had slavered upon his gas blisters took on a translucence. Peering down through the oculus portholes in the lid of his restorative Sarcophagus, the burned puckered skin on his face and neck smoothened and pinked. The fingers straightened. Where bare flesh had been exposed, we saw a coating of new skin slowly creep over the visceral muscle. As for his internal respiratory system, the charred nostrils, pharynx, bronchi and lungs, Dr Phunn and Wu Hu could make no prediction.

"We can only see what we can see," said Wu Hu.

"Yeah, well I can't see anything," complained Wicko. "And if anyone tries to lift me I'll bite 'em."

"Thank you, Manswick Smawl, be assured such unpleasantry for us and for you can be avoided." And Dr Phunn placed a chair beside the Sarcophagus for the dwarf to stand on.

He looked down through the glass oculus directly over Michael's congealing face and promptly wished he hadn't made such a fuss after all.

Michael's remarkable progress did not detract from the fact we were in serious trouble. Namely our commitment to supply the government with the design for our flying machine, The Ferrous Dodo. Yes, we could knock-up some sort of specifications for the body of the beast, but it would not be long before some officious engineer worth his salt would realise the nation's finest current-day systems of steam or electrical power generation could never overcome the weight-to-power and speed ratios required to make the Dodo take to the skies with the kind of nimble performance capabilities so many had witnessed outside the Abbey.

Supplying anything related to the Alytheium Generator propulsion system was a line which could not be crossed. It was engineering with which the people of this realm and of this time could never yet be trusted.

'Everything has its place and here and now is not the case' was the false-rhyme homily (yes, it was one of my compositions) to which we Adepts of the Invisible College strictly adhered.

The clock was ticking. Not in our favour. A convocation of the Invisible College was in order.

~15~

So, with that much in mind, I stepped aboard the Lift'n'Shift platform which juddered me three storeys aloft into one of the pair of matching ornate cupolas up on the roof of the theatre. Within the more important of the two, as you may know from my last volume, stand the trio of glass domes, big bell jars five feet in the height department and a full yard wide. All three were connected at their copper metal lids by droops of heavy cables which plug straight into the side of this heavy-duty grey walled cabinet housing racks of valvage and a snake-pit of flexes and pipes. It is the magnificent communication device I call my PSYKE: an acronym for: 'Private Speech Yield Kinetic Exchanger'. Well, *I* like it.

I threw the requisite circuit breakers, and adjusted the voltage knobs, jolting the beast into droning life and drawing just enough power to infuriate the local residents – again – as their own fuses flashed and banged. My, how the good people of Paddington suffered since we moved in.

Above West London black thunder clouds quickly barrelled in from every direction, generating forks of spiteful lightning which split the through the sky and speared our antenna. The bleachy ionised atmosphere grew heavy and oppressive. The PSYKE was searching for her friends. It was a spectacular palaver to commence a communication but so much more exciting than one of those Alexander Graham Bell-rings.

Mercifully William Thomson, Lord Kelvin of Largs, had not yet decamped from his grace and favour Glasgow University home to his retirement castle, so the black, rainless clouds which flashed and seethed above the University of Glasgow was his signal to step lively from that magnificent terraced house in Professors' Square across to the College's Hunterian Museum, opposite.

Four and a half thousand miles across the Atlantic in Colorado Springs, a similar electrical tempest exploded furiously above the surrounding scrubland. Great silver zig-zags of vicious energy spiked and stabbed at the copper antenna poking up from the roof of Nikola Tesla's barn-like laboratory.

Shuffling uncomfortably as I sat on the wooden chair within my glass confinement, I watched as the vacant dome to my left began to become less vacant. Its copper metal lid sparked yellow and fizzled blue and steamy smoke billowed up within the dome. Slowly, as the cloud dissolved, Tesla's vaguely translucent image began to form in a splutter of sepia spirals, revolving and building upwards, line by line from his battered boots up through his trousers and torso until … there he was.

Blurring in and out of focus, Nik was jacketless, tieless and with his white shirt sleeves rolled to the elbow. Despite the hissing and popping I was encouraged to see, as he sat in his equivalent dome in Colorado, that his dear, pointy-featured face did not possess the familiar testy-Tesla irritation one might usually associate with a Nik disturbed in the middle of his work.

The voice from the speaker horn within the dome was metalized, and despite his fifteen years living in the U.S. Tesla's sentence construction was still inclined to the Slavic. Admittedly, his American was way better than my Austrian. "Octopus! I hope you bringing the news most positive, concerning Michael!?"

He called me Octopus because he could never master the pronunciation of 'Artemus'. Also, because he thought I slopped and probed my tentacles – no, my tentacles – into all kinds of 'business most dubious'.

I shouted back that mercifully Michael was presenting a favourable reaction to the Phunn's' esoteric medicals.

Now the third vacant dome crackled and billowed into life as the rotund facsimile of Kelvin ascended by degree, his bearded face and bald head stabilising quickly from nearby Scotland.

"Gentlemen. That is fair good news to hear," yelled the great Scottish scientist. "All Save Robert Hooke!" He was a proper stickler for the traditions of the Invisible College, and Nik and I repeated the incantation. With formalities concluded to his satisfaction the noble lord continued: "So! The prime minister wants the Dodo!"

As the nation's highest-ranking scientist, the First Baron Kelvin would, of course, be privy to such classified information, but I do find his constant air of all-knowing superiority does tend to get up the nose a bit.

But! I do happily acknowledge and proclaim that he is truly a great and gifted genius because, as you know, it takes one to know one. I just thank goodness I am blessed with more in the way of humility.

"This is the truth, Octopus?" demanded Tesla, a little alarmed.

I admitted it was. We had hoped that landing the Dodo in the evening shadows of Westminster Abbey would not have caused such a...

"Kerfuffle," barked Kelvin. "A suitable Celtic expression for this kind of dilemma."

The use of my invented Pulsa Pistols and Dr Phunn depriving the Bank of England of many bars of gold bullion using Teslan technology, had alerted those in authority to the existence of such advanced knowledge, and the Dodo was the final nail.

"You have fluttered close to the winds more perilous these many years, Octopus," sighed Tesla. "There was for sure the inevitability of this exposure."

They both agreed that to hand over the Dodo's advanced knowhow would be disastrous. I advised them of our plan. To work on the design while awaiting the outcome of Michael's treatment. Whether Michael came through or not, Wicko and I would destroy, conceal and generally put the mockers on everything we had built at The Metropolitan Theatre of Steam, Smoke and Mirrors before disappearing into the night and continuing our work from the shadows. Remembering that our ultimate quest was to get ourselves home, to get Michael back to where he once belonged.

You know, in an entirely perverse way, all that unpleasantness at Westminster Abbey was precisely the boot in the glutes we required to spur us on.

~16~

Two weeks passed. As promised, coerced, however you wish to put it, we delivered to Superintendent Melville our freshly drawn blueprints for the design of the Dodo. Which looked very convincing. We even threw in a few aesthetic improvements, such as glazing the entire nose cone section, giving the aeronaut a better view of the ground. The engine? We were still working on that. We said.

At the theatre the auditorium grew more chilled and solemn. On stage the pre-set illusions stood sulking under oil cloths and the boards underfoot began to creak. Once a night Wicko would fire up the lights and run the Iron Safety Curtain up and down for something to do. Phoebe spent her time between the theatre, her railway carriage home where she honed her combat skills or maintaining a vigil at Michael's side.

It was all as if time was dragging itself to a complete and inexorable stop.

In fact, so stagnant had life become we looked forward to our nightly visits from Father Connor O'Connor, ex-communicated priest of this parish, which were a welcome relief from the drudgery. If only for their absurdity.

For example, one night he sat in the Pit Bar quaffing glasses of 'medicinal' port and brandy looking rosier than usual and flushed with contentment.

For so long as we had known him Connor had been the proud wearer of features made florid by the drink. In fact, so red was his face, while wearing a scarlet cassock and with that broad almost toothless grin, he might easily have been taken for a mobile pillar box.

When not lending his tireless support to the local distilleries or giving succour unstinting to the nuns of the diocese, none of whom were novices, he was generously attending to the needs of the local widows. One such middle-aged lovely of whom he told us that evening was a certain Mrs Flute, formerly of Cambridge, who briefly assisted the Director of the Fitzwilliam Museum, Dr M. R. James, in translating New Testament apocrypha. Despite his priestly credentials, Connor had to be told the apocrypha was writing by early Christians giving accounts of Jesus.

Mrs Flute gratefully repaid Connor's caring ministering by tracing his ancestral lineage and discovering that our dissolute priest could well be descended from one of the twelve disciples of Jesus.

"Sure, and that is most definitely the case," said Connor with pride. "'Tis a God-given fact."

"That is rather fascinating, Father O'Connor," purred Phoebe, genuinely intrigued. "And to which of the disciples did the remarkable Mrs Flute suggest you are you related?"

"Judas," he said proudly.

"That sounds about right," smiled Wicko, who continued to smile even as Father Connor O'Connor denounced him as the issue of an unholy union between a Satanic Leprechaun and an ass.

"Judas?" said Phoebe, with more than a hint of the query to her tone. "And, Father, you are comfortable with that?"

"Ah, now. I agree your man might not be the best loved of all the apostles. And was by far the most duplicitous. And reviled. But, look. In a decent light it cannot be denied I present the noble, aquiline features associated with the Iscariots." Connor proudly

47

offered his battered profile, slightly elevated as if to enhance his likeness to the betrayer of his Divine Master. "And I too am famed for my kissing!"

~17~

The next day a message was hand-delivered. The embossed coat of arms was familiar. From Buckingham Palace. In the absence of any immediate family, Michael's closest friends were to attend a presentation ceremony. The memory of the late Michael Magister was to be honoured with The Albert Medal first class, awarded for 'gallantry in saving life on land' – the civilian equivalent of The Victoria Cross.

Apparently when Prime Minister Salisbury's approval was first sought, he was less than enthusiastic. Buffoon. Michael's heroics saved a dozen lives, including the bearded old codger himself! Buffoon. Anyway, Her Majesty herself and the Prince of Wales were having none of it and both endorsed the recommendation. There was no official presentation. Just Phoebe, Wicko and I over for a quick cup of Darjeeling at Buckingham Palace and, in exchange for further signatures assuring the secrecy of the Westminster Abbey debacle, the Prince of Wales passed the medal under the table with a knowing tap of his red nose.

Having endured the company of her father, Phoebe felt it was correct to accept an invitation to the Cadogan Hotel for lunch with her mother. Which proved surprisingly civil and indigestion free, with Phoebe evading Mrs Langtry's subtle queries concerning the Flying Machine and plans for Michael's funeral, with ease and élan.

"Of course, I do still suspect Michael's death is all but a magnificent pretence for publicity," Lillie said, with confidence. Phoebe looked more puzzled than put out. "This is how I would plan the scenario. At his funeral, one imagines in Kensal Green, Magister is revealed with great reverence laying in the open coffin. There is weeping. Lamentations. The lid is then firmly nailed into place and the casket gently lowered into the cold earth of the yawning grave."

Phoebe flashed her eyes to the heavens. Go on.

"A brief and touching eulogy follows performed by, well, I suggest myself. But then in a moment of emotional and dramatic revelation, I foresee Michael is not dead and insist the coffin be raised again. That crowbars are taken to the lid. And once prised open – Magister is gone – but you climb out."

Lillie sat back and sipped water from the cut crystal tumbler, thoroughly pleased with her performance. "Is it not a most splendid idea?"

Phoebe was frankly stunned. Yes, she tried hard not to show it, but, in that overblown pantomime, Lillie Langtry *had* created a perfectly performable illusion.

And here's how it would work. Phoebe heads the mourners, but when Michael's lifeless body is revealed, faints and is carried away by, let us say, Wicko and myself. The mourners are then distracted by Lillie's histrionics.

Behind a bush, the fully conscious Phoebe drops into a specially dug tunnel leading to the grave. She waits in a hollow chamber beside the floor of the grave.

When the coffin is lowered, a sheet is flung across the mouth of the grave. At that moment, a false side panel in the coffin slides open allowing Michael and Phoebe to switch places. Michael rolls out of the coffin into the space as Phoebe slips under him into the box. Then, following the dramatic foretelling of life from Lillie Langtry, the secret panel is slid shut and the coffin raised. Phoebe can unclip her earth-streaked cape before the lid opens and she emerges. To great applause which echoes around the cemetery. And, no doubt, mourners fainting or clutching their hearts.

"You were most fortunate to have known Mr Magister, my darling child," said Lillie, when lunch drew to a close. "We both were."

*** 

Phoebe, hating herself for rather enjoying the encounter, rode a Hansom straight to the theatre, and was hurrying along White Lion Passage when she saw a man in a long fawn coat and a brown felt hat loitering by the Stage Door of the Metropolitan Theatre of Steam, Smoke and Mirrors.

He was rubbing the fingers of his right hand across the door and examining the Spectrascope lens, almost in appreciation. Behind him stood a good-sized black leather steamer trunk. None of which suggested he was police, Special Branch or a debt collector. Phoebe steeled herself as she approached, cleared her throat as she did, which made the man jump.

"Forgive me, sir," she said sweetly, "but I must inform you that all performances have been cancelled until further notice."

The startled fellow turned to face her. His eyes widened and in a shy fluster he removed his homburg hat. The man was olive skinned, sharply, darkly featured with the blackest of eyebrows, moustache, and luxuriant black wavy hair.

"Madam, perhaps I have the honour of addressing Miss Phoebe Le Breton?" His accent was strangely European, "At last we meet in the person. I arrive unannounced to visit with Professor More and Dr Smawl. And, of course, your good self."

"Well … now may not be the best time."

"Miss Le Breton, please understand I have journeyed a great distance on matters of importance very great. So please, if you would be so kind as to announce my arrival."

Phoebe found herself disarmed by the strange man's diffident yet insistent charm. "Whom shall I say is here to see them?"

"Madam, my name is Tesla. Nikola Tesla."

~18~

Inside the theatre I greeted Nik like a lost brother. It had been many years since I had physically held his skeletal frame against my chest instead of yelling at his blurred and fizzing image bouncing off the troposphere all the way from Knob Hill, Colorado. Wicko quickly joined the brotherly hug although, naturally, because of his stature could only snuggle his face into Tesla's stomach.

We refreshed the vegetarian, teetotal Nik as best we could in a theatre bar which sold spirits and bitter beer and Wicko's 'Mrs Lovett's Meat Pasties'. We then suggested he use Michael's vast dressing room in which to restore himself. But Nik was adamant, he had not spent a week braving the foaming fury of the Atlantic, then the smoky racket of the North Eastern railway just to then take what he called 'the sleep, most time wasting'.

Instead, he carefully unlocked and clicked open the latches on his steamer trunk and eased back the lid. First the reek of mothballs coughed into the air, then he removed several changes of neatly folded clothes, to reveal the first of his treats.

"I bring the gift for Miss Le Breton," explained Tesla. "For use in the hot city weather, or beneath the hot stage lights."

Tesla passed a beautifully wrapped package to Phoebe. It was revealed to be a Chinese hand fan; thin white silk mounted on metal slats, for which she expressed great joy and many thanks. Phoebe splayed open the fan and began cooling herself.

"Dear lady, it is while fanning the face one must exercise the most caution," warned Tesla. "Please now carefully close the fan."

She did.

"Now, at the arm's length, touch the tip of the closed fan upon this … item."

Nik pointed to the Mrs Lovett Pasty, which sat untouched on the bar. Phoebe did as she was asked. As soon as the tip touched the pie it sparked white and

FFZZT!

zapped the pasty clean off its plate, clean off the bar. Even the glasses on the shelves rattled from the force of the discharge.

The glorious reaction was everything Nik had hoped for, but Phoebe's delighted hug was not what he expected. "The simple discharge of the generated static electricity. For the self-defence. My gift to you."

She looked over at the pasty, lying stunned and forlorn on the floor. "You, sir, have been Tesla'd!"

Next out of the steamer trunk: a package the size of a loaf of bread, swaddled in white linen which, when removed, revealed itself as an object the size of a loaf of bread, nine inches in length and five in circumference. Perfectly cylindrical and skinned with burnished brass.

Now, when in doubt, I would often say at this point: "Is that what I think it is?" which is the question I always ask when I have not the faintest idea what something is, in the hope that the person holding the mysterious whatever it is, will say "Yes," and then explain exactly what it is, allowing me, now much the wiser, to then say, "I thought it was," and thus keep my genius intact.

But this object of simple artistic beauty, I knew precisely what it was. Two metal grills, two plunger switches, a lovely line of tiny rivets traversing the length of the cylinder, two more encircling the capped ends. From one end sprouted the stub of a tube. On the other, four circular dials, the largest inset low, with three smaller arrayed above, white-faced, glass housed. The large dial showed settings at the circumference, numbered from one to thirty-one. On the second dial, settings one to twelve. Next to that the dial showed twenty settings, and the final clock, far right, thirty.

It was a Tempus TimeKey. Tesla's Tempus TimeKey.

"Nik. You perfected it," Wicko whispered in awe, leaning close to examine the cylinder in detail. "Incredible. Nice to see our memories of Sir Nicholas Tesler's original Contrivance weren't far off the mark."

Tesla looked appalled. "It was your recollections most faulty which set me back these many years! The first version you had me build was the size of a carthorse. However, I refuse to be confounded by my other self."

A swish of breeze blew through the theatre.

"And it works?" said Wicko.

"Of course," said Tesla.

"And you trialled it where? The clock tower in New York?"

"In the practical sense, the Contrivance remains as yet, untried."

"Well, how do you know it works?"

Tesla gave Wicko a withering look. "Because I am Tesla."

Wicko nodded. "That's fair."

"Dr Tesla, may I please ask a question?" said Phoebe quietly.

"Why, madam, yes, please, of course."

"What on earth is a Tempus TimeKey?"

I began to tell Phoebe it was the key to our escape, but before I could continue, we heard a voice from the stage. A familiar voice.

"Professor More? Wicko Smawl? Chriiist!!"

The spavined man in bib-top dungarees was already standing in the middle of the stage in a state of great agitation, stiffening while he scanned the gloom of the theatre.

WHUMPH!

The beam of the spot cast him in a bright circle of light. He squinted and shielded his eyes.

Phoebe was walking down the aisle centre towards the stage. "Mr Spindleshanks? How did you get in without being detected, pray tell?"

Wicko scurried behind trying to keep up with her. "It's all right, Miss, he knows the magic passcode. Literally. We've got to change that…"

Spindle stiffened again when he saw them hove into view. "Chriiist! Dr Phunn and Miss Wu Hu say you're to come at once. It's Magister!"

~19~

The four-mile journey westward to the Scrubbs had never been convenient, but with Phoebe driving, the Steamo tamed the route in double quick time. Riding with her: Wicko, myself and Spindle. But not Tesla. Having been robbed in the past, Nik had no regard for the Chinaman.

In Dr Phunn's laboratory, hidden at the back of his pagoda, we all jammed in around the Sarcophagus watching him and his sister at work. Spindle balanced on his tiptoes at the back trying to get a peep at what was going on. Phunn busied himself taking readings from the gauges, while Wu Hu prepared a hypodermic of her green gloop.

"Thank you, ladies and gentlemen," said Phunn. "It is time."

I didn't see what controls he adjusted, but immediately the needles on all the gauges fell to zero. The continuous sigh of gas breezing into the Sarcophagus drifted to silence.

Phoebe glanced at me, then Wicko and then steeled herself. Wicko and I tried to adopt an air of insouciance but inside…

The Oriental shaman unlatched the heavy side clamp
TTTTTSSSsssss…

releasing a cloud of mist. The portholes fogged with condensation. The pressure now equalised, Phunn lifted the lid of the Sarcophagus and hinged it open. The air from the casket was cool and clean. Sterile.

The vapour thinned and swirled and then vanished, revealing Michael's body, entirely uncovered save for the dark goggles protecting his eyes. Wu Hu withdrew the rubber tubes from the veins in his wrists and bound them tightly with muslin seeped in some eastern potion. She hauled free the orange rubber tube which snaked from his mouth. Then administered the injection of gloop.

"Magister is independent of the machine," she said. "He now either lives, or he dies."

All of us, everyone, peered into the Sarcophagus. Curious. Fearful. Hoping. Silence.

Then…

"GAAAAH!" The wheeze was desperate and painful. Either Michael Magister's first gasp or his last. His muscles tensed. He tried to sit up. Dr Phunn restrained him, forcing his shoulders back down.

"Lie. Breathe. Relax. Breathe." They were firm commands not soothing advice. Michael did as he was told. Once Wu Hu signalled her approval, Phunn continued: "Thank you, Michael Magister, we are about to remove your protective lenses. But your eyes must remain tightly closed. Is that understood."

A dry rasp.

Phunn eased the goggles from his face. "Breathe. Gently. Gently, I said."

Wu Hu then snapped an order at Phoebe. "Le Breton. Here. Now. Let yours be the first face Magister sees."

Wu Hu shuffled to one side, affording Phoebe a better look down inside the iron casket, while she ordered Magister in no uncertain terms to: "Very slowly open your eyes! I said very slowly!! Open them."

Michael did not dare disobey. The dull light softened the image before him. His mouth tasted of carbolic. His eyes rasped as he blinked a dozen times, washing away what felt like sand. He knew he wasn't dead. But the face he looked up at was angelic.

"Welcome back," said Phoebe.

*** 

Half an hour later, Michael was out of the Sarcophagus, dressed in a maroon silk robe, one of Phunn's less elaborate dressing gowns. Four hours after that, convalescence continued, involving puffing unspeakably sharp herbal fumes from a Hookah pipe and sipping cups of vile amber sludge.

Already Michael was looking so much better. The scarlet flesh from the burns on his mouth and neck, hands and arms had healed so well as to be almost imperceptible. His breathing, though wheezy and gentle, was without discomfort. Talking remained a problem, although Wu Hu anticipated a return to full function.

"We do not know how to express our gratitude," said Phoebe.

"Thank you, Phoebe Le Breton, but you and Michael Magister rescued my sister. Saved her life. It is correct we should reciprocate."

"Return tomorrow," said Wu Hu. "Then you may take Magister home."

Before firing up the Steamo, we were again profuse in our appreciation. The Phunns and Spindle waved us away as we bounced and bobbed across the Scrubbs, through the trees and out onto Scrubbs Lane.

"Thank you, Mr Spindleshanks, what is the cause of your consternation?" asked Phunn.

"You have been bouncing from foot to foot ever since you brought them back here." Wu Hu was particularly terse.

"Christ!!! When I went to the theatre to tell them about Magister, I looked around. Heard them talking. Chriiist!"

"And?" demanded Wu Hu.

"Miss Wu Hu," said Spindle, as he tensed, "Tesla's in the country."

"Tesla? You're certain?"

"Chriiist, yes. He's at the theatre. And he's brought the Tempus TimeKey."

This time Dr Phunn and Wu Hu tensed. Then smiled. And it was she who said: "Christ!"


~20~


As predicted, Michael was sufficiently strong to be 'discharged' from the pagoda. The Phunns had generously delayed their journey to the Continent for quite long enough. We all agreed Michael should continue his convalescence at Phoebe's elegant railway carriage, down there in a Paddington Goods Yard siding, just by the Harrow Road.

It was warm, and, despite the shunting and shifting racket outside, remarkably peaceful.

I was in the kitchen area, brewing up another panful of Phunn's efficacious sludge tea while the two great scientific minds which were Dr Manswick Smawl and Nikola Tesla tried to fathom how to get the medicinal Hookah going.

Michael had regained some voice and looked much stronger, reclining, blanketed up, on the chaise as Phoebe reminded him of those dramatic events leading up to his heroic death. And, in her capacity as an illegitimate royal, presented Michael with his gold 'Albert Medal, first class'.

"You'll see the engraving states – For Gallantry in Saving Life on Land" Phoebe told him. He closely studied the honour. The enamelled red oval with the initials of the Queen and her late consort 'V and A' intertwined.

"Of course, it is awarded posthumously," said Phoebe. "From a grateful nation. So, once they discover you are still alive, they will grab it back in a heartbeat."

He smiled, distracted.

"Michael? I know you too well now. What is the matter?"

"Nothing. No. Well. I hope not. See, Pheebs, it's important I tell you this and that you hear it from me. It's something the Professor and Wicko and Nik have known for the last decade, probably even ten years."

Phoebe settled on the floor beside him holding his hand. "Go on."

We all joined them in the sitting area. Wicko, Tesla and me.

"I would have told you sooner, truth is I only just remembered it myself. See, you know my demon nightmares? All those slips of the tongue I made. Ridiculous stuff we could never understand. Now I know everything there is to know about me. Everything I forgot."

"Michael. Get on with it."

"So. Yes. And this might be kind of hard to take in, because it certainly was for me. The thing is, Pheebs – I'm from the future."

~21~

Phoebe sat and stared, then chuckled, looking at Michael and then up at us. "Now, is this some kind of post end-of-life hangover?"

"Magister is right, Miss," said Wicko. "He's from the future. One hundred years in the future to be not quite precise."

There was a moment's silence.

"That is … the most wonderful news," she exclaimed! I know, but that's how she said it. Wonderful news!! She patted her neck and said: "Oooooh, thank goodness for that!"

Well, frankly we were all stunned by the reaction. I said something about knowing this was a difficult concept to comprehend, but Phoebe laughed again, and flung her arms around Michael's neck, saying: "Absolutely the opposite! This is Mr Wells' story come true! I could not be more excited!"

"I can tell," said Michael, gasping a little.

"And, of course, it explains so much. Michael, not only your nightmares, the visions, but your exuberant manner which is nothing like anyone has ever seen before! And your shocking misuse of the English language, often spoken without any sense or meaning! I *knew* it was not simply down to the fact you were American!"

Michael winced.

Phoebe let him go with an "Oh, I'm so sorry. Are you all right?" Then she continued, now on her feet. "I truly thought I was the one who would one day wake up from a dream. I am so thrilled and it's such a relief, I can't tell you."

"This has gone a little better than I hoped it would," said Michael.

"So now. Now! Safe in the knowledge that Michael is from the future, I am rapidly forming the opinion, as I stand here in the midst of this plethora of scientific geniuses – that I am the only person in the carriage who is *not* from the future. Am I right?"

She looked around, expecting us all to agree. Which, after due consideration, we did.

"Ha! I knew it! Oh, this is all too wonderful. Come, you three, let me hug you." So, we let her. Although Nik was slightly awkward. Then she counted thoughts off on her fingers. "It also explains the Dodo. The Steamo. The power sources in the theatre. This carriage. Michael's barge. The mechanical illusions. And Mr Garrideb! Dear Lord, even our much-missed Pulsa Pistols. I do rather miss those, by the way. All of it based on knowledge you all brought from another time! Splendid! Does that include Dr Phunn's miraculous healing Sarcophagus? Are he and that sister of his from the future as well?"

"They are," said Tesla.

"I knew it. Far too untrustworthy for their own good."

I insisted Phoebe sat in a chair for a moment and took a breath to reduce her heart rate. Wicko even offered a puff on the Hookah, which she sensibly declined.

Then she crossed her legs, smoothed her skirt and adopted that ladylike, serious look. "So, now then, gentlemen of the future. As much as I love you, there is one major question I am compelled to ask you. What on earth are you all doing here in 1899?"

~22~

"Long story told short," said Wicko, jumping up onto a seat and shuffling to get comfortable. "Well, not that short. It's 1919. The Professor and me, along with Phunn and that sister of his, we were working in a laboratory beneath a clock tower, in New Jersey, and – there was an accident. A surge of uncontrolled energy, if you will. We were standing too close and got flung back to 1889. There are further elements which add complications to our situation which I won't bore you with right now. The Professor can do that when he writes about them one day."

(And I shall, I promise you.)

"Madam," said Tesla, meekly. "Permit me to confess … to accepting your hug, under the false pretences. Because I, like you, am not from the future."

I endorsed Nik's admission, but added it never showed in his work. Which pleased him. I went on to explain that Michael's situation was also a result of some 'surge of uncontrolled energy' accident.

Michael took up the tale, confident that for once he knew what he was talking about:

"I'm living in New York, in 2001. I wound up in a clock tower, with very little, and possibly at the same time *no* clothes on, do I need to explain..."

Phoebe held up a knowing hand. "I can imagine."

"But something happened there, or outside, while I was drugged, asleep, whatever I was, because when I woke up, it's 1889. There I am curled up beside a gravestone with nothing but my jacket and a pack of cards in the pocket. That's the only reason I knew my name. And that I could do magic tricks. If the

Professor and Nik hadn't found me, who knows what might have happened."

"You see, the Professor and me, and the Phunns, we could remember everything," said Wicko. "Who we were and where we came from, everything. And the reason for that anomaly, we believe, is because Michael wasn't awake when the event occurred, that's what caused the amnesia. The jacket and the cards jogged certain memories, but nothing else."

The complete memory recall of his life was triggered at the moment of Michael's death. Then Phoebe's question cued even further exposition.

"But you all gravitated from different years back to 1889? That surely can be no coincidence."

"Ah. That, madam," admitted Tesla, "is most likely down to myself. At that time, I operated three laboratories in New York. During that week I was conducting the first complex test experiments upon my power transmission Coil, the biggest built thus far. We hypothesise that the electrical atmosphere generated by the Coil attached itself to the energy pulse generated around each clock tower."

To continue the current theme of conversation, I grasped the opportunity to admit there had been no reason to share time travel information with Michael. Why confuse him further? Until we learned from which year he came, and we had developed the means by which we could take him, and ourselves, back.

We even enlisted the assistance of William Thompson, Lord Kelvin as he is known now, the most eminent scientist of this era, who naturally embraced the technology with the intellectual maturity to remain aware of its significance and respectful of our confidentiality.

"With the existence of the Flying Dodo now exposed, and the eventual arrests of Professor Octopus and Dr Smawl most likely, I said to myself, Dr Tesla, now it is necessary to deliver the working Tempus TimeKey. With this, you may all return to your former lives. And if this is the plan, and everyone is agreeable, I would very much like to come with you. To see the future."

"If you are planning on going, so would I," said Phoebe.

"Pheebs?"

"Michael, think about it. What would I possibly do if you and the Professor and Wicko were no longer here? I would not entertain going back to the Music Hall as Maskelyne's assistant. I have two parents who are far too famous to even dare acknowledge I exist. Yes, there are people I would miss. I can think of three. Each of them of certain age. My closest family is in this railway carriage. That is why I too would like to come."

I told everyone a decision of this magnitude requires a time reflection.

"I've reflected," said Michael. "Let's go."

"If the Tempus TimeKey is to function with total accuracy there is one additional component part which requires the sourcing," said Tesla. "That component, most important, is the Fugit FlyWheel."

I agreed. And like it or not – we had to visit The Grimm.

Wicko's shoulders sagged at the thought.

And both Michael and Phoebe said: "Who's The Grimm?"

~23~

Later that afternoon, Michael was dressed, hatted, scarfed and claiming to feel very much better on his reasonably unwobbly legs. He sat in the back between me and Tesla, who nursed on his lap the canvas bag which housed the TimeKey. Phoebe steered the Steamo, next to Wicko who was directing the route to St Albans. A straightforward journey. Turn left out of the theatre, up the Edgware Road heading north and keep going until, no surprise, the village of Edgware, where it becomes Watling Street. Through Elstree, stopping off at Radlett to take on water – and the price of water on the highway these days! Then a hold up where a cart had shed its load of offal, then bear right to St Albans. Two and a half hours! Which, to be fair, Nik Tesla remarked was necessary because the only person skilled enough to confect the component we required was The Grimm.

"And The Grimm is?" asked Michael. "We are still waiting on an answer here."

I apologised. He is Lord Grimthorpe.

"Grimthorpe?" Phoebe knew the name. "The gentleman who designed the huge clock mechanism for Big Ben?"

The very same. And it was that very clock mechanism we would use to facilitate our passage through time. Grimthorpe built it to drive Parliament's four clock faces, mindful that one day his mechanism would enjoy a secondary use.

"Oh, my days, that is tremendously exciting. But is not Lord Grimthorpe said to be a little…?"

He is.


It was early evening before we finally crunched along the gravel drive of "Batchwood", Grimthorpe's vast mansion set in twenty picturesque acres on the north western fringe of the city.

I tugged the chain which rang the bell. Or I should say bells, at least half a dozen all tuned to form some discordant din. While we waited we examined the exterior of the house. "Batchwood" was barely twenty-five years old, broad of frontage, built in the faux Georgian style, three storeys, five windows either side of the central door, and built and designed by Lord Grimthorpe himself. Or to give him his full title: The First Lord Grimthorpe, formerly Edmund Beckett Denison Q.C., formerly Sir Edmund Beckett, fifth Baronet.

"You call him The Grimm for short," said Michael.

"There is another reason," said Wicko.

"Is there no peace?" hollered the voice from inside the house. "Whomever comes a-calling at this time of night, you are not welcome! Get thee gone, lest I turn the dogs on you."

Michael understood. "And that's the other reason."

Exactly so. But fortunately it sounded very much as if we were finding him in one of his better moods.

I announced us all loudly, with the words 'All save Robert Hooke!' Which was met with a loud, unimpressed harrumph.

Nevertheless, a noise of myriad clicks and clacks then ensued while at least a dozen locks and bolts were released and the door swung open just enough. The man standing before us looked formidable. Wearing a wing-collar shirt done up to the neck, long-tailed black evening wear, with sleeves rolled back up over the elbow. Remarkable for eighty years of age, spectacles perched up on the brow of a long forehead, bright, beady eyes, lines creased down his face from a life of constant frowning and scowling, all topped off with a luxuriant shock of snow-white hair swept up and back in some absurdly high quiff.

"All save Robert Hooke, indeed," said Lord Grimthorpe as he weighed us up. One at a time.

"Professor More. Dr Smawl. And, what's this? Dr Tesla, is it not? I am honoured, sir." The Grimthorpe pattern of speech was clipped and haughty. He squinted at Michael. "You, sir, who be ye?"

"Michael Magister. Your Lordship," said Michael, removing his topper, and bowing. "The Industrial Age Illusionist."

"Poppycock," was Grimthorpe's firm and confident response.

"Erm. With respect, your Lordship, I am pretty sure who I am. Maybe my card will prove it." Michael stepped forward before the old boy could react and swiftly produced the King of Clubs from behind Grimthorpe's absurdly long right ear. And his ears truly were unfeasibly long.

"I heard tell ye was dead. And by the look of you, sir, those accounts were not without foundation."

Now, I know Michael still looked pale and peaky following his death, but it was not in The Grimm's nature to be sympathetic. Instead his blazing eyes widened further once they flicked to Phoebe. "And you! I say ye be that Young Woman of whom I hear. A paragon of stagecraft and mystification. The Music Hall's epitome of beauty, they claim. The Queen of Steam, they attest. Goddess of the Aethyr. If all of such said was so, 'that Young Woman' should not be sharing the company of these here scoundrels."

The Grimm flapped a dismissive hand in the vague direction of the rest of us, adding quickly, "I mean, of course, no disrespect to Dr Tesla."

Then suddenly he lost interest and consulted one of three gold pocket Hunters chained to his waistcoat pocket. "But there it is. Each to their own. And time and tide tarries for no man. I thank you all for calling. There lies the exit. Good night." And with that

SLAM!

he promptly closed the door.

Phoebe broke the brief silence by asking: "Am I alone in wanting to crack him across the head with a parasol?"

"Madam, you most certainly are not," said the normally mild-mannered Tesla.

"Miserable old git," said Wicko.

I had to agree that the noble Lord Grimthorpe was an acquired taste, and it was a taste very few could be bothered to acquire. In an over-crowded church hall, The Grimm would be easy to find. Just look for the man arguing with somebody. But perseverance was essential. And we had driven a long way.

"He's testing us," said Michael. "Notice he hasn't re-locked the door."

Very good point. So, this time I rapped on the black painted wood with my walking cane, while an irate Wicko shouted: "Edmund! Edmund, you miserable old git! Tesla's brought the Tempus TimeKey!"

The door swished open again, this time with ridiculous speed.

"The TimeKey? The Tempus TimeKey? Who are ye to come here? Claiming to bring the Tempus TimeKey?"

I told him we knew that he knew exactly who we were *and* we had already given the long-ago agreed password. "All save Robert Hooke". Hmm. Grimthorpe scratched his short, stubby chin. Hmm. Tough to dispute that.

Then he lowered his voice, as if spies were skulking in every shadow. "Tesla and Kelvin have finally come good?"

I told him Tesla had.

"Gratifying news that be. Gratifying news indeed. But far too late! All you idiots have been so slow." Yes, he really did call Nikola Tesla and Lord Kelvin 'idiots'. And Wicko and me! But then he would, wouldn't he? "I knew I should have worked the problem myself. Years ago. I would have cracked that conundrum in half the time they took. But still. Best that ye enter!"

So, we traipsed into the magnificent hallway.

"But!" Grimthorpe then held up a hand. "Not these magicians." He glared at Michael and Phoebe with disdain. "For I hear tell ye both be acknowledged as the finest escapees. Lock crackers of the utmost order. Be this true?"

"Yes, it has been frequently said," said Michael. "Admittedly by me."

"And on this occasion, he is completely correct," added Phoebe.

"Hah! But see here now. I am considered the finest of lock *makers*. Regard my own magnificence. Designed and built by these dexterous hands." Lord Grimthorpe proudly indicated the line of keyholes which ran up a third of the length of the door. "So then, Magister and That Young Woman, ye *may* join us within. But only *if* you can overcome *my* superior skills with *your* locksmith crackery. Good night."

SLAM!

...leaving Michael and Phoebe still outside. On the gravel drive. While they listened to the click and clacks of the locks being locked.

"I care little for your hospitality, sir," called Phoebe.

Inside, we none of us heard it and here is why.

The entrance hall of Batchwood was graced with two grand staircases sweeping symmetrically upwards to the first floor. The dark panelled walls did little to help the electric light penetrate the gloom, but, you know, the place was graced with the scent of smoke, polish and oil, an industrial cocktail we all found agreeable.

But none of these lovely distractions could compare to the noise! What a racket! Dear God, the interminable, rhythmical din of his collection of clocks! Hundreds of them. Grimthorpe was a known collector and keeper of timepieces of every age, style and persuasion: carriage, bracket, skeleton, ormolu, and lantern, silver, gold, brass, wood, all of them presented upon every available surface, table, mantel and shelf. Many domed in protective glass. All of them turning, swinging and spinning in some way or another, all of them ticking our lives relentlessly away.

Yes, they presented precisely the same time to the very second, but that in no way could mitigate the ruckus created by this unsynchronised, mind-fuddling 'clockophony'. The Grimm even stopped us mid-step so that we might enjoy this horological nightmare all the more. Arrgh.

"Of course, mathematics is my natural talent," declared Grimthorpe. "Ecclesiastical Law is my renowned expertise.

Architecture is my acclaimed ability. But, as you know, chronometry is my indisputable skill." At which point he thankfully led us from the hall and into a huge, high-ceilinged living room.

Gloomy, until he clicked on the electric light.

And the first thing we noticed as we walked in? The chill. And more tick-tocking, but softer. Less oppressive. Coming from clocks, all of the long case variety, all backed against every available wall space: grandfather, grandmother and assorted grand relatives.

On the fireless chimney breast above the mantelpiece a full-length portrait of Lord Grimthorpe posing on Westminster Bridge, resplendent in his coronet and scarlet ceremonial robes of Peerage, holding an open scroll depicting some sort of clockwork gubbins in one hand, and a large circular example of such dog-toothed gubbins in the other. In the background, beyond his right shoulder, stood the gothic Palace of Westminster and the great clocktower housing Big Ben.

In the centre of the room a refectory table, covered with hundreds of cog related parts which, when lined up and screwed, would form the movement of a town hall clock. The round face lying in the middle was smoky off-white and the size of a Spartan's shield.

Then, cutting through the visual distractions, a voice declared: "Ah. My Lord Grimthorpe. Come right in. After all, you do live here."

"We cannot think what kept you!" said the woman's voice.

~25~

Yes. The second thing we saw as we walked in was Phoebe lounging seductively in an easy chair, both knees hooked across one arm, and Michael standing behind her, leaning forward on the chair back.

Even I will admit to being startled by the sight. But Grimthorpe was horrified. His jaw fell and his brows knitted, dropping his spectacles down onto the bony bridge of his Roman nose. He quickly tried to fathom, with elaborate arm gestures, how such an impossibility could possibly happen. "But – but. I heard nought of the door. Saw nought of ye passing in the hall!"

Very pleasingly, the old boy was confounded.

"Sir! That Woman! I insist you explain this magicry."

"It's only magic if you don't know how it's done," smiled Michael.

"My Lord, your various locks and front door fasteners are all very impressive," purred Phoebe. "However, the latches which secure your downstairs windows…"

"…are very far from it," said Michael continuing the narrative, as he gestured with a sweep toward the two tall Georgian style sash windows which dominated the room. Sash windows were a Robert Hooke invention, by the way. All save him. "It's not difficult to slice a thin blade through the gap between the upper and lower frame and slide open the latch." Then with one hand he demonstrated by pushing the window up and closing it again. "So, what do you say, my Lordship? Call it a win for us?"

Grimthorpe squinted. Not happy. "I shall certainly not call it a win for thee! My door locks were the subject of the challenge and my door locks remain steadfast! That was the wager! Yours was burglary, not magicry! Such duplicity, sir, and that Young Woman, invalidates the trial! Here be the end to it!"

"That is very well said, your Lordship." Michael reacted quickly, in case Phoebe and Wicko expressed their outrage in word and deed. "Your door locks and your reputation remain intact."

"I am never bested," boasted Grimthorpe. "I accept your capitulation. You may remain to admire my horological craftsmanship."

"Edmund, are you going to play games? Do you want to see Nik's TimeKey, or not?" demanded Wicko, still smouldering.

"No, I do not," Grimthorpe told him. And how! "Too slow in the manufacture, was Dr Tesla. Too slow. I need waste no further time looking at ought from which I will now derive no benefit. You have denied me the miracle of time travel with your prevarication. And now ye have the gall to come begging for me Fugit FlyWheel."

Well, yes, why else would we be here?

"Ye cannot have her!" That stumped us. But before we could protest the old boy continued, "Go seek Dr William Percival Stockdale's 'Necessitti' device, let that aid thee."

No one knew where that device was located! Nor even Dr William himself, but that is entirely another story. Literally!

"But I shall grant ye the courtesy. Of trying to earn her ownership."

What?

He continued, very pleased with himself. "My magnificent Fugit FlyWheel holds her place in time. She *is* in this room. And if ye can locate said FlyWheel, then she is yours. Ye shall deserve her. But time is never a friend. And ye have but a single minute of time to seek her out."

"Gah, so help me, Edmund," said Wicko. "We are not here for games and riddles."

Grimthorpe consulted two of his waistcoat pocket watches. "Seek ye out the FlyWheel, then she is thine. That is the wager. And your one single minute of time begins to pass – now."

~26~

Where to look? Where to begin looking? Grimthorpe gestured to two dark wood dressers recessed either side of the fireplace while saying, "Make haste, ye doth not have time on your hands."

These side dressers either side of the fireplace were also covered with dismantled innards and stripped-down carcasses of brass and wooden clocks, each with their associated springs and cog-work innards laid meticulously by their sides.

I began by searching through those. Tesla worked the large refectory table. Wicko hauled open the doors of cases on the grandfather clocks and checked inside. One long swinging pendulum nearly cracked the side of his head.

"Be sure to admire my faultless workmanship as you search," goaded Grimthorpe.

Phoebe stood to join the search, but Michael told her to wait.

"Prof, exactly what is this Fugit FlyWheel," he demanded.

While sifting through possible parts I offered a hurried explanation. A fly wheel in a clock mechanism is the necessary component which regulates the passage of time, but this particular

FlyWheel, when operated in conjunction with Tesla's Tempus TimeKey, controls the passage *through* time. And the FlyWheel in question would be a certain size. Which he said was somewhere in this room.

Michael knelt painfully by the chair and whispered: "Pheebs, we don't have time to search. But I think I can figure this one out."

"Very well," said Phoebe, not exactly convinced. "So where would the great Lord Grimthorpe hide his Fugit FlyWheel?"

"We know he's pleased with his own workmanship."

Their eyes scanned the room, dwelling briefly upon we three great scientific minds, scratching our heads, and Grimthorpe rubbing together his hands.

"Loath as I am to admit, his work is all rather skilful," whispered Phoebe.

"He wants us to admire what he does. It's why everything's on show."

"Which rather suggests he's going to want to display the FlyWheel."

"Absolutely correct. It's not going to be tucked up tight in a box, a drawer or amongst any pile of stuff."

"Hidden in plain sight."

"Exactly that. And look at his face. Human nature. He's enjoying this. Knowing he can see it and we can't."

Lord Grimthorpe announced loudly: "Half of one-minute remains! I note you magicians be making no attempt to aid the hunt."

"This is a man," said Michael, "who clearly loves himself and what he does, which I know is something we both dislike. However – hidden in plain sight."

"Where we are looking, but not seeing?"

"Which is anything and everything. Narrow it down. Pheebs, other than himself, and this FlyWheel, what's this man's proudest achievement?"

"Surely it must be designing the clock mechanism which drives…"

They both whispered together "Big Ben."

They both turned to the portrait above the fireplace. Of Grimthorpe in his Upper House finery.

"'My magnificent Fugit FlyWheel holds her place in time'," she said, as inspiration hit. "That's what Grimthorpe said. Michael, what is he holding in the picture?"

"Ten seconds," announced Grimthorpe, most excited.

Michael smiled. "Best you go and find out."

Phoebe ran from the chair to the chimney breast. Rubbed her fingers over the canvas. Which was thick and rough with dried oil paint. Over the cogged circle of clockwork gubbins the noble Lord was holding in his hand. It was smooth to touch. Metallic.

"Two seconds!"

With both sets of fingernails she prised the FlyWheel from the picture. "Hello!" – and held it high in triumph.

~27~

The noble Lord was more gracious than you might imagine. Not by much, but in fairness he honoured the result of the challenge and gave up the FlyWheel.

Nik Tesla even showed the old boy the Tempus TimeKey. Grimthorpe peered through his spectacles, close up, examining the instrument from every angle. Tesla explained the input wheels which adjusted and set the needles on the gauges, controlling the precise target date, year and the direction of travel.

"Adequate for the job," said Lord Grimthorpe, which from him was high praise. "And the power source?"

The Tesla Coil within the TimeKey.

He drew himself up as best he could. "You would all benefit from my expertise if I were to accompany you on your travel. But I cannot. I am far too occupied redesigning St Albans Cathedral. Naturally it will be even more magnificent to behold when work is completed."

"Your Lordship, we'll benefit from your expertise with the FlyWheel," said Michael.

"You will all leave now. Leave! Good night and be gone." Lord Grimthorpe began ushering us out of the room. "Except    Mr TesIa. I wish to speak with you alone."

So, we bade Edmund Beckett, the first Baron Grimthorpe farewell, with an "All Save Robert Hooke". Well Wicko and I did, Phoebe waved the FlyWheel. Then we fired up the Steamo and waited for little more than two minutes before Nik Tesla too was shown the door and had it slammed shut behind him. He climbed back aboard, his canvas bag held close.

As we trundled the Steamo back to the theatre, Michael was the first to ask: "What was that about, Nik?"

"His Lordship, he demanded I look at how well his endeavours are still admired in the future. Most especially his endeavours on the St Albans Cathedral. And his work as the nation's greatest horologist."

"Michael, before you utter anything lewd it means the study of clocks!"

"I knew that," said Michael. He didn't. Not that it mattered. He just wasn't sure he believed a word of what Tesla had just said.

~28~

As I described in my previous volume, the Metropolitan Theatre of Steam Smoke & Mirrors had stood 'dark' for a month. 'No Further Performances' appeared on sandwich boards and the straplines pasted diagonally across the framed herald posters front of house.

The 'mystery' of Magister's disappearance, he calls it a 'Music Hall Urban Legend', which embroiders the situation a little I think, was the subject of alehouse scuttlebutt. But only until an advertisement appeared in the 'Paddington Mercury' announcing that at seven-thirty this evening Phoebe Le Breton, the Queen of Steam and Goddess of the Aethyr, would appear on stage to make a heartfelt announcement.

Interest, speculation and word of mouth was extraordinary. Complimentary invitations were sent out and just as quickly accepted, and by the evening, tickets were hard to come by. I should really have realised the attraction would have been so great. And I should have charged a price for the tickets. But my mind had been occupied with other plans.

Wicko and I held out for as long as we dared, until we delivered the blueprint designs for our Flying Machine. It would only be a matter of days before government engineers figured out that whatever they managed to build based on our specifications, the steam engine dirigible would possess all the aeronautical capabilities of an upright piano. And without the patent Alytheium Generator, the weight-to-power ratio could never be overcome. But I think I have always said that.

The plan was to stage this spectacular comeback performance, and as the end curtain fell, we would slip quietly away, to fulfil the promise Wicko, Tesla and I made to ourselves a decade ago, of delivering Michael back to the year 2001. In the very welcome company of Phoebe.

Here, in 1899, we would erase all evidence that any of us had even existed. Scorched Earth I believe they call it. That promised to be spectacular.

Snags we did not foresee, were three-fold. All of which conspired to converge on that night of the show. The first was Her Majesty's Government scientists turning out to be a good deal smarter, and faster, than anyone had ever before given them credit for. The second was a problem about which we knew nothing until much later, concerning our nemesis, the Black Bishop who dispatched Messrs. Drago and Skrill, his God-fearing murderous psychopaths to kill Michael and Phoebe in the name of the Lord at the end of this last performance.

But the most significant snag manifested itself in the form of Dr Phunn, his sister Wu Hu and the cast of their Carnival of Mechanical Miracles. During the show.

While Michael and Phoebe were enthralling the crowd with their steam-driven cavalcade of industrial strength illusions, and Wicko and I were occupied in our stage management roles, Nikola Tesla busied himself here and there back stage ensuring Scorched Earth was set to do what it was supposed to do.

He distributed envelopes containing equal shares of whatever money remained among our front of house staff, half a dozen of the most loyal, decent Paddington locals. We figured twenty pounds each would see them right for a year.

From the roars and applause he heard rumbling out through the stained-glass doors to the auditorium, Nik Tesla knew the finale was progressing well.

The difficulty started as he walked out of the ticket hall, onto the Edgware Road and cut back down White Lion Passage, heading for the Stage Door. On reflection, Nik thinks he heard the soft flick-flack sound while he was tapping the new Stage

Door entry code into the keyboard W R O N G. Well *I* thought it was amusing. Anyway, the flick-flack seemed to get louder.

CLICK!

The Stage Door clicked open and Nik suddenly felt a weight on his neck. Not so much a weight as a tension. No, a presence, borne out by the presence of the legs hanging down of the person who was sitting on his shoulders. "Gah? What...?"

"Chriiist!" cried Spindle in response, desperate to keep the Stage Door open while Tesla bucked and wriggled to shift him. And just as Nik twisted and pitched forward to tumble Spindle to the floor, a huge hand held the door and pulled it open wide.

Nik saw the huge bulk that was Lazarus. Then heard the voice. "Thank you, Lazarus. Dr Nikola Tesla. Good evening." The voice was firm and deep.

~29~

"Chriiist!" said Spindle, rolling up onto his feet in a single smooth action.

"Phunn," said Tesla bitterly. "I cannot think why I am so surprised."

"Thank you, shall we repair inside? Which, I should add is not a question."

Once Tesla was hustled into the Stage Door Lobby, Lazarus stood guard by the door. Arms folded across his mighty chest. You may remember Lazarus, the immensely strong black man, a sideshow feature born without limbs, but restored to mobility by the Phunns. He wore black dungarees, as did Spindle, except Spindle's were twenty sizes smaller.

"You stated to Octopus you were leaving for the Continent. This truth I did question."

"The Continent can be cold at this time of the year," said Phunn. "What would be more agreeable would be a voyage home. A return to my time and my place."

Phunn leant back against Wicko's Stage Door desk. Quite relaxed. His arms too were across his chest, but his hands tucked up into the cuffs of the opposite sleeves of his traditional Chinese silk blouse, Mandarin red, with an embroidered gold dragon. Upon his head, he wore a black skull-capped Wangjing hat.

"For such a voyage to take place you shall require the TimeKey and no such Contrivance exists."

"Ah, Dr Tesla, *that* truth *I* must question," smiled Phunn. Without shifting his gaze at Nik, the felon reached behind for the canvas bag which lay on the Desk and dragged it forward. "Oh, my. What is this? Mr Spindleshanks, if you please."

Spindle tensed his thin body, his knuckles inclined inwards.

Phunn pulled the brass cylinder from the canvas bag.

"Is this the Contrivance you witnessed Dr Tesla displaying in the theatre bar?"

"That's it, Dr Phunn, that's it. Chriiist!"

Phunn lifted the Contrivance for a closer examination. "I commend the beauty of the workmanship." Then he felt inside the canvas bag and with his other hand pulled out the metal ring. A foot wide. Black. "And what is this we also find? The FlyWheel." Phunn slowly caressed the teeth which formed the outer cogs on the rim with his thumb. "A generous bestowment from Lord Grimthorpe."

Tesla was white with rage. "You stole from me at Colorado Springs, and now you steal from me again!" He shaped to grab the TimeKey, but Lazarus stepped in to form a threatening barrier. "You are a disgrace to your medical genius, Dr Phunn."

"It is a burden," said Phunn. "But one I am content to bear."

He reunited the FlyWheel with the TimeKey in the canvas bag and casually tossed the precious content to Lazarus, who caught it with ease.

"Chriiist!" said Spindle.

"Our business here is done. I bid you good evening, Dr Nikola Tesla. And farewell."

There was nothing Tesla could or dare do to prevent Dr Phunn gracefully strolling out of the Lobby and into the night, his two acolytes following close by. Spindle grinning spitefully. And Lazarus carrying the precious cargo.

The Stage Door closed. Nik dabbed the sweat from his brow and moustache with a 'kerchief, then slumped into Wicko's chair. This was to be the explanation most difficult.

## 30

Out on stage, concluding a full hour's show of magic and illusion which left the crowd drained of all emotion, the giant projected face of Michael Magister, floated gracefully in the air above the stage, high and ethereal.

"I have returned from the dead," boomed his voice. "And now I take my secrets with me. As I bid you all a fond and a long – farewell!"

The image began to melt. Features and flesh appeared to dissolve, exposing the green and grinning skull lurking beneath. Eyes and nose now hard black voids. The crowd gasped in horror. The jawbone of the hideous image yawned downwards emitting a malevolent cackle. Then silence. Before the skull cocked itself quizzically to one side. A hollow voice from everywhere said: "But remember, my friends. It's only magic if you don't know how it's done."

The hypnotic skull then slowly broke apart, the pieces floating and drifting like snowflakes. Then the silvered sheet curtain dropped from above with an emphatic, heart stopping WHOOMP!

The audience rose as one and cheered, stamped and called for more. That we could not fail to hear. What we did not see, because we were occupied making our escape, was Superintendent Melville and Inspector Pym standing, not to applaud, but to make their way up the aisle to the back of the auditorium. Unfortunately, they were met with a gaggle of spectators' intent on coming in the other direction. Much jostling and complaining ensued.

Willzen and Beatty scrambled from their mid-row seats, the best they could get, and shoved and fell into patrons still standing and cheering.

"Oh, I say," said the ineffectual Assistant Commissioner, Sir Cumberland Sinclair. "Fine work, Special Branch. Arrest them all! Arrest them all! Don't you think?"

Drago and Skrill were similarly motivated to grab the ungodly Magister and his wanton Jezebel, though theirs was more inclined to murder. Lucky to nab the very last seats for the performance, the psychopathic undertakers were perched right up in the gods, much disgruntled at finding themselves in no decent position to chance a pot shot at the magicians, mid-performance. And they were slow off the mark because Drago was so mesmerised by the giant skull, Skrill had to restore the focus of his dull-witted associate with sharp elbow to the ribs.

"Have a care to make haste, Mr Drago! The fiends are bolting!"

Thus galvanised, the killers shoved and stomped over everyone standing in front of them.

"Mind your way, harlot," sneered the shrew faced Skrill, toppling back and sitting on the horrified face of a matronly nun from St Benedict's.

"Gitdardofit, hnur, hnur, hnur," chuckled the porcine Drago, heeling his hobnail down into some poor coster's lap.

Further chaos now erupted as the rest of the crowd, witnessing the various pockets of commotion, decided to battle for the exits, in an orderly fashion, with fists and elbows flying.

Having hoisted themselves up onto the lip of the stage, Willzen and Beatty were now squeezing themselves beneath the heavy silver Safety Curtain.

Way further back, Drago and Skrill dropped from the Upper Circle, callously using the shoulders and heads of anyone below to break their falls.

With the auditorium now in total uproar and police and murderers alike falling over themselves to storm the stage, Wicko, myself and Michael and Phoebe, scurried into the Lobby, babbling with delirium at the success of the show. And we found Nikola Tesla sitting there, passive.

"Nik, what's wrong?" urged Michael. "It's getting boisterous back there. Let's go, we need to go!"

Phoebe grabbed her valise. Wicko typed in the Stage Door code.

"Dok Tor Phunn was here. Not long ago. With two of his cohorts. They assaulted my person."

A cavalcade of questions. Phunn? Here? Assaulted?

"My dear Dr Tesla. That is horrible for you. Are you quite all right?" Phoebe rested a sympathetic hand on his shoulder.

"Shaken, a little."

"Nik, what happened? What did they do?"

"The Tempus TimeKey. And the Fugit FlyWheel. They are gone! Phunn has taken them both!"

## 31

The adrenalin drained from our bodies like a plug had been pulled. It was too much to process in clarity. The TimeKey? Our entire escape plan? Gone?

"First these brigands steal from my laboratory in Colorado Springs." Yes, I remembered. The Molecular Disintegrator they used to rob the Bank of England. "And now they steal from me here. Right here. In your theatre. In front of me. I knew Dok Tor Phunn was never one to have the trust."

Then came the avalanche of How? What? Where did they go? questions.

"That is outrageous," asserted Phoebe, banging her fist on the table. "We have to hunt them down."

"Fortunately, there is no need for such diversion," said Tesla.

More questions. What do you mean? What are you talking about?

Then Tesla shrugged. "You may rook Nikola Tesla the one time. But you never rook him again. The TimeKey the Phunns possess? It is my inferior prototype. And the FlyWheel from the portrait of Lord Grimthorpe? A replica, forged of inferior steel." He held up a self-same canvas sack. "The real Contrivances – are in this bag. Now I think we should leave."

Willzen and Beatty stormed into the Lobby, but not fast enough. We had just gone. Beatty saw the Stage Door shut. He pulled at the handle and hammered on the door. Whatever he shouted doubtless involved "Listen see," and much blaspheming.

We headed right, along the alley toward the narrow Road where the Steamo would be brooding, ready to go. Ahead, from White Lion Passage we heard the clatter of footsteps, and Pym shouting, "Stop!"

Inside the auditorium, amid the screams and cries, Drago and Skrill tumbled and toppled over the Grand Circle seats and bundled themselves like lemmings over the ledge and down onto the front half stalls, the fautiles.

Outside, in the Passage, Melville and Pym sprinted left past the Stage Door, toward the Harrow Road. They heard the wet hiss and throaty growl of the Steamo as, with a jaunty whistle and all of us crammed around Mr Garrideb, Phoebe jerked and chugged and then with a spin of the driving wheels charged the beast away.

"As an insult, I think the whistle was a nice touch," said Michael, looking over his shoulder at the far too late Special Branchers.

"I do hope so," beamed Phoebe, as she swerved the snorting Steamo through the traffic.

~32~

"They're going east. Toward the Marylebone Road," shouted Pym, watching them disappear into the night-time traffic

"A Hansom, Pym," said Melville, looking about for a cab.

"No time for correctness here, guv'nor," said Pym. He stepped into the road hollering "Halt!" and forcing the first vehicle to swerve and skid to a stop, its two horses rearing in fright. The waggon was a flat bed, an empty cargo carrier. I shall waste no time describing the malodourous young driver because he takes no further part in the story. Only to report he was not the only one left cursing that night.

Pym at the reins cracked the horses along. Melville held fast and stood, peering above the traffic. In the dark he could follow the tell-tale grey puffs alternating from the Steamo's smokestacks.

"Turn right onto Park Lane," ordered Melville. "Sweet Lord, Walter. What cargo does this wagon transport?"

It was a dung cart. Well, it had to be. One of many which transported mountains of equine waste to dedicated depots on the fringes of London. Pym pretended he didn't hear and continued breathing through his mouth.

This district was better. Carriage lamps and gas streetlights. Ahead, the Steamo roared smoothly past Dorchester House, straight on to where Park Lane becomes Hamilton Place. She slewed a sharp right onto Piccadilly, then a very sharp left beside the Wellington Monument, across Wellington Place where she skidded to stop under the Wellington Arch.

Phoebe told Tesla the Arch housed the smallest police station in London. And mercifully it was the least manned.

"Closed to all traffic," said the one policeman on duty.

But a grand presentation of Michael and Phoebe's official Special Branch Consultant Warrants Cards sufficiently impressed the Constable on duty to unbolt the iron gates and push them open. Phoebe shoved open the regulator and gunned the engine, whereupon the officer was all but blown off his feet by the vicious chuff of smoke.

Phoebe aimed the Steamo down Constitution Hill, which isn't a hill at all because it's flat, and was so called because King Charles the Second would stroll along this part of Green Park for his peaceful morning constitutional while walking those little dogs which shared his hairstyle.

"Yeah, can we all just concentrate here," pleaded Wicko, standing on his seat and looking back. "This is an escape, not a sightseeing tour."

For Tesla, squashed at the back beside Mr Garrideb, it was also not the most comfortable.

A good way behind, Pym cracked his horses to the end of Hamilton Place. Melville scanned ahead. Did they turn left onto Piccadilly? No belching smoke in that direction. To the right Hyde Park Corner was a jumble of conflicting traffic. Melville ordered Pym to go right. Then through the trees of Green Park he thought he saw smoky wisps, dissipating.

Moments later he saw the Wellington Arch, and the back of the uniformed Constable, minus his helmet, standing and shaking his fist at something in the direction of Constitution Hill.

It was enough of a pointer for Pym to swing the wagon hard left, through the open Arch and send the luckless Officer scuttling for cover once again. The gamble played out. In the distance. The smoke plumes. He had them.

~33~

Aboard the Steamo, with the regulator wide open, Phoebe was in her element. "This road has not been so kind to the monarchy in recent times, Dr Tesla. The Queen survived three attempted assassinations just along here," she shouted, wiping her goggles with the back of her lace glove. "Oh, and Prime Minister Peel suffered a riding accident while cantering along here."

"This road, it certainly is the jinx," managed Tesla, through a mouth stretched wide with fear. "The man Peel survived?"

"Only until he died," said Michael, eyes shut and pulling the same kind of face as Tesla.

With the stark, solid symmetrical mass of Buckingham Palace on the right, Phoebe slid the Steamo left onto Birdcage Walk. Another straight run, another full head of speed.

Way behind, in the manure wagon, absence of any other traffic was also a blessing for the Special Branch. Once Constitution Hill had curled around in front of the Palace forecourt, Magister and his cronies would take one of three routes. Melville saw the welcome smoke signals to the left along Birdcage Walk.

At the same time Wicko was convinced he saw the outline of a wagon. In the distance. "We've got pursuers. I think. Maybe."

The chase required all Pym's military training with whip and rein. If only that lot had given up the plans for that Flying Machine's engine, none of this would be necessary, he thought. He would not be overly concerned to see Magister go to gaol. Or the dwarf. Or the mute hunchback (meaning me) but he would hate to see Miss Phoebe locked up in Holloway for any length of time.

Along George Street the Steamo was now complaining about the constant speed. She was turning belligerent, cussing smoke and sweating steam.

Tesla gasped and pointed straight at the view ahead. "Such wonder!"

He was quite right. Before us loomed the gothic Barry and Pugin splendour of the clock tower – known as Big Ben – soaring high above the jagged roof of the Palace of Westminster. The gas-lit yellow circle of the clock face staring toward them was welcome and warm. A beacon of their impending sanctuary.

At least Nik was getting to witness some of the glamour, quirks and history of the great city during his brief but eventful stay. For example, the Ayrton Light set atop the clock tower, glowing to signal Parliament was still in session.

Phoebe skirted the north side of Parliament Square, swung a right and shuddered the Steamo to a fishtailing stop outside the gates to the Mother of Parliaments. The original plan was to roll the vehicle off Westminster Bridge and scuttle her like the Dodo.

But not with the suspicion that Melville was tracking us with remarkable detection skills.

We resigned to give the old girl up. Mr Garrideb's malevolent green glare and "Bugger off!" grumbling would have little effect on the Special Branch. Wicko agreed with my suggestion; the best thing we could do was lock her down.

With everybody out and off the vehicle, I thumped the navel of Mr Garrideb before scrambling myself down from the passenger cabin. In less than a minute the mechanical man would smoulder, flare, then combust himself to cinders.

Phoebe, Tesla and I slid iron sheets up the windows and latched them into place. Wicko had neither the height nor the inclination to assist and Michael was now beginning to struggle with the fatigue of the stage show and his recently restored lungs. The sheets ought to confound Melville's engineers, at least for a few hours.

Yes, I could have just climbed out of the Steamo and fled, but it wasn't for us to make life easy for the Government scientists. Unfortunately, my bloody-minded prejudice deferred our escape.

There were a pair of Constables manning the gate to New Palace Yard, the stretch of lawn which leads to the entrance to the clock tower. Both coppers held their lamps high and examined Michael and Phoebe's Warrant Cards with meticulous caution. But, swayed by the explanation of confidential police business and the prospect of disciplinary encounters with Sir Cumberland Sinclair and Sir Edward Bradford, they waved us all through.

The night-time dash across the fresh cut lawn of New Palace Yard must have presented a peculiar image. Phoebe racing ahead, Michael half walking, half running as best he could, followed by Wicko complaining about his dignity and, "If you ever tell other living soul about this…"

Well, he had a point, you see, because his legs were dangling between Tesla and me, as we lifted him bodily by the shoulders and ran.

"Such wonder," said Tesla, looking up at the soaring Clock above us.

Phoebe's Picker Nicker whirred and clicked while its digits oscillated within the five-lever lock, feeling out the correct setting to open the door. Inside, another door, half windowed. The brass sign screwed across the centre told us: "CLOCK TOWER".

Phoebe had the second door opened with ease. We could have broken it down, but we had far too much regard for the history of the place. Phoebe locked the door behind us. No sense in making life easy for Melville.

In the neck-craning blackness way above, a tiny slice of light, an L shape emerged from what I knew to be the Clock Room. Were Dr Phunn and his crew there? My voice bounced around on the hard stone surfaces. There was no reply. I called again.

Ahead of us the narrow stone staircase wound its way up to the most iconic clock mechanism in the world. So, we started to climb.

With his horses wilting, Melville and Pym were losing momentum and the Scotland Yardies had all but resigned to losing us. Pym slowed along Great George Street.

Until, "There!" Melville pointed to the right, across Parliament Square. The Steamo.

~34~

Melville and Pym drew up alongside the Steamo, leapt from their manure cart, only to be halted by the Bobbies.

"Special Branch, gentlemen," panted Pym, showing his card and suffering for his lead-weight arms from pulling those reins. "Did you witness the party of coves who alighted that mechanised vehicle?"

"Thems as wiv your outfit, boss?" said one of the uniforms. "'appy to 'elp 'em, sir. 'Specially as they was operatin' incognito."

"Where'd they go?" snapped Pym.

"Stepped through the arch, and up into the Tower, as I witnessed," suggested the other. "On the right 'urry-up an' all they was too."

"Climbing the Tower," puzzled Superintendent Melville. "Send for Sir Henry Erskine."

"The Serjeant at Arms? Gawd, yessir," saluted the first officer.
***
It is three hundred and thirty-four stone steps to get from the base to the Clock Room mechanism. Eleven floors occupy the Tower, including document storage rooms and detention rooms used

81

until twenty years ago for locking up drunken or recalcitrant MPs. "Woefully under used," Phoebe told us all.

We climbed at a rhythmic pace in the darkness. Feeling our way to begin with until we learned the shape of the stairs. With Michael in no condition to hurry. Tesla and Phoebe were by far the fittest to tackle the relentless stairs, despite the handicaps of Tesla's precious canvas bag, and Phoebe's valise. Wicko's legs struggled with the steps; it was painful work, but we needed to press on.

The impetus we needed came with the noise of the rattling of the door below. Melville had found us.

"You must tell me when you need a break," Phoebe insisted.

"I could do with one," panted Wicko.

"Wicko, I was addressing Michael," scolded Phoebe. "You're not recovering from death."

"He sounds as if he soon will be," panted Michael.

In fact, we had made extremely good progress; we were less than a hundred steps from the Clock Room when from below we heard the inevitable.

Melville and Pym could wait no longer for the Serjeant at Arms and his bunch of keys. They shouldered the door.

BLAM!

The echo rang up and around the stairwell. Truly, the chase was now on.

Melville and Pym looked up through the void of the stairwell. Heard the rhythm of our footsteps. They had lamps and danced the beams upwards. And saw our silhouettes. Three quarters of the way up. Slogging and staggering our way to freedom.

"You lot!" shouted the Inspector. His orders rang around the stairwell. "In the name of the law, stop!"

I was quaintly pleased people actually shouted "In the name of the law!" I thought it was just something said in those Strand Magazine stories. Then Pym yelled: "For cripes' sake! Stop where you are, don't move and come down!" I think he realised what he'd said as soon as he said it.

Naturally we took not the slightest notice, so now the stone steps resonated with the clacks of two more pairs of boots as the climb for us entered its final stage. I remember the cast iron railings being cold to the touch while our thighs and throats burned with the effort of the climb. Round and round. Relentlessly round and round.

"I implore you to give up! This cannot end well!"

It was Superintendent Melville. We continued climbing. Inspired now by the worry that boots below were sounding faster and fresher than ours.

The steps were relentless. One-two-three-four turn. One-two-three-four turn. We were all struggling now. Gasping and slowing, Phoebe stopped to let Tesla and me pass. Stopped to help Wicko, then Michael.

With every step Melville and Pym grew closer. Up ahead the L-shaped light getting bigger and bigger. Down below the jostling beams of the police lamps growing closer.

One-two-three-four turn. One-two-three-four turn.

Pym, the fitter man, had drawn away from Melville. Military training. His metal boot taps sparking on the stone steps. He was climbing two at a time. Two at a time! His remarkable determination matched his energy. His lamp light was now enveloping us all.

He was all but right behind us.

~35~

Two more flights to the Clock Room. I was following Tesla, hauling on the handrail. My thighs and throat blazing with the effort.

One-two-three-four turn. One-two-three-four turn.

Nik was there. So was I. The Clock Room. Remarkable. Lit by the lamps from the Clock Faces above.

Wicko and Michael and Phoebe were two turns, eight steps from the summit.

One-two-three-four turn

Then Phoebe felt the yank of the hand on her shoulder. Pym!

She yelled and shrugged and turned and shoved with her valise. Saw him topple backwards. His lamp strobed and spun wildly from his grip. His hands grabbed at thin air for support.

Phoebe, shocked, shouted, "Walter!"

Michael's hand stretched down past her. Grabbed the neck of the Inspector's waistcoat. Prevented his fall. Pulled the man up straight. It only took a moment holding the handrail for Pym to restore his composure.

"Pheebs," ordered Michael. "Now take my hand."

She did. Held it tight.

One-two-three...

Michael felt it. Phoebe's hand slipping from his. He was holding her black lace glove. Pym had hold of her now. Both arms. She tried to struggle.

"Magister! Halt!"

"Michael! Go!" screamed Phoebe. "Go!"

In the blur, Michael's head spun. Heard her say something like "It's not meant to be."

I dragged Michael into the Clock Room, and with both hands Wicko shoved the door shut. I thrust my walking cane in the gap at the base to wedge it shut.

"Pheebs!" yelled Michael as best he could, with little strength to fight his way past me. "We're not leaving her!"

The loud TICK-TOCK-TICK-TOCK was hypnotic. The cogs nudged on their frames. Above, the fly fans twirled. Below, the fourteen-foot brass pendulum swung back and forth.

Tesla aligned the FlyWheel cogs of Grimthorpe's mechanism, as per his instructions. The TimeKey was set in place. The day, month and year destinations pre-set.

Outside, Phoebe's struggle delayed Pym only until Melville arrived. Pym was shouldering the door. I leaned against it. Leverage and my cane were on our side. His confined space meant Pym could not get a run at it. Instead he hammered and shouted.

"Is everyone prepared," asked Tesla.

Michael did not answer. Tesla ordered everybody that, whatever happened next, we must keep together. And wished us all luck.

~36~

Tesla pressed the master switch on the TimeKey.

zzzzZZZ-KERRACK!

A slice of blinding silver energy zagged free from the TimeKey and speared the Clock Mechanism. The entire frame juddered.

TICK-TOCK-TI...

Parliament's clock had stopped. Below us the great pendulum froze mid-swing.

But the cogs still turned. Gathering speed. At an alarming rate. The whine was suddenly close to deafening. They started to smoke. The Clock Room rattled violently. Acrid with the smell of burning. Everything inside started to race! Michael, Wicko, Tesla and I held fast to one another.

But outside – in the slowest of motion, Pym was still striking the heel of his fist on the door with a dull

B A N G … B A N G …

Phoebe was still shouting something sounding like

"G O … "

In the Clock Room I felt my body lift. Witnessed the others rise. The last thing I saw was the line of inscription on the mechanism. Written in gold.

THIS CLOCK WAS MADE IN THE YEAR OF OUR LORD 1854 BY FREDERICK DENT, OF THE STRAND AND THEN ROYAL EXCHANGE, CLOCKMAKER TO THE QUEEN FROM THE DESIGNS OF EDMUND BECKETT DENISON

Then with a deafening CRACK! I felt myself flung – no – snatched away like a sheet! Into a black void of heat. Then cold. Then never-ending falling.

Then nothing.

Fifteen minutes later, out on the grass of New Palace Yard, Melville was placating an older man with a bald head and a full brown beard, resplendent in ceremonial uniform which included stockings to the knee. The Parliamentary Serjeant at Arms, Sir Henry Erskine, who was still demanding to know what in God's name had just happened.

On-lookers, call them witnesses, were swearing on their mothers' lives they saw a halo of silver light balloon outwards from Big Ben, then get sucked back in.

Phoebe, held firm by those two Constables, called to Melville. "Superintendent, do you mind? I assure you I cannot summon the energy to escape. And besides that, where would I go?"

He took no notice.

Pym ran out of the tower, dusting the arms and shoulders of his overcoat. Made straight for Melville.

"Empty, guv'nor. Looked up and down the clock tower. All over. Magister, the dwarf, the Italian, and the 'unchback Professor. Each and every one of 'em. Gone."

Melville said nothing.

It was coming up to the hour. Above them Lord Grimthorpe's faultless mechanism whirred and triggered the peel of melodious Westminster chimes which herald the striking of the hour. The long pause. Then the two-ton hammer struck Big Ben.

And the first sonorous DONG! rang out across London.

Midnight.

*"To travel is to live."*
*Hans Christian Anderson 1805-1875*
~PART TWO~

The silence was just as fearful as the tumultuous din. It was a profound silence. Vacuum deep. Endless. Until Michael wheezed and coughed. Then we all started spluttering. Gasping for air. Steamy white and oily blue.

Finally, I braved a furtive glimpse around the Clock Room of Parliament's great tower; at first dark, now flickering into painful light.

Not yellowed gaslight. This was harsh white electric. Tesla happily confirmed as much when he peered up at the square neon lamps. The room was the same. But different. It was spotless. Everything shone, the metals polished, the paintwork fresh and brickwork buffed and sharp. The legend across the frame still stated the Clock Mechanism was "made from the designs of Edmund Beckett Denison".

"We have been thrown forward in the time," he said.

Then…

TICK! TICK! TICK!

The repetitive engagement of the gravity escapement clicked in, and…

SWOOSH! SWOOSH! SWOOSH!

…the great pendulum below resumed its swing. Swooping back and forth, back and forth, once every two seconds as if nothing just happened.

"That…" whispered Michael, pointing around at nothing particular, "was every bit as bad as I remember." His tortured lungs rasped with every breath.

He was quite right. There is much to be said for time travel, apart from the actual travelling. Time sickness left us all giddy and retching, but mercifully with all our faculties and functions unimpaired. Well, not *all*. One or two of my functions have been a worry for years.

We all let go of the frame and slumped in our own utterly spent way. Wicko sitting with that thousand-yard stare and Tesla was on his knees. I weakly asked if we all remembered who we were, and why we were here. Our collective recollections remained unstripped.

"Pheebs," groaned Michael. Through bleary eyes he peered at the limp, black, long-sleeved glove he'd pulled from his pocket, prompting her memory. "We need to go back. Save her from Pym and Melville. Nik, fire up the TimeKey again. 1899."

"Would it be that I could be able," said Tesla. Then, yes, in true scientific genius fashion he said it. "Observe."

He pointed to the TimeKey, now protruding limply from The Grimm's Westminster clock mechanism. Its brass casing blackened with soot. The glass on the gauges, fogged and each a spider's web of cracks. A decade of Nik's work, of trial and error, the 'ire and terror' he called it, now spent and forlorn.

And The Grimm's all-important interfacing Fugit FlyWheel? Untouched. In fact, considering the rigorous drubbing every cog, chain, train, gear, bevel and winding barrel of his entire clock mechanism had just sustained, it still clicked, snicked and ticked in perfect gleaming order. The iron frame within which the five-ton gear-wheeled mechanism is set, resembles a flat single bed. It had been fixed in place and had performed without failure for thirty years. Thank God The Grimm hadn't come with us, we'd have never heard the end of it.

"Magister. Miss Phoebe's in the past," finally gasped Wicko. "It's where she always was. And she knew it's where she'd always be."

Tesla dabbed his bitter-tasting lips with a fresh 'kerchief before adding: "It was her courage most remarkable which enabled our escape."

Michael screwed his eyes tight in frustration.

For fifteen minutes we sat in contemplation. Summoning not just the strength but the courage to explore our journey's end. Currently we had no verified notion of quite where in the great Chronology we had wound up. We hoped this was 2001, Tesla's dialling up the correct figures would never be in doubt, but the variables were many. Even now a centenarian Melville and his elderly cohorts might be prowling outside, heating up the handcuffs and roughing up their truncheons.

I started to worry for the Phunns and how their own time travel experience might fare with stolen and substandard technology.

But my concerns were short lived. Mostly the result of malice, and partly because that ticking, at first hypnotic, does begin to grate after a while. So, I proposed we girded our loins and venture out. To see what 2001 had in store for us.

"Yeah. Come on," agreed Wicko. "Time to see where you come from Magister. See what all the fuss is about."

I pulled at the wooden door, the one I jammed shut with a lump of Kendal Mint Cake. That was long gone. The door showed no signs of repair. The wood was waxed and swung open with well-oiled ease.

It had taken five muscle-burning minutes to scramble up and around those three hundred and thirty-four steps to the Clock Room. And in the dark. And with raging Special Branchers giving chase and hurling abuse. At least now our descent could be enjoyed in a more dignified manner. Mind you it was still hard going, clinging to the newly painted cast-iron railing and gently easing our way down. At least this time the staircase was steeped in warm electric light and the grey stone steps were now treaded with a safety conscious non-slip material. Very considerate.

Also, you know, everything smelled fresh. Not a whiff of that damp concrete mustiness you associate with a thirty-year-old building. Or would it be now? A one hundred-year-old building. It was beginning to bode well. The foot of the relentless staircase was most welcome, then through those two further doors, and we finally emerged. 2001.

~2~

First impressions? The sweet, almost dry night air of the outside world. In fact, the atmosphere was so pure it made your head swim.

We gazed around, blinking. And everything was exactly the same. No, that's not exactly true. Everything was the same, but cleaner. Fresher. I mean, laid out before us was the lawn of New Palace Gardens, but a weed-free green manicured sward. Soaring behind us, the beautifully lit clock tower and the Palace of Westminster, its limestone construction restored to the original sandy colour. The weathered gold details surrounding the clock faces and the six heraldic crosses of St George lined above, all now clearly defined. In fact, everywhere was ablaze with light, so vivid and bright. It was only the black sky directly above and the blue coloured hands on the blue coloured clock faces pointing up at the '12' and down at the '30' that confirmed it was night-time.

"See all about us. My Alternating Current. It powers the city." Nikola Tesla gasped in wonder at the light sources, the lampposts and the arc lamps. He then happily added: "This is most certainly the future, my friends."

Ahead of us, Parliament Square. Over there to the left, Westminster Abbey, of such bitter memory. All beautifully maintained.

Wicko clambered up onto a metal bench for a better view. The reward was glorious. "Here. Artemus. Have a look at those carriages. They've come on some since even our time."

Oh, my, you know, he was right. There was not a horse, not a chimney stack to be seen. The vehicles were, well, works of art. All were exactly the same size and shared the same sleek elongated egg design. The only difference was in the colours. A subtle spectrum of pearlized shades, some I had never before seen. And all apparently at a total standstill in Parliament Square. Traffic chaos! You see, some things can never change. Fascinating. And the people. Several scores. Clearly in no hurry. Just marvelling at the views and bathing in the warmth.

"Mr Magister, the New York you recall from your 2001," whispered Tesla. "It was as remarkable as this?"

"No, Nik. Not a bit of it." Michael slowly shook his head while rubbing his aching chest. "I mean, where're the fumes? The smells? Wherever you go there's always burnt garlic. Who knew air could be this clean? And listen. Do you hear that?"

"Hear what?" said Wicko.

"That's what I mean," whispered Michael, looking all around.

He was quite right. There was barely a sound. The rustle of the trees in the breeze. And maybe the soft GLUBBLE! and occasional SCHLOP! from the Thames, somehow carried on the gentle, warm draught, but otherwise just – countryside quiet. In a major city.

"There's no honking or hooting," whispered Michael. "Nothing's moving. Not a soul on the sidewalk. Not a car on the street. It's like everything's just … stopped."

We looked and watched and waited. Again, he was right. There was not a movement to be seen.

Surprisingly, it was Michael who said, "Come on," and started walking across the lawn, as smartly as his tortured respiratories would allow. So, we followed his lead. And the closer we drew to the street ahead, the clearer and more puzzling everything became. Especially the people, who were not frozen in mid-step or in time or anything like that; they were just standing there. With their arms by their sides. As if they were waiting for – well, nothing that I could immediately discern.

First impressions? Well, hair loss must have achieved epidemic proportions. No barber could ever make a living around here. Everyone, but everyone, was bald. As a coot. And! And! Not only were the people bald, they were all fit and taut with clear muscular definition. Six feet tall, suntanned and dressed in exactly the same style of snug-fitting, and I mean *alarmingly* snug-fitting, one-piece trouser suits. The stillness, the silence, the similarity, yes, 2001 was starting to feel eerie.

As we reached the sidewalk, Michael called out to the individual closest, with its back to us. "Hi! Hello! Pardon me. Hello?"

The sun-tanned head smoothly turned to face us. Looking back over her shoulder, her face was stunning in its beauty. Lips pursed, nose, chin, cheek bones, perfect. She opened her eyes. The most sparkling cobalt blue.

"Why, good evening, gentlemen…"

With feline grace she turned her entire body to face us; which was when we were hit with another tremendous shock. The woman was not only utterly beautiful, she was unashamedly starkers. I mean not a stitch! Firm bust, flat belly, long legs, exquisite … well, you get the picture.

We could not help but stand there in slack-jawed awe.

Then she said:

"…I have been expecting you.

~3~

"Evading arrest," said Melville, tired but still calm.

"Aiding and abetting fugitives," chipped in Pym.

Phoebe was not a little vexed to be sitting across the desk from Melville. Scotland Yard was a dour, brown place at the best of times, and the early hours did nothing to help her mood. And Pym was rather irritating, prowling up and down behind her.

"Oh, Walter, for goodness sake, it has been a long night, do sit down," she sighed. Pym showed no interest in sitting so she continued. "Very well. Let me address your accusations. Evading arrest? Aiding and abetting fugitives? Fugitives from what crime? Any judge would deem us heroes upon learning we saved the life of Detective Inspector Walter Pym, who, if it were not for our prompt and selfless action, would have plunged down the stairwell of the clock tower, a plummet of almost sixty feet, and cracked his head upon the concrete floor like the egg of an Aylesbury duck."

Melville ignored the flowery analogy of a Bucks-bred mallard but had to admit, in a broader sense, she was right. It would be quite embarrassing enough to explain the unfathomable disappearance of Magister and his associates from a locked and barred room almost at the top of Big Ben without the additional headache of subjecting one of the Prince of Wales's illegitimate offspring on a less than convincing prosecution. Instead, he resorted to Melvillian pragmatism.

"Miss Le Breton. You are a stage magician of enormous knowledge and skill. How did they disappear? Where are Mr Magister, Dr Smawl, Dr Tesla and the cove who masquerades as a slobbering hunchback," said Melville. Masquerades?! I must have been less convincing than I thought.

"It was magic."

"Get off," scoffed Pym.

"Superintendent, Michael Magister is an illusionist. A conjurer. Disappearing is what he does. Wicko and the Professor are his consummate magical engineers. Dr Tesla is a scientific genius. In my time working with them I was privileged to learn many of their methods. But that vanishing trick from the Clock Room of Big Ben certainly foxes me. It is only magic if you do not know how it is done. And I do not know how it was done."

Melville sighed. "You may go."

"Thank you, kind sir," she said. "I wish I could say it had been a pleasure."

Phoebe picked up her parasol, adjusted her top hat fascinator, straightened her dress. Pym opened the door and she stepped gracefully through. "Good night."

"What will you do now, Miss?"

Phoebe went to speak, then it occurred to her. "Actually, Detective Inspector Pym, I really have no idea…"

And with that she walked away. Along the bland corridor, down the stairs, out of Scotland Yard, into the damp darkness.

And a new life.

~4~

The enormous, sparkling eyes of the tanned and naked woman studied each of us in turn. Then her full mouth softened to form a radiant smile. She placed her hand on her chest, well, her breasts really, and bowed her head in supplication. "Why, it is a great honour to at last meet you all. Dr Nikola Tesla, and of course, Dr Manswick Smawl and Professor Artemus More."

We were stunned. She knew who we were. And made no reference to Michael.

"Madame, you are most gracious," said Tesla.

"That's very kind," said Wicko, blushing modestly.

But, I suppose, even in these bewildering circumstances, stage performers don't care to be completely ignored.

"Okay, Miss, forgive me here, but this is important: why is it you know who these fine gentlemen are, and not me?"

The mouth smiled wider still. "Why, sir, I know very well that you are Mr Michael Magister, also known as The Industrial Age Illusionist, mentored by Professor More and Dr Smawl, you performed a magic act extensively at various national venues to great acclaim and finally established success and notoriety at The Metropolitan Theatre of Steam, Smoke and Mirrors."

The woman managed to flow her entire sentence in a melodious voice with clarity, inflection and without once having to draw breath. Michael was taken aback, but managed to admit, "I'm comfortable with great acclaim."

"You're welcome." The 'you're welcome' was delivered with richly enounced sincerity and enhanced by a coy inclination of the head. "Dr Nikola Tesla is revered as a scientific pioneer, and a monument to his remarkable achievements in almost everything we see about us,"

"Thank you, Madame."

"You're welcome; Dr Manswick Smawl's importance as an inspirational scientist, inventor and in his capacity as one of the two Principal Creators is also hugely revered..."

Wicko acknowledged the accolade with a look of false modesty.

"...along with Professor Artemus More, an inspirational scientist, inventor and in his capacity as the second of the two Principal Creators is equally highly revered."

Michael looked at everyone revered about him. Which was us. Amid the puzzled pointing, the best he could manage was: *"Really?"*

And I must say such praise was highly flattering. But at the same time disconcerting. Tesla had been rightly feted as the brain behind everything about us. But Principal Creators? Wicko and me? Of what? Unless...

Naturally oblivious to our overall perplexity, Michael was keen to assert some kind presence in the proceedings and told the beautiful woman she had all four of us at a disadvantage. Which was that she knew all of our names, but we did not know hers.

"Why, of course, Mr Magister. I am Debbi,"

At which point Nik, Wicko and myself, began harbouring the same misgiving. Much, I suspect, as you."

"Debbi, if I may say, that is a very lovely name," charmed Michael.

"Why, thank you, Mr Magister," said Debbi, "and now you are here, how may I sustain all you gentlemen first? With food, drink or physical love?"

~5~

Excuse me?

"Why, I asked how I may sustain all you gentlemen first? With food, drink or physical love?"

"That's it," said Michael. "I knew. We're really dead."

Wicko assured him we were all very much alive. His elevated pulse was the clue. I quickly told Debbi how generous she was but that our more pressing concern at the moment was to confirm where we were and in what year.

"Why, certainly, Professor More, your present location is precisely fifty-one degrees, twenty-nine minutes and fifty-seven seconds north, and zero degrees, seven minutes and twenty-nine seconds west, you are currently facing south on Parliament Street, Westminster, London, England; and the year, in the Gregorian calendar, is twenty zero zero one. Or, as preferred, two thousand and one."

Not that we ever doubted that The Grimm's Great Clock mechanism combined with Tesla's Tempus TimeKey would work. Or that Robert Hooke's theory all those years ago was ever flawed. But the stillness, the silence and the street populated with all these other people, none of whom moved or reacted. It was, well, faintly disturbing.

Wicko excused himself, shifted over and tapped one of the other people, the one nearest and facing away from us, on the lower back. The person he tapped flexed. Well, the dwarf got the shock of his life when the person who swung around quickly to face him was a totally naked man.

Wicko jumped back at the shock. "Oi, steady! You nearly had my eye out with that!"

"Why, my apologies, Dr Smawl, good evening to you Dr Tesla, Professor More and Mr Magister, it is a great honour to meet you."

The manly figure had an easy, smooth voice like deep velvet. He didn't speak, he announced. And his physique was defined, muscular perfection. In every particular. As Wicko, to his horror, discovered.

Tesla was astonished. "Sir, do you also have no clothes? For the modesty?" he asked.

"Why, Dr Tesla, it has never before been mentioned. My apologies."

Michael had to agree. "Impressive though it all is, if the Professor had his hat, we could maybe use that." Michael knew he was babbling, so changed the subject. "What I'm saying is … once again, you know who we are, but we don't know your name?"

"Why, sir, my name is Garri."

"Very good to meet you, sir. So, we have Garri and we have Debbi. And … Professor? Are you getting this?"

My stomach had tumbled as soon as he announced his name. I asked the names of the others hereabouts.

"Why, we are all named Debbi," said Debbi.

"Why, and we are all named Garri," said – well, you know who said it.

Michael rubbed his aching chest. "Professor, is this sounding as bad as I'm thinking it's sounding?"

I feared it was. Our scorched earth plan in the event of our secrets being exposed, 'Operation London Bridge', for whatever reason, had clearly not been the total success it needed to be. Not everything we left in 1899 had been destroyed. Couldn't have been. The evidence was standing before us. And over there. And over there. Power-driven men – and women. Remarkable in every detail. But without doubt named for our mechanical Garridebs!

Tesla pronounced it, more brutally than I would have preferred, when he said: "As a consequence of the failure of Operation London Bridge, I fear, my friends, we have just changed human history."

~6~

Lionel de Latour Wells. Well, with a name like that he was never destined for a life working down the mines or in the docks. No, Wellsy, as no one ever dared call him, was a retired naval captain. Decorated for bravery, too. But here and now, in 1899, and in his capacity as Commissioner of the M.F.B. (oddly enough, that is not an acronym for a phrase from Father Connor O'Connor's ripe language repertoire – instead it stands for the Metropolitan Fire Brigade), he stood, straight-backed and resplendent in his serge black tunic, double-breasted silver buttons shining bright, smartly topped with a silver-plated Trojanesque 'Merryweather' fire helmet.

Beside Wells, standing at the back of the auditorium, and looking dull by comparison in his signature black bowler and grey gabardine mac, Superintendent William Melville. But, you know, the head of Scotland Yard's Special Branch was very grateful for everything he was wearing that day as the water began dripping down upon both men, each drip causing an annoying TING! to ring from Wells's helmet.

The scene they were watching was sad in every particular. A dozen firemen burdened by their heavy, belted tunics and shiny brass helmets, damping down the smouldering embers of the gutted shell of what used to be The Metropolitan Theatre of Steam, Smoke and Mirrors.

With great spans of Frank Matcham's glorious roof destroyed, the murky sun could now cast down shafts of smoky, natural light, never before seen within the building. In fact, I believe my dear old friend Frank had just left, shaking his head having pronounced the structure beyond redemption, and murmuring less than flattering words about me.

From Melville's point of view, the rows of seatbacks of the stalls now resembled the rotten stumps of blackened teeth. The balcony of the cantilevered Royal Circle above had collapsed on one side and now slumped at a rakish angle, like a drunken sailor's hat. Straight ahead the proscenium arch was a bed of grey ash resting on a charcoal woodpile that used to be the stage. Everywhere, the air hung acrid and steamy.

Buckets, stirrups pumps and rubber hoses lay discarded in defeat. The solid building which last night echoed to the vibrant sounds of laughter and applause was now a husk of dripping memories.

"The place is well named now, d'y'see?" stated Wells, without emotion.

"Commissioner?" said Melville, in a tone which might have suggested what *are* you talking about, man?

"The property, Superintendent. It was the Metropolitan Theatre of Steam, Smoke and Mirrors, d'y'see?" The chief fire officer gestured accordingly. "Steam. And Smoke. But no mirrors. Shattered by the 'flagration, d'y'see?"

Melville's mouth barely flicked his irritation. "Everything is gone?"

"Quite so, by and large. Incinerated or smelted beyond all measure of recognition."

"Arson?"

"Oh, without doubt," Wells said quickly, as he stroked his walrus moustache with his gauntlet. "There's too much arson about. As we said in the Royal Navy."

Melville pressed on. "The evidence the fire was intentionally set?"

"The Safety Curtain inexplicably hoisted, d'y'see? Bottles of turpentine by the crate, strategically positioned hither and yon, maximising the blaze. No, this was intended, Melville. And reliably executed."

As if to underline the Commissioner's assertion –

SPLII - SCRUNCHHH!

amid strange shouted warnings of "Aye-aye!", a charred support spar from the roof shifted from beneath the collapsed Circle, landing not ten feet to the left, and showering orange-glow smuts briefly into the damp air. The lead roof, two hours ago a drooping lake, had cooled to sag now like the crust of a half-baked pie.

As best he could, given the death traps still threatening above and below, Inspector Walter Pym moved swiftly up the littered aisle to join Melville.

"Heck of a waste, gents," said Pym.

I imagined he was not expressing aesthetic or artistic sentiment at the loss of a theatre, more frustration that all of our technological trickery and knowhow had been consumed by the flames of 'Operation London Bridge'. In particular he and Melville, or more importantly their political masters, were banking on discovering the correct designs, blueprints or even notes concerning the construction of our flying machine, The Ferrous Dodo. And anything else of an advanced engineering nature.

But following our escape and Phoebe's short-lived arrest, by the time Melville and Pym had raced back through the early morning, here to the Edgware Road, all drawings and plans had curled and flamed in the face of our timer-triggered booby traps.

'Leave nothing but scorched earth,' Tsar Alexander the First had ordered his troops as they retreated from Napoleon's advancing armies. Advice we planned to heed.

At least – that's what we *thought*.

"A word, sir," whispered Pym. "There's something here you need to have to look at."

## 7

Melville made his apologies to Wells and followed Pym, picking their way down the mushy aisle.

"The Bucket Brigade found it."

Pym led Melville to what was the stage, then down a wooden fireman's ladder into the void below; the space we called the Dungeon.

"Remember, it's down here that shifty dwarf lurked much of the time. Along with his oppo, that Professor More. A wary looking cove if ever there was. Always kept his own counsel. I was never much struck on the pair of them, meself. Truth be told, I'm not convinced that Professor More fella was even a real professor."

"Indeed. And I was never convinced he was a real *hunchback*," said Melville.

Pym led the Superintendent though a clearing in the forest of twisted and contorted iron uprights which once supported the stage.

"So, this area here, this is where they constructed those contraptions for the magic acts and such."

Pym pointed to the sooted brick elevation at the rear of the Dungeon. "Now see this, guv'nor? Remember they told us this wall backed against the sewers and when we took the sledgehammer to it, some of the lads got smothered in foul effluvium?"

Is there any other kind?

"The wall has now been proved to be – a falsehood. Turns out there's not a sign of a Bazelgette sewer. Just a cunning booby-trapped bladder of filth hidden behind. But then – the Bucket Brigade discovered this."

Clearly defined in the centre of the wall was a rectangular gap, the height and width of a door.

"The lads wager it was the heat of the blaze as melted the rubber seals," continued Pym, running a finger across and down the gap. "Turns out to be a door. So then, I've given it a pretty good shoulder shove, and…"

He lowered his voice, "You best take a gander in this cupboard. You will not believe what's inside, sir. Have a mind for the unexploded fire bomb within. It's highly volatile."

"Thank you, Inspector, I shall."

Melville gingerly poked his head inside the cupboard. Which turned out to be a whole lot bigger. More a brick vault. Yes, by the door, a menacing wooden box racked with bottles brim full of clear fluid, a rubber pipe looping from neck to neck. Combustible, yes. But not as explosive as this.

"Well, now," whispered Melville, as soon as he saw what he saw. Decomposed bodies.

Five of them. Not lying. Standing. Shoulder to shoulder. Leaning back against the wall. Heads hanging limply forward. But they were decayed in such a manner Melville had never before seen. Instead of yellowed skeletal frames, they were non- reflective silver grey. And not really skeletal. With a gloved finger, Melville pushed one of the heads back up to gaze upon, not a skull, but just a pair of round-lens eyes and a square grill mouth. The eyes glowed briefly red, then flickered and faded away.

"I know," said Pym. "And you recall that 'novelty' who always sat in the back of the magicians' vehicle, that Mr Garrideb?" Pym was referencing the menacing figure which rode about with us in the Steamotivator, glowing his green eyes and growling pithy discouragement at anyone nosey enough to get too close. "Strikes me all these fellas are way beyond him. A good far way."

The head of Special Branch took in the detail. Bi-pedal. Lean, skinless, metal rods and hinge joints for arms and legs. Winches and pullies instead of muscle. The entire thoracic and abdominal area was a glorified silver box, patched with access panels, and from which every mechanised limb originated. The power source perhaps? Yes, because from the top of either shoulder poked the stub of a chimney. Stencilled across the front of each chest were the words "Type VII".

"Very fine work, Inspector. Very fine indeed."

"Means at least some good has come of this diabolic' mess up, sir," said Pym, proudly.

Melville backed out of the enclosed space. He looked thoughtful. Pensive. "I wonder, Walter, if 'good' will turn out to be quite the appropriate word…"

Yes, I know! I didn't tell you. But then neither did Michael tell Phoebe about our platoon of advanced mechanical men.

And, in truth, you must have wondered. How Wicko, a fellow of limited stature for whom anything resembling work is viewed with morbid suspicion, and myself, hardly a tower of strength even when I'm not masquerading as a mute hunchback, could possibly have constructed a Contraption as complex as the Dodo? And our other Confections: the Steamo, the Lift'n'Shifts, those Psyke long-distance communication domes? Yes, based on knowledge we brought with us from our Steam Realm we could design those scientific masterpieces, and be grateful for the additional advice of Lord Kelvin and Nik Tesla. But the heavy lifting strong-arm construction – all performed by those advanced Tesla-Aethyr-powered Garridebs.

The creations we consciously shared with the world, the Steamo and the basic SteamMark III Mr Garrideb, we knew we could justify as the overblown creations of eccentric engineers – and Lord knows there were plenty of those around – commercial marketing tools to publicise the entirely unique shows starring Michael Magister – The Industrial Age Illusionist, and Phoebe – the Queen of Steam and Goddess of the Aethyr. All of which drew curious, cash-paying crowds away from Maskelyne's Egyptian Hall.

More importantly, we felt the obligation to keep the SteamMark VII Garridebs hidden from the unscrupulous, the criminals and the politicians. We could never trust them to employ such powerful machines in an altruistic manner. They would be very quickly conscripted into becoming world-conquering war machines. The problems thrown up by the Pulsa Pistols (see 'Steam, Smoke & Mirrors: I' and 'The Windsor Curiosity') had proved such a point. That was very much my fault. Scientific vanity.

I should also admit at this point the debt we owe, not only to Nik Tesla and Lord Kelvin, but to our debauched drunken priest Father Connor O'Connor. I know. Connor O'Connor. Who would have ever thought that?

It was back in 1895 that the holy man was tending to the needs of Miss Lilly Brennan and Miss Anne Bailey, two housemaids in their twenties, both supplicant enthusiasts of Father O'Connor's religious approach to the laying on of hands. Lilly and Anne worked for a successful builder called Simpson, James Barron Simpson, who lived at number one Dorset Street in Marylebone. Mr Simpson's property was easily the most impressive flat-roofed Georgian mansion in that area of West London. Detached and guarded at the front by black wrought iron railings, the solid house shouted symmetrical perfection over three storeys, with a main entrance front and centre. Within the long garden at the back stood two substantial brick-built sheds, perfect storage for his construction business.

It was one afternoon while the builder was out going about his business and the priest had just concluded going about his, that Father O'Connor left the ladies reciting their Hail Marys and took himself into the back yard for private communion with our Lord. Which, of course, was nothing of the sort because Connor was keen to have a mooch around the bigger of the two outbuildings just to see what he might pinch. At first glimpse, other than cobwebs, sacks of damp sand, stacked piles of dusty red bricks, tiles and half a dozen shovels that had all seen better days, the pickings were all decidedly poor. Not to mention heavy. However, not to be outdone and with his knowledge that the Lord helps those who help themselves, the rogue rummaged around at the back of the building and happened upon an old sorry-looking Welsh dresser, standing in a dark corner, wormed and sagging and fit only for the fire. The drawers, opened with a yank, revealed nothing but scuttling spiders and a rock hard rat. The large cupboard was just as bare.

But when in desperation Connor plunged his arm deeply and blindly towards the back, his hand touched upon what was revealed in the broad light of day to be a stiff-lidded leather attaché case. The hinges were rusted shut but a quick shake told him there was something decent inside. Decent because surely attaché cases of this substance were always associated with the well-to-do. So, the priest snaffled the mystery prize and slipped out through the side gate.

Once back in his vestry, with the case sitting on his sticky kitchen table and the locks jemmied open, the contents proved to be more than disappointing. Not a pound nor even a farthing to be found. Just a wad of musty, brown at the edge, technical ink drawings, foxed with age, which no matter what way round he held them up, he could not fathom. The pile of notebooks, equally dappled, were filled cover to cover with neatly annotated handwriting and numbers, which made little more sense than the drawings. But it looked learned. Scientific, even. What were those words by William Blake? The dark Religions are departed and sweet science reigns.

"Holy Jasus, yes," said the Lord's representative in Paddington. "I know the very bustards mug enough to pay a decent coin for this ol' pile a'…"

~10~

The very bustards, of course, were us. Myself, Wicko and Michael. Now, you should know, this was four or so years before we took over the refurbished Metropolitan Music Hall on the Edgware Road. Michael was working his magic act, third top, doubling at the Royal Music Hall on High Holborn and the Marylebone Music Hall on Marylebone High Street. We were lodging above a small shop premises on the Portobello Road in which Wicko and I were displaying our collection of automata. Foot-high models of fez-wearing monkeys that jigged, flouncy ballerinas who twirled, trees which sprouted leaves and a life-sized fakir in robes and a turban; Sheik bin al Garrideb, who was supposed to perform the cup and bean routine, but was currently out of order.

This sorry situation was brought about when a raggedly desiccated old woman, roaring drunk and with no teeth, staggered into the shop and tried to substantiate her claim that the Sheik was really a man dressed up, by stabbing him in the chest with a bread knife. A squirt of black oil instead of blood proved her wrong.

The walls of our fancy Palace of Phantasmagoria, as the name above the shopfront proclaimed, were lined with colourful, posters advertising the venues in which Michael had performed and where he could be seen tonight. I silently haunted the inside of the premises, wearing a full length, threadbare, blue linen smock while adopting the character of my hunch-postured mute, purely for mysterious effect, while Wicko 'spieled' out front, drumming up trade, dolled up in a scarlet military tunic with lines of braided gold running across the chest and pantaloons, a costume he filched from his time in New York with Barnum. At least Phineas had it made to measure.

Very often Michael would perform card manipulations and banter with whomever paid their tuppence to come in through the door. With the exception of that dentally-deficient harpy, the patrons by and large marvelled at our animated toys. Oh, and another bugbear was that local priest. Father Connor O'Connor. In the frayed and grey dog collar and a shiny, greasy black cassock. Florid of cheeks, stubbled of chin and a hank of straw hair splayed over his bald bonce. He would wander past at least every other day, making the sign of the cross and denouncing the automata as disciples of the devil.

"None of this is natural," he roared at the passing crowds, pointing in our direction.

"Of course it's not natural, you idiot," chided Wicko, without patience. "It's mechanical."

Wicko even unlatched the access panel to the Sheik and showed the priest the inner workings. Which went some way to shutting him up. That, and the glass of communion gin we plied him with, and suddenly he was our friend.

Well, it was on that fateful morning that Father Connor O'Connor arrived, standing outside gently tapping the window with gnarled knuckles and hissing swear words before we had even lifted the shutters. Once I slid back the bolts he glanced furtively up and down the Portobello Road and slipped inside, holding the attaché case close to his chest. He drew us to the back of the shop where he lay down the case on a table.

"Now then. Am I right in thinking the pair of you ignorant anti-Christs be honourable men of a knowledgeable persuasion?"

I confirmed he was quite right to think such a thing.

Connor O'Connor jumped back. "Jasus, ya mute bustard, y'can speak!"

I assured him miracles do happen. He railed at my blasphemy, stating firmly he would have no further dealings with me, but because there was money to be made, continued anyway.

"So, what might be yous saying – to this?"

~11~

With impressive theatricality he hinged open the lid and spun the case with its exposed contents towards us. "A miscellany of learning, be it not?"

I looked on while Wicko stood up on tiptoe, then poked around the books and papers, nodding and humming approval before saying: "What is it?"

"How should I know?" confessed the holy father, scratching the stubble on his chin. "But upon the life of Abel, I reckoned you two scientists would at least appreciate the value of the philosophising found herein."

The priest happily gave his permission for us to remove the miscellany of paperwork and lay it on the table. I unfolded one of the plans, a drawing in grey ink on yellowing foolscap, blotched and mottled brown here and there. It smelled fusty. Material unseen in many long years.

Fading ink outlined what looked to be the promontory of a coastline. More interesting was the reverse side of the page, which displayed a careful design of interconnecting mechanicry. A Contrivance of rods, cams, bellows, pulleys and pistons, most of which I understood, and all which, when held up to the light, fell within the boundaries of the 'shoreline'. The other pages, and there were many of them, displayed indeterminate sweeps of the pen, backed with more mechanical intrigue. The hand-drawn notes suggested materials and the arrows itemised individual workings.

"Worth three shillings to a decent man of science," said Father Connor O'Connor, confidently.

"Hardy that," said Wicko, carefully flicking through the pages of one of the hide-bound tomes. The edges were greyed and frayed from knocks and wear, but the binding was secure. "Here, Professor, see what you think of this?"

I gave Wicko one of the blueprint sheets and he handed over two of the books. The cursive calligraphy on the unlined pages was elegant and flowing. The sketched diagrams were clear. As were the strings of highbrow calculations and equations which often ran over two lines of vigorously subtracted, divided and fractionalised 'x's, 'y's, all to the powers of whatever.

Oh, my goodness. We held history in our hands.

Purely out of interest, I asked Father Connor O'Connor how he came by this case. Remember, this was before we knew him as a debauched, commandment-dodging ne'er-do-well.

"A gift it certainly was. Bestowed upon me by the master of the house in Dorset Street where I pay a regular visit in ministry of the sacrament."

Wicko and I replaced the items in the case. I slid the case towards him and offered sixpence.

"Sixpence? Sixpence? Ya thieving bustard, robbing the holy church," growled Father Connor O'Connor. He coughed and hacked and spat on the floorboards. "That's what meself and the church be thinkin' of that derisory submission. Sixpence? That's how you insult a man of the cloth. I'm taking the match to the lot of it. Right here. Right now."

~12~

"How about," said Michael, appearing at the foot of the stairs. He was up and dressed, but his shirt was tieless and his waistcoat still unbuttoned. "How about a shilling and a full bottle of whisky."

The priest thundered: "The shaman himself emerges! I'll not be bought wi' whikky!" then he paused and licked his lips. "What blend?"

Michael looked at the label on the bottle. "It says here Glen Nevis. Whoever he is."

Michael handed the whisky to Father Connor O'Connor who checked the stopper. Unopened. Then held it to the light to study the colour. Suddenly, in his hands, it became a sacred relic.

"Strikes me we have ourselves an accord, shaman," grinned Father Connor O'Connor.

Michael flicked him a shilling coin.

"Always a pleasure dealing with men of education," said Father Connor O'Connor, who caught the spinning coin in mid-air, spat on it and thrust it deep into his cassock pocket. Then he parted the air with his hand up, down and across. "The Lord's blessings be upon you."

Then he left. Then, purely for the benefit of passers-by, called for the heavens to strike down everyone in this den of satanic sin.

"How did you come by the whisky, Magister?" wondered Wicko.

"A dowager left it for me at the stage door, last night. At the end of the Marylebone show. Tell me about the papers. I figured from your reaction they were important."

"Oh, they are," said Wicko, his eyes gleaming.

Holding open the sheets, I showed Michael the signature at the foot of each drawing. Ada Lovelace.

Then Wicko opened one of the notebooks and presented the inside cover. Which said: "Observations on Mathematical Laws, and the construction of Analytical Engines. Volume 2. By Charles Babbage."

"And that's good?" said Michael.

Oh, yes. Oh, very yes indeed. I closed the door of the shop, threw the bolts. In reverential tones I told him that Professor Babbage and the Countess of Lovelace were by far the finest proponents of mechanised calculating machines in this realm. By a very long chalk. And rumour was, before the beloved Countess passed away at an all too early age, she and Babbage were engaged in a project uniting mathematics and physiology, and formulating calculus pertaining to the nervous system.

"I see," said Michael. He didn't. But at that time nor did I entirely.

"Give me those sheets a minute," said Wicko.

He checked their shape and orientation, hummed and ha'd, and finally had them all laid carefully on the floor. Wicko looked deadly serious.

"This material we bought for a shilling and your bottle of Glen Nevis? It's the Babbage-Lovelace Mother Lode."

Michael looked at the rectangle of pages on the floor. The meaningless coastal curves and sweeps. But once Wicko had aligned them all correctly, the lines formed the shape of a person.

As Wicko suspected, hoped and then confirmed, the Babbage-Lovelace plans took the notion of functioning, pre-programmed mechanically-driven artificial human being. They abandoned the idea when a suitably-sized power source could not be built. But we had such a power source. Tesla's Coil.

"And Connor was just given it," said Michael.

I told him I fully expected a little light-fingered skulduggery was the more likely. But the priest mentioned Dorset Street. Charles Babbage lived at number one Dorset Street for the last fifty years of his life.

~13~

Now, more than a century later, in the here and now of 2001's London, it was clear. Those advanced SteamMark VII Garridebs had survived their destruction at the theatre. They had been stripped down, studied, and with trial and error over who knows how long, forced to give up their myriad secrets and inspire further generational improvements. I mean, what would Debbi and Garri's iteration be now, SteamMark CCXXVI?

As I have made clear, our primary suspicion was that such advanced technology would never be pressed into service for universal benefit. It was not in human nature to do so. But thus far, the Garridebs were proving holistic rather than hostile. The air, the tranquillity, the lack of urgency, the respect for the past and the present was positive.

There was, however, one growing concern we all felt, and which prompted Michael's query.

"Deb?" Yes, that was typical. To him she was now Deb. Ingratiating.

"Why, yes, Mr Magister?"

"Well, I think I'm right in saying you'll forgive four weary Victorian time travellers who have just appeared on schedule from the past for asking this question, but as I look around, I'm seeing a dozen versions of you and Garri standing here, quite literally hanging out. And, well, thing is, what I'm not seeing are people. You know, flesh and blood type people. Like us."

"Why, Mr Magister, you would not see the people, because they are all comfortably ensconced in their homes."

Really? All of them? I wondered if we might meet with one of these people Debbi talked about. Perhaps at their residence. As soon as possible.

"Why, certainly, Professor More." She tilted her head and paused for thought. Or to retrieve information from who knows where. "The person who would most like to meet you had expected you to rest following your journey; however, he is currently available to receive you at once."

"He?" spotted Michael. "So, it's a man?"

"Why, yes, and the gentleman is known to you; and for many years he has spoken with great warmth of you all."

"Wait, Deb, what, we know him?"

"Why yes, Mr Magister you all know him."

"From the year of 1899?" Tesla inflected our surprise perfectly. "Which leads me to ask, Madame Debbi, how precisely old is this person?"

"Why, the gentleman is one hundred and forty-one years of age; and like Dr Tesla, Dr Smawl and Professor More, holds a position of the highest esteem in history."

Who the heck had survived that long? That we knew? And was held in the highest esteem? Someone who predicted we would arrive here? The Prince of Wales? Salisbury? Queen Victoria? No, Debbi said a man. Melville? No! Not Dr Phunn!

"All right, Debbi," said Wicko. "Out with it. What's this person's name?"

"Why Dr Smawl, the gentleman's title is His Holiness Pope Innocent the Fourteenth; but you of course will all know him as Father Connor O'Connor."

~14~

What? Connor O'Connor? *Our* Connor O'Connor? The Pope? It was a shock too far for our already bewildered systems. Debbi insisted we sat on a bench abutting what she called Parliament Square Garden. Suddenly, the hypnotic attraction of a beautiful female android, naked and perfect in every particular had vanished.

Never mind the ascension of the Garridebs! Dear Lord, if Connor O'Connor had been crowned with the papal tiara then we really had mucked up history!

Debbi studied each of us carefully as we sat, stunned. Of particular concern was Michael. She even asked permission to place her hand on his chest; I presumed in doing so, she could evaluate his signs and symptoms. She wondered if we would not prefer to rest at a hotel of our choice, and continue in the morning.

"Thank you, Deb," said Michael, "but if a one hundred and forty-one-year-old Connor O'Connor is something we cannot wait to see, then Connor as the Pope is totally off the scale."

"All right, Debbi, when can we go?" Wicko stood up, resolute. "Come on, gents. But I tell you one thing. I'm not kissing his ring."

"Why, then, gentlemen, if you would care to follow me, your Motivator is over here."

Watching Debbi lead the way to the Motivator, none of us was left in any doubt that she moved just as she spoke, with a smooth sensuality. Our Motivator was the nearest of a sleek line of clear streamlined vehicles tightly parked nose to tail along Parliament Square. From a distance they looked ovoid and sleek. Close up they revealed themselves to be smooth works of art.

All four wheels were housed within the bodywork, which was one seamless moulding. The Motivator must surely have been inspired by an egg pitched forward. The passenger canopy was clear glass, the pearlized bodywork, translucent. With no prompting, one of the vehicles must have sensed our intention, gently easing itself into life by hinging the entire passenger canopy forward. The interior revealed six plump leather chairs, tan brown, arranged in pairs over three rows. A more functional solo metal seat took up the rear. Debbi's. Like the driver of a Roman chariot, but with no visible means to control the vehicle.

"Please, be seated wherever you wish," directed Debbi.

Our chairs raised themselves on scissor jacks, requiring little effort in the way of climbing on board, then retracted into their travelling positions. Whatever propulsion the Motivator required was hidden below the black padded floor.

I sat with Tesla, upfront. Wicko and Michael boarded behind us. It truly was the most comfortable chair I had ever sat in.

"Why, gentlemen, please do not be alarmed by the restraints."

The canopy door swung silently down to enclose us. Unbidden, the safety belts snaked over our shoulders and laps, emerging from beneath and behind the seats. Then something strange happened. I know, as if everything else that happened since our arrival hadn't been strange…

"The duration of our journey shall be two minutes and fifty-eight seconds."

Really? To Lambeth Palace? The first traffic problem I could foresee, how our vehicle could manoeuvre itself out of this kerbside jam, was resolved when the Motivator simply crabbed sideways into the road.

Once clear front and back, our carrier reversed, soundless and smooth, affording us a superb view of Big Ben. She then swung left and swept forward crossing Westminster Bridge. The vistas on either side were breath-taking. Ahead to the left, the south bank of the Thames was dominated by a huge bicycle-wheeled structure which must have stood an impressive four hundred feet tall, but apparently served no discernible water-pumping purpose. Craning further round to the left at least there remained the reassuring dome of St Paul's Cathedral.

At what looked like breakneck speed through the canopy, but with no feeling of movement within the cabin, the Motivator spanned the bridge and curved right. The momentum was so intense, my hopes of seeing St Thomas's Hospital on the right were reduced to a blur of multi-coloured light.

Tesla whispered: "Octopus. I submit there exists an unseen electro-telepathic link between the vehicle and Madame Debbi."

he certainly wasn't steering our Motivator, yet the thing knew precisely where to go. And having watched my friend pioneer the concept of unwired electrical transmission, I was in no mind to question his genius. Suddenly the vehicle decelerated to a halt, but we experienced zero forward sensation – ha! – happily mocking the 'first law of inertia' purported by that foul man, Newton.

Despite the midnight hour, the streets were still lit as day. Everything, everywhere was impeccable. Streets, sidewalks, the historic glories of Westminster glowed as rich and clean as the time they were built. Nothing eroded by weather or sullied by smoke. Everywhere was shining night-time splendour without a soul to appreciate it.

## 15

Lambeth Palace, and in plain sight of the Palace of Westminster across the river, is a dominant structure on the appropriately named Lambeth Palace Road. Bordered by a ten-foot red brick wall, the Palace presents a miscellany of period architectural styles. To the right stand two fifteenth-century red brick towers: Morton's Tower, a Tudor gatehouse which contains a small prison, and Lollard's Tower which houses a prison cell. They clearly liked taking their prisoners back then. Set in the middle, stands the Great Hall, rebuilt by William Juxon, the Bishop who read the last rites to Charles the First. Samuel Pepys described Juxon Hall as 'new old fashioned'. Whatever that meant. But then he also admitted kissing the mummified corpse of Henry the Fifth's wife, so each to their own.

I asked Debbi about Father O'Connor's – sorry, Pope Innocent's – tenure, in what to my knowledge was always the official residence of the Protestant Archbishop of Canterbury.

"Why, Professor More, the Pope harboured fine intentions to relocate to Rome to take his position there, but has, as yet, to do so."

"Too idle to make the journey," whispered Wicko. "Or too sozzled."

"Why, please do follow me, gentlemen; The Pope resides in Juxon's Hall. He is expecting you."

"Thanks, Deb."

"You're welcome."

Very odd. What was Connor doing living in the Great Hall? I remembered the Archbishop of Canterbury lived in chambers in the Palace.

Sensing Debbi's approach, the arched wooden doors of the Morton Gate swung out and we followed her in, all feeling a strange ambivalence of fascination and trepidation.

Again, everywhere was brightly lit. The air warm and clean.

The Garri standing, in all his manly glory, inside the arch was a dead ringer for the masculine android we encountered outside Big Ben.

"You're very welcome to Lambeth Palace, Professor Artemus, Dr Smawl, Dr Tesla and Mr Magister," he said in that same patronising tone of voice.

Ahead of us the stone-built Hall. The wooden door swung open.

"Oh my … what the…" recoiled Michael, suddenly heaving and his eyes streaming at the overpowering assault on his delicate nostrils and throat.

"I do concur, Mr Magister, the aroma is most disagreeable," said Tesla clamping a fresh 'kerchief over his mouth and nose.

Oh yes. Dear God, what a reek it was. Putrid. The old River Fleet when it ran as an open sewer would have honked less rank.

Debbi clearly had no olfactory sense whatsoever, but nevertheless apologised. "Why, gentlemen, if you find the quality of the breathing air too debilitating then do please make use of these Contrivances."

The doorman Garri was now by our sides holding a silver salver upon which lay four full-face gas masks. A filter dangled from the front of each mask like a stubby elephant's trunk.

"These must be modelled on you, pal," Wicko told the Garri, as he reached up to grab a mask, which was formed not of black rubber, but an entirely see-through material. With no straps, no ties, the Contrivance moulded and sealed itself to the contours of the face. They put me in mind of those fearsome gas masks worn by Scotland Yard's clandestine 'Clean-Up' Squad, but with these, conversations could be conducted clear of muffled interference.

Entering the Hall, the cool purity of the air within the mask was most welcome, and through the clear visor we could see the foul air shimmer.

Despite its great age, the Great Juxon Hall remained an impressive building, more than fifty feet long, floored in a chequer board pattern of black and white tiles. The walls were lined with dark wood bookshelves weighed down by learned ecumenical volumes. Above us were the beautifully carpentered trusses and cruxes of the massive hammer beam roof.

At the far end, blurred by the heat haze, well, there looked to be something there. Only as we drew closer did the something began to take form. And, dear Lord, the sight was horrific.

## 16

"No. That can't be him," said Wicko, wiping his mask with the bank of a hand.

The image before us was not so much a person, more a gelatinous mass of pink and grey leathered flesh. You remember the size of Cardinal Corvus from my last volume? Corvus was snake-hipped by comparison. The barely recognisable human form was gigantic. Its corpulence widened from the jaw line, spreading out like fleshy lava.

The face: florid cheeks, piggy milky eyes, up-turned nose, looked tiny in proportion to the rest of his body. The lower half of his face was dominated by a slobbering gaping mouth. Then everything below the first chin sagged under the weight of jowlsy fat. The fifth and final chin slopped low and wide over the bosomy chest which splayed onto the first of at least two dozen rolls of ever-widening belly flab, which in turn hung like a sore-streaked pink skirt down to the floor.

The arms were like pig skins of pudge, huge, with pathetic little fingers protruding helpless from the ends.

Lord knows what he was resting on, or how it survived the tonnage. Not that whatever it was had seen the light of day in a good long while, groaning beneath those enveloping folds of fetid, sweated flab which hung down between wide open legs which were the size of puckered dirigibles.

I suspect you probably get the giant baby picture by now.

"Jasus! Magister the magician," crackled Connor O'Connor. "The devil's imp ... Tesla the Italian ... And Professor Artemus More ... the foulest of the foul."

"It's him," sighed Wicko, in response to his own question.

Father Connor O'Connor. Now Pope Innocent the Fourteenth.

"He's let himself go," said Michael.

"Jasus, I suspected your arrival," Connor gasped. "When you nearly blew the top right off of Big Ben. Welcome, y'heathens, my finest friends, to the Promised Land. All the drink you take, and all the food you can manage and all the pleasure you can desire is yours, comes courtesy of lovely ladies of the likes of your Debbi here."

"Why, thank you, your Holiness," said Debbi. "You're welcome."

"And, my friends, thanks to you kindly making a proper bollocks of not destroying your theatre correctly, I find myself in my rightful position." Then he called for 'Celebration whikky!'

I told him not for us. Please, Connor.

"'Tis not for you, 'tis for me!"

Two Debbies entered immediately behind us. Walking in perfect step, the first was carrying what looked to be a metallic step-ladder, the second holding two bottles of Glen Nevis. Both androids perfectly identical to, and equally as nude as, the Debbi who was our guide. The first Debbi positioned the steps beside Connor, pushing the inclination of the ladder toward him, whereupon it leaned on nothing but air. No support whatsoever. Cantilevered, but without the cantilever. So to speak.

"Most remarkable. Gyroscopic gravity inclination," whispered Tesla. I just nodded, knowing he knew what he was talking about.

"Prof, that is a trick we need to use…" But Michael stopped before he could finish the sentence. That former life ended at the top of the Big Ben.

In supreme confidence of the physics involved, the second Debbi mounted the step-ladder, still holding her two bottles.

"Good health!" wheezed Connor, a living contradiction to the expression. He opened his mouth. The second Debbi held one bottle high and dribbled the amber spirit into Connor's slurping maw. Some of it glugged out and ran down his chins like an Italian water feature. Then with one bottle drained, the next was administered in the same appalling manner.

Connor then belched long and deep, like a baritone hog, while his body quivered like a cauldron of jelly in an earthquake.

Tesla quite rightly could stomach the sight no more and staggered back out to the open air before he retched. Wicko had been rendered slack-jawed and totally speechless, though from his point of view, peering up at the monstrous Matterhorn of blubber, the view must have been awful.

"Thank you … my lovelies," gasped Connor.

"You're welcome," chimed the Debbies.

"Food…" he then drooled.

"Why, Mr Magister. Please do excuse us."

Michael turned to be confronted by two more delectably identical Debbies, pushing tables. One bearing a silver salver piled high with steaming boiled potatoes larded in butter, melted cheese and, if I remember, dusted with chopped parsley and a breaded dill crumb. The second table was weighed down by an entire roasted hog, seasoned with sea salt and bathed in an apple jus.

Only then did we notice these tables also displayed no visible means of support. They floated, in defiance of gravity, waist high. Steered by the merest touch of the Debbies' hands.

"Ah. The first course. Jasus, my friends, you'll take a morsel or two yourselves will you not?" wheezed Connor.

Perhaps too readily we all declined his generous dining invitation. Whatever appetite we might have built had disappeared just as soon as we walked through the door.

I claimed concern for Tesla's post-time-travel nausea as our excuse to decline. Said it was proper we let the Pope enjoy his meal in privacy, then we should return tomorrow refreshed, to reacquaint ourselves at our mutual leisure.

Connor O'Connor reacted with indifference, gasping, "Suit yourselves. All the more for me," called for "Whikky!" and with great gusto belched again.

"Lovely," said Wicko.

~17~

We bade the Pope goodnight, but not before he graciously demanded we should all be afforded the finest accommodation and our preference of the most vigorous physical love.

Our Debbi assured him that would most certainly be the case.

Well, truthfully, I was so thankful to get out of the Hall. All of us were left mentally battered by the overwhelming sensory assault, gratefully peeling our masks away as soon as we made the sanctuary of the sweet, clean outside air.

We found Tesla still mopping his brow with another clean 'kerchief. Michael looked pallid. Every breath crackled and rasped. Wicko was still at a loss for words and more than once I all but swooned.

Our Debbi gracefully followed us outside, and she sensed our discomfort. "Why, gentlemen, kindly follow me to the vehicle; and

117

if you are feeling unwell, I should quickly transport you to the hospital, where the medical facilities are faultlessly efficient."

I assured her that would not be necessary but wondered if it was these faultlessly efficient medical facilities that were responsible for keeping the Pope alive to such a great age; he was, after all, living in defiance of every natural law of science and medicine.

"Why, Professor More, over the past four decades the Pope has enjoyed three replacement hearts and nine transplanted livers; and as a result, his appetite and thirst remain active, although his proclivities have markedly declined."

"Access *would* be a problem," whispered Michael, quite unnecessarily, I thought.

I ventured the assumption that such generous surgical indulgence was a privilege of the Papacy.

"Why, on the contrary, Professor More; every person enjoys successful medical treatment, as swiftly as requested; and for the past four decades disease has been totally eradicated."

Eradicated? Entirely?

She confirmed it had been.

Who would ever have foreseen such a remarkable development? Clearly not we scientific cynics! So, in broader international terms, what about disputes, or conflict?

"Why, they have been rendered redundant; no campaigns have waged since the swift conclusion of the Great War in 1915."

Really? Was this right? That humans had lived in Utopian peace and harmony? For the best part of a century?

"And you think you know people," shrugged Michael.

~18~

In the face of such a remarkable statistic it was a good long while before anyone spoke another word. As we approached the vehicle it seemed to wake, then glowed itself into life, lights outside and within, swinging forward its canopy and elevating its seats.

Sliding aboard, Wicko broke the silence by bringing up the matter of Connor's apparent fondness for a full dinner plate, adding, "Now that *has* to be a benefit of being Pope."

"Why, no, Dr Smawl, food production remains at surplus levels and every person may eat and drink as much as they demand; famine has been eradicated."

Wait. Famine? Also wiped out entirely?

"Madame Debbi," said Nik Tesla, always impeccably polite. "Please be so good as to tell us: all these remarkable accomplishments have been achieved, how?"

"Why, purely as a consequence of the advancements originated by yourself, Lord Kelvin of Largs, and of course, Dr Smawl and Professor More, in designing and programming our original incarnations."

Our collective brains could barely process such a deluge of information fast enough, and now, coupled with this remarkable legacy, disease, famine and war eradicated? Facilitated by the Garridebs. And they were affording us the credit.

Well, as you can imagine, to say we were suddenly consumed with pride and self-congratulation would be – the truth. And while we basked in our understandable glory, the canopy of the Motivator closed, the safety straps embraced us and the vehicle accelerated away.

"Why, gentlemen," said Debbi, "in which hotel would you prefer to reside? The Savoy, the Langham, the Dorchester…"

The Dorchester? Must have been built after we left.

"And the Hotel Cecil."

We leapt at the chance of the Cecil, sited on the Strand, almost next door to the Savoy. Immediately, without instruction, the vehicle swung right onto Lambeth Bridge, heading north across the Thames.

"Why, gentlemen, that is an excellent choice; it is Great Britain's most luxurious hotel."

Good to know a century after it was built the hotel retained such an honour, and as celebrated saviours of the world, we thought such splendour was something we deserved.

During our pleased-with-ourselves distraction, it was Michael, still puzzled by the empty night-time streets, who said: "So, Deb, how many people actually now live in London?"

"Why, Mr Magister, the latest census reports the present population of London is three."

Incredible! There was a populace of six and a half million when we left in 1899. So, factoring in all these health improvements along with exponential growth, Debbi was telling us three billion people lived in the great city. Or was that three *trillion?* I felt another accolade coming our way.

"Why, no, Professor More, three; three individuals."

"…Three?" we all shouted together. "Three people?"

"Why, yes, and His Holiness the Pope is one of them."

It was a kick-in-the-stomach shocker.

"But, Madame Debbi, this number of the population refers only to London," pressed Tesla. "But of the nation in general, the population is?"

"The population of Great Britain amounts to nineteen persons. No, correction, eighteen, a female in the Smethwick district of Birmingham has just demised."

"How can there be so few?" yelled Wicko. We all of us shared his shock.

"Why, demise by natural causes, coupled with zero procreation; you will understand, while supremely skilled in the art and practice of physical love, we cannot bear offspring."

I asked her about the population of the world. An estimate.

"Why, that information I cannot access."

Our heads began to swim again. Debbi was telling us that in little more than a century, the human population of Great Britain was actually on the brink of extinction?

"Wait, Deb, with all these medical facilities, and all this food they can eat whenever they want it, how do people ever die?"

"Why, Mr Magister," she said in her matter of fact way, "with their sedentary lifestyle and voracious appetites, they simply explode."

There was a pause. Then Michael said, "When we get to the hotel, I think I'll skip dinner."

RAP! RAPPITY RAP!

The pudgy fingers used unnecessary vigour on the brass door knocker. Enough to rouse many of the lofty residents of Victorian era London's most well-to-do Kensington squares from their carefree slumbers. But, you see, the thick-set, pig-faced oaf hammering the knocker was by reputation heavy-handed. Despite being told many times. He was just too stupid to change.

In his capacity as an undertaker, presently unemployed, Mr Drago had dropped many a cheap coffin and let its mortal contents spill out at the graveside in front of a throng of weeping mourners. Also, in his side-line capacity as a professional murderer, currently hired, Mr Drago had frequently wrenched the head clean off a victim, when a simple snap of the neck would have sufficed.

"Loud, hnur-hnur-hnur," grunted Drago, referring to the door knocker.

"But a true and proper indication of the urgency of our visit," claimed his partner in death, the shrew-faced, hand-wringing, flowery-tongued fellow undertaker known as Mr Skrill.

The impressive mid-terraced villa was the London private residence of one of the vilest enemies of the state. However, the bowed, elderly, gammy-legged gentleman currently limping along the wide hallway to open the door was the villain's liveried retainer and loyal butler; a man frequently referred to as Pockney. Largely because that was his name.

The old duffer patted the lengths of sticky grey hair splayed thinly across his pate in a futile attempt to disguise his baldness, then unlatched the heavy front door.

"Yes-th, gentlemen. How mighth I help you?" enquired Pockney, looking not a little alarmed at the sight of the mismatched angels of doom who stood on the step, dishevelled in their stained black tail coats, grubby waistcoats and once-white shirts. The smaller, thinner member of the pairing removed his battered top hat with a flourish. The bigger, porcine lout copied the example.

"My man, we are in receipt of this urgent missive requesting our presence at this most gracious residence."

Skrill waved the crumpled telegram at Pockney with unwarranted distain. Pockney insisted on carefully examining the note. The order read: 'HERE. IMMEDIATELY', giving the Onslow Square address.

"And having thus satisfied yourself as to the veracity of this document," sneered Skrill, "perchance you might, without further ado, inform the sender of the aforesaid communiqué of our presence, as demanded. My man."

"Manded, hnur-hnur-hnur," agreed Drago.

"Dear me. The bore and the boar," thought Pockney.

Then he said, "Of coursth, gentlemen. Please enter and kindly wait-th in the Reading Roomwhile I inform him." Drago and Skrill thought they saw a knowing look in the old boy's watery eyes.

"Thank you most civil, my man," smirked Skrill, as Pockney let them inside, bowed and limped away to set about their bidding.

The hall was floored in tiny white tiles, displaying a recurring mosaic design: a symbol picked out in black tiles of a sun circle emitting rays of light, while enclosing a crucifix and depicting the letters H I S. Mr Skill elbowed his associate in the ribs and pointed to the pattern. Once Drago had figured out what it was, which took a while, both unemployed undertakers blessed themselves with the sign of the cross.

To the left, off the hall, the Reading Roomwas dark and vast. A huge bay window had its heavy curtains still drawn against the insipid dawn. Pools of light glowed from half a dozen black candles on tall brass candlesticks.

Drago and Skrill had never before witnessed a room like it. Not that Drago had ever before set foot in a reading room, possessing neither the inclination or indeed the necessity so to do. But this Reading Roomappeared utterly unique in that it apparently contained not a single book. The walls were lined from floor to ceiling with mahogany shelves where books should have stood and might well stand one fine day. But at the moment, empty.

Copious reading matter was readily available however in the form of newspapers, laid neatly over the floor. All manner of publications: The Manchester Guardian, The Times. And the most recent weeklies: The Observer, Union Jack, The Illustrated

London News. Oh, and the only stick of furniture in the Reading Room was a wooden lectern, set before the grand marble fireplace, upon which laid a stout, leather-bound Holy Bible; its covers closed, secured with two brass latches.

"An interesting seat of learning, Mr Drago," said Skrill looking about.

"Learnin'n, hnur-hnur-hnur," he agreed.

The wait was a while before the door to the Reading Room swung open and with calm purpose, in strode the tall, imposing monkish figure, clad in a black habit with the hood swung up over the head, revealing nothing of his features save for the length of black beard which hung down to his waist. Drago and Skill both dropped to their knees, blessing themselves in supplication.

"My lambs," growled the Black Bishop. "My chosen apostles. I thank you. For your prompt attendance. And for how you have thus far served me."

"Thy will most certainly be done, Excellency," simpered Skrill.

"Dun, hnur-hnur-hnur," said Drago.

"But. On this occasion," rasped the Bishop, "you bring news of disappointment?"

"I can perceive how it could be construed as disappointment, Excellency, indeed so it could. We recognise the unholy magicians still drawing on this earth may be construed as a disappointment, but we view it more as a temporary postponement. And, in mitigation, the throng of uncooperative onlookers patronising the theatre of flagrant sin conspired to thwart our malevolence toward the oleaginous magician and his brazen slattern. But do be assured Excellency, their time will shortly come."

"Of that. I have. No doubt. And you have my sympathies. The circumstances. Were most trying."

Drago and Skrill glanced at one another in relief.

"So I beseech you, my lambs. Pray, lift your heads. To receive God's kindly beneficence."

Both Drago and Skrill looked up to gaze upon the face of the Black Bishop. Instead all they glimpsed was the glint of the sword which slashed though their necks with a single sweep.

As their heads bounced onto the spattered newspapers and rolled with vacant eyes across the floor, they may have heard the Black Bishop growl: "No one fails me twice."

But then, we will never know.

~20~

Our proud euphoria was now chastened by the news that the humans in Great Britain were on the brink of extinction. Strangely, Debbi confirmed she possessed no data concerning the population of the wider world. Which did not bode terribly well. We always predicted it would be war which destroyed the human race. Instead, it was seduced by lethargy and indulgence. And now here we were, being chauffeured in great style to the most opulent, luxurious hotel in the country.

Michael, Wicko and I had watched the slow construction of the Cecil during the '90s. Prime Minister Salisbury, whose family owned the land, sold the lease to a building developer, Jabez Spencer Balfour. This character was a churchman, a founder of a savings bank 'The Liberator Building Society', a Justice of the Peace and a Member of Parliament. Amazingly, despite those 'credentials', no one took him to be a crook. Which of course he was. Jabez Spencer Balfour was the biggest, nastiest embezzler this country has ever known!

In 1892, the company developing the property collapsed, the Hotel Cecil was abandoned and Jabez Spencer Balfour swiftly boarded a boat to Argentina. Taking with him the millions of pounds of savers' money he'd plundered from the Liberator Building Society and leaving nothing behind but debt, destitution, despair and death.

Scotland Yard, in the shape of Detective Inspector Frank Forest sailed to Buenos Aires, kidnapped Balfour and dragged him back to Blighty, where he stood trial and was locked up in Portland Prison for fourteen years with hard labour. He was still there when we left.

"The developer of the Hotel Cecil, Mr Jabez Balfour sounds to me a man most disagreeable," said Tesla. "One must hope he spent his final years incarcerated."

"Why, no, Dr Tesla," said Debbi, "Jabez Balfour served his entire sentence of hard labour and was released from custody in 1906, after which he enjoyed a decade of freedom before his demise aboard a railway train, travelling to Wales."

"That was Balfour's final punishment, never getting to see Wales," said Michael, who always enjoyed playing Stoll's Empire Music Hall, on Swansea High Street.

It was now, as our vehicle breezed quickly west toward the Strand, that Wicko started the trouble, when he said: "Here, Deb, seeing as you know a fair bit about what happened to people..."

"Why, yes, I do, Dr Smawl," she said.

"Whatever became of that Superintendent Melville? Of the Special Branch? I'm interested." Probably because Wicko considered Melville the bane of his life.

Debbi tilted her head, retrieving the information. "Why, Superintendent William Melville retired to become the first operative of the new British secret service."

"A spy," said Michael.

"Why, he was. William Melville expired in 1918. The cause of his demise was acute renal failure, shortly to become a treatable condition, and his body lies interred at the Kensal Green Catholic Cemetery, West London."

The news rather jolted Wicko. "Poor bugger."

"Why, we shall be arriving at your destination shortly."

The vehicle smoothly scooted across Trafalgar Square onto the Strand. It was then Michael who, I'm bound to say, was by now looking very tired, said: "Debbi..."

"Why, yes, Mr Magister?"

"D'you have any record of Miss Phoebe Le Breton?"

There was a head tilted pause before she said: "Why, yes, I have, sir."

Michael *had* to ask the question, didn't he? Just had to ask. And if you ask a Debbi, you get told. And what she told us was simply too horrendous to contemplate.


~21~


In the shock of the news, we barely noticed turning right off the Strand, driving under the stone archway entrance and braking on a sixpence in the forecourt of the Cecil.

"I need to get out," Michael panicked. "I need to get out."

As soon as the belts were released and the canopy raised, he was scrambling to get out of the Motivator.

He knelt, hands and knees on the roped and red welcome carpet. Michael's face, already sallow, shaded to clammy grey. His stomach hollowed and his head span. He saw black spots swimming, heard the pulse surging wildly in his ears as the feel of a vice crushed his chest and he dropped to his side.

At once, Debbi was there, her hand upon his chest, not pressing, just touching, assessing. Blood bubbled from the corner of his mouth and onto the carpet.

"What is it?" begged Wicko in total panic.

Her diagnosis was instant. "Mr Magister has suffered catastrophic pulmonic failure. His demise will occur in seven minutes and seven seconds."

"Sweet Lord. What can we do? Can he be saved?"

"Why, of course, if that is your instruction."

"Well, yes!" said Wicko, in a tone of exasperation.

Immediately, Debbi calmly said to nobody in particular, "Medical emergency at this location; subject is Mr Michael Magister, total thoracic organ replacement required and housekeeping assistance; blood group B negative on woollen carpet."

Debbi placed her palm back on Michael's chest.

Silence.

She pressed her two index fingers, one either side of Michael's heart and discharged a burst of energy through her fingertips. His entire body jumped in spasm. Debbi removed her fingers, then reapplied her palm to his chest.

Silence.

Total.

Until: BIP ------ BIP--- BIP-BIP-BIP.

We all exhaled in relief. At least his heart was working. I thanked her for it.

"Why, you're welcome."

Two male androids, Garries, suddenly smoothed their way out of the hotel entrance with an unhurried style, guiding with deft gestures a white floating casket. Yes, floating. It put me in mind of an evolved iteration of Dr Phunn's healing sarcophagus, more bespoke, curved to fit a patient snugly within.

The Garries gestured the casket to the ground. The lid was clear, until it fizzed to become frosted glass and then evaporated. Debbi,

126

with no effort, hooked one arm under Michael's neck, the other beneath his knees, scooped him from the floor and rested him carefully within the coffer. Again, the lid fizzed, frosted and restored itself to a clear-lid coffin.

"This is a condition most serious?" asked Tesla.

"Why, yes, it is, Dr Tesla; however, Mr Magister will now be transported to the medical facility where he will undergo complete pulmonary-bronchio-replacement therapy."

A full thoracic set? What, new heart, lungs, oesophagus, and stomach? They had such organs, blood group specific, in stock?

Wicko snatched a look into the casket just as the two Garries waved their magic signals and began floating Michael back beneath the entrance arch and out onto the Strand. The next few moments mirrored the events of Westminster Abbey. Out on the street, a silver sleek airship, tapered to a point front and back, and bellied in the middle, hovered inches from the road surface. No directional fins, no propeller, no sound and no doors. The Garries simply pushed the casket, and then themselves, straight through the side of the airship

GLOOOP!

and disappeared within, leaving the skin of the ship to ripple, then firm.

"Remarkable," said Tesla, recognising his Molecular Disruption creation, now in its latest incarnation. "Madame Debbi, we may follow?"

"Why, you will be most welcome."

We all breached the skin, as easy as passing through the membrane of a thick soap bubble. The airship cabin occupied a floorspace of twenty feet long, and ten across. Plenty of room. From inside, the lower third of the ship appeared solid and peak white, while the upper section formed a clear-view, all-over canopy. It was only the view outside which offered us any sense of motion. With apparently no aeronaut helming the airship, she swiftly rose, sailed over the top of the hotel, and crossed the Thames.

"Where are we taking him?" wondered Wicko.

"Why, Dr Smawl, there is our destination," said Debbi directing our gaze directly ahead.

A dark space? Then as if on cue, an entire building was flooded with light. A stunning design. A series of rectangles, built entirely of glass or some such see-through material, and arranged on top of one another at irregular angles. The structure was five storeys tall. Breathtaking. And surely occupying the site where I remember stood a world famous 1869 gothic beauty: St Thomas's Hospital?

Debbi replied: "Why, it was, Professor More. Now it is 'The Dok Tor Phunn Memorial Medical Facility'."

The what?

~22~

The Dok Tor Phunn Memorial Medical Facility? We all looked at one another. Really? But then the airship swung about, above the building and descended. The entire glass roof frosted over, then vanished, enabling the vessel to touch down within the top floor.

Immediately the two Garries steered Michael's casket through the membrane of the airship. Without instruction we chose to follow, emerging into a wide open space, quiet to the ear, brilliant to the eye and sterile to the nose. A dozen androids of either gender stood dormant, awaiting a call to action which, in view of the population, was becoming increasingly unlikely.

The Garries directed Michael up ahead with such urgency, Tesla, Wicko and I were in no shape to keep up. By the time we trailed them around a corner, our route was barred by two closed doors. The words embossed on the sign above read: Surgical Suite.

"Here, Debbi, what exactly happened to Magister back there?"

"Why, Dr Smawl, Mr Magister suffered multiple aneurysms, aortic and bronchial, caused by his blood pressure rising to 180 systolic, coupled with cardiac arrest within a cavity environment of severe organ degradation."

Wicko screwed his face up in a kind of wince. "How long is it going to take to replace all that?"

"Why, one hundred and twenty-three minutes."

I asked if we could sit down. Suddenly, overwhelmed by – well, everything.

"Why, certainly; please follow me."

We did. To a brightly-lit suite of contradictions. Classical pieces set against a stark modern backdrop. Antique easy chairs, settees and chaises, all upholstered in soft cream fabric. Set within the white walls, oval alcoves, displaying grey-mottled marble busts of great clinicians: Hippocrates, Lister, Bell, Garrett Anderson, Jenner, Barnard, Taussig, Janzekovic, Apgar, Saunders, Williams, Crick, Watson, Wilkins, Franklin, Curie, Nightingale, Ostler, Gore, Hughes and a full length larger than life size tribute to the great clinician himself, in full Chinese regalia, Dok Tor Phunn.

In keeping with the ethos of hospitality we were offered an extensive menu of epicurean magnificence to curb our hunger, along with private sessions of physical comfort, which even Wicko declined. Far too drained. Emotionally and physically.

Debbi stood by the door of the suite, a silent sentinel. None of us spoke after Tesla politely requested the bright lights all around to be softened by 50 percent. And we drifted to sleep, reflecting mostly upon Phoebe's news…

*"You can never plan the future by the past."*
*Edmund Burke 1729-1797*
~PART THREE~

~1~

Phoebe was at a loss. Michael, Wicko, and myself were gone, possibly dead, and the Metropolitan Theatre of Steam, Smoke and Mirrors destroyed by fire.

The railway carriage tucked away in the sidings of the goods depot beyond Paddington Railway terminus, much as it had been her home for the past year, had suddenly lost its appeal. The excitement, the clandestine lodgings, the audacity of hiding in plain sight, now had little meaning. Along with her life.

Phoebe's closest friend Lady Elsinore Belvoir, one of the Eton Belvoirs, was travelling with her pompous husband. Phoebe's birth mother was far too busy living her own life to care much for her first daughter, the child the entire world knew nothing of. And she could hardly roll up to her father's home, asking to be put up for a few days; the Household Cavalry guarding Kensington Palace might have something to say about that. Also, the last thing she wanted anything to do with was privilege. No. Phoebe needed to do something useful. Worthwhile. And the answer was Matron.

Phoebe sent a telegram from the Harrow Road Post Office, then spent her last day living in the sidings at Paddington by draping linen sheets over what she didn't need, packing a trunk of what she did, then exercising, sparred with the wardrobe, 'The Jabber-Blocky' (as mentioned in my first tome of memoirs). "Fighting the furniture" Michael had called it. Six hours later, a return telegram was delivered. The message said precisely what she hoped for.

She locked down the railway carriage, lugged her travelling trunk down the steps, through the metal gate, stepped out onto the Harrow Road and waited not too long for a passing Hansom heading east. If he'd been carrying a fare he'd have turfed his passenger out to stop for Phoebe.

"South Street, please. The Park Lane end," she told the biddable driver, who even helped her with the luggage.

She didn't look back.

The cab rattled to a halt outside number 10. A soaring four-storey house in the middle of an imposing Georgian terrace. As she stepped down from the Hansom, she noticed the white net curtain twitch. Up on the second floor. Matron. She missed nothing. The hefty black front door swung open before Phoebe got the chance to raise the knocker.

"Miss Le Breton," said the maid, Elizabeth Hubbard; a small woman in her thirties, starched and proper, of both dress and demeanour. "She asks that you go straight up."

"Thank you, Miss Hubbard."

Inside, the house itself could not help but be grand. Although there was nothing superfluous or ostentatious about its contents. Every stick of furniture, every item and object, served a purpose. And be it wooded, tiled, or glazed, everything was polished and buffed to a mirror's gleam.

Phoebe pulled off her boots, stood them in the hall, hitched her long skirt and scurried up the stairs. The knock on the bedroom door was greeted with a cheery bid to enter.

The old woman, wearing a cream linen nightdress, a white frilled bonnet, with her shoulders shrouded in a white cashmere shawl, was sitting at a writing bureau, the envelopes, paperwork and correspondence all piled orderly and high. She signed a letter with great care, laid down her wooden dip pen with the silver nib, and dried the ink with a roll of the blotter. "There."

"Matron. This is really very good of you."

"Psht. I expect it is, my child. But it makes me happy. Come. Hug."

Said Florence Nightingale.

~2~

Phoebe was shown her room by Miss Hubbard, then set to work almost immediately, slicing open envelopes, sifting the correspondence into piles of requests and enquires, all requiring polite replies; and event invitations all to be, with regret, declined.

"Has Arthur resumed writing about Holmes?" asked Miss Nightingale, as she scratched words on the page with her wooden ink pen with the silver nib. "If not, he is foolish."

"I really don't know, Matron. And don't like to be one of the many who keep asking."

"Don't, my child? Don't? The expression is 'I do not know'. Psht. You have already been too long upon the stage of the Music Halls, performing with the American gentleman."

"Wait until you hear some of the abuse of the English language I learned from Michael."

"Thank you, but I am in no hurry."

"Uncle Art is not a fool." Phoebe stopped what she was doing and looked up. "But he does rather find himself side-tracked. Faddish interests such as snow skiing and cycling. Being quite so ungainly, none of them conjure an attractive image. And there are other distractions."

"Of the fleshly distractions? Arthur Doyle?" Miss Nightingale shuddered. Now that was certainly not an attractive image.

"I was referring more to his new-found interest in proving the existence of fairies. And spiritualism, can you believe he joined the 'Society for Psychical Research'?"

"Psht. I expect he has."

"I understand he's even attending a séance this evening. Rather a cause for concern, would you think?"

Florence Nightingale smiled, "My child, I am a woman with whom God has conversed on four separate occasions. Thus, I am in no position to pass judgement on a few fairies and a séance."

~3~

In the dim half-light of the small, atmospheric wood-panelled room, you had to squint to make out the details. The circular table was draped in a worn, coarse black cloth which was patterned with what once were white symbols of the Zodiac. Above the table, a lamp hung low from the ceiling rose, served by a length of quarter-inch copper gas pipe. Two dangling chains adjusted the supply flow to the hissing mantle, which was cupped by a glass shade, casting a rich orange glow.

Around the table sat a disparate gathering of souls. Arthur Conan Doyle, twiddling one end of his waxed moustache in excitement. He was wearing a three-piece suit and tie for the occasion, his un-restrained symphony of country gentleman's coarse tweeds of every of shade of mustard. To his right, another Arthur. Arthur Morrison, an author and journalist of note, mid-thirties, slender, with round wire spectacles, black hair creeping back from the forehead and a just as black moustache.

On Arthur Doyle's left yawned the gap of a vacant wooden chair. Next came a man and woman. Sunday-best dressed, certainly not working class, both in their early thirties. The husband, Ronathan Chafeskin; bouffant hair with a floppy fringe, pinched of face and anxious disposition. His tongue flicked in and out. A nervous habit.

Beside him, Mrs Chafeskin. Eadie. Short, stout and serious, in a full-sleeved high-buttoned grey dress, all topped with a pinned grey Presbyterian bonnet. Next to her, another vacant chair.

Completing the mystic circle, an ill-shaven man, closer to forty. An ill-fitting black suit, with stained lapels and fly front, hung shapelessly from his frame, the elbows of the jacket shiny from wear. His white-collared shirt boasted a silver stud but no tie. Connor O'Connor. Priest of our parish, but tonight, just a godless civilian. As opposed to his usual capacity of godless cleric.

The door opened. An elderly woman stepped in, smiling, grey hair swept up a tight bun. The lined, but kindly, face of a maiden aunt, dressed for the opera in a charming white full-length evening dress and white gloves. Around her throat a white silk choker.

Miss Cordelia Ravenport. By profession, a Medium.

The gentlemen stood. Not Connor, well only after a glare from Doyle.

"Oh, please, my dears, how kind, but be seated and settle yourselves down," she said sweetly, squeezing delicately between the two Arthurs and the wall. Before taking the vacant seat between ACD. and Mr Chafeskin, Cordelia reached up, adjusted a chain on the gas lamp, and dimmed the glow.

"A reminder please for no speaking while I try to contact Nostradamus in the nether world. Do not be alarmed by anything you see, it is all quite normal. Just the way of Nostradamus. Now for the moment, may we all place our hands on the table and stare at your own sign of the Zodiac. Then, once Nostradamus possesses my body, you may ask of him any question concerning your future. And I know some of you have important questions to ask. So, shall we begin?"

Cordelia made herself comfortable. Placed her hands on the table and closed her eyes.

Silence.

Save for the hiss of the gas lamp.

"What a pile of heathen..." thought Connor, the sentence interrupted by...

"Spirit of the great oracle Nostradamus," called the old spinster. "I call upon you. Request your presence. Do not be shy, my dear. Pray do enter me."

Connor O'Connor smirked.

"Nostradamus, are you there?" Cordelia asked meekly. "I know you are."

She then began a long moan which started high and delicate and glissed down to a breathy murmur.

Then, like a judge's gavel:

BANG! BANG!

"Jasus!" barked Connor.

Everyone jumped.

Suddenly Cordelia gasped. Her eyes flew open in surprise. Her body jerked. Head thrown back. Mouth gaping.

The reptilian voice rustled like dry leaves in the wind. The voice from her throat. "I hear you, banshee! Sss. I hear you well!"

"Holy mother of all that is holy," whispered Connor O'Connor, peeping at the spasms of the Medium.

"Silence, while I enter the banshee," susurrated Nostradamus. "Sss. None shall gaze upon thissss mystic rite."

Connor quickly complied. Sheer terror. He gazed at the tablecloth. The symbol for Virgo. Then couldn't help but sneak another peek. But, in fairness, so did Arthur Conan Doyle. Wisely too, because at this point things began to get a little lively.

Hideous whispers circled the room and Cordelia Ravenport convulsed violently as the spirit of Nostradamus possessed her entirely. The gas lamp before them spluttered and flickered. Then blacked out.

Total darkness.

Doyle shuffled with excitement. Morrison gritted his teeth and clenched his fists. Mrs Chafeskin reassured her husband by patting her hand on the back of his. Connor O'Connor whimpered.

BANG! BANG!

"Jasus!"

The gas mantle brightened and glowed orange again.

"Mary and Joseph, the woman has gone," said Connor.

Now they all looked. The Chafeskins and the two Arthurs. And saw Connor was right. Cordelia's seat was empty.

"Those gathered here," hissed the voice of Nostradamus, now from the other side of the table. "Tell me what you wish to know."

Everyone shifted their gaze towards the voice. In the warm, low half-light, they saw her. Cordelia Ravenport. Still wide of eye and gaping of mouth. But now in the seat between Eadie Chafeskin and Connor O'Connor.

Arthur Doyle said he had never experienced such a jolt. Nor Morrison. Ronathan Chafeskin gasped and his wife put her hand to her mouth, all of them rendered speechless by such a wonder.

Except for Connor O'Connor.

He screamed. And screamed. And stood, no, leapt to his feet, sending his chair crashing backwards to the floor.

"Gahhh," gasped Nostradamus. Cordelia held her throat as if suffocated.

Darkness again! The sounds of chaos and alarm and Connor's terrified yells and ribald language.

BANG! BANG!

The gas lamp re-ignited and the radiance grew.

Cordelia Ravenport had moved again! She was now slumped in her original seat. A terrified Connor was yelling to be let out, hammering with both fists along the panelled wood, until he finally found the door, flung it open and staggered out.

Ronathan Chafeskin nearly swooned and was comforted by his wife while the two Arthurs, Morrison and Doyle, were now on their feet expressing dire embarrassment and profound apologies.

Cordelia seemed oblivious to the chaos as she recovered her wits and regained her naturally kind personality. She stared about the room smiling sweetly. "Well, my dears, that was an eventful experience, but as long as we are all unharmed. Oh, but what became of your friend, Dr Doyle? Was he taken poorly?"

"I do regret, Miss Ravenport, the occasion proved for him somewhat overwhelming. Mmm? Mmm?" said Doyle.

"Be so kind, dear lady, as to excuse us. While we attend to the wretch," said Arthur Morrison. Clipped and precise. And furious. He then included the shaken Chafeskin couple by adding, "Our sincere apologies. For the disruption. Good evening."

Arthur Doyle and Arthur Morrison found Father Connor O'Connor outside in the busy street, bent forward, heaving, one hand on the brick wall supporting himself. The splatter of six whiskies and a few bites of bread pudding lay between his boots. His face was a shade of colour unknown to artists' palette, pale beyond white.

"That…that…" he waggled a finger vaguely in the direction of the front door. "…what in God's holy name *was* that? The banshee moved. Did you see her? First she'll be sitting in that chair over there, then she's sitting besides meself in this chair here." His quaking hands wildly mimed the uncanny seating transposition. "And her with a voice from the very bowels o' Dante's Inferno. Jasus. None of that was right, I'm tellin' ya. Not a bit of any of that was right."

"The mysteries of the séance have forever defied logic, Connor," said Doyle.

"Compose yourself, priest," ordered Morrison. "Willingly we came here. I, to witness such a manifestation, and consider its authenticity for myself. A journey bespoiled by your theatrics!"

Connor placated Arthur Morrison by telling him what to get and where to shove it and that everything they had just experienced was an unholy abomination, which even Doyle thought was a little strong coming from a priest who believed in nothing sacred, except for women and drink!

"If y' re-enter that house of hell, and commune with Satan, do not come running to me for bustard absolution!"

Connor then wiped his mouth on his sleeve and stomped off down the road in high dudgeon. Museum Street, towards High Holborn, actually.

"The lady was attempting to commune with the spirit of Nostradamus, Connor," pleaded Doyle. "Michel de Nostradame. A seer from three centuries ago. Many of his visions of future events have come to pass."

"Well, Satan or Nostradamus, or whatever name your bustard man might claim," shouted back Father Connor O'Connor, over his shoulder, "he's no right to enter a spinster in that sort of way. And I should know!"

~5~

Inside Cordelia Ravenport's apartment, furniture had been righted and order restored. For Ronathan Chafeskin, what he considered to be timewasting hokum had turned into alarming madness. More than good reason to leave. But his forceful wife prevailed. They needed to know, she insisted, telling Miss Cordelia Ravenport they would happily pay for a further sitting.

"Oh, my dears, I do not know. Nostradamus was disrupted in his communication and he can be a temperamental spirit." Cordelia rested her head to one side. "Oh. But I sense your troubles. And, of course, my dears, we must see what we can do. Learn what Nostradamus foresees for you."

Eadie Chafeskin was hugely grateful and prompted her husband to endorse that gratitude with a sharp nudge to the ribs.

"Please now, retake your places at the table."

Cordelia turned the key on the gas mantle and dimmed the light.

"Now let us commence, shall we, my dears, by placing our hands back onto the table and gazing at your sign of the Zodiac.

Ronathan Chafeskin was still convinced this was all going to be hokum. But having seen what he saw, even as scientist, it took some explaining. Against all he believed, Ronathan stared at his star sign, Scorpio, and listened to the gentle burr of the gas.

"Spirit of the great oracle Nostradamus. I call upon you. Request you return to me."

Silence.

"I am sure you are still there, Nostradamus. I feel your presence. Come now, dear, do not be displeased. Please return to us, I do implore you. The very nice Mr and Mrs Chafeskin have a question for you, my dear."

BANG! BANG!

The Chafeskins jumped. Cordelia suddenly stiffened her slim body and rolled her head, then with a start stared sharply ahead. Her mouth flapped open and closed like Fred Russell's doll, Coster Joe. Then the gas mantle flickered and died.

BANG! BANG!

Blackness.

The lamp then spluttered back to light – and the voice came from another chair. And there she was, now opposite the Chafeskins.

Cordelia's face gentle and vague, was now hardened. The eyes closed. Her mouth opened.

"Again you dare trouble me, banshee," hissed the disembodied voice from Cordelia's throat. Then the eyes opened. Wide. Staring.

"I ssssee them," Nostradamus's words hissed like a hot razor's caress. "A woman of open mind. Ssss. Eadie, by name. And a man. Ronathan. Ssss. An unbeliever."

Both Chafeskins shuffled uncomfortably. Eadie shooting her husband a chastising glance.

The voice then demanded: "Present to me your enquiry."

Eadie swallowed, then cleared her throat, but still quaked. "My dear husband here at my right hand is a gentleman who laboured deep and long for the role of Chief Assistant to the Astronomer Royal at the Greenwich Observatory. But Mr Christie granted the post to a Welshman. By the name of Goronwy Dapper."

"Nostradamus knows all that has been and gone. Sss. And sees all which is yet to come. Sss. Continue."

"Our question to you, sir, is – in the future, will the role ever fall to my Ronanthan?"

Ronathan swallowed and started to sweat. This was uncanny.

Cordelia's eyes rolled. As if in contemplation.

"Harken well. Sss. On my portention. Ronathan Chafeskin should seek solace for his disappointment. Sss. This weekend. Away from London. Sss. And the position of Chief Assistant to the Astronomer Royal….sss…*shall* be taken by Ronathan Chafeskin. What I foresee, so mote it be."

BANG! BANG!

Blackness again.

The glow of the orange brightened and widened and found Cordelia back in her original chair. And when the rigid tension of Nostradamus had seeped from her body, she sat back, much relieved.

"Has he gone?" whispered Ronathan.

"Oh, my dears," said Cordelia. "Nostradamus predicts and then moves swiftly on. Was he helpful, was it good news he gave you?"

Eadie gripped her husband's hand and grinned with excitement. "Miss Davenport. I am in awe. We are so grateful."

Cordelia arose from the table, leaned forward and smiled. "Well now, the time to be grateful, my dear, will present itself when all that Nostradamus foretells becomes truth."

At the front door of the apartment, Eadie Chafeskin thanked Miss Ravenport and pulled a sixpence from her purse. Cordelia shook her head and told the Chafeskins: "Oh, do keep your money, my dears. If the Nostradamus prediction is proved false, then as charlatans, we must be denounced, as you first suspected Mr Chafeskin."

Eadie glared at her husband.

"But if what Nostradamus foresees comes to be true, he knows you will be generous with your reward."

~6~

Goronwy Dapper was a pot-bellied, round-faced, bald-headed fellow. He also possessed a permanent squint in one eye, caused by a lifetime's dedication to peering through telescopes. Most recently the brand-new Altazimuth telescope. Housed in the purpose-built pavilion atop the hill in Greenwich Park. His official title, as you know, was Chief Assistant to the Astronomer Royal.

Dr Dapper was a scientist of dogmatic dedication, unflinching in his study of the stars and the serious promotion of himself. As a young astronomer in Wales, he had once been asked how the heavens affected our fortunes. "The stars inform our past and our present. They do not forecast our future," was his lofty contention.

On reflection, forecasting the future by gazing at heavenly bodies might have come in distinctly handy for Goronwy Dapper, given the unfortunate circumstance in which he was about to find himself. And here's why.

He lived just by the Blue Coat Girls School on Maidenstone Hill, a narrow Blackheath side street, and only a brisk ten-minute step from the Greenwich Observatory. The Dapper residence was an end of terrace double-fronted cottage as befitted a learned figure of such stellar self-importance.

And being an unmarried gentlemen from Usk, as you might expect, his home was so devoid of any comfort that Charles Dickens would have said Tiny Tim's lodgings were a good deal more cheery. But Goronwy Dapper had no truck with cosy. His interest, his obsession if you will, was his work. A colleague was spending a few days holiday at the coast. Nothing could interest Mr Dapper less.

His many books were distinctly well ordered, and when there was no more room on the shelves, tomes and journals were stacked on the floorboards in a well regimented fashion. His collection was dedicated to the history of astronomy: works by Copernicus. Galileo. Halley. Keppler. The foul Newton. But not entirely. On occasions, Dapper had been known to dip into Mathematical Analysis of Logic by George Boole, for a bit of lighter reading.

In his spartan but pristine upstairs bedroom, Goronwy Dapper hung his day clothes carefully in the aged wardrobe and changed into his cleaned and pressed coarse cotton nightshirt. He thoroughly washed his hands and face at the bed stand, in a china bowl of cold water, dispensed from a large unmatching jug.

He availed himself of his convenient enamel chamber pot and gently slid the thing just beneath the foot of his dustless bedframe. Cupping his hand behind the flame, he blew out the candle on the polished bedside table and climbed into his firm single bed, fully expecting to drift quickly off to contented sleep, as he did every night.

It was as he felt the heavy darkness drawing him down, he heard: "Goronwy Dapper."

A voice which sounded like the rustle of Autumn leaves on the breeze. He thought nothing of it. Autumn leaves on the breeze.

"Goronwy Dapper," the voice repeated his name again. And again, and then added: "She sees you. Sees you, lain in your bed."

By now, Dapper was quite awake. He looked up from his pillow. "Whatever is that? Is someone there?"

"She sees you. Sss. From the street below. She stands there and sees you."

"She sees me, does she? From the street, does she?" Goronwy Dapper sat up. "High-jinks, is what this is." He threw back the yellowing bed sheet, swung his hairy legs out, padded barefoot to the window and looked out. The street was not so dark thanks to the blur of the fullish creamy moon. But there was neither man nor beast to be seen, left or right.

"See her below," rustled the voice.

Dapper looked directly down.

Good Lord!

Standing almost on his doorstep. A figure in grey with a bonnet. Looking directly up at him. With the face of an old woman. Benign and appealing. She raised her hands together to plead in some fashion.

Dapper knocked at the window.

"By heavens, woman. Whatever troubles you at this time of night?" His sing-song voice of the valleys was so soft he realised she should not hear him. He fiddled and fussed with the latch, then swung open the window. "I said whatever troubles...?"

But when Dapper looked down again she was gone. Vanished. Which was odd. Very odd. But not of his concern. He must be half asleep. The vague wisp of a clouded dream. He closed the window and returned to his bed.

"She sees you, Goronwy Dapper," the voice hissed. "In sss your bed."

Dapper sat bolt upright again. "I demand again, is somebody there?"

He struck a match, lit his candle and held it towards the sound. And there! The old woman in grey. Standing at the foot of his bed!

"Ahhh!" He jumped, nearly tumbling the candle from the stick. "How dare you... Leave this house immediately..."

The old woman was holding a battered leather Gladstone bag. She stepped forward.

DHONG!

She looked down at what she'd kicked. The chamber pot. "Oh, dear!"

Dapper quickly got himself out of bed in a tangle of legs and bedsheet, while saying, "See here, woman. First you are down there and then in a trice, you are up here. What..."

A great unseen force shoved him hard on the shoulder. So hard he spun in mid-air and crashed face down on the bed. He struggled to get up but found he was pinned. Face into the pillow. Arms spread, legs akimbo. Unable to move. He yelled but the pillow stifled the noise. He gasped for breath and tried to turn his head. To see what was happening. It was just as well he could not. He heard the opening Gladstone bag. What was that? Clicking?

He felt the old lady lift the hem of his nightshirt. What was the hag doing? He shouted something which only the horsehair in his pillow could hear. Then Dapper felt something between his knees. Brushing. Then it moved. Tentative. Gently feeling and probing. It had legs. What in God's name was it? He fought to struggle but the force pressing him down was too strong.

"It is a Velvet Swimming Crab, my dear," said the sweet old woman. "A most beautiful sea crustacean."

"Also known sss as the Devil Crab," said the malevolent sibilant voice. "A creature which becomes agitated. Ssss. In confined spaces."

The large crab moved up between his thighs. Now scratching and now climbing its way up. Relentless. High and higher. Then came the nips. Delicate. Then sharper. And higher.

Dapper shrieked another silent scream, as the crab latched its pincers onto whatever was soft and fleshy in the dark up ahead. And watching the convulsions on the bed, Cordelia Ravenport knew what the crab was now clamping down.

"Enjoy the pain, Goronwy Dapper," said the voice of Nostradamus. "As you breathe your last."

And the now *former* Chief Assistant to the Astronomer Royal felt the gentle embrace of the enveloping, velvet unwaking darkness.

"The prophecy sss is fulfilled."

"Quite so it is, my dear. Quite so it is. May Ronathan Chafeskin enjoy his new position."

~7~

"Your fee, Miss Ravenport? Your fee? Well. I assure you that your fee shall most certainly not be paid."

It was four days later, and although Eadie Chafeskin's words were whispered, her rejection of Cordelia's request was resolute. They were standing on the doorstep of the Chafeskin's Ormiston Road terraced house in Greenwich. Ronathan's wife was proving every bit the formidable woman everyone took her to be. A proper eminence grise. And she whispered not because of the lateness of the hour, it was gone ten, more that she wished not to draw undue attention from her newly middle-class neighbours.

A London bound passenger train chugged out of Westcombe Park Station, behind the house, the engine puking up a line of grey-smoke puffs which blended, then dispersed above the roofs.

"But, my dear, was not Nostradamus correct in his prognostication?" asked Cordelia. "I am quite sure you will find he was. Has your husband not been awarded the position you both craved? At the Greenwich Observatory? As predicted?"

"Dapper's heart gave out, banshee," scoffed Eadie Chafeskin, deliberately using the insult expressed by Nostradamus. "It was inevitable. Dapper was a man most unwell. Any fool with eyes could witness his condition. His death was nought to do with your Nostradamus prediction. So, no, charlatan. We shall not pay any fee. Not a ha'penny nor a farthing. And may that be a development your Nostradamus did not foresee."

"Oh, my dear, this is most distressing. Perhaps I might speak with Mr Chafeskin himself on the matter." Cordelia tried to peep over Eadie's shoulder in the hope of a more agreeable reception.

"No, you may not see Mr Chafeskin. Mr Chafeskin is at his place of work, charting the night skies. After all, he is now the Chief Assistant to the Astronomer Royal, you know. So I advise you banshee, to get you gone from here. Else I whistle up a constable."

Cordelia looked fearful. "Oh, no, no. Please. There shall be no need to whistle up anybody, my dear. But you did agree to settle the fee when your husband's promotion was announced. You did promise. Most sincerely."

"Answer me this, banshee," hissed Eadie Chafeskin, gripping Cordelia's wizened neck in one chubby hand: "Whose account are the Police Courts bound to believe? The lunatic claims of a decrepit old swindler like you? Or the noble word of the Chief Assistant to the Astronomer Royal?" She then shoved Cordelia away. "Now get gone from this house. And never return."

Shaken and uncertain what to say, Cordelia simply gulped and turned and hurried away.

"I'm watching you," hissed Eadie Chafeskin. And watch Cordelia she did, until the old woman had hurried around the corner. Satisfied she had nipped this nonsense in the bud once and for all, Eadie Chafeskin stepped back indoors and went to close the door. And got a chilling surprise.

There. Standing on the other side of the road. Under a street lamp. Highlighted in its a yellow glow. Cordelia Ravenport.

Eadie Chafeskin gawped. No. Surely not. She had just watched the old woman turn the corner twenty yards down the street. She looked again, expecting she was mistaken. But no. The Ravenport woman was still standing there. But gone with the sweet and simple maiden aunt. This time she was glaring with a face of pure hatred. Her eyes locked on Eadie Chafeskin.

And she began to walk across the road. Straight for the house. Strong, determined strides.

Eadie's spine chilled. She prayed this was not happening. But the crazed banshee woman was still coming. Straight towards her. Even quicker. Eadie rushed inside. Slammed the door shut and stood with her back to it, panting. Then quickly shot the door bolts across. Then knelt with both hands holding closed the letterbox, lest a bony arm thrust its way through to grab her.

Eadie leant her full weight against the flap, fought to suppress her alarm and listened. There was nothing. No hammering on the door, no rapping the knocker. Stoney silence.

It took Mrs Eadie Chafeskin several minutes to win the courage to release the letter box flap and stand. Then she hitched her skirt and scurried up the stairs to the front bedroom window. She looked right, left and straight ahead. Blessed relief. The street was empty. And later that night when Mrs Chafeskin eventually took her shaken self off to bed, it was not without wedging two of her best dining chairs against the front and back doors.

She would only remove the chair and unbolt the front door when Ronathan came home. Which in itself proved over-optimistic.

~8~

Having winched open a four-foot gap between the two halves of the grey dome, Ronathan Chafeskin knew exactly where to find the yellow crescent of the waxing moon. He adjusted the well-oiled wheels which realigned the New Altazimuth telescope a few degrees west to track the lunar transit. The action was smooth and soundless, brand new bearings rolling against the turning circle below.

A quick look through the observation glass. He then eased the pivot wheel which raised the angle of elevation. Another look. Following which he adjusted the focus on the telescope and the yellow edge first blurred then sharpened, presenting itself through the eyepiece as a vivid image. Celestial beauty.

Ronathan Chafeskin felt marvellous. Vindicated. This was his first night on duty as Chief Assistant to the Astronomer Royal. His rightful position. Yes, Goronwy Dapper's passing was most unfortunate. But only for Goronwy Dapper. Then it occurred to Chafeskin: the last person to use the Altazimuth was Dapper himself. Splendid.

Chafeskin bent forward, peered up through the eyepiece once again, then pattered down the short flight of wooden treads to the ground floor office to retrieve a sheaf of handwritten notes. Observations and numbers. Dapper's records were neat and precise. Typical of the man.

The office was circular and compact. A polished wooden writing desk and a rack of shelving for books and paper piles. In fact the Altazimuth Pavilion, a red brick and terracotta standalone observatory building on the ever expanding site of the Royal Greenwich Park, was no bigger than a two roomed cottage. Chafeskin heard the door of the observatory behind him but was distracted enough by the figure columns not to look around.

"Thank you, Mr Donaldson," said the astronomer. "Please be so kind as to leave the teapot on the desk, would you?"

Nigel Donaldson was the Observatory's porter. Chafeskin liked him. Everyone did. A fine worker. Industrious. Even Chafeskin's wife Eadie found the porter agreeable, and she was renowned for not much liking anyone except herself. And her husband, of course, but some of the time she was none too keen on him either. She was always complaining he had no gumption.

There was another noise. Different. A garbled whisper was how it sounded.

"Hmm? What is that you say, Mr Donaldson?"

This time Chafeskin did turn around. To find he was alone. No Donaldson. No tray with a cup and saucer and pot of steaming tea either. Chafeskin looked here and there, even opened the door and looked outside. Although it was dark, there was neither sight nor sound of Nigel Donaldson. Tugs chugging along the Thames a few hundred yards down the hill occasionally hooted and clanged the odd bell. They were the only discernible noises.

So Chafeskin went back inside, closed the door, climbed back up to the viewing platform, re-checked the Altazimuth's alignment and settled into the lean-back seat from which the newly appointed Chief Assistant to the Astronomer Royal could begin his observations. A wonder device this kind of mount, so called because it allows the 'scope to up and down in altitude, and left and right in azimuth. Apparently.

It was while he was peering through the eyepiece, accustomising his eye to the white lunar arc, that he heard the noise again. Chafeskin pulled away from the viewfinder, rubbed his eye and looked about the dark circular viewing room. "Halloa?"

Again, nothing.

Chafeskin returned to his telescope.

"Scorpiussss," hissed the voice from nowhere.

~9~

"Hmm," said the astronomer, vaguely.

"I said Scorpiussss, Chafeskin!"

Chafeskin's blood chilled. It was a voice he knew. After a long pause, just listening, he finally dared to withdraw from the eyepiece and looked around.

"Nostradamus?" he quaked. "Miss Ravenport? Are you hereabouts?"

"Sss. Train your telescope to view the constellation Scorpius."

"Now see here," started Chafeskin, "I shall call...."

"Train your telescope to Scorpiussss. You know precisely how!"

In terror, Chafeskin scrambled from his seat, bounded down the stairs, reached for the door to make his escape. Except the door refused to budge. The key jutted from the lock. Chafeskin twisted the key to open the door and pulled on the handle. Heaved. But the door stood firm. Chafeskin shoved it and barged it. Hammered on it and called for Donaldson. None of which achieved a thing.

Then, through one of the Georgian windows, he saw her. Outside. Miss Cordelia Ravenport. Dressed in grey. Glaring and furious. He staggered back from the window in shock. Turned to run across the office to the other door. But now she was there. In the room with him.

"Your wife refused to pay my fee, my dear. Flat refused and was most unagreeable."

The astronomer started to scream, then he felt a grip round his throat. But not hers. An unseen hand was squeezing and choking, before Chafeskin felt himself flung to the floor.

His face flopped with sweat as he gasped as best his throat could manage: "What devilry is this? Miss Ravenport? What is happening?"

She said nothing. But the voice spoke. Nostradamus. From everywhere. "The promised fee. Sss. Has not been paid."

"But that cannot be so. I am perfectly willing to pay the fee." He reached inside his jacket for his wallet. "Your prediction was correct. I was appointed to the position. The payment of fee was never in doubt. If my wife will not pay you then I shall."

"Yesssss. You shall. By observing the constellation Scorpius. Do it now. Ssss." The voice of Nostradamus was hoarse and horrific.

"I should do as he says if I were you, my dear, said Cordelia, sweetly. "And right away. You know what he can be like."

Chafeskin dragged himself to his feet muttering 'yes' and 'of course' while clambering up the treads as quickly as his jellied legs could manage. He watched in cold terror as the adjustment wheel cranked, turning the telescope through ninety degrees to point south west – by itself.

"Lower the elevation…sss…to the horizon. And train the lensss on Ssscorpiusss. Do as I decree, Chafeskin!"

So he did. Ronathan Chafeskin flumped down in the observation seat. Damp, trembling hands required several attempts to pull the image into the correct focus.

That was it. In the black circle, Chafeskin could see the red pinprick of Antares. The centre of the body Scorpio. Not as red as Mars but bright in the sky nonetheless. The stars which formed the constellation's legs splayed to north east, the tail pointing to the south east.

"I have it…" gasped Chafeskin, his throat dry. "Here. See?"

"Gaze upon the constellation, Ronathan Chafessskin," hissed the voice. "You see them? Sss. The stars which form the body of the Scorpion?"

"Yes…yes…" sobbed Chafeskin. "I do! I do!"

"Good. Sss. Now…. feel her *sting!*"

Chafeskin felt the unseen force shove his head forward, impaling his eye hard onto the eyepiece.

DANG! SHLITTT!

Chafeskin heard the noise, saw the white flash, then the red. And felt the stabbing. Hard and deep. He rolled to one side, out of the seat. Held his hands to his eye socket. The pain tore and seared. Chafeskin staggered to his feet. Felt the warm liquid stream down his cheek. He tripped and fell. The agony, it was now unbear….


~10~


"Your superior, Sir Edward Bradford insisted nothing should be touched until your arrival, Melville," said William Christie, making no attempt to disguise his exasperation.

That hairstyle, darkly oiled with a sharp, straight white parting to the left, even that black bushy moustache, none of it served to soften the sharp features and stern eyes of the Astronomer Royal. His black frock coat and cravat set against a peak white wing collar shirt gave him, and I am not being rude, the air of a professional mourner.

Superintendent William Melville of Scotland Yard's anti-terrorist Special Branch was standing inside the Altazimuth Pavilion, looking up at the steps and the sprawled corpse of Ronathan Chafeskin, halfway down. Halfway down, Melville concluded, because that was clearly his direction of travel.

The head was haloed in a scarlet puddle, now pretty much dry. The face was contorted in terror. The left eye wide and wild. The right, a black and purple void. The body was exactly as it had been found last night.

William Christie headed the research here at Greenwich. The Astronomer Royal was a position of great scientific importance, formerly held by Edmund Halley, the foul Newton and Nevil

Maskelyne – no relation to the Music Hall magician, by the way, and don't believe him if he tells you otherwise – and a man called Nathaniel Bliss, although none of us has ever heard of him.

"The Commissioner of Police is very wise," said Melville, quietly. "And nothing *has* been touched?"

"Not a thing," snapped Christie. "Other than closing shut the dome as a precaution against the weather. One must protect the telescope."

"Indeed."

"But all this, Melville. All this surely…" Christie shook a frustrated finger at the corpse, the mess and at Melville, "…tantamount to nought more than a tragic accident."

"Accident or otherwise, Mr Christie, The Royal Observatory, Greenwich is a significant scientific institution. Not one, but two Chief Assistants have died within days of one another, which raises more than an eyebrow in Westminster. You will recall the attempted bombing of this establishment five years ago by the French anarchist Bourdin?"

In '94, Marial Bourdin attempted a terrorist attack on the Observatory with chemical explosives, but as he wandered his way up the hill to his target, the bomb he was holding detonated, blowing much of him to pieces. The mention of the carnage served to chasten Christie's attitude.

"Of course."

"Very good. Tell me now if you will: were the two deceased gentlemen involved in any clandestine matters, secret projects?"

"Our work here is well documented, Superintendent. The present role of the Chief Assistant is specialising in the study of lunar transitions. Both men, Dapper and Chafeskin, were thus engaged in such work."

"And might anyone serve to benefit from the untimely departures of these two gentlemen?" asked Melville. "I am thinking of ambitious colleagues?"

"Not a soul," snapped Christie. "And therein lies a further tiresome irritation. With no suitable candidates, I am now compelled to seek a replacement from elsewhere."

"Mr Chafeskin's body here was discovered by whom?"

"This gentleman, guv'nor," said Detective Inspector Pym. "Mr Nigel Donaldson."

Pym had just strolled into the Pavilion, accompanied by a tall, substantial man with dark hair and a pale face. He wore a battered tweed jacket, tan overalls and was holding a cloth cap in both hands, which from time to time he would wring nervously.

"Mr Donaldson, is the Observatory porter." Pym invited the man to repeat everything to the Superintendent.

"Yes, sir. Last night I had restocked Mr and Mrs Christie's bedroom fireplace with logs up at Flamsteed House, then set off to deliver Dr Chafeskin's pot of hot tea. Nine of the clock it was."

"And you are certain of the hour?" wondered Melville.

Christie chipped in to say, "Donaldson's work ethic and timekeeping are impeccably dependable, Superintendent."

"What with this being Greenwich Observatory, sir, there's no shortage of clocks," said the porter, awkwardly.

"Of course," Melville all but smiled. "Please continue."

"Upon arrival here at the Pavilion, I found the door locked, which was a surprise. So, I rapped on the door but with no answer forthcoming, I assumed Mr Chafeskin had left to use the privy. But when offering my lantern to the window round the side, I espied Mr Chafeskin lying on the stairs. Assuming he'd taken a fall, I barged open the door, to discover the gentleman lifeless. I then hastened back up to the main house and reported the matter to Mr Christie."

"Very good," said Melville. "Help me again now please. Have you a thought on *why* Dr Chafeskin locked himself in the Pavilion?"

"None that I can reason, sir. It was not what he'd done previous. And he knew I would be attending him throughout the night."

Melville assured the porter that would be all.

As he turned to leave, Nigel Donaldson stopped and added: "Finding two dead bodies within days of one another can shake a man a good deal, I can tell you, sir."

"Indeed."

Once Mr Donaldson had gone about his business, Melville asked, "That gentleman was present when the local constable found the body of Chafeskin's predecessor, Goronwy Dapper?"

Pym confirmed that was the case.

Melville hmm'd his sympathy, then excused himself and tiptoed up the stairs, avoiding the body and the blood. Within the dome he examined the eyepiece of the Altazimuth telescope, then tiptoed down again.

"Thank you, Mr Christie. I have seen enough. We will arrange for the removal of Mr Chafeskin's body forthwith."

That news certainly bucked up the Astronomer Royal. "Your conclusion then, Melville? That both deaths were an unfortunate coincidence of circumstance and timing?"

"Dapper died from heart failure. Chafeskin, as the result of accident. Both gentlemen died alone, in rooms which were locked from the inside, suggesting no other party could have been involved. In either case it is impossible for me to find any evidence of foul play."

"That is a great relief."

"However," said Melville. "Before we close the file, I would be negligent if I did not solicit additional expertise. I propose to commission an investigation by our consultants."

Christie looked puzzled. And so did Pym.

"A formality. Second opinions to corroborate our conclusion. Until then, the scenes of both incidents, the Dapper property and the Altazimuth Pavilion must remain sealed."

Christie stated his frustration with expressions like 'Now, see here!', and 'I shall speak to Sir Edward!'.

"Quite so, Mr Christie, and when you do speak with Sir Edward, You may wish to mention that according to my diary there is currently a new moon and nothing to see."

Christie hurrumphed and conceded. "When may I expect your consultants?"

Melville consulted his pocket watch and cranked a few mental calculations. "At the earliest convenience, Mr Christie. Thank you for your time."

The two Special Branchers buttoned their barathea overcoats to the neck and held on to their hats as they braved the Greenwich Park wind. As they padded down the grassy slope to their waiting carriage Pym finally said, "You're thinkin' something's not square there, guv'nor."

"Possible."

"How about Donaldson? He found both bodies."

"The man is shaken to the core. If not, his performance is worthy of a stage appearance with Henry Irving."

153

Pym approved the removal of Ronathan Chafeskin's body with a waiting Constable. Then rocked the suspension of the carriage as he climbed aboard and joined Melville in the cab as the snuffling driver, Constable Coxhead, clicked the horses to walk on.

Only once he had settled himself opposite the Superintendent did Pym venture to ask: "What consultants, guv'nor? What consultants are you plannin' to commission? With Magister now scarpered, it's not as if we can send for the Magicians."

Melville was looking out of the window when he said: "One remains."

"Meanin' no disrespect, guv'nor, but she's going to be hardly of a mood to do anything for the likes of Special Branch."

"Of that, Walter," said Melville, slowly turning to face his colleague, "I would not be so certain."

~11~

Two hours later, framed in the large open doorway, Melville and Pym found themselves looking at the figure of haughty indignation they had come to know so well. One hand on hip. Lips pouting. She did look lovely though. At least that's what Pym thought. Frothy-fringed white blouse, synched brown leather waistcoat, and full, purple taffeta skirt.

The Special Branchers were standing on the doorstep where Miss Elizabeth Hubbard, the maid, had told them to wait while she summoned the new personal assistant.

"Really?" Phoebe had said, as soon and she saw them. Pym was convinced her teeth were gritted. "Well, unless you gentlemen are here to arrest me yet *again* – all I have to say to you is good day!"

SLAM!

The Special Branch men were now facing a closed black front door in which the flap on the brass letter box was still rattling.

"That went worse than even I expected," said Pym.

The last time Pym had been in South Street he was supervising the removal of the heavyweight dead body of a Cardinal from the house of gentlemen's entertainment owned by the exotic courtesan Catherine 'Skittles' Walters, just along the way. And at the moment, that was by far a merrier experience.

Melville poked a gloved finger at the letter box and called through the gap. "Miss Le Breton. I would value your time perusing the file which Inspector Pym is about to pass through. Nothing else. And please give my finest respects to Miss Nightingale."

On the other side of the door, Phoebe watched as the buff coloured folder poked and scuffed its way through the letter box. She caught the file in mid-air just before it spilled its papers on the coir mat.

The portcullis emblem of the Police of the Metropolis was embossed on the cover. TOP SECRET was stamped in red at an angle across the page.

Why would they still trust her with confidential material? Phoebe thought long and hard about examining the mysteries which lay within. Even just a cursory glimpse. But then tossed the folder onto the marble hall table, the one with the cut glass vase of fresh pink freesias.

"And what did Superintendent Melville bring, child?" called Florence Nightingale from above.

"His finest respects, Matron."

"Psht. I expect he did," she huffed, her voice echoing about the cavernous stairwell. "But what else? Melville was never a man to waste time making house calls without good reason."

As Constable Coxhead forced the carriage out into the traffic of Park Lane, Pym, leaning back in that dimpled leather seat, wondered aloud if she really would give the file a gander. "I mean, you know what she's like, guv'nor. She'll be demanding the vote next."

"If Miss Le Breton is not already experiencing boredom, she very quickly shall. She will read the file," said Melville. "She will not be able to stop herself."

He was quite right, of course. The folder sat on the marble hall table for all of two minutes. In which time Phoebe paced up and down a dozen times with her arms folded. And Miss Nightingale was being unusually quiet upstairs. *Finally*, tutting at her own lack of will power, Phoebe snatched up the file, sat at the foot of the stairs and lifted the cover.

Inside: three flimsy, cream coloured sheets. Typewritten, smudged carbon paper copies of the originals. Also slipped inside the docket, a localised map of Greenwich, skilfully hand drawn, highlighting the location of the Royal Observatory in relation to the surrounding streets and the home addresses of the two recently deceased astronomers who appeared to be the subjects of this enquiry. "No foul play suspected" was the typewritten conclusion at the foot of page three. After which someone had added a handwritten symbol. In blue ink. A large question mark. Underlined.

"Superintendent Melville, you are a despicable man."

~12~

Having quickly skimmed the gist, then absorbed the details, Phoebe now found herself back upstairs sitting on the bottom edge of Florence Nightingale's soft, plump bed, all white sheets and silk counterpane. On the wall at the head of the bed, an oval mirror and a shelf of books. Two hefty maple wardrobes dominated either side of the chimney breast. In the fireplace roared a coal fire.

A green leather-topped table, with inkwell and desk-tidy, piled orderly and high with correspondence stood in front of the multipaned Georgian window: the vantage point from which Miss Nightingale could observe all the comings and goings of South Street. To one side of the window, a roll-top bureau piled even higher with correspondence: letters, requests, invitations and proposals of marriage from old soldiers. Everything was neat, spotless, polished or freshly laundered and the air sweetened by the fragrance from another vase of pink freesias.

"Well, that was a waste of reading time," huffed Phoebe.

"Explain," demanded Florence Nightingale.

"If you're quite sure, Matron," said Phoebe patiently. "It will be interesting to see which of us dozes off first. It seems both deceased gentlemen took the position of Chief Assistant to the Astronomer Royal. One after the other. Both died within less than a week of one another. Their names were, let me get this right," Phoebe browsed the file again to be certain. "Goronwy Dapper and Ronathan Chafeskin."

"Pssht," said Miss Nightingale. "To lose one Chief Assistant may be regarded as misfortune. But to lose two looks like…"

"Skulduggery? If nothing else this has given us the opportunity to rewrite Mr Wilde." That brightened her face. Even Florence Nightingale allowed herself a smile.

"Melville must harbour his suspicions, child. For what other reason would he request you to examine the file?"

Phoebe looked at her remarkable counsellor. Aged sixty-nine, with arthritis and poor health beginning to win its creeping battle, Miss Nightingale was now pretty much confined to her bedroom. But mentally she remained sharp and agile. Her still-dark hair, with its centre parting, was swathed in a headscarf of white lace, tied below the chin. Clear eyed with not a line on her face. She wore a black nightdress trimmed with white at the cuffs and around her shoulders a white shawl cover with black dressing gown.

The sickening sights and sounds of war still haunted the revered ministering angel, memories which had inspired her personal industry and sustained her resolve over the four subsequent decades. The five hundred pounds annual allowance from her father also helped, financing her passionate campaigns for nursing reform and affording her the comfort of this Mayfair house, with its attendant staff.

Phoebe continued her appraisal of the file. "Dapper was promoted over the head of Chafeskin, but died shortly after his appointment, from natural causes. Chafeskin inherited the role, then he quickly died following an accident at his place of work. Whoever thought astronomy could be such a dangerous profession. Both causes of death are equally unexciting..."

Florence Nightingale flashed an icy stare. "Such disrespect is uncalled for, child. The details?"

"My apologies, Matron. Dapper passed away at home from heart failure. Chafeskin broke his neck falling down the stairs. Both died alone. Both behind doors locked from the inside. Even the official report says no foul play is suspected."

"Yet something troubles Melville enough for him to trouble you."

"I cannot for one moment imagine what those troubles may be, but they are entirely his affair and, I still believe, nothing whatsoever to do with me." She closed the file and tossed it casually onto the bed as if to underscore her point.

"How might Michael Magister respond to Melville's request?"

"Ha. Michael would have leaped at the opportunity to once again help Special Branch. He had a knighthood to pursue." As soon as she said it, Phoebe felt guilty. She gathered her thoughts. "I suppose both victims in the same job, the timing and the locked rooms might have piqued his interest. Michael never believed in coincidences."

"And while Magister took himself off to Greenwich by himself to investigate, you would have sat quietly reading another book?"

"Ye gods, no. Who knows what sort of pickles he would have got himself into." Phoebe shook her head at the thought. Then thought some more. "While it is flattering to be consulted and, I admit, it would have been rather satisfying to prove Melville's concerns were entirely without foundation, none of it would prove exhilarating."

"And working with an old woman on her correspondence *is* exhilarating?"

"Matron, that life of the Music Hall and solving baffling curiosities while baiting the Prince of Wales and Lillie Langtry and the entire British Establishment was *enormous* fun while it lasted! But that part of my life is over. And now, assisting you is what I like to do."

"Very well, child. Let us get back to work." Florence Nightingale returned to her bureau, picked up her pen and returned to her writing. Phoebe returned to her desk, picked up a sheaf of unopened envelopes, sliced them open one by one, sorting them into piles of subject, and then importance. With a pencil she neatly summarised the contents, suggested a response and a few salient phrases Matron might wish to consider.

They had been working in silence for the best part of an hour when Miss Nightingale looked up out of the window for what seemed like the thousandth time and smiled. "We have another caller, child. Elizabeth will be busy, so please answer the door."

"I do rather hope it is not Melville again," said Phoebe.

She was at the foot of the wide staircase before the door knocker finished sounding its gentle rat-a-tat-tat.

Phoebe opened the door. To a slender gentleman in his early sixties. Clean shaven with pointed features. He rested his case on the doorstep, removed his top hat. He looked rather distinguished with his full head of silver hair.

"Hello, m'princess," he said with a gentle smile.

Phoebe took a step back. Her jaw dropped. All she could managed in return was, "Hello, Papa."

~13~

It was eleven years ago.

And the brisk early Sunday morning walk through affluent Edinburgh streets just west of the Castle, across the dark ribbon of river known as Water of Leith, to Dean Cemetery, always took ten and a half minutes.

The burial ground had opened forty years earlier, said to be the most fashionable and one of the most secure. Secure, you may wonder? ("Why do they build walls around graveyards, ladies and gentlemen? The people outside don't want to go in, and the people inside can't get out!" That was one of Michael Magister's less savoury lines.) Well, back in 1846, it was a precaution against shovel wielding resurrectionists. Covens of Burke and Hare inspired ghouls would heave the freshly dead from out of their not-so-final resting places and offer the corpses to unscrupulous anatomists. No, not for profit, Your Honour, purely for the furtherance of the medical sciences.

It occurred to the hawk-faced gentleman now gazing upon his late wife's headstone, that before the 1832 Anatomy Act became law, he was precisely the kind of surgeon the Scottish grave-robbers might have woken in the night, carting an unripe corpse: "See you thus, doct'r. Newly exhumed! Gi' it a sniff. An' yours fer jus' six o' yer finest pennies!"

The air was still in the cemetery. As if the leaden morning sky was holding its breath until it turned blue. The gentleman removed a bunch of faded red roses from the base of the stepped plinth and replaced them with a fresh bouquet.

The grave was a simple stone cross. The dedication inscribed:

EDITH KATHERINE ERSKINE MURRAY
BORN ABERDONA 4th OCTOBER 1840
DIED AT EDINBURGH 9th NOVEMBER 1874
*"I THANK MY GOD UPON EVERY REMEMBRANCE
OF YOU"*

Thirty-four years of age. She was lost far too young to the incurable uterine killer, puerperal peritonitis – horrific, when you consider the number of lives that had been saved by her loving husband's steady hands, keen eyes and remarkable surgical skills.

A few whispered prayers and a soft blown kiss. The doctor ran a graceful finger across an arm of the cross, bade his beloved farewell until next week and turned to walk briskly back home.

Despite his fifty-three years, the doctor was still tall, spare, and in no way stooped. His skin was swarthy, and his body naturally energetic. The houndstooth weatherproof Inverness coat, billowed behind like a cape as he strode.

Once the gentleman turned onto Melville Crescent, a small circle junction bounding the crossroads of Melville Street and Walker Street, he spotted the anonymous horse and carriage standing before his impressive Georgian town house. And immediately formed an opinion of his visitor. Which would be undoubtedly correct.

As the doctor bounded up the five steps, the front door was opened wide with precise timing by a matronly maid. Before she could speak, the man burred: "Thank you, Margaret. And I believe our caller is a high-ranking policeman."

"Quite so he is, doctor."

"And I have kept him waiting at least fifteen minutes."

"As is the case, doctor." Her reply totally unsurprised by the man's statement. "But he is not at all impatient."

The hall was cool and airy, a white and black tiled floor, a dark wooden hat stand, set to one corner and a large blousy aspidistra stretching upward from a shiny copper planter standing at another. As Margaret took the doctor's travelling cap and cape, the tall, impressive visitor hove into view from the parlour and saluted.

"Chief Inspector Lester, sir," said the fellow. English. From his assured manner, Scotland Yard. His was a firm but kindly face framed with black hair and mutton chop whiskers. Smart in his brown three-piece suit and cravat, Lester held a bowler hat to his chest in one hand and offered his open warrant card with the other.

The doctor waved the card away in a 'no need' fashion. "Good morning, Chief Inspector. Your visit from London suggests a matter of considerable importance. But thankfully not the usual bad news which comes to my door."

"And you know this how, sir?"

"My dear good fellow, I must apologise to you for knowing so much about your visit before granting you the courtesy of explaining matters for yourself."

"Not in the slightest, doctor. I am intrigued. Please do continue."

"A fine black carriage waiting outside with a patient and well-groomed black horse in harness, driven by an equally well-attired coachman. Anonymous, but pristine. Edinburgh City Constabulary. Only a senior officer would be granted the courtesy of such fine transport, while any rank lower than Inspector would have been dispatched on foot. The manure-pile 'neath the hind quarters of the gelding was fresh but emitted no steam indicating a waiting time of no less than a quarter of one hour."

"Very impressive, doctor."

"Of course, you are from London, but before you spoke your tired eyes and pleated creases across the lap of your trousers suggested you had been seated long, and had travelled far. Police officers arriving at my door are without fail the messengers of bad news. Your demeanour is professional but in no way solemn, thus bad news is not a factor. Your mission concerns the important missive you carry within the inside pocket of your jacket which you have patted twice now with your hat for reassurance of its continued presence."

"I, for one, doctor, deem that remarkable."

The detective then awkwardly juggled his hat and warrant card to fish the stiff envelope from that very pocket. "I was instructed to ensure you receive this letter by hand. In person. I am also commanded to inform you this communication is…"

"Of a highly confidential nature, I understand," The doctor took the envelope and without even looking at it said softly and melodically, "I take it His Royal Highness, the Prince of Wales, demands a swift response to this message."

"You know that much, sir? With barely a glance?"

"The quality of the stationery informs me, Chief Inspector Lester." The doctor smiled benevolently and continued: "Additionally, with my thumb I felt the insignia embossed upon the flap, the fleur-de-lis, which very much confirmed my presumption. But I crave your forgiveness. Observing and analysing, they are the habits of an old surgeon."

"No, please, yes, thank you, doctor," the policeman flummoxed and babbled. "The sender is... he... I shall await your reply outside, doctor. And may I express the honour of having met you."

"Ohh, tush, Chief Inspector," said the doctor, modestly. "But thank you. Go safely about your business. And have a care for your left knee."

The Inspector looked surprised. "That I will try, sir, thank you, sir."

The doctor bade the policeman farewell, making no attempt to explain that the heel of his right boot displayed the greater wear as it bore majority of his weight. The wince of the policeman as he climbed aboard the carriage was further confirmation.

Now then. This letter. The slanted barely legible scrawl bore a vague approximation of the words: "Dr J. Bell FRCSE".

~14~

Dr Joseph Bell, a Fellow of the Royal College of Surgeons of Edinburgh, and Queen Victoria's personal surgeon in Scotland, sat quietly in his dining room staring at the envelope. And with no idea as to what the contents might hold. Hard as he tried, not a clue to be seen. All he knew was by whom it had been sent. Oh, do get on with it, Joe, said the soft voice in his head. With delicate precision, he took up a butter knife and sliced open the flap.

Dr Bell unfolded the cream velum and studied the single page. Scribbled in a hurry, but with long prior thought given to the details.

"Well now."

According to the letter, he was being invited to consider, which translated from Royal into English definitely meant 'commanded', to oversee the educational development of a child, the birth of whom he had so skilfully overseen. "In no finer hands..." blah blah, the usual Royal flattery. "And no better an educational benefit could the child enjoy than..." et cetera, et cetera.

Scrawled at the foot of the page in an indecipherable style that only a crazed code breaker could figure out was an approximation of the name "Albert Edward".

Well now. Joe Bell certainly didn't see this one coming. But at least his deduction of the author's identity was spot on. Albert Edward. Bertie. The Prince of Wales.

In subsequent discussions the eminent surgeon was to be assured that the child's Edinburgh-based schooling would be independently financed, and the suggested seat of education was to be the Queen Street School. Dr Bell knew it, of course, a vast eighteenth-century five- storey terrace, the longest in Edinburgh, with an impressive reputation. The ethos was teaching imperative female skills, painting, drawing, music and dancing. Languages, mathematics and science were also listed on the curriculum, but they were secondary considerations in the upbringing of a young girl.

Dr Bell's patronage, in view of his status in the City of Edinburgh, a leading figure in pioneering medicine, would ensure the very best for the child. His role would be purely advisory, supervisory. Mindful, of course, that his personal life had been rendered less burdensome now the parental responsibilities of his two daughters Jean and Cecilia and son Benjamin had been removed, since none of them now lived at home. And professionally he no longer held the position of editor of the 'Edinburgh Medical Review'.

So, the poor child was being shunted up to Scotland, into the shadows, away from awkward questions. The demand on Dr Bell, of course, was audacious, outrageous and typical. Bell was a widower, he was middle-aged and he was still far too busy to oversee the education of a young girl. At least Joseph Bell had the courage to decline the Prince's kind offer.

But then he imagined that voice again. His wife whispering in his ear. "Come now, Joe, the poor bairn has ne'er a soul who really cares about her, least of all those parents."

Deny the Prince of Wales? In this matter, Dr Bell would do so in a heartbeat. But disappoint Edith? No. It could never be done. The surgeon then struck a Swan Vestas match, holding first the letter to the yellow flame, then the envelope, he watched the paper flare and curl black.

So be it.

Two minutes later, Margaret the maid was in the street handing the reply through the open window of the carriage. The Inspector nodded and saluted Bell who was standing at the dining room window, and then smartly tapped the carriage roof to 'drive on'.

The newest member of the Bell family.

Now, more than a decade later, those vivid pictorial memories flickered through the mind of Dr Joseph Bell as he tapped on the knocker of the grand Georgian Terrace house at the Park Lane end of South Street in Mayfair.

The shiny black door opened.

"Hello, m'princess," said Joe Bell to the beautiful young woman standing there. Who took that step back. Whose jaw dropped. And who, in return, could only manage to say "Hello, Papa."

~15~

"Who is there?" called the woman upstairs, as if she did not know.

"It's Papa Joe, Matron," called Phoebe.

"Phsst. I expect it is, child." Above they could hear the floorboards creak while she moved about.

"Would you care for me to bring him up to see you?"

"Certainly not, child," came the firm, precise reply.

"Oh, very well then," whispered Phoebe.

"'Child', then it still is?" whispered Bell with a mischievous grin.

From above they heard scraping and banging, shortly before Florence Nightingale, like an apparition, appeared at the top of the stairs. Supporting herself on two walking sticks. "Dr Joseph Bell is one gentleman for whom I should always make an effort."

Joe Bell climbed the stairs two at a time and held the heroine steady as he kissed both her gnarled hands while they gripped the ebony walking stick handles. If she was in any way flattered, she did not let her face know. It remained darkly creased from each cheek down to the corners of the pursed mouth.

Bell said: "Matron. I am happy to see your undulant fever is much improved. Although I am saddened your spondylarthritis remains an irritant."

"Pssht. I expect you are, doctor. And *I* am happy to know your vision remains as perceptive as your mind," said Florence. "That

I am up out of bed indicates the improvement in the one condition while my curvature stoop dictates a less satisfactory tale. Those are the clues which inform your diagnosis, I presume."

Bell smiled and said: "Matron, you presume correctly."

"Pssht, I expect I do," Florence Nightingale dismissed the great surgeon with a wave of the hand. "Enough of your parlour games, Joseph Bell. As you are about to learn, your timing is propitious, and your visit will take on a far greater purpose. So away with you now. Lest you no longer remain my favourite Scotsman."

In the front parlour Bell sat straight upright on a hard chair while Phoebe sat on the arm of the plump floral sofa.

"The Angel of Mercy still pens her copious letters," observed the doctor. He clearly noted the black stains on the finger and thumb on Florence's right hand.

"Often three dozen," said Phoebe.

"Per week?" said Bell, impressed.

"Per day. I am rather convinced she has seen far more ink upstairs than blood in Scutari." Phoebe then changed the subject. "Matron knew you were coming to London this week?"

"There is little that woman does not know. I have lectures at St Barts and her telegram suggested I arrive two days early."

Phoebe apprised Dr Bell of her recent breakneck experiences, culminating in Matron happily offering a roof and a role. He sat back and considered his 'adopted' daughter with immense pride. Then said: "Matron suggested the timing of my arrival was of benefit."

Phoebe passed him the Special Branch case file, complaining about the audacity of Melville, as he read.

Bell sat deeply back within the armchair, the tips of the fingers of both hands together to form a steeple. He recognised the sheer frustration of coping with Phoebe's loss when Michael, Wicko and I, apparently, inexplicably, vanished. Bell too felt the same aching, hollow loss when his wife Edith died. The only visual evidence of the depth of his grief was his once thick dark hair turning to iron grey in three days, but his therapy was to steam straight back into his medical work.

"Melville's question to you is: I suspect these two deaths are related, but have no idea why," said Bell.

"Well, yes quite so… And, my question to you is…."

165

"No, Princess. *My* question to you is: when do we begin?"

"We?"

"Why ever not?"

"Papa, are you certain you have the time? And the inclination?"

"On both counts, of course."

"Am I about to investigate a possible crime with the man who inspired Uncle Arthur's Sherlock Holmes?"

Joe Bell smiled. "I prefer to think of you investigating a possible crime with your new Michael Magister."

~16~

Of course, what he needed after a long trek down from Scotland was yet another railway journey, but Dr Bell found the three-stop journey from London Bridge station to Greenwich fascinating but at the same depressing. Elevated above the streets for most of the route, the views of the blackened smoke-billow terraces packed cheek by jowl were simply a stark reminder of why he had never moved from Edinburgh. The carriage ride to Goronwy Dapper's house on Maidenstone Hill was by comparison positively bucolic.

The only Contrivances Phoebe still possessed were the new Aethyr generating self-defence fan with which she could 'Tesla' assailants, and my device to confound all locksmiths, the Picker-Nicker.

It was with that little clockwork beauty she quickly un-picked the catch of Goronwy Dapper's house and swung open the door. Bell admired the skilled carpentry which had repaired the frame around the lock and the top and bottom bolts.

Phoebe read from the file. "Which bears out the insistent claim of Mr Donaldson, the porter from the Observatory, that the door was secured from the inside. Apparently, Donaldson was dispatched here when Dapper failed to arrive for work for two successive days. Donaldson knocked, failed to summon Dapper, but when peering through the letter box detected a strange smell. Presumably decay. He found a patrolling Constable and between them they shoulder-barged their way in. Donaldson and the Constable discovered the deceased body upstairs in the bedroom."

"From the general appearance of the cottage, Mr Dapper was a well-organised gentleman. A creature of habit," said Bell.

The bed was stripped leaving only a striped horsehair mattress. His suits and shirts still hung with rigid, almost military order in the wardrobe. In fact, the dense waft of mothballs released when Phoebe looked inside was a blessed relief because, frankly, the bedroom air was not unlike the stagnant miasma which pools around Father Connor O'Connor's socks. I think we can assume.

"Bacterial decomposition takes great delight in outstaying its welcome," said Bell. "The windows were closed and latched too when Mr Dapper was discovered?"

Phoebe waved a black, lace-gloved hand under her nose while she leafed through the file. "They were."

"And the position of his body if you please?"

"Here we are," she read aloud the police surgeon's report. "The body was discovered lying face down on the bed and clad in a nightshirt. The cause of death was myocardial infarction. A heart attack?" Bell nodded. "And asphyxia. It says here he was in general good health, although there was some scoliosis. Curvature of the spine?"

"Borne of his profession. Years peering through a telescope," said Dr Bell. Phoebe noticed that, although he was listening and talking, his true focus was on scanning the room, analysing every detail. It was always clear to his students, and to Phoebe, that her adoptive father never looked at anything. He *saw*.

"Oh, I say, this is rather special! The body also displayed recent bruising and lacerations to the testicles. Even the most ordered of gentlemen have their own bachelorhood peccadillos, I suppose."

"Should you be reading such things, m'princess?" asked Bell. "More importantly, should you be *knowing* such things…"

"Papa Joe, I was a magician's assistant on the Music Hall stage."

Bell shrugged. But it was true of his own children too. What he didn't know, he couldn't worry about.

"Are the testicles important do you think?"

Bell's response was to ask: "The details of Mr Dapper's weight and height if you please?"

"Let me see. Oh, I say. Rather big chap. Sixteen stones and twelve pounds, and his height recorded at five feet eleven and a half inches."

"Well, then. I am of a mind to suggest, despite the locked door and closed window, our late astronomer may not have been alone when he departed."

That perked Phoebe up. "Foul play is afoot. I knew it."

"Ah. You did not *know* there was foul play afoot," corrected Dr Bell, "you and Superintendent Melville merely suspected it. Like so many policemen who first form a theory, and then reject any facts which do not subscribe to that theory. Only when you have accumulated all the facts, may you formulate your theory. M'princess, you are employing some indefinable 'Magister-esque' instinct."

Phoebe had far too high a regard for Joe Bell to argue that Michael's uncanny instinctive knack during both the Mesmer and the Lazarus investigations was rarely off the mark. Instead she hitched up her purple velvet skirt and squatted on her haunches, creaking her black leather boots, to try to identify for herself Bell's observation.

"Okay, you were looking at the floor."

"Okay?"

"It's a Michael word," she said dismissively. "Don't tell me what you saw."

"I shall not. You tell me."

"Most obviously – this. An indented circle on the raffia matting."

Phoebe pointed to the ringed impression, about four inches in diameter, pressed into Dapper's simple bedroom carpet.

"A chamber pot! Which always stood here below the foot of the bed, slightly protruding, but has recently been shoved further under. May I?"

With Dr Bell's nodded approval Phoebe shrivelled her nose and, by the handle, pulled the white and blue china pot from beneath the rusty bedsprings.

"Oh, how very charming. Someone had a full bladder that evening." Had Phoebe pulled the chamber pot more forcefully it was clear that some over-the-rim sloppage would have occurred.

"And what else do you see?" asked Bell.

From the odds and ends which adorned her black lace thigh garter she unclipped a small magnifying lens. Bell raised both eyebrows and looked away. Oh, dear, dear. The entertainment industry had much to answer for.

~17~

With her thumb, Phoebe played the jeweller's lens over the matting, highlighting the dark outline of a dry stain splashed either side of the indented circle.

"Oh, yes! Papa Joe, how could you see that? The carpet is stained this side of the indenting ring. Confirming the chamber pot was shoved in the opposite direction, which is further under the bed."

"Very good. What else?"

"Discolouration of the mat due to the fresh spillage ... but, yes, here." Phoebe trained the lens closer. "There is an unstained area. In the shape of a letter U. Two inches across. With the bend of the U facing the indented circle."

"Imagine now a scenario," said Bell, "which could have resulted in the creation of that unstained patch."

"It is the shape of a shoe! Or a slipper? Yes! The chamber pot was accidentally kicked. Their foot was then soaked, creating this U-shaped dry patch." Phoebe stood and played out the action. "Dapper entered his bedroom, kicked the protruding pot. How does that suggest another person was present?"

"What do we know of Mr Dapper?"

Phoebe gave it some thought. "You asked about his size! He was big fellow. No doubt with feet to match! And the dry stain is small. Which suggests the chamber pot was kicked by someone with a smaller foot!"

"Might it not have been the boot of the Constable who discovered the body? Or the porter Mr Donaldson?"

"No!"

"Your reasoning?"

"Because both of those professions require big-built men who would be in possession of correspondingly large feet."

"Bravo!"

Phoebe continued play-acting her exposition. Someone stood at the end of Dapper's bed. Someone who did not notice or see, perhaps in the darkness, the protruding vessel, and accidentally nudged it with their foot. "Papa Joe, you're quite right. There was another party present in Mr Dapper's bedroom. Somebody small. But, Papa Joe. How can that be possible, when the windows and doors were locked from the inside?"

"That is a puzzle," admitted Bell. "Mr Dapper's mortal remains were transported to where?"

The file told Phoebe, "Lewisham Infirmary".

"Is that a great distance?"

"Barely three miles."

"Excellent," said the great man of medicine. "Not a moment to be lost. I have genitalia to examine."

Phoebe nodded. "That is not an expression one hears every day…"

~18~

That's the thing, you see. No matter how unlikely you look to those in charge, when one of you is a famed Forensic Expert for the Crown, albeit in Scotland, and the other can flourish a Metropolitan Police Warrant card ("I cannot enter because I am a young woman? I believe you'll find this rather says I can!"), then doors are quickly opened, and objections overcome. Until other doctors heard Bell was in the building and dropped their thermometers and stethoscopes to rush down to meet him. Once again Phoebe found herself in the company of a highly recognised personality.

All of which was why, little more than an hour after leaving Goronwy Dapper's house, Phoebe and Dr Bell, with his coat now removed, white shirt sleeves rolled up over the elbows and hands freshly scrubbed, were both standing over the man's linen covered corpse.

The bright, white mortuary of Lewisham Infirmary was sharp to the nose with chlorine. The body had been iced and retained only while searches continued for any next of kin. Otherwise the poor fellow would now be lying in a brown wooden box under a hundredweight of damp earth instead of lying on top of a cold white ceramic slab.

Joe Bell pulled away the linen cloth, damp with condensation, to reveal the grey, shiny cadaver. "Very interesting. I imagine the autopsy reported petechial haemorrhages?"

Phoebe flicked through the copy of the report which accompanied the corpse and confirmed the findings.

"You see. Purple blotches here in the eyes and on the face. Indicating air deprivation to the lungs. Suffocation."

"Wisps of duck feather were found in his nostrils," said Phoebe, reading from the notes. "Papa Joe, if Dapper was face down into the pillow, might he have been deliberately stifled?"

Bell shook his head. "Theories and facts again, m'princess. You see here? No evidence of ecchymosis on the posterior of the neck or shoulders. Bruising is always present when force is applied. Much as you would wish, at the moment we cannot show with certainty that Mr Dapper is a victim of murder."

Phoebe hmm'd her disappointment. "Now may we see his testicles?"

"Aye, thank you, *I* shall examine the testicles," said Bell. "You should avert your gaze."

Phoebe smiled, stepped back to please him, but still peeped a look.

With a pair of forceps Bell lifted the square of linen covering the corpse's nether regions, then used the instrument to gently adjust, rearrange and prod at Goronwy Dapper's appendages.

Peering intensely over Bell's shoulder, Phoebe could clearly see the genitals; which to all intents and purposes resembled a shrivelled grey whelk dozing on a pair of plumped up yellow cushions in a raven's nest.

"Oh my days. That looks far more than the reported bruising and lacerations," said Phoebe. "It is as if they were rather squeezed with nut-crackers. Which, these days, I hear is quite the pastime among the Kensington elite."

Bell raised his eyebrows, looked over his shoulder and was horrified to see Phoebe observing. "Are you quite certain London life suits you, m'princess?"

"Papa Joe, you train nurses who are younger than me," she sighed.

Yes. A fair point well made.

"Interesting that the scrotal area has continued to swell," said Dr Bell. "Which for our benefit appears to accentuate these painful wounds."

It was evident that the line of even-spaced red livid blotches only appeared on the underside of the sac.

"Crabs."

Bell shook his head. "Mr Dapper presents no evidence of pediculosis pubis."

"No, Papa Joe, the marks. Do you not think they rather resemble the grip marks of a claw?" She remembered being frequently nipped on the foot when rock pool fishing on the beach at Ayr.

"Mayhap." Bell pointed with the forceps. "And regard these. What began as minor grazes to the medial thighs." The grazes on the insides of both hairy upper legs were now fiercely raw.

"They do now look alarmingly sore. What would cause that?"

Bell shrugged. "Possibly an allergic reaction. Or the presence of a toxin."

"That is very encouraging," said Phoebe brightly. "Isn't it?"

Dr Joseph Bell stood up straight and stretched his back. "The autopsy report is quite correct. Death by natural causes. A heart attack, and suffocation, a consequence of sleeping in the prone position."

"Excuse me?"

"At the time of the original examination, I too would have drawn such a conclusion. However, this inflammation has developed post autopsy. You should encourage Superintendent Melville to authorise further forensic tests on the body."

"Does that mean you and I are sharing the same thought?"

"M'princess, without further results it is best not to present an hypothesis which is at worst absurd and at best outlandish."

"Oh come now, Papa Joe, these are exactly the peculiar circumstances which prompted Melville to seek the advice of Michael and I in the first place."

"You should await the results."

Phoebe pulled that face. The pouty, frustrated one. "Well, if you are not prepared to say it aloud, Papa Joe, then I shall. Goronwy Dapper was very definitely murdered in his bed. With a poisoned crab. By a small person. Who can escape from a locked house."

Dr Joseph Bell raised his eyebrows. Again. "I believe it is time we visited the Greenwich Observatory."

~19~

"Yes, yes, forgive the unannounced intrusion, Miss Ravenport," the man with the clipped tone of voice removed his top hat. His voice always sounded sneery but, in fairness, this was entirely unintended. "You may have a recollection of me. From the other evening. Mr Arthur Morrison."

"Oh, my dear, I probably do," said ever-so-sweet Cordelia Ravenport. "Yes, of course. The smartly attired gentleman in the dark suit as I recall. Why, you accompanied the charming author. Very famous. Oh, what *was* his name? I remember. Arthur Conan Doyle."

Arthur Morrison was standing in the hall outside Miss Ravenport's mansion flat in Tavistock Chambers on Bloomsbury's Hart Street. And truthfully, was not a little put out by the old lady's reaction. Her only remembrance of his presence was his dark suit. Not his distinctive dark looks, black hair and style of speech, emphasising words in the middle of a sentence for no apparent reason. Nor even remembering the hysterical ravings of the blasphemous Irishman. No. Most firmly lodged in her mind was the memory of Arthur Conan blooming Doyle.

Morrison strongly felt like advising the woman that he too had penned a successful novel. The acclaimed exposé of poverty in the East End of London, "A Child of the Jago". But he was far too proper, too dignified for that.

"Yes, yes. Miss Ravenport, I call this evening to personally apologise for the unfortunate disruption which bespoiled the proceedings last time we convened..."

"Ohh," Cordelia laughed merrily. "You must not trouble yourself with such trifles, my dear. It was certainly not the first time old Nostradamus has been disrupted and I daresay it shall not be the last. Fetch yourself in, my dear. I suggest a nice hot cup of Mr Lipton's darkest brew is required. The kettle is boiling."

"No, no tea please, thank you, madam. You are already too hospitable," he raised a hand in gratitude, "but I will agree to enter, if I may. You see, truth be told, because of the disturbance the last time we met, I return to crave your indulgence and to beg another consultation. In the privacy of a singular sitting as it were."

Morrison lowered his voice. "It concerns a matter I could never have broached during our previous encounter."

Cordelia lifted her head in understanding. "Ahh, well you can be assured of my confidentiality, my dear. And of course we may reconvene. You take yourself through."

She followed Morrison along the dim corridor to the séance chamber. The gas mantle in the centre glowed brightly, granting Morrison a better look at the room. Small and windowless, which explained the warmth. Wooden panelled walls, top to bottom in faux Elizabethan style, and the round table swathed in the worn black cloth patterned in white with the emblems of the zodiac.

"Do settle yourself down, my dear, and let us see what Nostradamus can do for you, shall we."

As she adjusted the brass tap on the gas mantle, reducing the orange glow, Morrison rubbed his hands together with nervous excitement. Cordelia eased herself slowly into her usual seat, rested both hands palms up on the table and closed her eyes. "As before, my dear, I ask you place your hands on the table and concentrate on the image of your astrological sign, while I summon Nostradamus."

There was silence for more than a minute. Just the purr of the gas lamp and the steady breathing of Cordelia Ravenport. Finally, she said: "Nostradamus. Nostradamus, my dear, are you there? I believe you are. Pray, enter me from your spirit world. I am your vessel."

Nothing. She waited another good minute then repeated her request. Still nothing. Morrison held his breath in hope. Cordelia relaxed and returned to the land of the conscious.

"Oh dear, that is a nuisance. Nostradamus appears reluctant to join us. He can be such a temperamental spirit. And I've spoken with him about his attitude on more than one occasion. But let us persevere."

"Yes, yes, if we may," said Morrison, keenly.

Again, Cordelia closed her eyes and opened her mind.

"Nostradamus are you there? Be gentle with me."

Nothing.

"Nostrada.."

BANG! BANG!

Which made Morrison jump. He had forgotten that spectral gavel.

Cordelia stiffened and jerked. Her eyes flared and her mouth gaped as the gas lamp spluttered and died.

"Silence, sss, banshee," hissed the spirit. "Who dares to commune with Nostradamusssss?"

The mantle spat and popped and glowed again.

Arthur Morrison looked toward the voice. Instead of sitting at his side, Cordelia was now directly opposite. Which again was remarkable. She was rigid. Her mouth was gaping.

"Y-yes, yes. It is I who wishes to commune, sir," said Morrison, weakly.

"Arthur.....Morrisssson. The author. The champion of the poor. Nostradamus knows all that has been and gone. Sss. And sees all which is yet to come. Sss. You seek to know the future?"

"Y-yes, yes, I do."

"Make. Ssss. Your enquiry."

"Yes, yes, you see my enquiry concerns my friend. Dr Doyle. Arthur Conan Doyle. Also a writer. Of detective fiction. Much like myself. I created the criminal investigators Martin Hewitt and Horace Dorrington…"

"Continue! Ssss…" Nostradamus clearly had little patience with canons of literary creation.

"Yes! Yes… my question is, will Doyle ever return to writing his stories of Sherlock Holmes?"

Nostradamus hissed. As if in contemplation. Then said: "You desire thisss knowledge why? Ssss."

"Yes, yes, I, er, I admit for purely commercial reasons. You see, Arthur has not published a Sherlock Holmes story in these past six years, and if he continues with this fallow period, in Holmes's absence, I wonder if my Horace Dorrington detective character might achieve the Holmesian status he, er, deserves."

Cordelia's eyes rolled.

"Harken well. Sss. What I foresee, so mote it be. Arthur Conan Doyle…sss…shall never write another word."

Arthur Morrison was slightly stunned. "Another…? What? Ever?"

"Arthur Conan Doyle will never write…Sss…another word."

~20~

"One was assured one could expect bona fide investigative consultants," said the Astronomer Royal, peering down at Phoebe's warrant card. The young woman was bright and confident in her manner and her dress, traits many a man struggled to cope with. So, William Christie addressed the thin grey-haired man. "One cannot possibly imagine what you and your assistant here can achieve, Dr Bell."

"Ah. To correct you on that point, Mr Christie. Miss Le Breton is the investigating consultant and *I* am her assistant," came the reply.

Christie was now agitated. First Superintendent William Melville, and then Commissioner Sir Edward Bradford, had ordered that the Altazimuth telescope could be neither repaired, nor even touched, until the consultants arrived, And, he had been made to wait until after sundown for the arrival of these Scotland Yard people. Furthermore, one of them turned out to be this brazen slip of a girl.

The three of them were squeezed into the circular observation gallery beneath the metal green dome of the Altazimuth Pavilion. The telescope itself was an impressive, chunky affair taking up much of the room.

"I imagine the observation roof has been closed since the incident," said Phoebe. "May we please have the roof open?"

Christie huffed, shuffled around and hauled on the looped chain, hand over hand, causing the two halves of the dome to separate. Rattling and squeaking, the gap widened to three feet along the length in the roof, exposing the Pavilion to a waft of cool air and the dark sky above.

"Mr Christie, is it common for astronomers to injure themselves quite so violently upon telescopes?" asked Phoebe.

A ridiculous question. "Young lady, never."

"Until now."

Intolerable. Being spoken to as such.

Bell examined the eyepiece of the telescope. The eyepiece which had inflicted such a catastrophic, horrible injury. The surgeon tried to imagine the force required to impose such damage. "Mr Christie, the last time you saw the victim, was he suffering from a head cold?"

"Not as far as I knew," said Christie. Another ridiculous question. This time from the old man. And look. Now the girl was examining the telescope!

"Mr Christie, this thin brass tube bolted to the body of the main telescope. Does that serve a purpose?"

"It is called the 'sighting scope', said Christie in a tone which assumed everybody should know that. "It aligns the main telescope with the stellar body one is observing. Do be careful, girl, that is a precision instrument."

Bell whispered quietly as he slipped past the Astronomer Royal: "Mr Christie, it is worth bearing in mind that Miss Le Breton's warrant card is endorsed by your friend the Police Commissioner."

Phoebe looked up through the opening in the roof, then bent forward and squinted up through the so-called 'sighting scope'. Before Christie could complain again, Bell asked: "I too have experience in promoting staff. What was it convinced you to appoint Goronwy Dapper to the role of your Chief Assistant over Ronathan Chafeskin?"

Christie sighed. "Dapper was by far the superior candidate. He was more orderly of mind. More methodical of practice. In character, Dapper was also dedicated to work, less driven by ambition than Chafeskin. Or rather, Mrs Chafeskin."

Bell examined the stained wooden steps. After picturing the fatal chain of events from impalement to impact, he asked if locking the Pavilion door from the inside was a common practice among astronomers, an implied 'do not disturb' sign, while making celestial observations.

Christie admitted it was most irregular. "As I said, Donaldson, my porter, had to barge through the door to afford access."

"Mr Donaldson has had a great deal to contend with lately," said Bell. "May I enquire after his well-being?"

"He does very well," Christie told him. "One supposes. Look, are we to be much longer?"

Phoebe ignored the question. "What was Mr Chafeskin studying?"

177

"The moon. It is our current program of observation."

"And are you quite certain this telescope has not been moved since the incident?" demanded Phoebe.

"Locked into position," groaned the Astronomer Royal. "As most inconveniently requested. By your superiors."

"Can you please indicate for me the transition of the moon across the night sky? Point it out for me."

"East to west," huffed Christie. Then upon Phoebe's insistence, reluctantly swung his arm in an arc to indicate the direction.

"I thought as much," nodded Phoebe.

"Then why ask?" demanded Christie.

"Only because I am wondering why the telescope is inclined to such a low angle and pointing toward south west."

Well, that shut him up. He looked at the telescope. Up and down. Scratched his head. Stroked his chin. Flummoxed. And hated to admit it but the girl … was correct.

"If this *was* the last position of the telescope, and we have your assurance of that fact, Mr Astronomer Royal, what on earth, or rather what in heaven was Ronathan Chafeskin looking at?"

Christie quickly squinted through the sighting scope. "It is difficult to accurately determine with this instrument."

"Allow me." Bell stepped forward and wiped the eyepiece with his 'kerchief. Removing most of the mauve crust. "I trust this will sufficiently help?"

The astronomer winced at the prospect of using the eyepiece, but felt the need to respond to the collective, glaring insistence. So, with his stomach churning, Christie sat in the observer's chair and chanced a quick peep. Adjusted the focus. Just a tad. Looked again. Then sat back, relieved the ordeal was over.

"Antares. Chafeskin was observing Antares."

"What is so special about Antares?"

"It is a star. A red supergiant, appearing as vivid orange and discovered by Johann Burg, eighty years ago. It is also known as Alpha Scorpii. A prominent star in the constellation Scorpius."

~21~

On their way back to Greenwich railway station Phoebe and Bell, according to their Bradshaw's timetable, found themselves with sufficient leeway to detour their carriage and visit the house of the widow Chafeskin, to offer their condolences for her husband's tragedy. And perhaps garner additional insight into her husband's state of mind.

"Is it important that Mr Chafeskin was looking at a completely different part of the sky?" asked Phoebe.

"The relevance, while puzzling, does not compare with the greater mystery. The inexplicable impact of the gentleman's eye with the telescope," said Bell.

"Which is why you asked Christie if Chafeskin was suffering with a head cold? Wondering if he might have sneezed while observing the sky?"

Bell shook his head. "Even the force of a sneeze would prove insufficient to inflict such trauma. But look, we are at the house. It is best we do not continue our deliberations in front of Mrs Chafeskin."

The timing of their arrival at the neat Ormiston Road property proved fortunate. As did Dr Joseph Bell's reputation in the medical world, which once again trumped Phoebe's warrant card in terms of heft and persuasion with Eadie Chafeskin's doctor, a young sallow-faced fellow named Skene. A usually pleased with himself Scotsman, he found himself thoroughly overawed to be standing in the presence of medical greatness. Whatever were the chances? And so far south of Edinburgh.

Dr Skene took the trouble to straighten his tie, tidy his hair and roll down his sleeves as he reported Mrs Chafeskin's medical condition, and how he favoured the familiarity of the living room over the idea of confinement to the bed, with its redolent emptiness. In fact, he was also about to administer a dose of morphine to aid her rest.

When Bell explained the circumstances of their visit and requested a brief postponement of the injection, Dr Skene slipped the hypodermic back in its case.

"My poor Ronathan worked so hard for that position," wheezed Eadie Chafeskin. She was lying back on the settee, head resting on a cushion, wearing a yellow winceyette dressing gown. Her hair was tousled, unkempt. Tear-stung soreness circled her defeated eyes. The ferocious ambition, the pushing, the cajoling, the scheming, all now vanished.

179

In Dr Bell's experience, the reaction to unexpected widowhood differed dramatically from case to case. At the extremes, some wives are so crushed by their husband's demise they all but lose the will to live. Others express their grief by dancing a merry jig and clapping their hands with glee. Clearly Eadie Chafeskin did not fall into the latter category. In fact, Bell commended Skene on his diagnosis of a woman so bereft she was on the brink of mental collapse.

"We should proceed with caution," Bell told Phoebe.

With great care Phoebe talked about Mr Chafeskin's great astrological achievements, his standing in the profession and how much he deserved the promotion to Chief Assistant to the Astronomer Royal.

"Precious little good that position brought. For my Ronathan. Or Goronwy Dapper." Eadie Chafeskin's eyes were wide open, but she was looking at nothing. The pictures were all in her head. "We were both shocked by Goronwy's death. Even though it was ordained my poor Ronathan would soon take his place. But the gentleman's passing was truly mourned."

"Were you and your husband here at home the night Mr Dapper died?" fished Phoebe casually.

"We were away. Visiting the coast," whispered the widow, reliving the happier time. "The De Crespigny Boarding Establishment on the East Cliff. At Bournemouth. The railway is convenient and the demand for off season accommodation easy to come by. I made hasty arrangements to take Ronathan away for the weekend. A distraction to assuage his disappointment at being overlooked."

Phoebe glanced at Bell. One of those knowing exchanges she often shared with Michael. The Chafeskin alibi would be sound, with witnesses, many and several.

"Mrs Chafeskin, you remarked that your husband's promotion had been 'ordained'," said Bell. "What did you mean by such an expression?"

"Ordained, assured. All but guaranteed." Eadie dabbed her red nose with a wet handkerchief.

"Assured by the Astronomer Royal?" asked Bell.

"Oh, no. You will be amused," Eadie Chafeskin flashed an embarrassed smile. "Nostradamus told us."

Bell raised both eyebrows. "Nostra-damus?"

As opposed to Phoebe's frown: "The French seer?"

"Of course, we never for one moment believed Ronathan would be granted the position so quickly following the prediction, and under such circumstances."

"Mrs Chafeskin, Nostradamus has been dead for two centuries," said Phoebe. "How could he tell you?"

"He speaks from the spirit world. Through an elderly woman I heard tell about. She consults with Nostradamus. She is his vessel. His conduit."

"You mean she is a Medium," suggested Phoebe.

Eadie nodded.

"And this was during a séance?"

"He spoke to us. Nostradamus. With his strange voice. He said 'what I foresee, so mote it be'. And like a miracle – it was."

Bell stroked his chin. "Forgive me, Nostradamus predicted Mr Chafeskin would soon take on the new position?"

Eadie nodded. "And he was right."

Extraordinary. Phoebe wished Michael were here now to witness this conversation. A séance. A prediction that came true. She ventured to ask if Nostradamus's elderly Medium went by a name? At all?

"Why, yes. She is a delicate lady. Ravenport. Miss Cordelia Ravenport." Eadie stopped mid-sentence. The mention of the name triggered a reaction. A black mood descended. Fear and anxiety became quickly overwhelmed by hysteria. Eadie sat bolt upright. "She is a hag bitch banshee. Even he calls her 'banshee'. Nostradamus. Banshee, he cries. And she is. She can travel. Oh, yes. She can travel. The banshee. In the blink of an eye. From one place to another. From there to there. And back. Around the table. And here. Out in the street."

"Dr Bell?" Skene looked for reassurance.

"A care for a moment longer, please, doctor," said Bell, who was quickly on the settee. Sitting behind Eadie. Holding her arms.

"I should have paid her," Eadie shouted at everyone. "When she came here. The banshee. It is my fault he's dead. She is a banshee from hell. Ask anyone. Anyone who was there. A banshee!"

"Doctor, the sedative now if you please," said Bell, holding the widow, restraining her from thrashing about. Skene charged the syringe from a tiny glass bottle.

Phoebe shouted: "Please, a few more moments!"

"This patient is in danger," said Bell, firmly.

Phoebe stood back and watched as Dr Skene joined Dr Bell in the struggle. Bell trying to pull up a dressing gown sleeve. Looking to expose a vein.

"Ask anyone," gasped the woman. "Anyone there. They will say it. What she is. An evil banshee."

With the plunger depressed and the opiate surging ice cold up her arm, Eadie's eyes dilated and she relaxed. Still babbling about the séance. But quietly now. Bell laid her back down on the settee. And before drifting away she mumbled: "The author. Ask him. Arthur Conan... Ask... He knows..."

~22~

Dr Arthur Conan Doyle was keen to be seen as very much the literary luminary about town, which is why he agreed to meet Phoebe and especially his old Edinburgh medical school mentor Dr Joseph Bell for lunch in a conspicuous restaurant of some swank. ACD planned to impress at one of his favourite temples of epicurean excess, where he was so well known. But as he discovered, while staff at Simpsons, 100 The Strand, were perfectly happy to admit Doyle and Bell, the young woman in their company could not be allowed to join them. Least of all one dressed like that. And they would make no exceptions, not even for the great man who created and killed off Sherlock Holmes.

Which was why an embarrassed Dr Arthur Conan Doyle and Dr Joseph Bell were now sitting with a most indignant Phoebe Le Breton, reading the menu not a five-minute walk away at the more flexible Rules Restaurant on Maiden Lane.

Bright, and glittering with starched white table cloths, the air in the restaurant was thick with the aromas of all manner of roasted meats, sliced generously on plates or packed densely into pies and puddings. But the miscellany of brightly coloured fresh vegetables in silver tureens was more than enough to accommodate Phoebe's dietary preferences. The last time she came to this restaurant was with Michael, upstairs, when they met with Lillie Langtry and the Prince of Wales. (As mentioned in my last tome of memoirs.)

Now, here's where I briefly digress. I know. Again. This departure concerns Richard D'Oyly Carte. You know, that bearded producer who was raking in a fortune from those phenomenally successful Gilbert and Sullivan singalong operas at the Savoy Theatre? Who then built the hotel next to it! Well, only recently he had forked out Lord knows how much to purchase Simpsons.

Anyway, clearly he had caught wind of the awkwardness outside his restaurant and quickly scooted across the street from his Adelphi Terrace apartment to make amends. Bow-tied, immaculately suited, with a cashmere overcoat trimmed with fur draped about his shoulders, the apologetic impresario was charm itself not only ordering a pricey bottle of Bahans du Chateau Haut Brion, Pessac-Leognan (no, me neither) for Dr Doyle's table, but also offering Phoebe the part of Yum Yum in his next production of 'The Mikado'!

With the wine uncorked, along with promises that the men-only policy would be reconsidered, and Phoebe graciously declining the chance to pursue a singing career, Richard made his grand exit in agreeable good order.

"Bah, mmm," grumbled Arthur in his old-before-his-time way. "I can recall when the fellow was known as plain Dickie Carte! Did you know that? Mmm? You see, D'Oyly is his second forename. Oh, yes! Added later. Dickie Carte became Richard D'Oyly Carte to befit his new elevated position. Mmm? Pure affectation."

Said Arthur *Conan* Doyle.

"Not a man enjoying good health is Mr D'Oyly Carte," said Joseph Bell. "Your diagnosis, Dr Doyle?"

Doyle nearly choked on his wine. Oh, my goodness. Medical expertise sought. And from his mentor! If only he had not arrived in London early for these lectures. Oh, dear. Think now. What would the old boy look for? "Yes. Mmm? Let me see. Um. I... I did perceive a shining of the face. And oedema of the hands. And from his gait, possibly of the legs."

"Indicative of?"

"Oh. Mmm. Indicative of dropsy?"

"Your prognosis?

"Um. Shall we say ... three years?"

"Regretfully. Two at best," said Bell.

At which point also Phoebe said: "Yes, thank you, doctors, but we are about to eat, and *I* would much rather talk about the predictions of a Medium – named Cordelia Ravenport."

ACD's surprise and discomfort was deflected by the three waiters who, with military precision, brought three bowls of steaming tomato and basil soup to the table.

"Miss ... Cordelia Ravenport, you say?" asked ACD. Michael had taught Phoebe to recognise peoples' guilty giveaways, slight tics or twitches. Arthur's giveaways were more a full facial animation: the quizzical look with the raised eyebrow, the sniff and the nervous index-finger brush of the moustache.

"Yes, Uncle Art, Cordelia Ravenport. I understand you recently attended a séance at her establishment?"

"Why, well, yes, as a matter of fact I did," blustered ACD. He looked uncomfortable, defensive, in front of his logic-driven Edinburgh mentor. "Although I'm bound to explain it was pertinent to my present research investigations. Into esoteric matters such as the paranormal. Mmm? Mmm?"

Joe Bell raised his eyebrows. It was his giveaway tic, which also said so much.

"Séances and speaking with the dearly departed have become quite the vogue in Knightsbridge circles, Papa Joe," explained Phoebe.

Bell smiled benevolently. Of course they have.

Arthur explained that Cordelia Ravenport was attracting a growing following because of the accuracy of her spirit guide's predictions. "The entity with which she communes is Nostradamus. The French soothsayer?"

"Yes, we know who he is," said Phoebe, patiently.

"When summoned, the spirit of Nostradamus answers questions and delivers the benefit of his foresight. He speaks through Miss Ravenport. For a fee, quite naturally."

"And pray what did Monsieur Nostradamus foretell for Arthur Conan Doyle?" asked Bell.

Arthur reluctantly admitted: "Well. Um. We did not actually get around to predictions. Mmm? Mmm? But only because of the fracas." Off the looks of his two dining companions, ACD was compelled to explain. "Yes, you see, I know it was wrong but I took him with me."

"Took whom?" asked Bell.

Arthur cleared his throat. "Father Connor O'Connor."

~23~

Phoebe all but choked on her soup. "Connor O'Connor?!"

A sharp silence cut through the restaurant as nearby diners stopped and looked; then slowly returned to the burr of conversation and clattering and scraping of silver cutlery on bone china.

"Good grief, Uncle Art," she whispered, "you don't take Connor O'Connor to a séance. You don't take Connor O'Connor *anywhere*."

"Ah. Well, you see," blushed ACD, "I simply made mention of my intention and Connor insisted upon joining me, not for ecumenical support or anything of that sort, you understand, he was looking to learn of any progress he might make within the Catholic hierarchy. As if! Mmm? Mmm? I ought to have realised his presence would become disruptive."

"He tried to seduce the elderly Medium over the séance table," suggested Phoebe with some confidence. A remark which earned a reproachful glance from Joe Bell. Music Hall talk, no doubt.

Arthur eyed the heavens. "Would that it had been so simple. During the ceremony Miss Ravenport is required to adopt a state of trancelike reverie to contact Nostradamus. Convulsions then come upon her. Nostradamus seems a particularly vexed and truculent spirit when disturbed. He calls the poor woman 'banshee', all of which, for the inexperienced observer, can be alarming. Mmm? Mmm?"

Arthur now settled keenly into his narrative. "But when totally controlled by the spirit, Miss Ravenport then partakes of Astral Travelling. Mmm? Mmm? Remarkable. In the first instance she was seated in one chair to my left, but in the next she appeared in the chair opposite. Then travelled back again. It was an aberration of the natural world to which I assure you I bore witness. And it was at that point Connor could take no more. He fled from the apartment screaming the foulest invective, and the meeting was abandoned in total chaos. Most disappointing. And my question, I fear I never got the opportunity to ask. You take me for a fool, Dr Bell."

"Quite the contrary, Arthur. We learn only by investigation and experience," said Bell. "But while you explore these dark avenues, I counsel caution. And the accompaniment of a colleague of greater repute than your priest."

"Ah. Mmm. Yes. Of course. But, in mitigation, do you know I'm bound to say I was also escorted by a man of thoroughly more standing. Mr Arthur Morrison. The social reforming journalist and fellow author. And he was equally disappointed by the outcome."

Phoebe and Joe Bell sipped more soup while they contemplated Doyle's account.

Only then did it occur to ACD to ask: "Here's a mystery. Mmm? Mmm? How came you to know of my visit to Miss Ravenport?"

Bell dabbed his lips with a linen napkin. "You may recall a young couple also attending the séance? Mr Ronathan Chafeskin and his widow Eadie."

"Indeed I do. He, shy, she more robust. But wait, his widow, you say?"

"The night before last, Chafeskin lost his life while working as Chief Assistant at the Greenwich Royal Observatory," said Phoebe. "In rather unorthodox circumstances, quite possibly a case of 'murder by telescope'. And Chafeskin's curious demise was prefaced by the equally puzzling death of his predecessor, a man called Dapper, just a few days earlier. The connection of both incidents was deemed appropriately curious for Melville to invite me to take a dig around. And from what little we have uncovered, we believe his concerns are not without foundation."

"Oh, that is splendid," Arthur Conan Doyle ejaculated. Don't. I know! But it was a verb ACD frequently used to express excitement or astonishment in his own writing. "Mmm? Mmm? And in the sad absence of Michael I am sure you require some assistance in your enquires and … oh, I say…"

Arthur Conan Doyle's enthusiasm suddenly evaporated as the thought occurred to him. He looked across at Joseph Bell, then to Phoebe. She had already used the word 'we'.

"Oh, dear," thought Phoebe. Of course, Doyle's reaction to Joseph Bell's involvement in the investigation had occurred to neither Phoebe nor Bell. Heavens, they both understood the man well enough. But they were both so caught up in the clues and the theories and the circumstances, they overlooked Arthur's inevitable disappointment on learning that Phoebe's first thought for detective assistance was Dr Bell, and *not* the great detective writer himself.

ACD's eyes glistened and his face sagged. Albeit briefly. Tics and giveaways.

"Arthur," said Bell.

"No, no, good sir," brightened Doyle. "Our girl has displayed the sound, exceptional judgement we expect of her. Mmm? If there is a mystery to unravel, there is no finer fellow with no greater mind in the world to have by your side. I raise my glass to you both."

And so he did.

~24~

Cordelia Ravenport sat quietly at the table in the séance chamber. The gas mantle was turned up brightly. Gone was the worn black cloth with the faded white symbols. Now it was just a dining table.

Another woman, another Cordelia Ravenport, pushed open the door with her elbow, and carried in two china plates of buttered bread and crumbled slices of white Cheshire cheese.

"Luncheon, my dear."

Both looked the same. Both were dressed the same. This time in grey.

"Oh, my. Thank you, my dear. That is most kind of you."

"Not at all, my dear. It was my turn after all." The woman settled into the chair opposite. "Now, the good news is that Mr Arthur Conan Doyle lives not a quarter of an hour's walk from here."

"Oh, that is a most welcome change, my dear."

"Is it not so? Most welcome. And further news which you will find to be just as marvellous?"

"Oh, do please tell, my dear."

"Arthur Conan Doyle's birthday is the twenty-second of May! Which makes him…"

"Oh, my dear – of all the things! A Geminian!"

Both elderly women then giggled. Girlishly at first. Then hysterically.

~25~

There was no doubt that Phoebe's decision to work with a new partner in crime solving had cut Arthur deeply. Mercifully, Uncle Art didn't know she had not even given him a thought. But she could understand his thinking. It must have felt like a betrayal. Which accounted for his loss of appetite for steak and kidney pudding.

"I am bound to admit at puzzlement. Why my attending a séance has any relevance upon your enquiries. Mmm? Admittedly the Chafeskin couple were present. But the man Dapper was not. Mmm? And the gathering rapidly concluded in chaos, with no conclusions drawn or predictions made."

Phoebe trod gently. "Yesterday, Eadie Chafeskin admitted that following the pandemonium they remained behind with Miss Ravenport who conducted a subsequent séance, in private. Apparently, Nostradamus predicted with certainty that Ronathan Chafeskin would be awarded the role of Assistant to the Astronomer Royal. The following evening, the man who held that position, Goronwy Dapper was dead. Then, shortly afterwards, the newly promoted Chafeskin himself was found dead, with his wife babbling to us her regrets about not paying the banshee."

"I see," said Arthur quietly. "Banshee. That is how Nostradamus addresses Miss Ravenport." He swirled his post-luncheon Remy Martin around the balloon glass, then took a sip, then sighed: "I believe you were correct. By not including me in your investigation. I am far too invested in spiritualism to offer an objective view. Quite right."

"Which does not preclude us from craving your advice, Doctor," said Bell. "What should be our next course of action?"

Which made ACD perk up. "Ah. What next?" he gave it a moment's thought. "Do you know, I'm bound to suggest you first speak with Arthur Morrison. A fellow of reasoning. And integrity.

You must solicit his unembroidered view of the séance debacle. Afterwards, I would visit Miss Ravenport herself. Mmm? Mmm? That would be my advice."

"Then that is what we shall do." Bell excused himself from the table on the unspoken pretence of making himself more comfortable, but in reality, to quietly settle the bill.

Phoebe broke the thoughtful silence.

"Uncle Art."

"Yes, my dear?"

"Had the séance gone rather more smoothly, as you hoped, would you have asked Nostradamus for a personal prediction?"

"Mmm? Oh, yes, most certainly. I would have asked the spirit a most pressing, serious question."

Assuming it would have concerned either the health of his wife, Phoebe's Aunt Touie, or if the sales of his latest book of poetry 'Songs of Action' might ever improve, or heaven forfend the singing career of his friend Miss Leckie, Phoebe was intrigued enough to ask, "Which was what?"

"On our behalf, you and I, I would have asked if we would ever see Michael again?"

You know, if Phoebe felt badly about disappointing Arthur Doyle, she now felt very much worse.

~26~

Armed with Arthur Morrison's address, Phoebe and Bell caught the first available Great Eastern Railway train from Liverpool Street station on a branch line to Loughton, a village deep in the Essex countryside.

Salcombe House, on Upper Park Road, off the sparse and quiet High Street, was barely a ten-minute walk from the station. The Morrison family home was a sprawling and substantial redbrick-built home set within half an acre of boundary-walled land. Handsome brick chimneys, half a dozen leaded windows on every side, a fancy bicycle standing under the ivy clad porch which spanned the heavy oak front door. The kind of rural idyll that does not come cheaply. Arthur Morrison's life was now enjoying the benefits brought by hard work and literary success. Not bad for someone born into the poverty of London's East End. Not bad at all.

The walls of the cluttered but expansive bay-windowed parlour displayed just a part of his collection of framed Japanese art. Woodcut drawings and paintings which included delicate portraits of ladies with powder-white faces, hair knotted into shiny black bunches, their hands crossed and tucked into the sleeves of long elegant silk kimonos; or at the other end of the scale, careful studies of chickens.

Phoebe and Joe Bell stood politely listening and pretending to show interest in Arthur Morrison's passionate explanation of the subtle artistic differences between 'The Kano School' and 'The Koyetsu-Korin School'. He even demonstrated his fluency in the Japanese language, although truthfully, he could have been spouting Martian and Phoebe and Bell would have been none the wiser.

At the front door, a very long half an hour ago, Phoebe had apologised for the uninvited intrusion and explained her role as Scotland Yard consultant and her connection to her godfather Arthur Conan Doyle. Yes, yes. Morrison was very delighted to finally meet the young woman who had spent those summer breaks in London with the Doyles, who had even worked as a secretary in ACD's failed ophthalmic practice.

He also recalled Doyle speaking kindly of his medical tutorage at the Royal Infirmary of Edinburgh under the wise guidance of Dr Joseph Bell, all of which served to warm their welcome.

Arthur Morrison continued his fulsome appreciation of Japanese art by explaining how he had started his collection by visiting the London docks and buying pictures cheaply from Oriental sailors.

All very interesting, but Phoebe really had some questions to put to him concerning the last time he saw Arthur Conan Doyle.

"Yes, yes. But before that, let me move you on and explain 'The Zen Revival Period'…"

Gah!

As if in answer to a prayer, relief arrived when Arthur's wife Eliza, a slender lady, fussed and flurried into the room apologising and directing the plump maid to lay the tray, heaving with authentic tea and currant cake slices, on the table, and then fussed and flurried them both out again, in a slapstick diversion worthy of a Fred Karno skit.

By contrast, Arthur Morrison was sophistication itself. As smartly dressed as ever in a black suit and tie, as if coordinated to match his hair and moustache. He also wore a pair of pince-nez on the bridge of his nose, which now and then caused him to incline his head up and back so he could peer through the lenses. He also drew puffs from a cigarette held between the first two fingers of his left hand in a somewhat effete manner.

"Dr Doyle appreciated your support on his visit to the female, Cordelia Ravenport," said Joe Bell, now gratefully sitting in an armchair. "He is developing quite the fascination with abstruse sciences. And the..." finally he bought himself to utter the word, "supernatural".

"Yes, yes. But, you see, I do believe it is so healthy we writers pursue our extra-curricular distractions," opined Morrison, again adding weight to the import of his words. "In the past, I too have had dealings with the 'Society of Psychical Research' in London. When compiling my first book, an anthology of fifteen short ghost stories entitled 'The Shadows Around Us: Authentic Tales of the Supernatural.'"

Oh, as bright and decent and friendly a fellow as he was, dear Lord, Arthur could be pedantic.

"Yes, well, you see," he continued, "when Dr Doyle requested that I accompany him to the Ravenport apartment, I felt compelled to oblige. Yes, see, frankly, I was keen to learn more about this latest whim which was the gossip of the chattering classes. Or the chatter of the gossiping classes. Whatever you prefer."

"And so having made the journey into London, I imagine it was rather a disappointment you did not get to witness Miss Ravenport in full psychic flow," said Phoebe.

Arthur Morrison looked at her blankly. "By which you mean?"

"I'm thinking about the commotion caused by the Reverend O'Connor."

"Oh, my, yes, yes, that, that," said Morrison, in that way people do when they're about to make an admission, and here it came. He even lowered his voice. "Yes, well, you see. In that matter... I have a confession to make."

"Truth be told, I have subsequently witnessed Miss Davenport communicate with the spirit of Nostradamus. Without interruption. When I returned to the apartment. Yesterday."

"You went back?" said Bell. This was something of a turn up.

"Yes, yes. Purely to test Miss Ravenport's reputation for myself, you understand. She granted me a private séance. And most convincing it turned out to be. Yes, yes."

"We have spoken with people who describe the woman as a banshee," said Phoebe.

"Yes, well, no, you see, she herself I found to be most personable. Kindly and genteel. It is only when she communicates with the spirit of Nostradamus that her demeanour becomes unnerving. *He* is the most tiresome and unfriendly spirit and, yes, yes, he does refer to the woman as a banshee. But despite such hostility, Nostradamus did answer my question concerning the future. But whether or not it comes to pass we shall of course, in time, see."

Phoebe and Bell both paused. Their teacups halfway twixt saucers and lips.

"Nostradamus cast a prediction for you?" asked Bell. "Sir, may one enquire as to the nature of the prophesy?"

"Yes, yes, well you may think ill of me, for the information I sought was, I fear, a tad self-serving."

Yes…

"You see, in fact, I sought the future of a third party per se. For purely literary reasons you understand."

*And?*

"Yes, yes. You see, I enquired of Nostradamus if Arthur Doyle would resume writing his Holmesian tales any time soon? Because as a recent author of detective fiction with some success, the continued absence from the market of Doyle's Sherlock Holmes fair benefits the profile of myself and my own sleuthing characters."

Phoebe tried not to sound too impatient, or desperate, when she asked: "And what was the response?"

"Oh, yes, yes. Well, you see, Nostradamus told me that Arthur Conan Doyle will never write another word."

"Oh, my days," said Phoebe. "Nostradamus said that?"

"Yes, yes. I recall precisely those very words," said Arthur Morrison. "Naturally, I was surprised by the news. But not a little buoyed, you understand. But of course, with Miss Ravenport, payment is only required if the prophesy comes true, and given the open-ended nature of the arrangement... Oh, are you leaving?"

~28~

The London-bound railway train rocked and slogged its way out of the Loughton station, slowly gathering speed in a trail of black smoke. Phoebe and Joe Bell sat facing one another in an otherwise empty compartment. The door to the carriage's side corridor slid shut.

"Our exit was both hurried and rude, m'princess," said Bell, still breathless from their run along the platform in pursuit of the departing train.

"Papa Joe, I am quite sure Arthur Morrison will understand."

"You have eight railway station stops in which to explain your thinking."

A good hour and a bit, Phoebe could not contain her urgency.

"This is plainly and simply murder for money. Ignoring, of course, the fact it is neither plain nor simple. The common factor are the séances. The Chafeskins visit Cordelia Ravenport to ask if Ronathan will ever secure his rightful job. Nostradamus predicts he shall. Better still, the spirit apparently guarantees it. Shortly afterwards, the man who holds the position, Goronwy Dapper, is dead; the prophecy comes true and Ronathan is awarded the role."

"Supposition, m'princess. Without those test results, there is no firm evidence supporting Dapper's death being murder." Bell rested his chin on steepled fingers. "But please continue."

"Despite the prophesy coming true, Eadie Chafeskin refuses to pay Cordelia the agreed fee. Later that night, Ronathan Chafeskin is found dead, also in dubious circumstances."

Bell said: "But the death of Ronathan Chafeskin was never foretold."

"Because it was a revenge killing. Punishment for Eadie not upholding her part of the agreement."

"Very well. You contend Dapper and Chafeskin were both murdered. By whom?"

"The Medium. Cordelia Ravenport."

"Cordelia Ravenport, who by everyone's admission is a slightly built, mild-mannered, elderly woman."

"Yes. Along with her twin."

~29~

Bell sat back in his dusty seat. "A twin?"

"An identical twin."

"And your evidence for the existence of this twin?"

"The séances. Everybody present said Cordelia vanished from one chair only to suddenly reappear in another seat on the other side of the table. Astral travelling, claimed Uncle Art. Knob rot. It is a Music Hall magic trick."

"Intriguing."

"Picture this. From the beginning, Cordelia Number Two is hidden beneath the table. Identically dressed, Cordelia Number One sits in a chair and begins the dramatic séance. When the light blacks out and everyone is distracted, she slips beneath the table. At the same time, Cordelia Number Two slides up and into a chair opposite. Up come the lights. Oh, my days. She has moved. How did that happen? A magic trick. A well-rehearsed, beautifully executed magic trick."

"Fascinating. And the voice of Nostradamus."

"Performed by whichever twin is hidden beneath table. Perhaps using a speaker horn to help distort and disseminate the words."

Bell nodded. It was hard to fault the logic. "And the murders. Both, 'victims' if you will, died behind locked doors. Locked from the inside. More secret Music Hall trickery? How were the murders committed?"

Phoebe leaned further forward. Took a deep breath. And said: "I have no idea."

"I see."

"Hard as I try, Papa Joe, I cannot work out a method which doesn't involve elaborate pre-dug tunnels. Michael would figure

194

some unlikely gimmick which no one would believe but would then turn out to be right for all the wrong reasons, but regretfully I do not have his mind… Or him."

"No," said Bell, quietly. "But you appear to have embraced his cavalier reliance upon intuition. And if your unproven theory for the murders is in any way correct, and Arthur Morrison has just been assured by Nostradamus that Arthur Conan Doyle will never write another word…"

"We have to warn him. He could be in mortal danger."

~30~

"And see this, my dear Regan," said Cordelia to her twin. "Doyle's abode could not be more conveniently situated."

"Just around the corner, my dear Cordelia," said the twin. "It saves our poor legs."

"It certainly does, my dear. And what a lovely evening it is for a stroll too," beamed Cordelia.

"Beautiful," agreed Regan.

As they turned into Montague Place, with the back of the grey blocky British Museum over on their right, these two cheerful little old dears were quite the matching pair. From their bonnets to their tiny shoes, they were dressed entirely in black. Passing women would smile and gentlemen would tip their hats at this charming picture of joyful innocence. Totally unknowing that they each concealed a loaded double-barrelled Howdah pistol in the pocket folds of their dresses.

***

"Knob rot?" said Dr Joseph Bell. "Another of Michael Magister's expressions?"

"Ye… that one I did make up on my own," admitted Phoebe.

The first-floor apartment within number twenty-three Montague Place at the back of the British Museum was not a grand affair. More a convenient London bolt-hole. Naturally, the locked front door to the street did not pose a problem, but out of courtesy Phoebe knocked at the door of the ACD abode.

However, the singing from inside the lodging was terribly loud, she thought. No. Make that terrible and loud.

The voice of an angel, Uncle Art had described it. The voice of an angel being strangled by Satan were the words he conveniently left out. Phoebe knocked again, more firmly. And steeled herself.

"This will not begin well," she told Bell.

The din from within stopped and, following a surprisingly lengthy wait, the door opened. Just gap-enough for an eye and a nose.

"Miss Leckie," said Phoebe, in a friendly tone.

"What do you want?" said the woman in a manner more hostile.

"I was rather hoping we might be allowed in," said Phoebe, smiling sweetly.

"Dr Doyle is very much not here," snapped Miss Leckie. "You should come back later. Good day."

~31~

The woman tried to shove the door shut, but Phoebe's nifty use of her well tried boot-in-the-door trick did not let her down.

"Do you mind," huffed Miss Leckie.

"Not in the slightest. Because I have brought with me – Dr Joseph Bell."

Bell loomed into view. He tipped his top hat. "Good evening to you, Madam."

Well, 'madam' quickly changed her tune; from grim to gushing, adjusting her hair and swinging the door open wide. "Ohh, Dr Bell, such a glorious surprise. Please, please, come in." She left Phoebe to pretty much see to herself, and close the door behind her, while 'madam' fawned over the great surgeon Arthur had apparently told her so much about.

"Oh, my days, woman," Phoebe sighed to herself.

Dark haired, tall and delicate, this was the Jean Leckie of whom Dr Bell had heard. Arthur's platonic friend. Willowy now, thought Phoebe, but time will bring a coarse chubbiness to those cheeks. And that mouth, almost permanently downturned, served only to make her long face even longer. Even now, when she was trying to smile so broadly, her lips resembled those of a disapproving cod on a fishmonger's slab. But that was Phoebe just being mean.

Why did Uncle Art indulge this person, barely four years older than Phoebe herself? But then, Uncle Art was a man of strange contradictions. A graduate of one of the leading Roman Catholic schools in the country, yet he was accepting of the unholy rantings of Father Connor O'Connor (You may remember from my last volume, he even nursed the priest to back to health in this apartment). And a man utterly devoted to his ailing wife, Louisa, whom Phoebe called Aunt Touie, and yet pursuing this two-year clandestine friendship with Miss Leckie. Creating one of the most widely read detective characters in literature, then killing him off. Arthur was also a man of character steeped in the lore of logic, but was at the same time fascinated by the supernatural. Contradictions.

"It is most gracious of you to come to visit Arthur, Dr Bell, he should be back shortly, and he did so enjoy your luncheon together," Jean Leckie shuffled and tidied the sheets of music on the piano, a splendid half grand Schubert from Chappells. "Let me offer you tea, or perchance a whisky."

Nothing offered to Phoebe.

"Thank you, no refreshment, Madam, our visit is fleeting," said Bell. "I see you are a songstress. Have you graced the boards of the stage much like Phoebe?"

"Oh, mine own performance career will differ considerably," she gushed. "It shall not be reliant upon the sensational."

Which prompted Phoebe to snipe. "Quite right, Miss Leckie. Sensational is not a word the audience would associate with you."

~32~

Cordelia and Regan Davenport watched as the Hansom drew to a halt just ahead of them. The rotund man stepped awkwardly down from the carriage, then paid and tipped the driver. The brown fur collared overcoat was a stand-out, the brown homburg hat, and the brown bushy moustache a giveaway. He fiddled with his keys to number twenty-three.

"My dear, it is the very man himself," gasped Cordelia.

"My dear, so it is," gasped Regan.

They watched as the cab clattered away. Then looked around. The street was not exactly busy.

"Fortune favours us this evening, my dear," trilled Cordelia.

"Oh, it most certainly does," trilled Regan.

"Oo-ooh, Dr Doyle!" called Cordelia, waving her arm.

Arthur turned to the sound and saw a face he recognised. Miss Cordelia Ravenport! The Medium! What a delightful surprise. But his ready 'Halloa' was quickly stifled by confusion. At Cordelia's side ... was a second Cordelia. Really? Perhaps he was seeing double. No-no, there were certainly two of them. Extraordinary. He had no idea. Then he watched both women move their hands. Simultaneously. Like living bookends.

In less than a moment their faces turned from benign, beaming happiness to hard narrow-eyed fury. Well, Arthur did not like the look of that. One little bit. In an ungainly flurry of fingers and thumbs he fumbled with the key to the front door. He looked at the women again and yelped.

Both of them were reaching into the folds of their dresses. At first snagged, then freed, then awkwardly revealed: twin-barrelled Howdahs. Long and unwieldy. Doyle recognised the pistols.

"Die, Doyle!" hissed the voice of Nostradamus. From everywhere. From nowhere. "By the hands of The Twins!"

Arthur almost snapped the key in the lock as the front door opened. He flung himself inside, slamming the door behind him, locking the latch then scrambling as best he could up the purple carpeted stairs to the first floor.

"But doubtless now you are unoccupied, you may choose to spend more time with your acquaintance, the good Lady Belvoir."

Her birth mother was a far more skilful antagonist than this woman, nevertheless Joseph Bell watched Phoebe swallow and smile, suppressing the nascent urge to pin this scrawny creature to the piano, with a parasol across the throat.

In fact, Bell was about to rebuke Miss Leckie's disagreeable attitude but was interrupted by the hammering on the door of the apartment, loud and frantic; the cries for help, desperate. Instantly, Phoebe was at the door to throw it open wide. There in the corridor, doubled forward, panting and clutching his chest, was Arthur Conan Doyle. His face was scarlet, his hands shaking, eyes wide with sheer terror! He staggered past Phoebe, begging her to shut the door! Quickly! They were after him!

Jean Leckie screamed and held her hands to her mouth.

Phoebe looked down the corridor. Empty. Then closed the door as he had pleaded.

Bell shook Doyle by the shoulders. "Pull yourself together. You are hysterical, man. Who is after you?"

"Was it Cordelia Ravenport?" said Phoebe, glancing at Bell. Just as Jean screeched something like "Oh, my darling man," and wrestled Bell from Arthur so she could embrace him.

"It was," wheezed ACD, "Outside. In the street. Good heavens, how did you…?"

"And there were two of them?"

Arthur was stunned. "They have pistols. I saw them. And by their cold, hard expressions, I'll wager a dozen guineas their intention was to shoot me."

"Oh, my dear poor darling," said Miss Leckie, tangling her arms around Arthur's neck, like a Gordian Knot. Which didn't help his gasping for breath.

Bell was now by the window, twitching the net curtains and peering down to the street. "Arthur, are you quite certain of whom you saw?"

"Upon my word, Doctor. I even heard the voice of Nostradamus. Saying 'Die, Doyle'."

"Och, I have to admit this is precisely what Phoebe surmised," Bell told Arthur before gently raising the sash-window and easing out his head, just enough for a quick look left and right and across the street. "Your two Ravenport females are not to be seen now."

"Do have a care at the window, Doctor, I beg you," panted ACD.

"My poor darling," whimpered Jean Leckie.

"Uncle Art, did you secure the door downstairs?" Phoebe demanded, firmly.

"I believe I had the wit to do so. But … I cannot be sure."

"I had better see."

"No!" implored ACD.

"Arthur, let her go," urged Jean. "It is imperative we keep you safe." Her arms enveloped the man like a squid on a submersible. He struggled to object but found himself restrained.

"I will accompany you," said Bell.

Phoebe assured Papa Joe in no uncertain terms that she would be careful. And, gesturing with her parasol and her Tesla fan, reminded him she was better equipped to take care of herself.

She spent a moment gathering her thoughts and waving the fan to charge it. As quietly as possible, she eased open the front door of the apartment. Just a little. Nothing.

"Lock the door behind me."

She then slipped out.

The corridor was just like a swanky hotel. Phoebe tiptoed with her back sliding close to the wall. It reduces the target, so her Bartitsu self-defence teacher Mr Barton-Wright had once told her.

She looked down over the black-brushed metal bannisters into the stairwell below. Two flights of stairs. Five feet wide. Nine treads each, leading to the vestibule and the front door.

Phoebe stepped back. Held her breath. And listened deeply. And waited for a minute. Any noise from outside was muffled. The building, silent.

Step by step she tiptoed down both flights. Reached the entrance vestibule. Tested the latch and rattled the door. All secure. Good fellow, Uncle Art.

Reassured, Phoebe bounded up the stairs, two at a time, parasol still poised, still keen to mete out dire retribution. Old ladies or not, these women were cold-hearted, greed-driven killers.

By the time she tapped on Uncle Art's front door, Phoebe could afford to breathe again. Joseph Bell let her in.

"Well done, Uncle Art, the building is secure."

Arthur Doyle afforded a smile, happy with the praise and a little more relaxed now the danger was averted. Jean Leckie's contribution left Phoebe dumbstruck. She clutched a candlestick telephone and complained loudly at some poor operator at the British Museum Bloomsbury exchange about the time it was taking to connect with Scotland Yard and didn't they know who she was?

Phoebe exploded. "A telephone? Since when did you possess a telephone here? Why did I not know this?"

ACD was taken aback by her outburst, which was entirely forgivable. The frantic rush from the wilds of the countryside could have been averted by one telephone call.

"Miss Leckie, listen to me," ordered Phoebe.

Miss Leckie did not. She was too busy berating.

"Miss Leckie, you will stop babbling and listen to me!"

That shut her up.

"Do not question me, just listen. You will ask the switchboard operator to connect you with Whitehall One-Two-One-Three. It is a dedicated Scotland Yard number. When the voice asks you for your designation you will say 'Thurmatagist'. You will then be connected with office of Superintendent Melville. You will tell him where we are and that we are in danger. That is all. Is that clear? *Is that clear?*"

Jean Leckie whispered a yes.

"They have a telephone," she said to Papa Bell, while waving her arms. "All that rushing about and they have a telephone…"

Arthur was now sitting, leaning forward, elbows resting on knees, hands supporting the sides of his round head. "What did I possibly do to upset the wretched woman? The wretched women!"

"It is a rather convoluted explanation," said Phoebe. "Just be assured Melville will move on this very rapidly."

CLICK! CLACK!

Phoebe looked at the front door of the apartment. "That was the locks."

SLAM!

The front door swung open so violently it all but snapped the hinges. Framed in the doorway, two figures in black: Cordelia and Regan. Both with eyes blazing. Both with Howdah pistols levelled to shoot.

"Sss – your time is now, Arthur Conan Doyle. To die!" The voice of Nostradamus was everywhere.

Phoebe sprang forward to hurl herself at Cordelia.

BLAM!

The pistol round exploded into Phoebe's chest, erupting a shower of gore and kicking her backwards. She was dead before she hit the floor.

Jean Leckie screamed.

Arthur tried to haul himself to his feet hollering, "No!"

BLAM!

Another puff of grey smoke and Arthur Conan Doyle's head popped like a raspberry balloon.

"No witnesses," hissed the voice of Nostradamus

Joe Bell dropped to his knees in total shock, to cradle Phoebe.

BLAM!

The vicious impact spun him around, showering his shoulder all over the wall.

BLAM!

The telephone shattered into a dozen Bakelite pieces, along with Jean Leckie's forearm. Both she and Dr Joseph Bell were dead. Exsanguinated. Long before the police arrived.

*"Any sufficiently advanced technology is indistinguishable from magic"*
*– Arthur C. Clarke 1917-2008*
~PART FOUR~

After precisely one hundred and twenty-three minutes, as predicted, Debbi lifted her head to wake us with a start, by announcing firmly that Mr Magister's procedure had been completed.

"And?" said Wicko. Debbi required further detail. Which Wicko testily explained was very much the essence of his question too. "Is he going to be all right?"

Debbi paused briefly, then replied: "Why, naturally the surgery was successful, and Mr Magister will be fully recovered in six days, and if you wish to see him now, that is possible."

This was getting to be a habit. Looking down on the comatose body of Michael Magister. The last time was through a mini-porthole in Dr Phunn's Victorian-technology sarcophagus. Now, our confidence was inspired by the remarkable medical advancements apparently achieved by 2001.

The platform which encircled the large clear-glass viewing dome was set high about the glaring-white Recovery Room. We all craned forward to see Michael suspended in the centre of the Room, again defying gravity with no visible means of support. He gently revolved, affording us a three hundred and sixty degree view, which every once in a while was a little fulsome considering he was totally naked. A lack of dress code apparently favoured by the Garridebs.

The only colours in the peak white environment were his skin tone, a healthy warm pink, and his eyes, protected by black ovals. From every orifice, including both ears, a tube, of mercifully not too excessive girth, emerged and snaked down into whatever machinery functioned beneath the floor. Michael's helpless condition put me in mind of a marionette before the puppeteer had threaded up the strings.

The only clue to the surgery was the barely visible plus-shaped incision, down, up, and across his chest. And not stitched. More melded.

"Why, all respiratory, coronary and associated tissues within Mr Magister's thoracic cavity have been replaced; all are functioning correctly and a complete recovery is assured..."

I interrupted Debbi to tell her I knew we were welcome, but on behalf of us all I still wished to express our gratitude for saving Michael. I also now believed that in thanking Debbi I was thanking every Garrideb involved in the procedure.

Our Humannequins, from the Mark 1 models we cobbled together using whatever was available in the late 1890s, had evolved into these infallible ... well ... entities.

Having learned of the stunning decline in the population and witnessed the result of Connor O'Connor's fully expected, but nevertheless shameful, submission to total decadence, we loftily agreed to behave with professional integrity until we more fully understood the circumstances in which we now found ourselves.

Well ... that was the intention. Until we were each allocated our individual Debbies. Exact replicas of our generous hostess. Which effectively meant her familiar face and form could be in more than one place, all of the time, for all of us.

It may surprise you to learn that despite our pact to maintain our propriety, Wicko was the first to succumb. Pretty much immediately. In fact, he was barely though the door of his suite! And, you know, given the extremes of experience we had endured in the hours since we departed 1899, quite how he found the appetite, or the energy, was frankly impressive.

I required more in the way of rest and reflection, but a day later even my much-vaunted self-control was found wanting... and wanting... I suppose it is what makes us human. Unfortunately.

Only Nikola Tesla remained dignified and true. With our Victorian garb taken for cleaning and repair, Nik's only concession to our new situation was to agree to wear these remarkably comfortable, and flattering, one-piece trouser suits.

Marine blue in colour, the fabric was soft, breathable, cuffed at the wrists and with inbuilt footwear. And an optional hood. The outfit you did not so much put on, as climb into. Which involved stretching the neckline, slipping your feet into the hole, then shimmying, as much as I could shimmy, your body down, like pulling on a giant sock.

Of course, removing the suit was less of a rigmarole. You simply laid back and upon request, your dedicated Debbi would grab the feet and pull. Much like a magician yanking the tablecloth from under a full dinner service, without so much as rattling the crockery.

And on the subject of dinner – the food! Endlessly available and consistently cooked to the highest gourmet standard. Escoffier, before he was sacked from the Savoy for cooking the books, would have seen the Garrideb kitchens as a real threat to his epicurean career. Even Nik had to admit his daily macedoine of cauliflower, broccoli and Brussels sprouts were always plated to al dente perfection.

I have to admit to you, if this was to be our future lives, we would certainly enjoy it.

~2~

Living in the grand opulence of the Hotel Cecil, we passed the week very comfortably. Each morning hospital visit we made was met with a pleasing improvement in Michael's recovery.

Once the life-sustaining pipework had been eased from wherever it had been inserted and Michael started unassisted breathing, he was moved, well, floated, to a suite of very comfortable proportions. I would say he was in the best place, but honestly, *we* were in the best place. But I digress.

The bed was a marvel. Single sized for nursing purposes, it thrust out, cantilevered from the wall. The mattress and pillow-support were formed of precisely the same material as ours in the hotel. Comfortable and malleable. Able to adapt itself to the shape of the body, adjusting with each move.

But set on the walls above the bed was a medical revelation: five tall, life-sized screens. The first was osteopathic, displaying Michael's full skeleton, white and clear, within a blue body outline.

The second screen, cardiovascular, revealed his new perfectly pumping heart and the associated pipeage of his entire blood-circulatory system.

The third displayed all things respiratory, from trachea down to his deeply inflating lungs.

The next screen presented Michael's brain and the elaborate far-reaching tendrils of his neurologicals, all of which fired a fascinating kaleidoscope of synaptic sparks in response to any of Michael's movements or thoughts.

The fifth screen was dedicated to all things digestive, showing his alimentary canal and its attendant organs, in all their vivid colour and fully-functioning glory. Wicko was not impressed, squinting and muttering something like, "Oh, do you mind, we've just eaten."

According to the displays, numbers, levels, statistics, ratios, height, weight and systolic whatevers, Michael's body was now seventy-four percent towards total health restoration.

Gone was the grey pallor, the quick to tire frailty, the frothy cough. And apparently multi-organ rejection would never present a problem because, according to Debbi, the stock of donated spare human parts available in the Medical Facility's Replacement Bank covered every known variation of tissue type and blood group.

The next improvement was Michael starting to speak. In fact, his first words to Wicko and I were particularly heart-warming: "Look at you two piling on the pounds."

"Here we go," said Wicko. "He's feeling better."

Of course, Michael was quite right. My dwarf cohort was now threatening to become so broad across, resemblance to 'Mr Wobblyman' self-righting toys would soon become a reality.

Michael's first sustenance, for which he developed a very fond taste, was a white tea called Snow Buds. The warm, pale drink so cleared his mind he started to call it his 'thinking tea'.

The iron-willed Nik Tesla, however, remained abstemious, as slender as a racing snake. He told Michael, "I have recommended Dr Smawl reduce his calorific intake to a minimum of the half dozen square meals per day, but my advice it still goes unheeded."

"Look, I'll know when to cut back, all right," insisted Wicko. "But, Magister, you cannot believe our Hotel! Luxury like we've never known. Debbies at your beck and call. But never mind what Tesla says. I'm getting my exercise. Three times a day. Four if I can manage it."

I must admit, my waistline was also reflecting this pampered lifestyle. And, believe it or not, for a man of my unattractive physicality, I too was frequently comforted. I know! Who could have imagined such a thing? I like to think I too shared Tesla's iron will. It was just that mine was getting a little rusty.

In weaker moments I found myself believing Connor O'Connor's pulpit fulminations back in 1899, when he raged that those two Commandments concerning the not committing of adultery and the not coveting thy neighbour's, whatever it was thy neighbour had, should be totally ignored on the simple grounds that God made them far too unreasonable!

And, on the subject of Connor O'Connor, following our Michael visits, Wicko and I felt obliged to pay respectful calls upon the irreligious old scoundrel, in his capacity of Pope Innocent the Fourteenth. But, in truth, that deference did not last very long. We stuck it for three visits.

On the first, he started snoring within three minutes of our arrival. The second occasion, he spent most of the time slurping Irish stew, fed to him by two Debbi's who ladled the nourishment into his gaping chops from a huge cauldron. It smelled delicious, by the way, but none was offered. As for the third time, well, whatever was occurring beneath that overhang of his many bellies, proved sufficient distraction for him to ignore us both completely.

We found that a light seven-course lunch could keep us going throughout the afternoon, while being relaxed, then following an evening visit to Michael, we returned to the hotel for a very fine and substantial dinner. And that was pretty much the pattern of our days.

Rather than join Wicko and myself on fruitless Papal pilgrimages and fine dining, the monkish Nikola Tesla spent his days in the company of his personal Debbi, out and about quietly, marvelling at the silent streets of the clinically pristine London.

What Wicko and I did not know was that Nik spent his late afternoons at Michael's bedside. At first in silence, then as the miraculous recovery continued, in conversation, apparently sharing the knowledge he had discovered.

On the ninth day, sitting with Tesla, Michael asked Debbi to show him the pages of Scotland Yard's Red Dossier, a highly secret file, designated "The Montague Mansions Massacre".

Mindful that it was the shock news of this appalling crime which predicated Michael's seizure when he arrived in 2001, Debbi determined his health restoration had improved sufficiently to know the details – if he wished. He did.

The projection light from her open palm cast clear images on the wall. Page by page, the report showed how the killer of Arthur Conan Doyle, Dr Joseph Bell, Jean Leckie and Phoebe Le Breton was never discovered because the investigation had been quickly closed down. In fact, on orders of the Crown and Government, news of such a sensational mass murder was suppressed. Covered up.

Nothing of the incident was reported to the public. The tragic shock of Arthur Conan Doyle's 'fatal heart attack' was international headline news. Holmes fans in their sobbing thousands lined the streets of ACD's funeral cortege as it processed to Westminster Abbey.

Dr Joseph Bell's unexpected demise from 'a ruptured appendix' was, for many a year, the talk of medical circles. It was exactly the condition which had taken his son, Benjamin; how ironic.

Newspaper obituaries of both men were fulsome in praise of their remarkable achievements. Miss Jean Leckie's passing was listed among the Births, Deaths and Marriages columns of The London Times.

And, of Miss Phoebe Le Breton? There was no mention. As if she never existed. The Establishment she vowed never to trust had more than lived up to her expectations.

Michael just frowned. Then patted Tesla's knee in agreement.

~3~

It was one morning three weeks after his surgery, that we were astonished to arrive at the Dr Phunn Memorial Medical Facility to find Michael standing in the reception hall waiting for us, shuffling a deck of cards. He was vibrant, fresh-faced, alert and dressed as we were, in a marine-blue one-piece.

"Gentleman, good morning. And as ever, I thank you for coming to visit an ailing conjurer."

He shook our hands with a firm squeeze.

"And this is something you will not believe."

Living in this future world, that was a statement we were used to. But this news was a belter.

"Up in my suite. Even if I told you right here and now, you still wouldn't believe it. So, I need you to follow me. And we'll take the stairs. We need to start getting you two back into shape."

And he was looking at Wicko and me when he said it!

Michael stepped out ahead of us in a lively fashion. It was a great pleasure to see him moving so comfortably. So much like his old self. It was not so pleasing when he and Nik were already waiting for us outside his medical suite when Wicko and I finally arrived sweating and panting, but that is beside the point.

Michael lowered his voice. "Okay. In case this gets a little awkward, here's what I'm going to do. I am going to tell you who's inside."

"Hold on, Magister, downstairs you said you weren't going to because it was a surprise," whispered Wicko.

"I know, but the fact is, I *have* to tell you because," he lowered his voice still further, "at first, even *I* didn't recognise them."

"So, who is it?"

"Ready for this? It's Wu Hu."

What? Wu Hu Phunn? Dr Phunn's sister? She was one of the London survivors? That was remarkable. Tesla was less enthused to learn this but having been robbed by the Phunns twice he had good reason.

"Just so you know, she is sixty years old. And believe me when I tell you – she does not look it. She looks a whole lot worse. So, just get yourselves ready for a shock."

"Oh, Magister, pur-lease," said Wicko, "give us a bit of credit for decorum, why don't you."

Michael gestured at the door of his suite. It slid open. We walked inside. And saw her.

"Eurgh, my God!" shouted Wicko.

Just before he turned round and staggered out again, holding his mouth and retching.

~4~

My. It was hard to blame him. Do you remember that feisty sister of Dr Phunn, so tall and slender with that long dark hair and those naturally lovely Oriental features? Well, now? She was the size of a whale.

I kid you not. Slumped back on a vast bed, much like Connor's in fact, angled forward just enough that she could see ahead, wheezing and slobbering and attended by two eager-to-please Garries. And she was just as naked as Connor – but not that that mattered because the draping folds of flesh more than concealed her womanlies.

Oh, dear. And while the features on her comparatively tiny face retained some of their original loveliness, they were overwhelmed by a great fleshy tyre of a forehead, and hanging, meaty jowls.

"It's all right, I'm back," whispered Wicko, wiping his lips with the back of his hand. "I don't think she noticed."

Whatever was Wu Hu's reaction to Wicko's reaction, it was hard to tell. Hopefully my effusion of good wishes and joy at seeing her would…

"Professor More … be silent," she ordered.

So I did. And while Debbi and one of the Garries quietly and efficiently tended to Wicko's mess directly behind us, Wu Hu continued.

"I have waited four decades in this future … for this moment … and I watched your arrival … from my suite … upstairs…" Wu Hu made a heavy 'up there' gesture with chubby fingers. "I witnessed the … Magnetic Time Storm … above the Big Ben clock tower…"

Wicko said, "Yeah, I imagine that was spec…"

But she quickly shut him up too. "Because … on behalf of myself and … my brother … I wish to apologise … to you all, especially … to you, Dr Tesla."

Nik was taken aback.

And I will not test your patience with a verbatim gasp-by-gasp description of her regrets at their filching the Molecular Integrator Contrivance from Nik Tesla's laboratory in Colorado Springs, and the final insult, their invasion at the stage door of the theatre, the coercion and making off with the Flywheel and the TimeKey.

Of course, had the Phunns and their crew succeeded in propelling themselves through the Nexus and returning to the Time Realm whence they came, they would not have been sorry at all.

But, to his credit, Nikola Tesla sought no schadenfreude, I think that is how you spell it, in telling Wu Hu both the TimeKey and the FlyWheel they stole were flawed, substandard prototypes and no wonder they blew themselves irrevocably to pieces. Instead he said, "Madam Wu Hu, be pleased to know that rancour is time wasted."

Knowing Wu as I do, I'm sure she would have merely shrugged if the flab on her shoulders would have allowed. Instead she recited the fates which befell her associates.

None of them enjoyed a happy ending. Apparently, Mel and Colly, the formerly conjoined twins, and Lazarus, the huge gentleman born without limbs, immediately embraced the life of hedonistic excess offered by the Garridebs. Even Spindle, in the first week, found his weight quickly ballooning to a portly eight stones.

Only Wu Hu and her brother, Dok Tor Phunn, ignored such kitchen-and-concubine distractions and dedicated themselves to working with the robots, sharing their ideas and experiments to further improve their regenerative medical practices. Eventually, the Garrideb's exponential growth of mechanical learning and steady-handed mastery of human surgery reduced even the Phunns to honorary bystanders.

With little requirement now for their medical genius, the Phunns also found that their alternative area of expertise, wholesale larceny, had been rendered redundant in a world where anyone could order whatever they wanted, needed or desired, and have it willingly supplied and delivered at great speed by the Garridebs. Without cost.

Wu Hu told us, playing up her capacity as one of the leading medical consultants in the country, she did convince the Garridebs that balanced, nutritious diets were urgently needed necessities to enhance and extend the life expectancy of the rapidly dwindling human population. So, the robots obediently made available extensive menus of heathy cuisine. But when they were met with universal resistance, and abuse, it was pointless to pursue Wu Hu's policy further. The Edwardian Obligation must be obeyed.

The Edwardian … what?

"Remind me to talk you through that little beauty later," said Michael quickly, before urging Wu Hu to continue.

"Inevitably, first my brother … and then myself … laid back and … yielded to the repulsive … orgy of pampered intemperance. It was all … that life here … could provide."

Wicko rubbed his hands together excitedly.

"Tell us what happened to Dok and everyone," said Michael

Well, Dr Phunn was the first to die. Five years ago. At the age, and weight, of sixty-two. When his stomach finally stretched to way beyond its limit and burst in a rip-roaring explosion of noodle-gas that rattled windowpanes more than a mile away.

Like you we winced at the image. The damage was inoperable, even for the Garridebs.

Once the flames of his three-day cremation had dampened down, Wu Hu requested that St Thomas's Hospital be re-dedicated in her brother's honour. Hence The Dr Phunn Memorial Medical Facility.

Not long afterwards, while dining on fifth helpings to suppress his grief, Lazarus loudly passed away in a blast of fried plantains and crab souffles. The Twins then died in similar circumstances, although their demise might well have been exacerbated by the requested passionate attention of half a dozen Garries at the time.

As for Spindle? Horrified he was tipping the scales at twenty-one stones, he vowed to return to his original weight. His ambitious fitness regime involved recreating the agile acrobatics which made him such an effective cat burglar.

Balancing on the parapet of Waterloo Bridge, he executed a series of somersaults, at first with great skill. Until he missed a footing and plunged headfirst into the Thames, where he found he could not right himself. A rescue team of Garries were with him in moments.

After a fast diagnosis, new heart and lungs were requested in what would have amounted to almost exactly the same procedure that saved Michael. But Spindle gave a firm refusal. Despite a careful explanation of the transplant's guaranteed success, his direct request was 'no treatment'. The Garries could only comply and watch him die.

And that was what became of Dr Phunn's Carnival of Mechanical Miracles.

Like us, Wu Hu dwelt a moment on the thought, then Tesla asked if she ever saw Father Connor O'Connor, Pope Innocent the Fourteenth. After all, he only lived just down the street.

She pulled a sour face which suggested she did not. Then said, "He is a foul, disgusting, gluttonous disgrace!" which pretty much confirmed she did not.

"Magister," she wheezed. "Demonstrate to me one … of your card conjuring … distractions. And I insist the trickery … you employ … includes the King of Diamonds … and the Ace of Clubs."

A deck of cards had been Michael's first request when he regained his faculties. The pack was boxed with the manufacturer's name 'Bicycle' on the cover. The fifty-five cards, including three jokers, were nicely laminated for smooth handling; not too slippery.

Michael fanned the cards face up, squared them off, sifted through, then riffle shuffled. Holding the deck in one hand he showed his audience, us, the top card, again face up. It was one of Wu Hu's choices. The King of Diamonds. Michael revealed his second hand to be empty, then placed it over the King of Diamonds, and using his palm, gently massaged the King. He then quit, took his empty hand away and showed everyone the top card again. No longer the King of Diamonds. Now it was the Ace of Clubs.

Although we had seen him pull that card stunt before, we all hummed our approval. The execution was not as effortlessly fluent as we were accustomed to, but given that the surfaces of Michael's burnt scabbed fingers had only recently been entirely renewed, the performance was encouraging. The dexterity was still there. Just a little more practice.

*Basically, Michael loaded the top of the deck with the King while making sure the card directly beneath it was the Ace. Naturally, the massaging was the mischief. As Michael rubbed the King, he pushed the card slightly upward, exposing the bottom of the card below, the Ace. Using the base of his palm, that soft section just above the wrist, he gripped the edges of the Ace, and gently drew it down clear of the deck. To Wu Hu it looked as if Michael was then massaging upward, when in fact he was carrying the hidden Ace and dropping it on the top of the pack – ready for the big reveal.*

"Okay, Wu, this next one is a better trick…"

"That is all," gasped Wu Hu, emphatically. "Now, I leave."

And that was that.

We all made the right noises, about how pleased and surprised we were to see her, but Wu Hu Phunn was not remotely troubled by what we thought. In fact, as the Garries floated her away, a half-hearted wave of the fleshy hand was all the departing gesture we were offered, along with the whispered remark: "Remember, Magister … if I ever see you again … that will be up to you."

Out and along to the lift then up and away to her penthouse, she was quickly gone.

"Really?" said Wicko.

We took another moment of reflective silence.

"No. I can't believe it," Wicko.

"If anyone knows, she does," said Michael.

It had been cryptic. Her message. Something known only to us. When Wu Hu insisted on those specific playing cards for Michael's magic trick.

The King of Diamonds and the Ace of Clubs.

She had sent us a grave warning. We were in serious danger.


~6~


While Wicko, Tesla and I prevaricated, wondering how best to address Wu Hu's bombshell, Michael seized the initiative.

"Deb, I know it's earlier than usual, but right now I do feel the time is right for my daily – whatever it is you call it."

Steady, Michael.

"Why, Mr Magister, it is known as your recreational ambulation."

Ah.

"Yes, gentlemen, I am going for my daily stroll and insist you come with me."

"Is it far?" demanded Wicko, not a little alarmed at the prospect of exercise.

"Down to the river," said Michael. "And, Deb, you will have noticed today I have not just Dr Tesla, but two other Principal Creators to keep me company. How good is that?"

"Why, sir, it is very good."

"Yes, it is. Which makes it not just one but three good reasons why I shall not be requiring your lovely company. With three of the finest minds in scientific history, do you know what that means, Deb?"

"Why, no sir, I do not."

"It means if I do have any kind of medical relapse, these three gentlemen will know exactly what to do. Panic and send for you."

Well, I must say, the urgent walking pace Michael set reflected well upon the extent of his recovery. With his tall, loping stride, Nik kept up with the multi-organ transplant convalescent, but frankly, my portly self and the ever-stoutening Wicko really struggled.

The rear entrance of the Dr Phunn Memorial Medical Facility led straight out onto a garden area laid to lawn and dotted with benches upon which to enjoy its magnificent view of the river just beyond. As a perfect canvas of pastoral tranquillity, right here in the still-heart of London, it could not be beaten.

Directly ahead, the Palace of Westminster, imposing in its spikey gothic splendour. To the left, the empty but predominantly red-painted arches of Lambeth Bridge. Just to our right, the green arches of Westminster Bridge. Each corresponding to the bench colours found in the two Parliamentary houses. Red for the Lords. Green for the Commons. Not that either had been used for any kind of law-making gobbledegook for decades. But I digress.

No sooner had we relaxed into the soft seats of the hospital garden than Michael set the agenda. "Okay, Nik and I have found if we all keep our chat down to a murmur and cover our mouths, the Garridebs don't know what we're saying."

"Why would we do that?" asked Wicko.

"Because we don't want them to know what we're saying," said Michael.

I asked what it was we *were* we saying?

"I'm thinking it's more to do with what Wu Hu said. Or rather didn't say. Or couldn't say straight out."

Right. Perhaps I should take a moment to share with you the meaning of Miss Phunn's enigmatic warning. It came when she insisted Michael's card trick should involve the King of Diamonds and the Ace of Clubs. It was a direct reference to our time in Manhattan. Back in 1889. When circumstances of life-threatening danger compelled Wicko, Michael and me to flee New York and set sail for England as fast as we could. If you are interested in the details, I shall fully relate those East Coast of America exploits in my next volume "The Conan Doyle Curiosity". Of this I most solemnly promise.

Now, where were we?

"Wu Hu is, for some reason, saying we need to escape from this," whispered Wicko, admiring the surroundings, and just beginning to hanker for a Cornish pasty. Again, the gentle SLOP! of the crystal-clear upstream tide against the concrete embankment and the perky bird chirrups in the trees, were the only sounds to be heard. "And should we take notice of a single word Wu Hu Phunn has to say?"

I very much agreed with Wicko. Here we were being feted and sated and revered as gods. Michael's life had been expertly granted a fresh new lease. And Nik could enjoy the immense satisfaction of witnessing all his electrification theories being proved unimpeachably correct.

Now match those positives with Wu Hu's unsubstantiated warning, not forgetting the Phunns' motives were always self-serving.

"Very well, my friends, let us for the moment accept that the Madame Wu Hu's warning is without merit and dismiss such an idea most spurious," said Nikola Tesla. "Let us also cast from our minds that this world of comfort, a world for which we may bear some responsibility, has contributed to the extinction of humankind, but in a manner so much more blissful than any of the alternatives. There does remain, however, a reason of the greatest motivation for us to leave this place and return to the time whence we came."

"What's that?" asked Wicko.

To which Michael replied firmly: "To save Phoebe."

\*\*\*

Ouch. We had not even considered that. Wicko and I. In fairness we had been consumed, no, distracted by everything around us. I asked Michael when he started scheming this.

"The moment I woke with all those pipes poking out of all those places out of which no pipes should be allowed to poke, I knew I needed to get back for Phoebe," he said. "At least stop her getting shot. Stop the Montague Mansions Massacre from ever happening."

There was little need for whispering or hand covering. None of us was saying anything. Instead, we sat there. Thinking. Contemplating. Looking around. Enjoying the peace. The warmth of the sun and the fresh breeze in the air. The prospect of another magnificent luncheon.

"Listen. Professor, Wicko. You don't have to come," said Michael. "I fully understand that. The chances are it all goes wrong and we wind up getting killed in the process. Or worse. This is my choice. And Nik's. You just needed to know."

I looked at Wicko. He looked at me. Then Wicko rubbed his forehead, sniffed and said, "What's the plan?"

~7~

"We've got the makings," said Michael. "Our good friend Dr Tesla just spent the last four afternoons scouting out what we're going to need to tear us body and soul all the way back to 1899."

The question was how to return. A torrent of first thoughts cascaded into our heads. But all of them obstacles. Oddly enough, one of the most concerning tied directly to Wu Hu's warning. Were the Garridebs a source of danger? And if so, would they really stand and watch as we flew back in time and altered events which might well compromise their own existence? The fact we were whispering not to be overheard demonstrated our suspicions.

I asked about The Edwardian Obligation and I am glad I did. It turned out to be an eye-opener.

From the information offered by his Debbi, Nik Tesla told us that the conclusion of a Great War, dubbed The War to End All Wars, in 1915, resulted in the surrender of all foes and antagonists of the Empire and the restoration of world peace. The 'Obligation' itself was named for King Edward VII, and was a simple rule imposed by a Royal Commission regarding the increasingly mechanised and cognisant robots. The Obligation stated that 'Garridebs will serve and benefit all humans'. Apparently, it took many months of discussion and waffle to draw that conclusion.

During the 1920s and 1930s, reliance on the labour force-capabilities of the Garridebs in agriculture and industry grew rapidly, providing greater time for human leisure and recreation. Even worthy scientists became so pampered that their work ethic slipped. Research and knowledge were now prefaced with the words culinary and carnal. Which I could fully understand – look at Wicko and me.

Wicko pulled a guilty face. "I suppose we can assume that everywhere else they're living in this kind of paradise."

"No idea," said Michael.

"Can't we just ask?"

"I did. Deb said she has insufficient information on that subject."

Tesla added that he too enquired as to how and why The British Empire proved so victorious in the first year of The Great War. "Again, on this subject most important, there was insufficient information available. Was victory in this 'War To End All Wars' a conquest of the world? Is such knowledge being withheld knowingly?"

You know that was quite correct. In our time here, we had not seen one book. The Garridebs were the only source of data, the only repositories of information, past and present. Yes, it was likely the peoples of the world beyond these islands also enjoyed lives of pampered excess provided by the robots. Equally possible: the world beyond these islands was a smoking, arid wasteland, draped with the bleached skeletons of billions.

Gah. If only those vital incendiary charges at the Metropolitan Theatre of Steam, Smoke and Mirrors had not failed.

"In the matter of the assistance from the Garridebs, Octopus is quite correct. Their Obligation cannot be tested with knowledge of our plans. Thus, I have conducted my research in a manner most clandestine. And in order to succeed our primary requirements are the FlyWheel and the TimeKey."

"Won't they still be where we left them?" said Wicko, gesturing across the river. "Over there in the clock tower."

Tesla shook his head. "Regretfully, that place I visited already. Both Contrivances had been removed by the robots."

Dammit.

"But not to be down hearted, my friends. I have located precisely the whereabouts of both Flywheel and TimeKey."

Tesla looked for approval at Michael, who said, "Go right ahead, Nik, you found them."

"They are on the display. On the top floor of the Science Museum in the South Kensington."

The Science Museum? I had no idea one had been established. There was a building I knew as the South Kensington Museum Science Division, a thin-built edifice stretching along Royal Institute Road, off Exhibition Road. In 1899 it was not an elaborate affair. Times change.

"And get this, gentlemen," said Michael, encouraging Tesla to continue. "Tell them, Nik."

"To flatter ourselves still further, the full name of the establishment is 'The More, Smawl and Tesla South Kensington Science Museum'.

Wicko and I were stunned. A building? Dedicated to us?

"Naturally, Nik's not crazy about the billing," whispered Michael, who then suddenly loudly said, "but he says this place is an essential visit which we have to see!"

Ah. I quickly understood. Whether it was his re-sharpened senses, or restored peripheral vision, Michael had spotted Debbi sashaying herself onto the terrace to join us. No doubt to offer tea or gin or food or whatever mid-morning whim took our fancy, and ask if we would like it right there and now?

We all adopted reposes of feigned innocence concerning our conversation.

"Deb, the Principal Creators have been thinking. Dr Tesla tells them your exhibition in their honour over at the Science Museum is something they have to see. Can you organise a visit for us? As soon as possible?"

"Why, yes, Mr Magister, I can arrange that excursion immediately."

"And, Deb, I believe I'm feeling more than well enough to tag along."

Debbie cocked her head, then said: "Why, Mr Magister, yes you are. Your arrangements have been made. You're welcome."

"Deb, I have one more request, on behalf of my extreme friends, the Principal Creators."

I think Michael meant 'esteemed' but reflecting on everything we had experienced just lately perhaps he was right.

"Why, certainly, Mr Magister."

"Before we go, do you think we can maybe get our own clothes back?" He gestured at our marine-blue fatigues.

Nik Tesla endorsed Michael's request adding that he believed they would settle even more quickly if they were comfortable in their own clothes. "Is this not the case, Professor More and Dr Smawl?"

We confirmed it was.

"Why, of course, gentlemen, your comfort is of paramount importance," said Debbi.

"And opera capes," said Michael. "Who wants opera capes? On the shoulders? Very fetching."

We did not. Well, Tesla did.

"That's two opera capes, please, Deb."

"Why, certainly, Mr Magister, it is all being arranged as we speak."

"Oh, and here, Debbi, there is one other last thing," said Wicko. "Before we set off for the museum. Can we have lunch?"

~8~

After large cups of Snow Buds 'thinking tea' for Michael and Nik, and a quick four-course snack for Wicko and me, including two helpings of the phyllo lobster and cream cheese appetiser, we now sat in the Motivator, replete and resplendent in our usual clothing. All of it fresh, the colours restored where fading had occurred, and I am ashamed to say in the case of Wicko and myself, with our trousers gently re-tailored to accommodate our new waistlines.

With their black opera capes draped about their shoulders, Michael and Nik looked impressive. And in the absence of a

Dracula costume competition to attend, which Tesla would have won hands down by the way, I assumed their motives had little to do with looking dandified.

The Motivator swept us smooth and silent, despite the astonishing speed, north along Whitehall. We passed a beautiful Portland Stone monument we had never seen before which Debbi called 'The Cenotaph', designed by Edwin Landseer Lutyens, commemorating those lost in the 'War To End All Wars'. Lutyens waived his fee, she told us. Yes, Debbi was with us, standing in her usual place at the back, and announcing our journey time to the 'More, Smawl, and Tesla South Kensington Science Museum' to be fifteen minutes and however many seconds. Not that I was really listening, instead thinking that a Museum named in our honour, afforded Nik, Wicko and me a status attained only by Lord T. Alva Edison. Even our esteemed Emeritus Polymath Professor of Genius, the late Robert Hooke, all save him, could point only to a Laboratory displaying his name. And that kept blowing up. I must tell you about all of that next time, as well.

As we approached Trafalgar Square and Lord Nelson's pale granite Column, a flutter of pigeons took flight, presumably startled by the motion of the vehicle. We watched them jink left and curl right, when suddenly from the grey, puckered dome atop the National Gallery, a dozen needle-thin beams of intense yellow light pinged through the air...

EEEEEZZZ – SHISsssss...

...decimating the flock to a shower of blazing feathers with chilling efficiency. The surviving ninety percent scattered for shelter every which way.

"Deb! What the hell was that?" shouted Michael, seeing the charred cinders of the zapped diminish on the breeze.

"Why, Mr Magister, that is a vermin cull," she explained, "carefully maintaining pest levels for the continued well-being of our charges."

An act of brutal maintenance, dismissed in a manner devoid of emotion. We were all surprised, no, shocked by Debbi's callous reaction, but more worryingly, we had witnessed the first indication that the Garridebs possessed any form of weaponry. And it was our Pulsa technology.

The remainder of the journey we spent in quiet reflection until the Motivator began to slow and Debbi announced: "Why, gentlemen, welcome to 'The More, Smawl and Tesla South Kensington Science Museum'."

Stepping out of the vehicle, we looked up at the brutal, grey, flat- roofed building. Industrial. Like a grand-scale pumping station. Not that that mattered. The carved stonework along the length of the building displaying its name? My name. And Wicko's and Nik's, of course. It was worth the journey just to see that.

Once inside, Tesla with his finest mid-European charm said: "Perhaps, Madame Debbi, you would allow myself the honour of acting as the personal guide for my associates. For the simple reason this may prove a visit most emotional."

"Why, certainly, Dr Tesla," said Debbi. "and should you require my assistance, or further information, you need only say my name, and – you're welcome."

Then she shut down, right where she was.

"I remember when I had that effect on the ladies," Wicko told Nik. With a bit of a swagger.

~9~

We followed Nik Tesla up a grand staircase into a wide rectangular room with faux marble columns and proper marble flooring. From the glitter of the chandelier lamps, to the gleaming oak on the bow-shaped box office booth, which displayed the seating plan and ticket prices, this was an almost perfect recreation of the entrance hall of The Metropolitan Theatre of Steam Smoke & Mirrors.

"The foyer," Nik said, with an off-hand wave, adding, "Please to keep moving," before leading us at a fair old lick through the stained-glass double doors and into a good-sized Victorian style art gallery, floored in a carpet of geometric design in pink and grey and walled in a rich sea-green flock paper.

Adorning the walls, a framed collection of publicity posters. Reproductions of silk-screen printed sheets, various designs, iterations, all daring the crowd to enter The Metropolitan Theatre of Steam Smoke & Mirrors and 'Experience the exotic, deadly magical, Inter-Dimensional world of Magister the Industrial Age

Illusionist and Phoebe, Queen of Steam and Goddess of the Aethyr'. Over-wrought slogans extolling the Goddess's power over gaseous erotica – no, Aethyr, steam and smoke – illustrated with clouds of swirling fumes, haunted by human skulls with red glowing eyes and their mechanised cog-driven jaws gaping with hideous laughter. And no, the skull heads were not based on me.

"The poster gallery," said Nik, with another gesture of indifference and a brisk walk through and into the next in an urgent, determined manner.

Admittedly it would have been hard to summon up any real nostalgic or historical interest in exhibits we had seen for real less than a month ago, but even so, as a tour guide Nikola Tesla was frankly terrible. And Wicko was struggling to keep up.

"Now, my friends, it is in this gallery we may take the brief pause."

"Thank God," said Wicko.

"For it is here you will find some interest."

You know, Tesla was quite right. The space was given to another grand Victorian drawing room, this time depicting material with which we were totally unfamiliar. All of it printed and published after our departure to the future. A pictorial history of the destruction of The Metropolitan Theatre of Steam, Smoke & Mirrors, as reported by the press. The stand-outs for me were same-size facsimiles of newspaper front pages. The local Paddington Mercury headline yelled: "BAFFLING BLAZE RAZES OUR MET".

The Evening News: "FIRST THE MAGICIAN, NOW THE THEATRE. GONE IN A PUFF OF SMOKE".

The Daily Sketch: "FIRE ENDS THE MAGIC. BRINGS CURTAIN DOWN ON MUCH-LOVED MUSIC HALL".

With an expanding gesture with his hands, Nik demonstrated how required blocks of text, or details of photographs could be magically lifted from the page, enlarged and viewed in mid-air.

"Terrible. Shocking," said Michael, scanning the pages. "Can you believe this?"

I agreed it made for very sad viewing.

"Not once. Pheebs and I are not mentioned once in this entire coverage. Look at it. Not a picture, not a word. If I'd have known about this at the time, I would have complained. Don't they know who we were?"

Um. If they did, they were not letting on. So we all coughed and made sympathetic noises while he stood there tutting about the building being the star. From his trouser pocket Michael pulled Phoebe's black glove. The glove he had pulled from her hand in desperation at the top of Big Ben. The tangible memory of her existence in this day and age. Michael kissed the glove as if it were a holy relic.

And talking of photographs, also adorning the walls, a vast assemblage of exposures taken at the time. Grainy original monochromes which, if you waved your hand across right to left, clarified and colourised the pictures. All of them different views, illustrating the roofless charcoaled husk of the theatre. Crumbled walls standing forlorn behind huge piles of steaming ash. A line-up of firemen in dusty tunics and heavy moustaches posing in front of what used to be the stage.

"Oh, gentlemen, take a look at this vanity picture. That is a very himselfly photograph," said Michael.

We huddled and peered where he was pointing.

"Detective Inspector Walter Pym. There he is. Right there. At the end."

Yes, he was. In the dark overcoat and holding his bowler to his puffed-out chest and grinning broadly for the camera.

"For certain, the Inspector does not appear to be the man who is burdened with sadness," said Tesla.

Wicko, up on tiptoe, was furious. "I don't think I could hate him any more than I do right now."

"Shall we continue?" This time it was Michael urging us on. He had seen quite enough.

Passing through the third set of double doors, produced a dramatic revelation. The centrepiece of the exhibition. The main gallery. A huge area occupying the rest of the available floorspace. Careful under-lighting skilfully set the authentic mood.

The first and largest feature was a restoration of a salvaged section of the theatre's auditorium. The partial ceiling and walls, Frank Matcham's beautifully scrolled and moulded plasterwork, gilded and glorious.

Beyond the three rows of rebuilt, reupholstered crimson seating, stood a full-size stage and proscenium arch. Stark and dark, until we climbed the set of access steps which led up to the recreation of the performance platform. It seemed our movements triggered spotlight beams which illuminated a series of Magister-Phoebe illusions. Rebuilt and mounted on plinths, the much-loved classics included: 'The Throne of Disintegration', 'The Steam Saw of Gore', 'The Guillotine of Deadly Beheadment', 'The Iron Monger's Coffin' – with authentic rubber-sharp spikes, and 'The Vitruvian Chamber of Agonised Dismemberment'. Each was such a grisly crowd-pleaser, it made you feel warm just to look at them.

Further upstage, toward the rear, one of the central features, which glowed now with great pride, was our Mr Garrideb. There he was, posing in his black overcoat, top hat, and gas mask with his green eyes permanently blazing. And he was the original! A true collector's rarity, with an added bonus. If you pressed the plunger protruding from the base of his stand, the old faithful mechannequin growled his entire guttural repertoire of discouraging abuse, including such favourite threats as: "Clear orf, ya bugger! I'll 'ave ya!" and "Clear orf, ya bugger! Gertcha!" Oscar Wilde? Pah.

The next display was a disappointment. Beside Mr Garrideb the lights fell upon an elevated stand, befitting, I suppose, their significance. There stood two of the original SteamMark VI robots; arranged in the manner in which we stored them. And looking remarkably developed when compared with the original Garrideb. We had made a very good fist of putting these heavy-lifting fellows together, but Nik, Wicko and I could not view them without a feeling of resentment.

This unhappy, untouched-by-fire diorama was further illustrated by a tableau of large actuality photographs, floating in mid-air, showing all six surviving SteamMark VI's exactly where they had been hidden. And discovered. Once again, in each image, smiling for the photographer, the men who made the discovery. A brigade of courageous firemen. And Detective Inspector Walter Pym.

"You know when I just said I couldn't hate him any more..." snarled Wicko.

The commemorative plaque beneath the display read: "The Originals. With grateful thanks to the remarkable technological advancements made by Principal Creators Professor Artemus Napoleon More and Dr Manswick Smawl, in association with Lord Kelvin of Largs and Dr Nikola Tesla of New York, and based upon the original conceptions of Professor Charles Babbage and Augusta, Countess of Lovelace, discovered by Pope Innocent the Fourteenth…"

Gah! I could read no more of that twaddle. For me the eulogy was not so much an affirming of credit, as an apportioning of blame. And if this was Michael and Tesla's hope, that showing Wicko and I this museum would harden our resolve to return to 1899, their plan had succeeded.

~10~

"Please to follow me over here, my friends," whispered Nik.

He led us straight to a plinth, set beside the SteamMark VIs, which displayed the museum's latest exhibits. Newly labelled. Set against a backdrop depiction of the Big Ben clock tower. The brass plate signage read: 'The Lord Grimthorpe (Edmund Denison) Fugit FlyWheel' and 'The Nikola Tesla Tempus TimeKey'.

Well, the last time I saw the TimeKey it was looking decidedly poleaxed, limply hanging from the Timing Train of The Grimm's clock mechanism and streaming black smoke from where black smoke should not ought to come. Now its brass and wooden casing was clean and the glass on the gauges, clear.

"The Madame Debbi, she invited me to approve the restoration of the Tempus TimeKey and supplied me with the tools most sophisticated to achieve such a result," said Nik. "She was most content I should fiddle and repair to ensure the TimeKey exhibit possessed the finest details of authenticity."

"That's a lovely job, Nik," said Wicko. "Will it work?"

To witness Tesla's look of contempt was a joy. But to then witness the audacious act of larceny which then took place was frankly a shock.

"Time to go home," said Michael as he lifted the FlyWheel, while Nik took up the TimeKey, and then both shoved their prizes under their capes! I braced myself for the onslaught of wailing sirens, strobing lights and Pulsa-packing Garridebs descending furiously upon us from all sides.

But instead there was – nothing.

"Please for you all now to follow me," whispered Tesla.

So, we did. In what we hoped was nonchalant innocence, although Wicko's raised eyebrows and tuneless whistling was hardly a performance to trouble Sir Henry Irving.

Nik led us to through to the rear of the stage, past a glass case containing a fob watch we called 'The Timepiece of Hyperion', and an illusion billed as 'The Graveyard of Death', both grimly ironic, given whatever plan were about to set in motion. We followed him up another plush flight of stairs, only twenty carpeted steps, but my knees ached with every one, leading to a glass atrium.

"Prof, what did you make of that roast pigeon incident back there at Trafalgar Square?" wondered Michael quietly.

I admitted I found both the cull and the firepower shocking.

"Me too. Which might prove a problem. Nik and I didn't figure on those Pulsa beams," said Michael, "which kind of means our foolproof plan to get to Big Ben might get shot down. Literally."

"What do you mean," said Wicko.

At the top of the stairs, Nik opened a glass door directly into the flat roof of the museum. "Because, Dr Smawl, you are going to fly us to Big Ben."

Wicko's reaction started loudly, before he changed to a whisper. "Fly? If we got hold of one of their airships, I couldn't get to grips with it." He waved his hands in front of him, like a Garrideb pilot. "All that malarkey."

Michael said, "But you know how to fly this little beauty."

Wicko turned. And when he saw it his mouth fell open.

~11~

Right there. On the roof. Our airship – The Ferrous Dodo!

The last time Wicko had seen her she was sinking to the bottom of the Serpentine in Hyde Park, more than a century ago. And right here and now in 2001, there she was, looking magnificent! Not a spot of rot or rust to be seen. Somehow, most likely, the

Garridebs had found, salvaged and fully restored our favourite dirigible. With her silver-smooth skin, rivets glinting in the sunlight, Windowscreen crystal clear, oh she was a beautiful sight.

Mounted on a slowly revolving dais, The Ferrous Dodo was clearly intended as the centrepiece finale of the entire attraction.

While Wicko gawped with joy, unable to speak, Tesla assured him she was ready to go. "This I can confirm with much confidence," whispered Nik, explaining how yesterday he had climbed aboard, heaved himself up into the aeronaut's seat and tested every switch and lever he thought he understood. And those he did not understand, he fiddled with anyway. Most importantly, he reported, The patent Aethylium Purger started first time. "I determined most certainly that in the past, visitors to the museum enjoyed the flights of pleasure aboard the Dodo."

"A circus side show," snarled Wicko, who had some experience of such a thing. "That's not right."

The red carpet laid out our direct pathway to the Dodo. On either side, more of those floating screens which flickered into life, displaying archive photographs of the Dodo, drizzling water as she was winched out of the Serpentine by a steam crane.

Michael and Tesla's capes fluttered in the warm breeze as they led our procession across the roof, straight to the Dodo's side entry doorway. The door itself was swept up on two arms, curled over the fuselage, while the entrance was accessed by a three-step metallic platform and a handrail providing assistance to the museum's visitors. Visitors who stopped coming a good while ago.

As we filed aboard we let Wicko take the lead; he was after all the captain. And, oh, the joy of seeing how beautifully the interior of the Flight Saloon had been restored. So faithful to our parlour design indulgence. The settee with its dimpled cushions, upholstered to perfection. The green carpet was plush and deep. Even the fringed velvet drapes hung beautifully.

"How long to get us skyborne?" asked Michael.

"If she goes like Nik reckons, the usual half a minute," said Wicko, now struggling to clamber up into the elevated aeronaut's seat. "Once I get up here." Having snuck their purloined instruments of time travel behind the settee, Michael and Tesla then saw fit to get behind our dwarf and give his lardy ass a helping shove.

As he shuffled into the familiar but slightly tighter seat, I asked how it looked up there. Wicko scanned the dials before him. Their faces gleamed white. The Helmswheel turned freely. Ahead, the Windowscreen had never been clearer.

"Right then. Fingers crossed. Here we go with start up."

He pulled a few levers and twisted a couple of knobs, pushed a button and at once the needles on the gauges bounced as the airship kicked into life.

Tesla and I settled onto the settee. My legs, grateful for the rest. Michael looked at us, relieved. "So far…" Then his face changed. "…oh."

The voice said: "Why, gentlemen, what are you doing?"

We turned to face the voice. And there she was. In the doorway. Debbi.

~12~

Michael hardly missed a beat before he snapped into performance mode. "Deb, where have you been? What kept you? Isn't this terrific? We were saying you have a done such a terrific job with this exhibition. These three Principal Creators are thrilled. Isn't that right, Principal Creators?"

We all parroted how thrilled we were, with weak smiles. Michael's invoking the name of the Principal Creators was clever, but if Debbi had figured our plan, we could wind up the way of a flock of vermin pigeons.

"And they are especially impressed with what you've done with the Dodo," continued Michael. "Especially her first aeronaut, the esteemed Dr Smawl."

"I was just saying that," lied Wicko.

"Yes, he was. And *I* was about to say, Deb, I don't think you'd mind on this great occasion if the best man for the job, Dr Smawl here, took this little beauty for a nostalgic flight, celebrating your fine restoration work and testing the old lady's metal."

It was the kind of wall of words Michael used on stage to bamboozle the audience into his way of thinking. Debbi cocked her head to one side. "Why, certainly, Mr Magister, that is a very good idea, however, I believe I should accompany you."

"And, Deb, we would be reassured if you did," said Michael.

"Welcome aboard, Debbi," said Wicko, as he clicked up the power. From the engine compartment at the rear, we felt the nudge and heard the suppressed whine of the patent Aethylium Purger. Another click and the Dodo lifted smoothly from the roof. "Beautiful."

Wicko teased the helmswheel to the starboard and the dirigible leaned an easy right, heading north. Ahead of us lay the grey, muffin-topped roof of the Royal Albert Hall. A hundred and thirty years old now, and just as solid as we remembered. Another turn of the wheel set the Dodo's course to the east.

Standing like a sentinel in the gaping doorway, Debbi pronounced that, in view of the altitude and the air speed, our continued safety and the security of the Grimthorpe Fugit FlyWheel and Dr Tesla's Tempus TimeKey would be ensured by closing the door. Which was interesting. And alarming. While still implying a concern for our well-being, Debbi's attitude had stiffened. First she had posed a direct question, and now she was stating her intention when, until now, Garrideb responses had been entirely reactive and suppliant to our requests.

Michael faced the robot head on. "Deb, what are you talking about?" He turned to face us. "Professor? Nik? Any ideas about what Deb's…"

Michael did not finish his sentence. Instead he launched a mighty back-heel to the robot. And caught her a purler. Straight in the belly. The shock toppled Debbi backwards and clean out through the yawning doorway.

~13~

Tesla and I stood in shock. I demanded to know what Michael had just done.

"What Pheebs would have done," said Michael, himself suddenly shaken by the gravity of what he had just committed. "Deb knew we had the FlyWheel and the TimeKey. If she didn't already know, she would have figured our plan and stopped us."

"You don't know that for certain, Magister," doubted Wicko from his elevated position.

I had to agree with him. And born of instinct or otherwise, Michael's actions were tantamount to murder.

"Octopus, listen to your emotional attachment," snapped Tesla. "Can one murder a machine?"

I said she was a thinking entity. Sentient.

Tesla was firm and forthright: "Michael Magister's action is but nothing when compared with the greater consequences of our return to 1899."

Ah. A point I had not considered. By going back, we would change the future and eradicate not one, but this entire Garrideb population.

Michael called for Wicko to hurry her up. Surely the Garridebs' collective response would not be slow in coming. Wicko clicked her up a few notches. The Purger whined. And the Dodo surged.

"She was right, Magister," called Wicko. "We had best shut that door."

The faster air flow now fluttered the velvet drapes, along with Michael's opera cape as he gingerly edged toward the open door. He stretched for the required lever. Then felt a vicious cramp in his left calf. Then felt himself being yanked off his feet. He crashed to the carpet. Before being dragged out of the open door.

Michael half turned and clawed wildly. Hooked his fingers on the door jamb, only just. Glanced down. Debbi was clinging to his knee. One-handed. Trailing through the air. Then began climbing his leg hand over hand

He heeled at her face with his right foot...

DOOF! DOOF! DOOF!

...and she let go.

Free. Until he felt the sharp jolt in his neck and the throttling. She was holding one-handed to the hem of his flapping cape. That damned opera cape. He felt his own fingers slipping.

Wicko banked the Dodo to the right just as first Tesla, then I, grabbed Michael's wrists, then arms. Held him firm. Tesla fumbled desperately at Michael's neck. His face was florid. Then finally, finally, Tesla unhooked the gold chain clasp.

Immediately the pain was gone as the opera cape ripped away. Back and down. And Debbi with it. Arms and legs flailing at nothing.

As we hauled Michael into the Flight Saloon I looked back and saw Debbi smash headfirst onto the lead-sheeted roof of Westminster Abbey. Of all places!

A shower of silver sparks spat and spluttered from her gaping mouth as her body buckled, then slid and scraped down the pitched roof, before tumbling and spearing her back onto one of the vicious up-pointing finials decorating the roof of the Lady Chapel. Her head and limbs hung while continuing to spark and twitch. Tesla and I reported the sickening impalement.

"That won't help her mood," said Michael, still rubbing his throat.

"Coming up on Big Ben!" yelled Wicko. "I'll put her down in the Old Palace Yard."

"Observe the Garridebs," said Nik, looking down and pointing. "In the streets below. They are moving."

Michael sat up straight, asking how many Garridebs were moving.

"All of them."

Michael joined Nik and I at the open door. Below, on Broad Sanctuary, were two dozen figures. Garridebs which had stood dormant for who knows how long were now turning to face the Lady Chapel roof.

"Taking her down!" called Wicko.

On the ground the Garridebs stared, as if trying to comprehend, or receiving instruction. Then they turned. Again, all of them. To stare directly up at the Dodo.

~14~

The Garridebs then turned to face the Palace of Westminster. They looked. And having weighed it up began, in perfect step, to march.

"Wicko!" called Michael. "We can't land! They'll catch us!"

"What do you want me to do?"

"Take her up! Aim for the clock face!"

"Clock face? Which one? There's four of them."

"The nearest!"

Along Broad Sanctuary, Abingdon Street, and across the lawn of Parliament Square Garden, the Garridebs streamed in determined military rhythm. Heading for the base of Big Ben.

"Coming up on a clock face, Magister!" called Wicko.

The off-white dial now filled the Dodo's Windowscreen. All twenty-three feet of its diameter. The time was on our side, but only just. Both huge clock-hands, the plain minute hand, all fourteen feet of it, and the shorter, more ornate hour hand were both pointing bottom right, between the numerals V and the VI. The time was five twenty seven.

Up close, the inner circle of the clock face was a jigsaw of irregular glass panes, set within a web of cast iron tracery. All of them far too small.

Radiating out to the circumference, the glazed panels became more geometric. Each hour-pane segment measured a one-foot by two-foot oblong. Out at the edge, the minute sectors were a foot square. The oblongs. Hardly ideal, but they would have to do.

"Bring her alongside the dial!" called Michael. "Down by the six o'clock mark. Sideways-on. Butt her door against the clock face."

"Blimey, Magister. I don't know if I can manage that."

"Pheebs always said you were the finest aeronaut in the world, Wicko. And I believe her."

The dwarf eased the power and deftly helmed the stern of the airship about. The Dodo swung broadside and slammed against the clock face. Not quite as deftly as I'd thought.

"Sorry!"

The Dodo drifted back and forth, up and down, like a ferry in a squall at the quayside. When she nudged up close enough, Michael kicked at the first pane of glass, that one to the left of the numeral VI. The impact blow splintered a diagonal crack.

The second stove in the brittle glass which shattered into a dozen pieces.

Jags of glass teeth edged the frame until Nik Tesla too lent his boot to tidy up the opening.

"Nik. You're up first. Show us how it's done."

Just as Tesla leaned out to step across and inside, a breeze caught the Dodo and gusted her away, opening a chasmic plunge of two hundred feet.

"Sorry," said Wicko.

"Concern yourself not!" called Tesla. "Miss Le Breton's opinion of your skill was not without foundation."

Wicko coaxed the Dodo back alongside, aligning the doorway with the opening.

Tesla again stretched across, leg first. One hand on the door jamb, one hand on the aperture framework. Hitched himself sideways then, ducking down, committed his body weight back and through, pulling his trailing leg behind him. Within the tower, the engineer's platform for cleaning and maintenance was firm and solid.

When the undulating breeze allowed, Michael and I carefully passed across the Fugit FlyWheel. Then the Tempus TimeKey. And then – oh, heavens – it was my turn for the leap of faith. More like a shuffle of hope.

With encouragement and careful timing, the experience of stepping across and through was reduced to only stomach-churning terror. A tight squeeze, but I passed across with little in the way of drama, or screaming.

Below, the Garridebs continued their purposeful trudge.

"Wicko!" called Michael. "We're up next!"

~15~

Our dwarfish friend again nudged the Dodo close to the clock face, locked off the Helmswheel and the engine regulators, rolled out of his aeronaut's seat and dropped to the carpet.

"You first, Magister," he insisted. "The skipper's always last to leave his ship."

Michael quickly and smartly slipped across and through, and turned to look back at Wicko, while Nik and I carried the FlyWheel and the TimeKey down to the Clock Room, a floor below. Michael watched as the Dodo pitched and yawed. Wicko tried to step across but his legs weren't long enough. Michael leant from the window, stretching his arms toward the doorway. Then the Dodo started drifting.

"Magister!" yelled Wicko.

Michael shouted "Jump!" Wicko cursed badly. Said he couldn't. Then we heard:

eeeeEEEZZ – WHUMP!

The Dodo bucked violently, as if struck by something.

"What's happening?" screamed Wicko.

"Nothing to worry about, old friend. But they're shooting at us."

Wicko screamed again.

Instinctive human reaction to danger is either 'fight or flight'. Like Michael, Wicko was more inclined to plain and simple 'flight'.

eeeeEEEZZ – WHUMP!

This time the impact shoved the Dodo closer to the dial.

Wicko reached out and leapt. Michael caught his arms. Pulled him in, head and shoulders. Outside, the Dodo took another direct hit and began to plume smoke. She swung her tail out. The nose-cone dropped, raking out the stonework below the dial.

Michael tried to heave Wicko all the way in, but his hips were too generous to squeeze though the frame, leaving his legs outside, dangling and waggling. An easy target for the Garridebs' Pulsas. Michael turned Wicko sideways-on and pulled again. It was like a breach birth as Wicko's belly and buttocks squeezed and squished – and he was delivered.

"Ooh, that's going to need some cream," moaned Wicko, pulling himself to his feet and rubbing his backside. "And I've torn me trousers."

They both chanced a peep out of the window and saw the Dodo spiralling downward. With every turn, her tail sheared great showers of stonework from the tower, tearing silver slivers from her fuselage...

SKREEE! SKREEE! SKREEE!

...until she belly-flopped, mid-spin, onto the grass of Old Palace Yard...

DOOPH!

...and broke her back.

"Blimey, Magister," said Wicko, welling up. "That's the second time I've lost her in a month!"

But Michael was more distracted by the five lines of Garridebs, at least a hundred in number, marching relentlessly across the yard towards the base of the clock tower.

Down in the Clock Room, Tesla and I had already married the cogs of the FlyWheel to those of the Timing Train of Grimthorpe's mechanism. Next came the TimeKey. Nik was thumbing through the enamel number dials, The Horological Settings, scrolling through to the required day, month and year.

It was twenty to six in the evening. Ideal. Between us, Nik and I agreed that being dragged back to 1899 at this time, we could thwart the Brimstone Gas attack on Westminster Abbey and solve myriad problems.

The only sounds were the reassuring, repetitive…

TICK! TICK! TICK!

…as the clock mechanism nudged itself round, cog by cog, in never ending circles, time driven by the…

SWOOSH! SWOOSH! SWOOSH!

…back and forth of the brass pendulum below.

Then came another noise. Just as rhythmic, but harsher. An echo from below getting louder all the time.

CLUMP! CLUMP! CLUMP! CLUMP!

I scrambled out of the Clock Room and peeped down the stairwell. And there they were. Climbing the stairs. More than halfway up. Garridebs. Marching in unison. With relentless, intimidating resolve. I called for Michael and Wicko, wondering what in hell was delaying them.

At the sound of my voice, the march of the feet on the stairs suddenly got faster.

CLUMP! CLUMP! CLUMP! CLUMP!

Finally, Michael was stepping down the stairs from the floor above. He was all but carrying Wicko. "All this living-on-the-edge excitement," said Michael. "I'll never know what Phoebe ever saw in it."

Tesla hit the button to fire up the TimeKey's internal Aethylium Generator. Built to suck the Aethyr from the air and convert it to fierce, clean power. The Garridebs were only a dozen turns from reaching the top of the stairs. Michael and Wicko staggered into the Clock Room.

I slammed the door behind us and grabbed the clock's frame. The noise from the TimeKey built and the wheels on the Timing Train engaged. Turning slowly at first, then gathering speed. And more speed, until blue-grey smoke fumed the smell of burning oil.

I remember Wicko hoping it would work. I remember Nik shouting something like, "Of course it shall work! I am Tesla!"

I remember the Clock Room turning and my legs lifting with the centrifugal force. The noise rising. Then being flung like a rag doll…

…as Garridebs threw open the Clock Room door with a mighty…

CRASH!

~17~

At the Metropolitan Theatre of Steam, Smoke and Mirrors on the Edgware Road, Phoebe Le Breton was sitting in her dressing room, adding a line to her carefully written Commonplace Book of Magister witticisms. Downstairs in the Dungeon, he had quipped: "We had all better remember the first rule of chemistry … Never lick the spoon". Another example of remarkable self-belief masking astonishing naivety. But that was Michael Magister's style. She was still to decide whether or not it was for effect. An attention-seeking affectation.

Phoebe had left Wicko and myself to apply our scientific expertise to the fathomation, as Michael put it, of the chemical formula C4 H8 C12 S.

Phoebe dried the ink with a blotter, clattered down the wooden stairs, then down into the Dungeon, my workshop below the stage.

"How goes the fathomation … gentlemen?"

Oddly, the Dungeon was empty. Michael, Wicko and myself were most certainly not there. She called out. Nothing. She rode the Lift'n'Shift up through the trapdoor onto the stage. She called again. Nothing.

"Is this a new vanishing trick?" she shouted, almost patiently. "Because if so, it is rather convincing!"

Nothing.

"Where are you?"

There was no noise at all backstage. So, Phoebe cranked the Safety Curtain, the Iron, raised it a foot or so, locked it off, shimmied underneath and stood on the lip of the edge, scanning the seats of the auditorium.

Nothing.

She sat on the edge of the platform and swung her legs down. Behind the frosted glass of the Pit Bar to the left she could see a dark figure. Which naturally turned out to be Father Connor O'Connor, perched on a stool, sampling a large whisky in one glass and an even larger 'medicinal' of port and brandy in the other.

"Ah, me lovely," he said guiltily, as Phoebe pushed open the door and looked in. "Am I not just testing the stock here for quality."

"Have you seen them? The Professor, and Wicko? Or Michael?"

"Sure, was not the unholy trinity with you beneath the stage?"

"Precisely what I thought," Phoebe pouted. "But now they appear to have vanished."

"Jasus, sure but they cannot have gone far."

Phoebe did not see it from inside the theatre, but a little more than two miles to the south east, a spectacular Magnetic Time Storm was sparking and crackling above and around the clock faces of Big Ben.

\*\*\*

At the same time in 2001, Wu Hu Phunn was propped up on her bed within the elegant penthouse suite at the Dr Phunn Memorial Medical Facility. She was gazing across the Thames through her vast glazed window. Across to her left she witnessed the fireworks display, spitting and flashing about the clock faces of Big Ben. Heard the great cracks of electrical discharge. Then saw the smoke and sparks sucked viciously back into the clock tower. And all was then silent.

Wu Hu Phunn nodded and moved her mouth as best she could to form the shape of a contented smile.

"Splendid," she whispered to no one.

Then with a final wheeze, her eyes rolled back and her head lulled forward, into a void of perpetual darkness. She never heard the medical alarms repeating and whining.

You know, this was my third experience of being dragged by the scruff through the fabric of time. The second was forward to 2001, and this third shocker, back to 1899. And I still do not have a good word to say about it. Ask Michael and Wicko. I mean, what is to enjoy about being viciously wrenched like a rag doll out of one time. Because that's what it feels like, my friend. You are wrenched at great speed. And that is the best part. Still to look forward to is the numbing chill and the searing heat. The dread of the fall which refuses to end. The blinding visual phantasmagoria of spectrum-split colours burning into the eyes, even when they're closed tight shut.

And then, above all else, there is the noise. That deafening flickering, like a thumb riffling a deck of cards, which speeds to a crescendo, then slows to the rhythmic…

TICK! TICK TICK!

…then, you're slammed down, hard and vicious, and it's done.

And we were definitely done. My joints were complaining and my skin was clammy. The air was musty, made bitter by the whiff of scorched machine oil. Then came that moment of dread. When we opened our eyes.

Into darkness. Then light. Fluttering at first, as the gas jets recovered their flow. The hard yellow glow from above. The dozens of gas jets which shone the reassuring beacon of time across London through those four iconic clock faces towards the top of this symbolic tower. Gas jets! Not Tesla-generated electricity. Tesla's Tempus TimeKey, The Grimm's Fugit Flywheel. I prayed they would deliver us from evil. As much as I pray.

"I still reckon that Necessitti makes this game easier." He was still banging on about that mythical magical orb. "Or that elusive time-tunnel. Not being rude, Nik, but surely that must get you back and forth a lot smoother," said Wicko, still sprawled on his back, panting.

Tesla said nothing.

"*I*, for one, am in no hurry to find out," said Michael, dusting down his trousers, then pulling himself to his feet. "Because *I* am never doing anything like that ever again."

I enquired about Michael's brand-new heart and lungs. How had they stood the test of time? Beating and breathing like he had never known before, came the reply.

I looked across at the great Nikola Tesla, pale-faced and kneeling on jelly legs, while tending his smoking TimeKey as if it were a new-born baby. I thanked him for all he had done.

"It is I who must thank you all, Octopus. But for your company. To take a glimpse of the future by myself? This is a journey I would never have undertaken."

Wicko puffed and pulled himself to his feet and then complained because the vigour of being wrenched back through time had caused the top button of his trousers to pop under the strain. And then he said he was hungry!

"We need to make a move," said Michael. "We've got a future to change."

~19~

At the theatre Phoebe was opening doors on stage cabinets and backstage cupboards, searching for Michael, Wicko and me. "Gentlemen, this comic escapade is beginning to wear thin."

Then a buzzer rasped. And rasped again.

Someone was at the Stage Door. Had Michael and Wicko and I *all* got ourselves locked outside? No, that was a ridiculous thought, all of them knew the pass code.

The buzzer rasped again and again to stress the urgency of the person outside doing the pressing. Phoebe pushed through the Pass Doors into the Stage Door Lobby, fired up the Spectrascope and stared at the fizzing image on the screen. It was a bearded man of a certain age, bald, bent double and gasping and sweating in his waistcoat and shirt. It was no one she recognised. Nor much looked like a bailiff, a debt collector, a Scotland Yardie, or for that matter a fan.

So she leant toward the screen, saying into the TalkiTube: "Good evening. May I help you?"

On the screen, the face looked straight at the bellows camera. "Praise be. Is that the voice of Miss Le Breton?"

"Yes, sir, I am Phoebe Le Breton."

"Miss Le Breton, forgive my angst. My name is William Thomson."

Lord Kelvin!

"Yes, of course. The Professor and Wicko often speak of you."

Phoebe tapped out the code on the qwerty keyboard. The Stage Door had barely clicked open before Lord Kelvin staggered in. "Thank you, thank you, dear young lady, thank you. But if you please, I must speak with Artemus. Or Wicko. With great urgency. I have done a truly terrible thing."

***

Wicko and I followed Michael and Tesla, descending the interminable stairs of the Big Ben clock tower; Lord knows how much I hated those steps, even walking down. By the time we reached the ground floor Wicko and I were desperate for breath. A desperation we quickly lost as soon as we stepped outside and tried. Oh, my Lord, the smell! And the noise. And the thick atmosphere. I promise you, in contrast to what we had become used to, this was like walking into a smoke house.

We all coughed and spluttered on air so claggy that if you breathed in through your mouth too quickly you would most likely chip a tooth.

"That is foul," hacked Wicko. "Rank."

It took a minute to reacclimatise ourselves, to look around. It was dark and grey, with fuzzy pools of orange lighting the way. People, carriages and omnibuses, bustling and busy.

"We're home," smiled Michael.

"We must confirm we have arrived home on the correct date," said Tesla.

A crowd had gathered around the perimeter fence of New Palace Yard and, along with half a dozen police constables, were all still looking upwards, some scratching their heads, discussing the lightning flashes and the fireworks display above and around the clock dials. The Magnetic Time Storm looked spectacular against the dusky backdrop sky.

By the time we reached the exit gate, the debate was in full flow.

"I wager 'twas divine guidance for our representatives therein," I heard a policeman say.

A buxom, well-oiled lady won a chuckle from her immediate crowd when she quipped: "Divine retribution is more as like."

242

Nik Tesla figured she was exactly the person to ask about today's date. While she was still buoyed by the spirited reaction to her remark. Instead, she laughed, and shouted that if this foreign gent did not know what day it was, he was mostly likely a Member of Parliament.

Oh, how they all laughed again.

"First rule of audience management, Nik," whispered Michael. "Never pick a drunk showing off to their friends."

The crowd's gaiety was short-lived when one of the policemen rebuked the lady for disrespecting her betters in Parliament and threatened to cart her off to pokey. Wherever that was. At that moment, another officer was helpfully assuring Michael it was most certainly the twenty-seventh of September, sir, before one of the drunk woman's disgruntled confederates punched the policeman's helmet clean off his bald head.

Belligerent shoving and name calling in and around the crowd quickly became a commotion and escalated to such a fist-flying ruckus that the policemen were required to wave their truncheons and blow their whistles for support.

We all managed to slip quietly away, shortly before the full-scale riot took hold. Oh, it was so much simpler when you could just ask a Garrideb and get a civil answer.

Yes, we were definitely home.

~20~

Above us, the Big Ben chimes began their prelude to ringing out six o'clock. Time was pressing to get to the Abbey. We knew the last time he was there, a century ago, the canister of Brimstone Gas which cost Michael his life had been planted in advance within Westminster Abbey, behind the transept known as Statesman's Aisle. We also knew the Parliamentary Committee discussing the placement of the W. E. Gladstone memorial statue had entered by the North Door.

Nik's presence would complicate matters, requiring further explanation with police, and Wicko and I, even at a brisk waddle, would hold him back, so it seemed prudent for Michael to hurry on ahead. It was from this moment on that the future would change.

The walk across the street and down by St Margaret's Church, even dodging unhelpful traffic, took less than five minutes. As expected, the line of plush carriages with fine horses were parked patiently outside the Great North Door of Westminster Abbey. Above, coloured light flickered from within, through the magnificent stained-glass Rose Window. Someone was home.

As he scurried by, Michael patted one of the pair of horses tethered to the grandest carriage. Still hot.

Michael recalled that Special Branch's Detective Constable Willzen was on sentry duty outside, and sure enough there he was. Still thick-set with thick hair, thick handlebar moustache, but intelligence-wise, not as thick as Detective Constable Beatty. At least Michael could understand Willzen, not like Beatty with his impenetrable "Ay, listen see" accent.

Professional and alert, in his black tailcoat and pinstriped trousers official evening wear, Willzen squinted and strained to see who was striding quickly towards him, before recognising Magister, and holding up a hand.

Michael remembered Willzen's look of bewilderment, but this scene would not play out as before. Last time Michael had Phoebe with him, and they had just crash-landed in an airship.

"Detective Constable Willzen. When did the Prince arrive?" demanded Michael, straight to it.

"The Prince, Magister? I think you might have been overdoin' the Cherry Pectoral, Magister," said Willzen. A reference to a cough mixture for infants brewed from twenty percent alcohol and opium. Very effective apparently. "There's no Prince here tonight, sir. Nothin' happenin' whatsoever in them regards."

"Which is exactly why one of Special Branch's finest is standing outside Westminster Abbey, surrounded by magnificent carriages, because there's nothing happening here whatsoever. And Mr Willzen, if there's nothing happening, you won't object if I straight go in."

"I can't let you do that, Magister," Willzen's arm became a barrier to Michael. "There's no one inside."

"Okay, you see I really do need to go inside and tell everyone they need to get out, because they're in danger if they stay there."

"And why's that?" sighed Willzen

"There's a deadly gas bomb about to be set off."

"Says who?"

Michael looked around, puzzled. "That would be me."

"Do you think they'll listen to a Music Hall turn? I think not."

"I know the Prince of Wales and half the government cabinet are inside right now discussing a statue to William Gladstone, along with Mrs Gladstone, Pym and Melville and a whole bunch of other people I've never heard of."

Willzen could not disguise his amazement that Magister possessed such accurate information that was supposed to be top secret. However, "Can't do it, Magister," was Willzen's decision.

"Perhaps then, Mr Willzen, I can amaze you further by this…"

"A glove?"

Michael had reached in his pocket and grandly produced Phoebe's glove. "Naturally I didn't mean that, what I really meant was – this."

In his less conspicuous hand he held a pack of cards.

With speed and style, Michael pulled the cards from the box, flung the box on the floor and shuffled the cards one-handed. Oh, yes. The old dexterity was back for sure.

"I haven't got no time for no conjuring, Magister."

"That is quite right Mr Willzen, because neither have I."

Michael, with a riffle, then splayed the entire deck in Willzen's face. It never failed. The detective recoiled more in shock than pain, and Michael was in.

CLACK!

The iron latch echoed as the door pushed open, stopping the Prince of Wales's hollering mid-anecdote. In the next moment, the well-to-do semi-circle in their evening finery, pretending to enjoy every word the future King was emoting, turned to face the intrusion of street noise – and saw Michael Magister.

The bearded Lord Salisbury, the baggy-eyed Arthur Balfour, the charming widow Gladstone, the white cassock'd nasty looking Dean and his gaunty-faced assistant, along with the ineffectual Assistant Police Commissioner Sir Cumberland Sinclair, the gloating Inspector Walter Pym and Superintendent William Melville, not to mention the handful of very-important government nobodies, all turned to look. Pym and Melville drew their pistols.

"A tough audience," thought Michael.

"Magister?" said Melville.

"Absolutely, and good evening Mrs Gladstone, Your Royal Highness, Prime Minister, Mr M. and whoever else the rest of you are, I need your attention please. All of you have to…"

CRUMP!

…Constable Willzen barged in from behind and bundled Michael to the marble floor before he could say another word.

~21~

Instantly, Melville pushed through the group to stand himself between the Prince and the 'threat', while pistol-toting Pym rushed forward to help Willzen.

From his awkward, cheek-pinned-against-the-cold-floor position, Michael heard the familiar kerfuffle of 'What the deuce', 'Outrageous interruption', 'Highly irregular', 'Top secret' and, a whispered 'Shit', which this time round convinced him it really was the Dean.

"Threat is restrained, sir," pronounced Pym, dropping to his knees beside Michael.

"Walter. I've missed you."

"Magister," whispered Pym. "Are you off your bonce? Busting in 'ere. That's the Prince over there. And the Prime Minister."

Willzen whispered: "He claims there's a gas bomb in the Abbey, boss."

"A what?" Pym cussed with impatience. "Are you acting the giddy goat?"

"I know. Hard as it is to believe, about the goat thing, whatever that is, all you've got to do is ask yourself this, Walter. Would I really come all this way, so close to show time, if I didn't know there was a gas bomb here? And if you don't believe me, at least let me wait outside. I don't really want to get a face-full of that again."

Melville loomed into view, sideways-on. "Gas bomb, Mr Magister?" he said calmly.

Michael tried to nod. "Only worse. It's Brimstone."

Melville did not react. Instead he ordered Willzen to keep the intruder restrained, then said: "Inspector. With me now, if you please."

Pym stood up and followed Melville.

"Between ourselves, we should really be making a move to the exit," Michael told Willzen.

Then he heard a hubbub of conversation. And several gasps. Then from his next-to-the-floor, sideways-on, dis-advantage point, Michael watched as, he presumed, Melville and Pym swiftly and firmly ushered the Prince of Wales, Mrs Gladstone and the Prime Minister toward the open North door.

"Good evening, Mr Magister," bellowed the Prince of Wales. "Splendid work down there."

"Pleasure, sir."

"I will now invite everybody to vacate the Abbey," announced Melville. "Follow us please. Quietly and calmly."

Michael said to Willzen. "The Superintendent said everybody. I think we're part of 'everybody'."

Willzen generously responded by taking no notice whatsoever.

Michael could only watch the Committee members making their hasty exit to certain safety. A clacking of polished spats, brogues, flapping pinstriped trousers, the tails of their black morning suits. And there! What was that? A fleeting glimpse. Of the puckered black rubber trunking hanging within a coat. The filter of a gas mask. It was the assassin. Foiled, but making his calm escape. Michael strained to lift his head. To see the face. Reveal the identity of the scheming…. Gah. Willzen proved immovable. The moment was lost.

~22~

Michael heard carriages jangling and clattering away. The draught from the open door was starting to chill, and his arms were aching from the weight of his captor's bony knees. Then the door closed with a dull, heavy…

KLUUUM!

"Thank you, Detective Constable Willzen," said Melville's voice. "You may kindly assist Mr Magister to his feet."

Which Willzen duly obliged with much ill grace. "Assaulting a police officer with a deck of playing cards is a serious offence, Magister."

"I wouldn't lean too heavily on that, Willzen. Letting the assassin walk straight out of here trumps anything I did with playing cards," Michael's frustration showed he was past dealing with subordinates. "Mr M., we need to get out there, chase down the assassin. We're looking for a man with a gas mask hidden under his tailcoat."

Melville thought for a moment or two.

"Detective Constable Willzen, you may take yourself outside and with discretion look to see if any gentleman is in possession of such a respirator."

Willzen wanted to protest. Instead he quickly did as he was told.

"Mr Magister. Whence came you to learn of this peril?" Melville's articulation could tend toward the arcane when he was deadly serious.

A good point.

"In addition to my uncanny instinct, and in my capacity as a highly acclaimed consultant to Scotland Yard's Special Branch, I am also trying to develop the skill of psychic prediction."

"Prediction!" scoffed Pym.

"I knew you'd say that, Walter."

"Predict, then if you will Magister, where this alleged gas bomb is supposed to be secreted."

Michael re-ran his death scene, as best he remembered seeing it. During the Prince's speech, the assassin must have slipped away, round the back, pulled on his mask and gloves, snatched up the bomb and then reappeared to throw it into the group.

"Certainly, Walter. It has to be the other side of this wall." Michael pointed to the stone screen on the left, which divided the Statesmen's Aisle from the small enclave of memorial chapels, running off of one another.

"Are we really goin' to hark at this prediction tripe, guv'nor?"

Willzen's return to the Abbey was helpfully timed.

"Sir," he said, not a little sheepish and holding up what looked like a small elephant's face made of black rubber. Two goggle eyes. A long, puckered filter hanging down. Whichever way you looked at it, it was a gas mask. "A uniformed Constable just found this. Lying on the gravel outside."

Melville told Willzen to retain the evidence. "Perhaps Mr Magister's new power of prescience will provide a more precise location for the device."

Michael applied a magician's logic. If you planted a bomb to throw at your target, it would need to be hidden, but fast and easy to access.

To the left, beside the North Transept, as you will see when you visit the Abbey, stands The Chapel of St John the Evangelist, almost claustrophobic with grey and brown gothic or classical statuary, brass inscription plates and slabs, naming the gone but almost forgotten.

But without doubt, in the St Michael's Chapel, off St John's, the most dramatic shrine is dedicated to the late Lady Elizabeth Nightingale – no relation. This elaborate memorial, really worth a look, stands at least ten feet tall, and depicts the manic, hooded skeleton of Death emerging from his gated prison, aiming to plunge his spear upwards into the heart of Lady Elizabeth, who lies slumped and dying in the arms of her horrified husband, who despite being a vicar's son tries in vain to ward off the stroke of death.

"Inspector Pym. You might want to look into Death's cabinet," said Michael, pointing to the only out-of-the-way real hidey hole in the chapel.

Pym looked at Melville who nodded his approval. So the Special Branch Inspector hitched his trousers, crouched and positioned himself awkwardly between the bony knees of Death, peering awkwardly into the black void beyond the gaping, iron gates. A waste of time, he thought. He reached blindly inside and felt around. No. Wait. Damn. There was something. Pym hooked his arm around. And gently withdrew a grubby knapsack.

"Unless that's Mr Death's lunch…" said Michael.

Pym eased open the flap of the bag and peered inside. He inclined the bag to Melville. Inside: the glint of a stubby silver cannister-bomb. As predicted.

"…my work here is done," said Michael.

"Indeed," said Melville.

"No, I mean really done," said Michael. He was firm and adamant. "After all this and everything else that's happened, I quit."

"This ain't exactly the time, Magister," said Pym, nervously.

"Inspector. This is exactly the right time. Because there's something very wrong when your consultant is being held down to the floor while the assassin who planned to use that," he pointed to Pym's bag of death, "walks straight out. If no one's listening, what's the point? It's what Pheebs would do. Inspector Pym. Superintendent Melville."

Michael turned and walked quickly out of the Abbey.

"Oh, and good luck with Greenwich."

His echoing voice was followed by the echoing…

CLACK!

…of the Great North Door.

Michael emerged from the Abbey alone, happy to leave this time alive. The official broughams were long gone. Only Coxhead, the driver of the Special Branch carriage remained. Along with an anxious Nikola Tesla.

Wicko and I were out on the street, waiting in Hansoms, ready to trundle west to The Metropolitan Theatre of Steam, Smoke and Mirrors.

Half an hour later, and with much relief, we entered by the Stage Door to find Lord Kelvin and Phoebe waiting for us in the lobby. It was ten minutes before show time. And neither looked impressed.

In fact, for effect, Phoebe pouted and folded her arms. Before demanding: "And where do you think you have all been for the last two hours?"

*"Time, the devourer of things."*
*Ovid 43BC-AD17*
~PART FIVE~

## 1

"Hello ... Dr Tesla, I presume," Phoebe had said, peering round at the thin man with the jet-black hair and sharp moustache half hiding behind Michael and myself.

"I have that honour, Miss Le Breton," Nik had said, shyly.

"My, this will take some explaining," she had said.

Lord Kelvin's concern over the volume of deadly Brimstone Gas he had distilled under duress, was relieved by Michael's news of the discovery of the cannister bomb. And Phoebe's ire rapidly turned to admiration upon the news of Michael thwarting the plot to murder the Prince of Wales and half the Government at Westminster Abbey, and then resigning their positions as police consultants! She could not have been more proud.

"And there's just a little more you should know…" admitted Michael.

***

Quite how Michael managed two performances that evening was a testament to his stagecraft, experience, self-belief, muscle memory, his perfectly functioning respiratory system and utter relief at being home to avert Phoebe's brutal death.

The timing on 'The Steam Saw of Gore' could have been tighter and the Saw itself a little less close, but the crowds were satisfied that their usual money's worth had been had.

In fact, all night, only one loudmouth required the: "Sir, if ignorance is bliss, then why do you look so miserable?" treatment.

But once the metalised final curtain had slammed down and the floating green skull had gargled its usual caution to the crowd to "Stay safe and keep an ever-watchful eye over your shoulder. Does the Goddess walk amongst us at will?", we repaired to the Pit Bar.

But with Michael's adrenalin spent, and Wicko and I jellied with time-lag, it was Nikola Tesla who regaled Phoebe, Lord Kelvin and the slack-jawed Father Connor O'Connor with an unembroidered description of the future we had enjoyed, or endured, for the past few weeks.

Kelvin nodded wisely, satisfied his oft-shared concerns for a possible future were not without foundation. Connor liberally toasted his role as the de facto Pope with delight. "Ah. The lineage of the Iscariots is vindicated," he said, before sliding off his stool.

Phoebe sat quietly listening throughout.

Nik's account kindly omitted the shameful eagerness with which Wicko and myself embraced the 'additional' benefits that the future with the Garridebs had to offer. And in the matter of the Montague Mansions Massacre, where Phoebe herself, along with Dr Joseph Bell, Arthur Conan Doyle and Miss Jean Leckie all perished, he was wisely coy. Such details, as you have discovered, were for, and of, another time.

At the end of the Tesla testament, Phoebe's summation was of perfectly measured surprise. "Well, gentlemen, it strikes me that your gallivant offered you a unique experience of a future which, after tonight's high jinks at Westminster Abbey, now no longer exists," said Phoebe. "None of it happened."

"So long as we remain disciplined and diligent," warned Kelvin.

"Bustards, denying a man his rightful place as Pontiff..." whispered a disappointed Connor, from the floor.

"Pheebs, I know it's a lot to believe," said Michael.

She frowned. "Why would I doubt you? To begin with, I do not need to see the SteamMark VI Garridebs to know they exist, loitering behind the Dungeon in some hidden lair."

She admitted she could never fathom how Wicko and I could be responsible for constructing all the elaborate Contrivances and the obscure modes of transportation, the Steamo and the Dodo, which governed our lives, without assistance. Especially as we were hardly built like the famous German strongman Eugen Sandow. But, you know, she put it so politely we could hardly take offence. Well, Wicko huffed a bit.

"I believe you totally and absolutely because we agreed we would keep no secrets from one another, and because I love and trust you, and take you at your word."

Such faith made us all feel better.

Until she added, "And frankly, how *else* could you two have put on quite so much weight in such a short space of time?"

## 2

RAP! RAPPITY RAP!

The pudgy fingers were heavy-handed, if that makes sense, on the brass door knocker. At that time of night it could have been construed as disturbing the peace of London's most well-to-do South Kensington square. But the hefty, pig-faced oaf would never have considered such social courtesy.

In his capacity as an undertaker, presently unemployed, Mr Drago, had fumbled and dropped many a coffin during many a funeral and then turned on protesting mourners with flying fists and boots. An edifying send-off for the dearly departed such behaviour did not make. Memorable yes, but not edifying. Little wonder in the world's most consistently busy profession, Mr Drago found himself unemployed. Along with his associate Mr Skrill. Both were, however, God-fearing folk, and currently enjoying a period of gainful employment as professional thugs and murderers to the crazed catechist colloquially known at The Black Bishop.

"Late, hnur-hnur-hnur," grunted Drago, referring to the hour.

"But a visitation demanded of our Excellency," whined his shrew-faced, hand-wringing, flowery-tongued partner.

Eventually, the front door was opened by the stooped, aged, shuffling, slightly deaf and shortly-sighted butler. Pockney.

Drago and Skrill were dressed almost identically to the old chap, except their shirts and suits would have looked sharper for a scrub with a sponge and a press with a flat iron.

The smaller, thinner, pointy-faced half of the visiting pair removed his battered top hat with an exaggerated flourish. The bigger, porcine lout copied the example but with less aplomb.

"My man, we are in receipt of this urgent missive requesting our presence at this most gracious residence."

Skrill waved the crumpled telegram at Pockney with unwarranted distain. Pockney insisted on carefully examining the note, holding a pair of pince-nez between his watery eyes and the message. The order read: "HERE. IMMEDIATELY", and gave the Onslow Square address.

"And having thus satisfied yourself as to the veracity of this document," sneered Skrill, "perchance you might, without further ado, inform the sender of the aforesaid communiqué, to wit, your master and our excellency, of our presence, as demanded. My man."

"Marnded, hnur-hnur-hnur," agreed Drago.

"Of courst, gentlemen. Please enter and kindly wait-th in the Reading Room."

"Thank you, most civil, my man," smirked Skrill, as Pockney let them inside, bowed and set about their bidding.

The hall was floored in tiny white tiles patterned with a recurring black mosaic design. If you knew what you were looking for you *might* have have recognised the image as a 'christogram': a sun circle emitting rays of light, while enclosing a crucifix and depicting the letters I H S, all picked out in black. Drago and Skill blessed themselves.

To the left, off the hall, the Reading Roomwas dark and vast. A huge bay window with the heavy curtains still drawn against the insipid dawn. Pools of light glowed from half a dozen black candles on tall brass candlesticks.

Drago and Skrill had never before witnessed a room like it. Not that Drago had ever before set foot in a Reading Room, possessing neither the inclination nor indeed the ability to anything associated with reading. But this Reading Room appeared utterly unique in that it apparently contained not a single book. The walls were lined from floor to ceiling with mahogany shelves where books should have stood and might well stand one fine day. But at the moment the room was bereft of literature. In the centre stood a wooden lectern, set before the grand marble fireplace upon which laid a stout, leather-bound Holy Bible, its covers closed, secured with two brass latches.

"An interesting seat of learning, Mr Drago," said Skrill looking about.

"Learnin', hnur-hnur-hnur," he agreed.

The wait was a while before the door to the Reading Room swung open and, with calm purpose, in strode the tall imposing monkish figure, clad in a black habit with the hood swung up over the head, revealing nothing of his features save for the length of black beard which hung down to the waist. Drago and Skill both dropped to their knees, blessing themselves in supplication.

"My lambs," growled the Black Bishop. "My chosen apostles. I commend your prompt attendance. And how you have thus far served me."

"We pray the foul Antichrist Prince of Wales and his heretic government writhed in agony and now lie dead courtesy of the Brimstone Gas, Excellency," simpered Skrill.

"Gazzzn, hnur-hnur-hnur," said Drago.

"The unholy filth still live," growled the Bishop, furiously. "All of them."

"But-but, Excellency, might one be so bold as to enquire how such circumstances prevailed?"

"Magister! The perverse Music Hall conjurer. Who disclosed knowledge. Of the existence of the cannister bomb."

"But-but, Excellency, Mr Drago and I find ourselves at a loss for words," said Skrill. But not so much that he could not prattle on: "How came this repugnant peacock to be cognizant of such a secret?"

"Betrayal, my lambs! I was betrayed!"

Skrill suddenly felt a cold chill. And did not much care for the direction in which the conversation might now be heading. Especially when the Black Bishop drew a long straight sword from behind the lectern, wielding the blade two-handed, aloft.

"Excellency, in the name of the blessed Almighty," gabbled Skrill as both men made the sign of the cross, "be assured of our fealty to you and your righteous cause. I would never express such craven sacrilege and Mr Drago possesses little facility to express much of anything at all."

"Be assured, my lambs, I acknowledge that your loyalty to our cause knows no bounds. I must suspect the heretic scientist. Kelvin."

Skrill breathed a sigh of relief. Of course! And with The Black Bishop correctly spitting the blame in the direction of the noble scientist, both supplicants felt they had dodged a blade. Until their bearded master laid the sword on the shoulder of Skrill.

"The heathen who escaped. From your clutches."

Drago and Skrill shared a terrified look. They knew they were dead.

The Black Bishop raised the blade, saying, "But we must now bide our time, my lambs. Consider a fresh course. The unholy Prince of Wales shall die in penitent pain and suffering. And the Magister and his slattern shall be cast into the fires of hell. Until then we must bide our time. Await a new opportunity."

The sword swung. Sliced clean through the stand of the lectern. The heavy Bible dropped like a stone to the floor. But was caught by Drago.

Both men thought they glimpsed a smile in the dark recesses of The Black Bishop's hood, as he growled, "Excellent. Your faith is most humbling."

~3~

Of course, with the timeline so completely redrawn, who could ever have predicted the great man of science Professor Lord Kelvin of Largs and our profane priest Connor O' Connor would find anything in common and bond so completely. I expect that both men surviving violent abductions at the hands of psychopaths had something to do with it. But in comparing ordeals and descriptions of their respective captors, it became clear that the mastermind behind the recent Brimstone Gas plot, in both its incarnations, was the character who had become our nefarious nemesis – the 'bustard Jebbi' as coined by Connor with such eloquence – the Black Bishop.

In Connor's case, you may remember from my first volume, the Black Bishop's confederate, Special Branch's Inspector Skindrick, was captured and hanged. But according to Kelvin's experience, the renegade high cleric had now recruited a duo of supplicants with infinitely more zeal. And they remained at large, to plot their next atrocity.

Most importantly, Michael, Wicko and I could all rest easy in the knowledge that Phoebe's continued life was assured because 'The Montague Mansions Massacre' had now never happened.

For all of us, the next few weeks of restorative peace and quiet at The Metropolitan Theatre of Steam, Smoke and Mirrors back here in 1899 were particularly welcome. Save for our sudden celibacy, of course.

Dr Phunn's Carnival of Mechanical Miracles had vacated Regents Park, sailed the English Channel and were making tracks to Paris with a carefully laid plan to hit another jackpot by cracking the safe of the Societe Generale Bank on the Rue de Provence.

Nikola Tesla was bound for the US aboard the RMS Lucania. His experience with us had convinced him that the cut-throat scientific world of New York was far preferable and more sedate than life in London, present or future. He left promising to speak with us via the Psyke communicator whenever we needed. He even presented Phoebe with a parting gift. From scratch, he rebuilt his Aethyr-charging lady's fan. You will remember, a few cooling flutters of the fan generates enough Aethyr charge to flatten an ox. She was just as thrilled as the first time Tesla presented that particular weapon, although she did not know it.

Lord Kelvin had also found his time in the capital far too exhilarating for his seventy-six-year-old bones, and headed back to Glasgow where I was sure he was still lying in a darkened room, in his house on Professor's Square at the University of Glasgow.

\*\*\*

Down at the Royal Observatory, Greenwich, the Astronomer Royal, Mr William Christie, announced the name of his new Assistant. It would be that diligent and dedicated member of staff Goronwy Dapper. Christie had fully anticipated the hectoring he received, not from the other candidate, Ronathan Chafeskin, but from his harridan wife, Eadie Chafeskin. What William Christie did not expect was that the striving Mrs Chafeskin would seek celestial guidance concerning her husband's career from a long-dead astrologer.

And although Arthur Doyle, along with Arthur Morrison and Father Connor O'Connor now had no need to visit Cordelia Ravenport to enquire about the likelihood of Michael's return, Eadie and Ronathan still attended the séance. They spoke with the spirit guide soothsayer Nostradamus and Eadie and Ronathan Chafeskin still set in train a series of events which culminated in bizarre, agonised tragedy.

\*\*\*

Standing outside the Altazimuth Pavilion, with Ronathan Chafeskin's blinded and broken body still warm, slumped on the stairs inside, Cordelia Ravenport felt compelled to return to

Ormiston Road and dispense with the newly widowed Mrs Chafeskin. She was a loose end which needed to be tied off.

"Oh, my dear, what an infuriating oversight," said Cordelia. "Vengeance clouded our thinking."

"No! Ssss," said Nostradamus, nowhere and everywhere. "The Chafeskin mare liesssss trembling in her bed. She beginsss the dessss-cent into in-sssanity … which shall be compounded when she learnssss of her husss-bandsss death."

***

The elite of the Special Branch had been ordered to Greenwich to investigate two deaths in quick succession at the Royal Observatory. The Commissioner of Police, Sir Edward Bradford, and the Astronomer Royal, William Christie, demanded assurance that there was no sinister plot to undermine the fine work of the world's leading astrological institution. And while Superintendent Melville and Inspector Pym were satisfied that there was no dire conspiracy afoot, the fact that both Goronwy Dapper and Ronathan Chafeskin had died alone of unnatural causes and behind locked doors gave Melville's belly a tweak.

There was doubt enough to call upon his specialist Scotland Yard Consultants to confirm nothing was amiss.

As they descended the grassy slope to their waiting carriage, Pym had reminded the Superintendent that their Consultants were now no longer inclined to assist the Special Branch.

"Of that, Walter," said Melville, slowly turning to face his colleague, "I would not be so certain. There is always a way."

~4~

Wicko and I were not only working on our waistlines with a pitiless culinary regime designed by Phoebe, we were also building and perfecting a new illusion. It was on the third night since our return that Michael and Phoebe felt confident enough to include the new variation on a transposition theme in the show. Appropriately named, under the circumstances, I thought…

"Ladies and gentlemen," announced Michael to the audience, "The Steam Digester!"

He swept the blue cloth from the tall upright cabinet: comprising four glass sheets set within wooden frames painted silver and weathered to resemble metal.

"Invented in the late seventeenth century by Denis Papin, a pupil of the great Robert Boyle and Robert Hooke – all save him – the purpose of this Contrivance was to remove fat … from bone."

Phoebe took up the narrative: "The intense pressure of the steam removes more than fat, it digests the flesh, leaving bones picked white … and clean. So tonight, I, Phoebe, the Queen of Steam and Goddess of the Aethyr, shall not only revive this vicious practice and the scalding science involved. No, this evening I shall tame the merciless powers of the Steam Digester!"

"You don't need no fat removed, girl, just your clothes!" hollered an uncouth admirer.

"I see sir is a fleshy gentleman himself," said Phoebe, pointing a gloved hand directly at the man. He *was* well covered. "Magister and I would certainly invite you up to try the experiment for yourself, but unless you have brought a large pat of butter for your hips, we could never squeeze you inside the Digester."

The crowd liked that. Even the fleshy butt of the joke laughed, stood and gestured salacious gyrations in Phoebe's direction with his girth.

Michael stepped forward. "But as you quite rightly say, sir, the Goddess has no need to step into the Contrivance. And such is my trust in her mighty powers, tonight I shall be defying the Steam Digester!"

The lights crashed to darkness. The key light pierced the gloom and pooled over the Digester and its immediate surroundings, into which stepped Phoebe.

"Before I commence to tame the power of the steam, I must command the Magister to … remove his clothes!"

Well, you can imagine the drunken reaction that statement won from the crowd. Especially when Michael really did step out of the darkness into the light. None of your leopard-skin strongman leotards here. This was bare, naked flesh. Well, except for a towel wrapped around his waist. Cream coloured. Michael posed, flexing whatever he could and the audience cheered and whistled.

"Phoebe, magic that towel be gone!" and "Give us a wave of his wand!" and other bawdy witticisms were yelled by the female element of the audience, invariably followed by shrieks of ribald cackling.

But even Phoebe, when she first saw Michael bare-chested yesterday afternoon during the rehearsal, had to admit to being quietly impressed. The sun of the twenty-first century had kissed more than his cheeks and not an inch of post-surgical scar tissue could be seen.

"And, ladies and gentlemen, I trust you to not say a word to the Lord Chancer," Michael told the crowd. The Earl of Halsbury was the Lord Chancellor and the nation's censor. "He takes a dim view of flesh."

"And a well-lit view whenever he gets the chance," tagged Phoebe.

More raucous joy at the expense of authority.

Phoebe sauntered and slunk around Michael, trailing a gentle gloved finger across his chest and around his back. More cheers and lewd hilarity. Even Wicko thought it was a little racy and far sassier than any Debbi could ever have managed. It quite made him realise how life in the future was so superficial and unemotional in comparison. But still nice work if you could get it.

Phoebe waved an arm, demanded silence – and got it – before declaring, "Ladies and gentlemen. Because the agony of the scalding steam is so intense, I now command the Magister to – sleep!"

Another elegant wave of a gloved hand was all the power the Goddess required to close Michael's eyes and drop his head to one side.

Phoebe hinged open the glass front of the Digester, guided the 'fluenced magician into the tank and turned him to face the audience. With seductive eloquence she explained how and why she was hoisting both his arms and handcuffing his wrists to the shackles dangling from the roof of the excarnating Digester. The Goddess then stepped out of the Contrivance and...

SLAM!

...the door was shut tight and latched.

"I summon the principal vital element within my power – I call upon scalding, flesh eating Steam! Vaporem invoco!"

And sure enough, steam did come forth. But only when, beneath the stage, I wheeled open the appropriate valve and released a spiteful...

HISSSSS!

...of blistering white steam which clouded upwards from a dozen nozzles.

As soon as the glass front and two side panels had fogged and Phoebe had commanded "Enough!", I closed off the valve.

"I must now warn you, ladies and gentlemen, the Digester knows no mercy. So prepare yourselves. Vapor abi!"

I fired up the extraction pumps, which sucked the mist from the tank ... the rivulets streamed down the glass ... Phoebe hauled open the door to reveal...

"The Digested Magister!"

The skeleton was bleached white. Devoid of flesh. The jawbone gaped slack from the skull, the eye sockets glared deep and dark, the nasal triangle, the arms stretched upward, hanging only by the handcuffs while the knees buckled with no muscle to support them. Only the damp towel remained intact, now preserving the modesty of Michael's pelvis.

Heads swam and oaths cursed as Phoebe let the crowd take in the full horror of the image. The commotion continued for a full fifteen seconds before she then...

SLAM!

...swung shut the door, a punctuation point which immediately refocussed the crowd's attention upon her.

"I ask every man, woman and child here tonight: do you wish to see him restored?"

Always a dangerous question, but under these circumstances the cheer was positive.

"Be assured. Only I, the Queen of Steam and Goddess of the Aethyr, can restore the corporeal body of the illusionist. Only I can return the Magister!"

"I love that no one has time to question how the towel survives," Michael said to me, standing beneath the stage, in the Dungeon, waiting for the precise moment to rise on the Lift-n-Shift and swap places with the shellac skeleton. Yes, it was a flaw in the presentation, but then deep down does the crowd really buy the idea of Michael being Disgested? It was a bit of Old Madam. A diversion from the reality of their lives.

From above, we heard the slightly dampened voice of Phoebe declaiming the convincing Latin, "Vaporem invoco!", my cue to re-release the valve wheel.

HISSSHHH!

The cloud of vapour surged upward, again apparently filling the Digester in that moist white cloud, while simply coating the surface of the glass.

"Enough! Vapor abi!"

Again, the steam was sucked from the tank. Phoebe flung open the door. "Ladies and gentlemen, the Regurgitated – Magister!"

And naturally there he was. Body and soul, still shackled to the roof of the Digester, his towel around his waist. The ladies stood and whistled while Michael posed and flexed.

"Regurgitated?" said Michael, as he and Phoebe took their bows. "That may need a re-write."

The next morning came the official knock on the Stage Door.

Wicko saw the face on the Spectrascope. Inspector Pym.

"I need to come in," said the Special Brancher. "The Lord Chancellor has issued a writ." He held said writ up to the bellows camera. Folded sheets of officialdom. "He is closing down your show."

~5~

Michael and Phoebe arrived at the theatre faster than Pym or Wicko and I could have imagined. Neither of them pleased. Least of all Phoebe, sporting what Michael called 'her resting bitch face'.

Had some petty prude reported the Steam Digester illusion to the Lord Chancellor's office and the ban-order been quickly issued?

No. Too quickly. It was more as if the Special Branch had secreted one of their number, maybe even Beatty or Willzen, among the audience, simply and eagerly awaiting the inevitable transgression.

We had settled the Inspector in the Stage Door Lobby. Sitting around Wicko's Stage Door Lobby desk. You see, with Michael and Phoebe no longer officially involved with the Special Branch, we saw the need for only perfunctory courtesy.

"What is the bargain here, Inspector Pym?" said Phoebe, oozing vitriol. "'Oh, Special Branch can magically intervene on your behalf, Miss. Ensure that judgement vanishes with the wave of a police truncheon, in return for your help in another crime which once again has us plain baffled'?. Well, shame on you, Walter Pym. And your coercion." She flung the writ back at the Inspector. "And kindly tell His Lordship, he can be damned and send us all to gaol."

Ah! Yes. Well. Steady on a minute, Phoebe, was my thought. Along with Wicko and Michael. Even Pym was taken aback when her ooze of vitriol quickly became a torrent.

"This will be about those deaths," said Michael quietly. "Down at Greenwich Observatory."

Pym sat up, intrigued. "You mentioned Greenwich the other night."

"Am I right?"

Pym admitted Michael was perfectly right, but demanded to know how? How did Magister know there was an incident of some curiosity thereabouts?

"I also told you at the Abbey, in addition to my uncanny instinct, I'm developing the skill of − 'psychic prediction'." Michael sharpened the vowels to great effect.

It was the words 'psychic prediction' which prompted Phoebe to give him one of her "Excuse me?" looks.

"Can we see the file you have hidden under your overcoat?"

Pym slid the manilla file across the polished Stage Door Lobby desk. Phoebe stopped the docket with a gloved hand. The cover bore the embossed portcullis emblem of the Police of the Metropolis. The words TOP SECRET were angled in red across the page.

She immediately slid the file back to Pym.

He looked perplexed. "You are not going to read it?"

"It is of no interest what this inexplicable curiosity might be," glared Phoebe, whose demeanour then softened to resigned indignation. "However. If our assistance keeps the show from closing…"

"I'll get the Steamo," smiled Michael.

## 6

The eight-mile run to Greenwich required enormous shoving and pushing and swerving of The Steamo across almost all the busiest roads in London. Wicko said it would be a bugger. Which is why Phoebe insisted on driving and Michael was seconded to reading the map, while Pym was made to sit behind.

The route took them south over Westminster Bridge, past 'The Canterbury Musical Hall', its tall and narrow façade smudged and blackened by filthy smoke, then right, along the elegant tree-lined tramway that was St George's Road, past the palatial colonnaded 'Bethlem Royal Hospital Lunatic Asylum' there on the right, all but opposite the smaller Georgian-built 'Asylum for the Indigent Blind'.

"One thing about these Victorians," thought Michael. "They tell it like it is."

With intrepid determination, Phoebe tamed the haphazard crossways at Elephant and Castle, then guided the Steamo along the New Cross Road, another free-running tree-lined tramway, which took an easy bend south, avoiding the pubic urinal built in the centre of the street, onto the Old Kent Road and past the very grand three-storey 'Asylum for the Deaf and Dumb', there, on the corner of Mason Street.

She continued following the tram tracks scored into the tarmac, past where the trees thinned and the traffic thickened, across the bridge over the narrow sludgy Surrey Canal which served a clutch of whiffy bankside factories: the 'Hair and Felt Works', the 'Soap Works', the 'Grease and Disinfectant Works' and the 'Glue and Size Works'. Each of them topped with belching chimneys.

Oh, and not forgetting the eight giant roundel gasometers which rose up from the 'South Metropolitan Gasworks' nearby, while a little further on to the right, on the corner with Gervase Street, stood the substantial 'Tramway Horse Stables', which added further flavour to the heady cocktail of appalling odours. And which served to explain why there were so few trees capable of growing alongside these particular streets.

The excursion continued under the brick-arched South London Line Railway Bridge, with the Old Kent Road Railway Station up on the embankment to the right, which stood beside the 'Royal Bleaching and Cleaning Works' – Royal, mind – which accounted for the sudden and welcome sharpness in the air. Handy too for the enormous 'South Eastern Fever Hospital', set just behind the terrace of Georgian villas on the left.

The New Cross Road eased left, then over the Deptford Bridge crossing the Ravensbourne River and a gentle right-hand bend which leads onto Blackheath Road where the open countryside – finally! – beckons.

The experience of enduring such a vibrant mix of appalling stenches prompted Michael to question Pym's investigation into the foiled Westminster Abbey assassination.

"Any clues on the gas mask you found?"

"Not a one."

Hmm.

"But we know someone at the meeting carried the mask, which has to mean they were the killer."

"Yeah, all of those people are high-ranking pillars of society," scoffed Pym. "Giant cogs in the engine of Empire, if you will."

"All the more reason to suspect them, Inspector," sniffed Phoebe. "And for you to share their identities."

Confidentiality only appertained prior to the meeting, thought Pym, who then named: "Royal Highness, the Prince of Wales; Lord Salisbury, the Prime Minister; the Superintendent and meself. The four of us can be discounted, being the first four to vacate the Abbey once Magister started the commotion. Let me see, who else? There was Mr Gladstone's widow…"

"We can strike her off the list," said Michael, "on the grounds she is a woman, and the gas mask I saw was tucked up inside a coat, not a crinoline."

"There was the Dean of Westminster and his assistant."

"Strike through those. I saw their white dresses."

"Michael, you saw their surplices," said Phoebe.

"I didn't get *that* good a view."

She screwed up her nose for trotting straight into that.

Pym continued chalking off his list of players: "Assistant Police Commissioner Sir Cumberland Sinclair; the First Lord of the Treasury, Mr Arthur Balfour; the Home Secretary, Sir Matthew Wright Ridley; the First Commissioner of Works, Mr Aretas

Akers-Douglas; and the secretary of the Political Monuments Committee, Sir Goliath Meatus."

Michael thought for a moment. And not specifically about that particular name. No, the one he meant was 'Mr Aretas Akers-Douglas'.

"All of those we can discount," suggested Pym.

"That's twelve," said Michael. "Twelve people."

"And?" asked Pym.

"And – from my uncomfortable sideways vantage point, pinned on the floor, I very definitely counted thirteen. Thirteen people walked past me on the way out. It strikes me you have an extra pair of pinstriped trousers and shiny black brogue shoes you can't account for."

If Magister was correct and given his irritating knack for such details there was every reason to believe he was, the Special Branch's much vaunted security had been thwarted. That kind of embarrassment would not please the old man, thought Pym.

On the plus side, it was unlikely that any of those named would be the traitor, with the guilt resting squarely on the shoulders of the mysterious gate crasher. Pym tried hard to relive the scene, to picture the assassin, but the images in his mind's eye would never be as vivid as Magister's.

"And what of the basement laboratory in Tottenham Court Road?" asked Phoebe. "Where Lord Kelvin was held captive?"

"Yielded nothing, Miss," said Pym. "The address had been rendered spotless."

"But surely Lord Kelvin's description of his captors was sufficiently detailed?"

"We ascertained the kidnappers were ugly beggars, the pair of them," said Pym.

"Which points the finger of suspicion away from you and me, Inspector," said Michael.

Pym would never admit to pride in flattery from Magister. But nevertheless...

Onwards the Steamo chugged through the freshness of Shooter's Hill, and that great green expanse of Black Heath.

"Turn right into Charlton Way," said Michael. "Arriving at your destination on the left."

## 7

The southern entrance to the Greenwich Park, one hundred and eighty acres of greenery, was marked by the Blackheath Gate, which opens onto Blackheath Avenue, running north toward the Thames, straight and true right to the doorstep of the Royal Observatory.

Do not listen to what others claim. It was Robert Hooke, all save him, who in 1675 selected this position on the site of the old Greenwich Castle, in response to Charles II's desire to set up a research establishment dedicated to 'rectifying the Tables of the Motions of the Heavens, and the places of the fixed Stars, so as to find out the so much desired Longitude of Places for perfecting the art of Navigation'. Which was a flowery royal way of saying 'Let us do something to assist our courageous men at sea to find out where the devil they are'.

It was Robert Hooke who designed the first observatory, with the assistance of Christopher Wren, and it Robert Hooke who should have been appointed the very first 'Royal Astronomical Observator'. But the usual gossip and conspiracy prevailed, and the role was slipped-on-the-sly to the Assistant to the Committee, one John Flamsteed, a pouting sour-face from Derbyshire, with a flamboyant wig of overly powdered curls. Apparently the only good thing to be said of the man was that his wife Margaret was worse. But I am biased. And in spite of this slight, it was Robert Hooke who was invited to source and install the astronomical equipment for the Observatory before Flamsteed took up his position.

The original observatory-cum-residence, now called Flamsteed House, was an impressive octagonal and turreted building, all red brick and white stone quoins, with its north side looking out at the Thames.

Improvements to the Observatory buildings were constructed to the south, including a domed edifice known as the Great Equatorial Building, built forty years ago, housing what was billed as the largest telescope in the British Empire.

Phoebe told Michael that the two most recent stargazing constructions, both still further to the south, were equally grand.

One, a substantial red brick and terracotta building topped with a grey dome and known as the New Physical Building, was almost complete. The other, the far smaller Altazimuth Pavilion, was already operational and already possessed a history of grisly death not normally associated with the science of astronomy.

It was outside this beautifully symmetrical structure that Phoebe drew the hissing Steamo to a halt, just behind Melville's police carriage. Driver Sergeant Coxhead, all long dark shoulder cape and neck muffler, was brushing the black backs of the two snorting geldings to a glistening shine. The breeze scything up from the river was keen and did nothing for Coxhead's notorious nasal soreness.

"Good morning, Mr Coxhead!" called Phoebe, from the driving bench while removing her driving goggles.

The driver tipped his bowler and told her the Superintendent was waiting inside. Pym pressed the case file into Phoebe's hand, announcing he would wait outside.

The Altazimuth Pavilion, built in red brick and dressed with terracotta, was simply a decagonal two-storey construction supporting a large grey dome. Two tall rectangular entrance halls were keyed onto the building front and back, north and south. The word 'ALTAZIMUTH' was carved neat and large into the terracotta lintels above both doors.

"A great architect," said Michael. "Mexican."

Phoebe patiently indulged him. As an illusionist working with props, she knew full well that Michael was aware of the 'altazimuth mount' and its properties of varying and supporting the aspect of an instrument along the vertical and horizontal axes. My apologies for troubling you with the technical vernacular.

As they walked, Phoebe made no effort to read the file Pym had given her. "Oh, tell me, Great Psychic Predictor. With your uncanny knowledge from the twentieth century, can we quickly conclude this case and return to the theatre?"

Michael cast his mind back to the reports of the Greenwich crime he had read in the future. So to speak. "The case was never solved. But Mr M was always convinced there was foul play."

"Foul play?" William Melville was suddenly standing in front of them. Overcoat buttoned to the neck; he too tipped a polite bowler. "Miss, Le Breton, Mr Magister, why would you think that?"

"Why else would you confect such an elaborate blackmail ploy to assign us the case?" sniped Phoebe.

"And two astronomers from the same world-famous observatory dead within days of each other? If that isn't foul play…" Michael said, "it deserves to be."

~8~

Melville led them single file into the Pavilion.

They were met by a man standing just inside. A big, dark haired fellow in coarse, brown overalls and a woollen workwear donkey jacket.

"Mr Nigel Donaldson is the Porter here at the Greenwich Observatory. It was he who discovered both bodies. Goronwy Dapper at his home, and Ronathan Chafeskin here in the Pavilion."

Michael and Phoebe expressed both their pleasure at meeting Mr Donaldson and their sympathy at his ordeals.

"It was you who broke the window to gain access?" asked Michael.

The ground-floor room within the Pavilion was a circular space, well-lit by the eight Georgian sash windows encompassing the room. Michael had noted that one of the small panes was neatly sealed with newspaper. A temporary patch. And a point of entry.

Nigel Donaldson looked awkward. "I admit to administering the necessary brute-force entry, which is becoming something of a habit, madam and sirs." His voice was of a baritonal persuasion.

"Mr Donaldson," said Melville, "please be so kind as to inform the Astronomer Royal that the Police Consultants have arrived."

Nigel Donaldson said he would do so straight away, bowed and scurried out.

"If Mr Donaldson is on your list of possible suspects, Mr M, you should take him straight off," said Michael.

"Mr Magister, at this stage I am disinclined to rule out anyone," said Melville, quietly. "Not least the man who was present when both bodies were discovered."

"Trust me, Mr M," said Michael, scanning the Pavilion. "That man is not involved."

"And your reasoning for this?"

"He's too nice. Far too nice."

"I shall bear your deduction in mind," said Melville.

Michael estimated the circular space in which they stood to be about twelve feet in diameter. Off the room, north and south, were perfectly identical corridors, both guarded by stout, matching outside doors. The curved walls were lined with cleverly carpentered shelves and a desk upon which paperwork could be stacked, books stored, and calculations compiled. The air was fresh with a gentle tinge of machine oil.

Dead centre stood the base of a robust structure of cast metal mechanicry. Hefty legs standing on rollers set within a turning circle bolted into the concrete floor, all geared to support the weight and movement of the great telescope resting directly above.

"Finally, they are here," said the voice from nowhere. Cultured, well-to-do and loud. "These Police Consultants." The words 'Police' and 'Consultants' were enounced bitterly. The word 'these' sounded pretty frosty as well.

The owner of the voice stormed into the Pavilion in a whirlwind of impatience. He glanced at the Superintendent and said "Melville." He glared at Michael and Phoebe and said, "Consultants."

Behold, The Astronomer Royal. For it was he.

Wearing not only a high-buttoned blue serge frockcoat with a wing collar and huge blue cravat, but also a face untroubled by merriment and dominated by an inverted Kaiser Wilhelm moustache. Which made his limp sandy hair look all the more lifeless.

No, William Christie cut a pale and slight figure. In fact, the only thing high and mighty about the man was his attitude.

He then stopped and looked at Phoebe again. "Good grief on Earth! You are a girl?"

"Sharp eyesight is an excellent quality in a stargazer, sir. Hello. I am Michael Magister the Industrial Age Illusionist, and consultant to Scotland Yard, having the honour to present Miss Phoebe Le Breton, the Queen of Steam and Goddess of the

Aethyr, who possesses exactly the same police credentials, but whom is, without doubt, the real brains of the outfit."

While Phoebe smiled her cynical smile, the Astronomer Royal's expression betrayed no reassurance whatsoever.

Michael whispered, "Should that have been who or whom?"

Melville chipped quickly in with: "You will have noted that the report in the file lists the circumstances of events which led to Mr Chafeskin's demise in this Pavilion. The victim accidentally impaled himself on the eyepiece of the telescope, resulting in severe optical damage. He then rose, staggered, then tumbled headlong down the stairs, coming to a halt almost at the bottom. Fatal head wounds were sustained. As you will observe from the evident blood spatter."

Melville directed Michael and Phoebe to the side of the room – if a circle can have a side – where a concrete staircase, contoured around the curve of the wall, led up to where the telescope was rigged.

Michael sighed. Why was there always blood? "Is it spatter or splatter?"

"Spatter," said Phoebe.

"Indeed," said Melville.

"You can see the spatter. Splattered on the wall," said Phoebe, very pleased with her joke.

William Christie looked on, bewildered.

"Thank you for that, Pheebs," said Michael. "Shall we slip upstairs and see the killer?"

William Christie reacted immediately. "Let me! *I* shall lead the way," he insisted. "The telescope is a precision instrument."

~9~

Michael and Phoebe followed, gingerly easing themselves sideways as they stepped around the purple-dried puddles on the treads of the stairs.

"I have to say, Mr Christie, I think the work you do here is terrific," said Michael.

"This, I know," came the lofty reply from above.

"Predicting people's futures with how the stars line up and such, really, that is just so clever."

"That, sir, is *astrology*! The important science research we conduct at here Greenwich is astronomy! *Astronomy!*"

Under different circumstances, Phoebe would have jabbed Michael in the ribs and told him to behave, but she appreciated, even approved, of his nerve to jibe Christie. Payback for the man's attitude towards her.

Compared with the Big Ben tower, these stairs were not so much a climb as a saunter: a dozen or so steps winding a quarter of turn to open up on a platform the same diameter as below, enclosed by a ribbed, grey metal dome. The centre of the circle was dominated by the telescope. A visual treat in every way. An instrument which in this timeline we can consider in more detail. If you are interested.

Ten feet in length, cast in bronze and resembling a pair of cannons welded end to end, the Altazimuth could be inclined up and down on its central pivot, and at the same traversed through the full three hundred and sixty degrees. The lower end which housed the deadly eyepiece was angled down towards a lean-back seat, braised onto the ironwork.

"I urge you to make haste with your appraisal," said Christie. "The quicker we are allowed to reinstate this vital equipment the better!"

"You are quite certain this telescope has not been moved since the incident?" demanded Phoebe.

"Locked into position," declaimed the Astronomer Royal. "As most *inconveniently* requested. By your superiors."

Like many men in authority, or indeed many men, Christie resented being quite so answerable, first to a woman and secondly to one so young. He had put up with quite enough female insolence from that pushy wife of Chafeskin, thank you very much! Gah. Even this flibbertigibbet girl climbing the stairs to stand upon the viewing platform was the very height of audacity!

Christie looked down his nose to share his own conclusion. "One must concur with the *official* police appraisal that Chafeskin accidently thrust his face into the eyepiece."

"Accidentally thrust his face?" queried Phoebe.

"Yes, girl, accidentally thrust his face. By dint of a sneeze, or a cough, mayhap a nervous spasm caused his head to jerk forward. There may be innumerable explanations."

273

Phoebe did not respond. Instead she, and now Christie, were distracted by Michael as he pantomimed the sequence Melville outlined. Chafeskin's face striking the eyepiece. With considerable force. The clutching of the agonised eye. Twisting out of the viewing seat. Blindly staggering a few steps. Then rolling his index fingers over one another suggesting the tumbling down the stairs, illustrated by quiet though appropriate sound effects.

"The sequence makes sense, Mr M," said Michael, satisfied.

"Indeed," said Melville from below.

Christie looked on, incredulous.

"Do you perform general observations with this telescope?" asked Phoebe.

"Mmm? Oh. No, certainly not," replied Christie, refocussed after the extraordinary distraction. "This entire Pavilion is dedicated to the study of the moon and its transit."

Surely everyone knew such a fact! Good grief, if this girl was considered the 'brains' of the outfit…

Michael pointed to the seat, "And this is definitely where you sit, when you want to 'astron'?"

*"When you want to what, sir?"*

"Mr Christie, I may be American but I have been in this country for ten years and although English is still only a second language to me, I know that if a robber 'robs' and a murderer 'murders', the astronomer surely … 'astrons'!"

Christie looked increasingly astonished, baffled, perplexed. He was quickly drawing the conclusion that Melville's experts were raving lunatics.

"I imagine the observation dome has been closed since the incident," said Phoebe.

"Well, of course. Against the elements."

"May we please have the roof open?"

Christie huffed, shuffled around and with much ill grace hauled on the looped chain, hand over hand, causing the two halves of the dome to grind and squeak, yawning open a gap three feet wide along the length of the roof and exposing the Pavilion to a waft of cool air.

"Is it a common accident? Astronomers injuring themselves so violently upon telescopes?" asked Phoebe.

A ridiculous question. "Young lady, never!"

"Until now," said Michael and Phoebe together.

As close as he dared, Michael examined the eyepiece of the telescope. It was still crusted in purple. How was it possible? That Chafeskin could impale his eye on the telescope with such a force? Then the solution came. It was obvious.

"Mr Christie, how long had Chafeskin been a Peeping Tom?"

~10~

*"I beg your pardon, sir?"* blustered the Astronomer Royal with shocked indignation.

"I said, how long had Chafeskin been a Peeping Tom?"

"That, sir, is *outrageous*," exploded Christie. "A calumnious slur! Chafeskin was a married man! Melville, I say, down there, Melville! Your consultant is a disgrace! Speak with him, I demand it!"

"Be assured I shall," sighed the half-hearted voice from below.

Phoebe rode to the rescue. "Come now, Mr Christie, there is little need for histrionics. My colleague was merely making a classical reference to the eleventh-century legend, where the original Peeping Tom gazed upon Lady Godiva and was struck either blind or dead. Totally apposite given the circumstances." She looked at Michael, firmly. "Isn't that right?"

"Absolutely – not, Pheebs. Chafeskin was clearly one for hiding up here at night, when he should have been looking at the moon, and viewing ladies from a distance. Down there in that direction. Towards Wimbledon. Where they're most likely to be getting undressed ready for bed beside a window with a glowing lamp…"

"Melville, remove these people from this place at once! *I demand it!*"

"Indeed," said the half-hearted voice from below. "Mr Magister!"

"Pheebs, even I know the moon is up there." Michael pointed vaguely at the heavens. "Look now at the low angle of the telescope. It's not looking at the sky. That is not astronomy. That is pure Peeping Tommery. I'm thinking Chafeskin got lucky looking at a lady, couldn't believe what he saw, jumped forward for a better look and pop – squished his eye."

"Melville!"

Phoebe followed the shallow inclination of the telescope. "Mr Christie, please do be quiet and kindly indicate for me the transition of the moon across the night sky. Now please. This is important. Or we shall take great pleasure in arresting you for non-cooperation in a fatal investigation."

Red-faced, William Christie stopped his huffing and upon Phoebe's insistence reluctantly swung his arm in an arc to indicate the direction. "East to West."

"Mr Christie, you will agree the direction of the telescope as it currently lies bears no relation to the lunar orbit?"

Well, that shot him right up the fundament. He looked at the telescope. Up at the sky. Then again. Stroked his chin. And finally, reluctantly, admitted this girl … was correct.

"Mr Christie, assuming you wish to spare your late assistant such indignity," snapped Phoebe, "what on earth, or what in heaven, do *you* suppose Mr Chafeskin could have been looking at through the telescope at such a low angle?"

~11~

Christie quickly squinted through the sighting 'scope, checked the direction against his pocket compass, the angle of inclination, yes, it was shallow, then brushed past the Magicians and hurried down the stairs. Michael and Phoebe shared looks of raised eyebrows and followed the Astronomer down.

Already he was running a finger along the spines of a row of notebooks stacked on the shelf, found what he wanted, pulled out the volume and flicked through the book to the relevant page.

"Antares…" announced Christie, not a little puzzled.

"Antares?" queried Melville.

"In that sou' westerly direction, at that twenty degree elevation, the last celestial object Mr Chafeskin trained his telescope upon before he died, was Antares. Although I cannot imagine for one moment why…"

"Anything special about Antares?" asked Michael.

Christie said, "All the stars in the sky are special. Antares is a red supergiant, appearing as vivid orange and known to the ancients. It is, in truth, a binary star, possessing a twin which appears in close proximity, a fact discovered by the Austrian, Burg, a mere eighty years ago. Antares has been allotted a Flamsteed Designation of 21 Scorpii, being a prominent star in the constellation Scorpius."

"The heart of the scorpion," remembered Phoebe from a book she'd read way back when.

"A colloquial reference," dismissed Christie.

Michael stroked his left ear. A stage cue to Phoebe that they were finished here.

"Thank you, Mr Christie, that will be all," said Phoebe. "We require nothing else from you."

The Astronomer Royal did not much care for such an off-hand dismissal. From the girl. But he was very glad to see the back of her.

"One more question," said Michael. "Why would Chafeskin be looking at this particular star?"

William Christie shook his head. "I have no idea. Do see yourselves out. And Melville. A word before you leave."

"Indeed. Miss Le Breton. Mr Magister. I will see you outside."

\*\*\*

I think everyone there knew the Astronomer Royal would be registering an official complaint concerning the disrespect and consummate stupidity he had been forced to endure at the tongue of Melville's so called 'Special Branch Consultants'. Probably planning to extend his protest as far as the Commissioner of the Metropolis, Sir Edward Bradfield.   Outside, Phoebe hooked her arm through Michael's and wheeled him out of the Pavilion.

"Tell me, tell me. What did you see that I failed to spot?"

"Nothing," said Michael, plainly.

"Then why did you signal me to leave?"

"I was bored."

"You really are a shocking fellow, Michael Magister."

"He was being sniffy with you. He got what he deserved."

It was just as Michael was helping Phoebe up onto the driving bench of the Steamo that they heard scampering footsteps from behind. Far too fast for the Superintendent. They both turned to see a breathless figure. "Begging your pardons, Miss, Sir."

"Michael, it's lovely Mr Donaldson," said Phoebe.

The porter glanced back over his shoulder, anxious to know if he had been noticed. Or followed. It was neither. But nevertheless he kept his voice low.

"I shall regret it evermore if I do not seize this opportunity to share something I trust will be looked upon evenly by yourselves. Something I know shall be dismissed by others as fanciful whimsy."

"Please feel confident to tell us whatever you wish, Mr Donaldson," assured Phoebe.

"It concerns what I saw when I happened upon the body of Mr Dapper in his bed, and of Mr Chafeskin upon the stairs."

"What did you see, my friend?" asked Michael, gently.

"I would swear upon holy writ, both gentlemen possessed on their faces wild looks of terror. Genuine total terror."

~12~

With a gasp, the brakes on the Steamo released and Phoebe pressed the regulator arm forward for a flamboyant wheelspin departure. The vehicle quickly picked up a decent turn of speed on the straight run south to the Blackheath Gate. With Melville, sitting comfortably in the back, helpfully furnishing the magicians with details concerning the discovery of Goronwy Dapper, even Michael failed to sense Walter Pym eating their dust, shouting and waving something, presumably of importance, but disappearing into the distance behind them.

The chug around the corner to Dapper's end of terrace two-up-two-down on Maidenstone Hill was so fast the Steamo barely had time to clear her smoky tubes.

First impressions of the house? Brick built. Solid and secure in window and door. In fact it was only the clues of the cleverly dovetailed blocks of unpainted wood, making-good the forced-entry damage, along with the shiny new lock on the front door which suggested much of anything had happened at Goronwy Dapper's.

It occurred to Michael that Mr Donaldson and the local Peeler, a P.C. Gnosh, must have expended a good deal of energy in breaking down this door. And most likely still had the bruises to prove it. Thankfully, on this occasion, such exertion would not be required. Melville had brought along the key.

"And why is a lock like the scab on the back of a magician's hand?" asked Michael.

"Because it's impossible not to want to pick it," said Phoebe, patiently.

"You see, Mr M, she learned from the best."

"Michael, I think very few people would ever consider what I have learned from you as anything to be proud of. But then whenever did I care very much about what ... oh, my days!"

Ah. Yes. Well, in fairness, Mr Dapper's body had lain, shall we say, fermenting, upstairs for a couple of days prior to its discovery. So, even with the corpse removed, when the Superintendent swung open the front door, the haze of flesh-rot, trapped inside the house overwhelmed like a sensory tsunami.

Phoebe dug a bottle of precious lavender oil from one of her many pockets. A gift from Florence Nightingale, as a matter of fact. She and Michael shared liberal dabbings below each nostril to keep the fug at bay. Melville declined such cologne-irrigation, preferring to cover his nose with his all-purpose official 'kerchief.

Wisely, Michael rejected the notion of telling Melville that the last time he pulled a handkerchief from his pocket a dove flew out, on the grounds it would be far more annoying than amusing. Instead he busied himself swinging the front door back and forth, examining the hinges and the edges.

"The damage here shows the door was not only locked from the inside but also bolted shut, top and bottom," said Michael, pointing out the ragged pairs of screw holes, top and bottom on the jamb. The two cast iron bolts attached to the inside of the door remained intact, while the retaining catches into which they slid had been shoved free by the forced entry.

Melville handed Phoebe another folder. His pockets must have been as capacious as hers were abundant. The writing on the front read: 'G. Dapper, deceased. Autopsy'. Which struck Michael as hopefully a statement of the obvious

"Be so kind as to follow me upstairs to where the body was discovered."

The bedroom, as you know, was spare with just a nightstand, wardrobe and neat piles of books. The bedstead was iron and had been stripped of sheets and pillows leaving only a grey mattress. The indent formed by Dapper's regular sleeping position was clear. Less so, halfway down, were the four tiny red dots. Melville was quietly impressed at Michael's speed of observation.

Phoebe scanned the two pages of the file to find the paragraph she wanted. "When discovered, Mr Dapper was clad in only a nightshirt, and was lying face down. According to the autopsy, causation of death was deemed natural causes, myocardial infarction, a heart attack. And – oh, my, this is rather peachy! The body also displayed recent lacerations to the inner thighs and marks and bruising to the scrotum."

"Along with the blood spots, it is that which raised my interest," admitted Melville.

"I can understand that," said Michael.

Phoebe continued: "The autopsy surgeon suggests, in view of these marks and subsequent swelling, the testes had been squeezed with pressure by something akin to nut crackers. Each to their own peccadilloes, I suppose. These days, I hear it is quite the pastime among the Kensington elite. The surgeon adds a footnote – reporting he is continuing his research into a more precise causation of this testicular trauma."

"What should we do?" asked Michael. "Maybe scour the house for nutcrackers? Or maybe a pair of tongs?"

To which an unseen voice said: "Crabs!"

~13~

"A very nice entrance, Inspector," said Michael. "You should try that more often."

"I could never have put it better myself," agreed Phoebe, without knowing she already had.

Michael, Phoebe and Melville looked to the hall outside. There, red-faced, bent double, was Inspector Pym. He was panting hard and wishing he didn't have to, as he felt for his police handkerchief. "Blimey, it's still rank in here."

"But what do you mean 'crabs'?"

"Truthfully, just the one crab." He held up a brown envelope. "According to this, just sent across from the autopsy surgeon. Tests on the scratches on the victim's legs, and the swellings to his undercarriage – begging your pardon, Miss – show they were caused by a crab with poisoned claws."

"And the surgeon can confirm this how?" wondered Melville.

"Ah, well." Pym slipped the folded sheet from the envelope. "He records here that a crab which secretes poison is unknown in nature. However, he states he compared the claw marks of several species crab sourced from Billingsgate Market, where his two uncles still work as porters' managers. The almost perfect match for the injuries came from the claw of the Large Velvet Crab. A substantial beast measuring all of six inches across the back of the shell. This particular crab is possessed of pincers of considerable strength. The conclusion he draws is that this unfortunate encounter 'down below' caused the heart attack which, along with the suffocation, killed the victim long before any poison took effect. I'll wager the autopsy surgeon bought a wide range of crab claws and offered them up to the marks on Dapper's 'nads. So to speak."

"There are worse ways to go," said Michael. "But I'm having trouble thinking of one at the moment."

"The surgeon is to be commended for his diligence," said Melville.

"Inspector, one assumes your colleague Constable Gnosh along with Mr Donaldson, upon discovering the body, made no mention of finding a hard-to-miss Large Velvet Crab crawling about this bedroom?" wondered Phoebe.

"None whatsoever, Miss," said Pym, his breathing now easier.

She looked at Michael. "And judging by the subject matter, his books and his passion for the sky above, I rather doubt Mr Dapper had much time or interest in keeping a crustacean as a pet."

And he agreed.

"Let's face it, anyone who smears poison on a crab is not doing it from the goodness of their heart. The same goes for any person who brings a crab and makes it scuttle up a man's nightshirt. Mr M, you were absolutely right, there is nothing about these Greenwich curiosities which rings true. I salute your instinct."

"And what does your infamous instinct tell you about these deaths then, Magister?" said Pym, his question laced with derision.

"One thing for absolute certain."

"Which is?"

"I have no idea," he admitted, before adding thoughtfully, "but, only for the moment."

"Well, there's a thing, guv'nor. The Magister stumped," said Pym, a little too smugly. "Perhaps you can fall back upon your newfound prescience. A bit of the old foretellin' of the future."

Michael was smiling, but he wasn't happy.

"Prescience?" Phoebe's face brightened as the notion struck. "Yes. Michael, you said it. Back there at the observatory."

"That is quite correct, Pheebs, I did. And … if you'd like to share that with the gentlemen of the Special Branch…" bluffed Michael, with absolutely no idea what she was going to offer.

"What you said to Christie! Astrology!"

"Astrology?" Melville was confused. As was Pym. Especially Pym.

"More specifically, Starsigns. Consider both these deaths. One night Dapper is intimately clawed by a crab. Another night Chafeskin is blinded while observing Scorpius."

"True," admitted Pym. "But much as you'd like it, Miss, not all crimes involve mumbo jumbo. At the moment it's just creatures with claws."

"Arthropods," said Phoebe.

"Steady," blushed Pym.

Dammit, she thought. He could be an idiot, but perhaps this time Pym was right. "Arthropods are exoskeletal invertebrates, Inspector, common to scorpions, crabs, spiders, so…"

"Dates of birth," interrupted Michael. "In the files. Do they give the victims' dates of birth?"

Melville consulted one file, Phoebe the other. She went first.

"Here we are. Goronwy Dapper was born on … the twenty-second of June."

Michael clapped his hands. "Which makes his starsign?"

"Oh, my days. Cancer the Crab!"

"And Mr M, I'm thinking now that Ronathan Chafeskin was born sometime in November?"

Pym checked the date and looked up. "The fifteenth."

"Scorpio the Scorpion," yelled Phoebe. "Oh, yes! Superintendent, there is your tangible link between the two victims. Both men suffered violent deaths in the manner of their astrological starsigns."

A shrug was the best Melville dare admit. "Administered by whom, Miss Le Breton? And how? Given both victims died alone. Behind doors locked from the inside."

Which was fair …

~14~

The safety curtain had been rung down and the final dribs and drabs of the second house audience were chattering their contented way out of the auditorium, having stormed the stage and vociferously complained about male nudity – no, the *lack* of male nudity – in the performance.

You see, exaggerated word of mouth had rapidly spread and many of the ladies, well-to-do or otherwise, had dragged their husbands, lovers, whatevers, along to see the birthday-suited Magister, waving his flauntibles, or flaunting his wavibles – only to discover The Steam Digester finale had been cut from the act!

It was an admittedly reluctant decision of mine, but at a stroke it removed our beholding to Melville, and his Lord Chancellor's leverage over us.

Such was the storm, Michael had had to go out front and placate the irate ladies with winning charm and hugs all round, while their husbands, lovers, whatevers, tapped their watches and tutted about the pubs and clubs closing soon.

To replace the 'Digester' we reinstated the 'Gas Chambers of Suffocation', which was a fag. More elaborate to stage, requiring two glass tanks instead of the Digester's one, and for Michael to dress exactly as Mr Garrideb, in gas mask and cape, allowing him to apparently 'travel' from a tank on one side of the stage to another in the blink of an eye. Certainly much faster than it took to read that last sentence!

To give the illusion a fresh look, we gussied up the chambers with a lick of verdigris paint and introduced the performance as 'The Diabolical Tanks of Diogenes'. I know. Cynical, but at least it would please Arthur Doyle.

"Here, Magister, don't let Miss Phoebe do all the pushing on that," said Wicko, sitting on a travelling trunk and offering no help whatsoever as Michael and Phoebe both wheeled the second of the Tanks upstage.

"Quite right, old friend," said Michael.

"I would help, Miss Phoebe, but that diet you put me on robs me of all energy by the end of the day."

"He says the trouble with vegetarian food is you don't get enough meat," whispered Michael.

Phoebe rolled her eyes.

"You two making merry at my expense?"

"Discussing the quirky Greenwich case, Wicko," said Phoebe.

Which prompted me, as I rose to the stage aboard the Lift'n'Shift, having stowed the stagecraft Mr Garrideb in the Dungeon, to enquire about those two deaths. Surely they were murders.

Michael was convinced of it. "I told Mr M 'London's Starsign Serial Killer' would make for a terrific headline. But that didn't go over much of a storm."

"Also, to achieve serial killer status, one needs to murder three people, which I must say I thought was rather interesting."

I was starting to believe Phoebe was correct when she spoke about working with us and the questionable influence it was having upon her.

"Bloody hell," said Wicko sitting bolt upright. "The Starsign Serial Killer."

"I thought it had a rhythm," said Michael.

Wicko asked Michael and Phoebe to run through the astrological clues for him again.

Michael concluded with the questions: "Why was Chafeskin looking at Scorpio when his brief was to study the moon? And why did Dapper have his 'nads chewed by a crab?"

"Michael, you should not use that word," chastised Phoebe.

"Apologies, Pheebs."

"Accepted. The correct expression to use is: 'His 'nads were *clawed* by the crab. Crabs claw, cows chew."

There was a lesson in there somewhere for us all. And I was now completely convinced Phoebe was correct when she talked about the questionable effect that working with us was having upon her.

It was then I noted Wicko also sitting in a thoughtful brown study, and so pressed him to learn why.

"This could be something, could be nothing," said Wicko, thoughtfully. "But it might be pertinent to your Starsign Killer."

Well, that hooked everyone's attention.

Wicko shuffled on the trunk to make himself even more comfortable and continued.

"Y'see, first time round, after Magister was gassed at Westminster Abbey, and we dropped him in Regent's Park at Dr Phunn's, I knew there and then we were finished. It was over. Plenty of people, police and everybody, had seen the Dodo and the whole house of cards was going to come down around about our ears. I flew here, left Spindle to give the Professor the 'London Bridge' warning, then I carried on with the plan, across to Hyde Park, to sink the Dodo in the Serpentine."

Wicko closed his eyes to help him picture the night-time scene.

"Right, now here's the bit I've been thinking about. This was late evening. Dark. Gates locked. Park as empty as it gets. I scuppered the Dodo and after I paddled to the shore, I watched this old woman, black bonnet, black cape, push a cart onto the Serpentine Bridge."

"Wait up, you said she was an old woman. If it was dark, how did you know?"

"The voice, Magister. She had this whiny '*Hello, my dear*' old woman's way of talking. Now if you're going to question everything…"

Michael insisted he continue.

"So anyway. I watched her as she hefted something off the cart, over the parapet, and tipped it straight in the water. From where I was it looked like a man's body. Now, how the old girl managed it," Wicko put his hands up in surrender. "Don't be asking me."

"The man put up no struggle?" asked Phoebe.

"Saggy as a sack. A dead weight. On account he must've been dead. But without a word of a lie, Miss, although I only saw the old girl, I know I heard two voices. She was chatting away with someone. Someone with one of those hissy, snaky voices. But I couldn't see the other party. As far as I was concerned, there wasn't another living soul on the bridge with the old dear. But here's where it gets proper strange…"

"It's been nicely strange already," said Michael.

"No, here's my point. Get this. Both of them said the same thing. The snaky voice and the old dear. 'Death to the Aquarian'. Clear as a bell. And pretty pleased with themselves they were when they said it. 'Death to the Aquarian'."

~15~

Michael made the telephone call from the Stage Door Lobby, and announced his "Thurmatagist" code word, fully expecting Melville to be at home and in bed in Colliers Wood. Instead, the Scotland Yard overnight plugboard operator Miss Eileen Spillage, quickly patched Michael through to Melville's office.

"I only sleep when I am tired, Mr Magister," in answer to Michael's concerned query.

"When were you last tired?"

"Eighteen ninety-seven. Please continue."

So Michael did. Asking if any bodies had been recently fished out of the Serpentine. Specifically, on the night of the Westminster Abbey business, which should be memorable as that evening he had saved the Prince of Wales and half the Government. A point he hardly laboured at all.

Ten minutes later, Melville returned the telephone call courtesy. Sitting in his small Scotland Yard office with the large desk and the portrait of Queen Victoria glaring down from the chimney breast, he read from the records of 'The Royal Humane Society of Boatmen' who policed the Serpentine.

In addition to the ten attempted suicides, there were so far this year two fatalities. An impressive record considering over one hundred thousand bathers enjoy the Serpentine per annum.

"The body of a gentleman was drawn from the lake the morning following the Westminster Abbey incident. Bearing signs consistent with drowning. No identification has yet been made, and until such time, no date of birth can be confirmed to support your Starsign Serial Killer theory."

Superintendent Melville's tinny voice emerged from the black Shellac listening horn I had hooked up against the telephone earpiece, enabling Michael and Phoebe, and Wicko and myself, to listen, much like 'Nipper' the dog in Francis Barraud's painting 'His Master's Voice'.

We all shared a look of disappointment.

"However. There was a puzzling anomaly," continued Melville. "The post-mortem recorded that the water discovered in the victim's lungs was comparatively clean and consistent with a horse trough. Markedly different to the water found in the Serpentine. Which may suggest murder, but the body presents no physical signs of employed force."

Splendid, we all thought. In a manner of speaking.

"Mr M," said Michael, into the mouthpiece. "How about Ronathan Chafeskin's widow? The woman's a more ambitious social climber than her husband. Christie all but said as much."

"Indeed. But questioning Mrs Eadie Chafeskin proved fruitless. Her grief is so profound, the doctor advises that unless her mental capacity rapidly improves, there will be sufficient cause to issue a Reception Order. Under the 1890 Lunacy Act."

"Would you object if Phoebe and I had a word with her? See if she responds to me? I mean, us?"

"If you are prepared to make the return journey to Greenwich, Mr Magister, and you believe progress may be made, I shall not discourage you."

~16~

Scotland Yard's most ineffectual Assistant Commissioner, Sir Cumberland Sinclair, with his responsibilities to oversee the machinations of the Special Branch, finished his balloon glass of brandy-milk and licked his lips. The warm glow from the spitting and popping fire in the marble fireplace bathed his sharp-featured face and reflected in his eyes. After a long hard day at the Yard, chatting about nothing in particular, and asking fellow officers what they thought about ongoing cases, Sir Cumberland was grateful to finally get home for a fine, fireside supper and a well-earned feet-up.

Superintendent Melville did apply himself with such vigorous dedication to the most extraordinary working hours at Scotland Yard, keeping the nation safe, and Sir Cumberland Sinclair for one did find that ever so tiresome. It meant that every once in a while, Sir Cumberland felt vaguely obliged to be seen also staying late. At least once a week. Or a fortnight if he could wangle it.

At least these midnight oil sessions enabled the Assistant Commissioner to catch up on the progress of on-going Special Branch cases. The recent fireworks display above the Houses of Parliament, specifically Big Ben, remained unexplained. Those disagreeable Boers were still playing high cockalorum in Bloemfontein, but he concluded little would come of that to trouble Great Britain.

Of far more fascinating reading, however, had been the official file marked TOP SECRET, the one now closed and resting on his lap. The report confirmed that Melville's early misgivings concerning that nasty unpleasantness down at the Royal Greenwich Observatory had been endorsed by that very lovely Miss Phoebe Le Breton, oh yes, and, of course, her charming companion Michael Magister. In fact, the latest entry recorded Melville's approval for them to continue their investigations in Greenwich tomorrow. He wished them every success.

Sir Cumberland Sinclair scribbled a few words on a sheet of paper and rang the handbell to summon his aged butler, the ever reliable and slightly bemused Pockney.

"Our Pockney, another splendid meal, mmm," gushed Sir Cumberland. "What do you think?"

"Thank you, sir." Pockney inclined his bald head as best as his arthritic neck could allow. "In terms of heat-th, sir, are you warm-th enough?"

"Oh, quite so, quite so. Mmm. Do clear the tray, if you could be so kind, there's a fine chap. And I have a missive to send. Not too late is it? What do you think, our Pockney?"

Pockney cleared the tray, assuring sir he would arrange to have the telegram sent-th immediately.

~17~

The bright early start the next morning, coupled with Michael now knowing the route and enabling Phoebe to anticipate the traffic, trams and jams, ensured the journey south west was far smoother than their previous drive.

They were keen to question Ronathan Chafeskin's widow while she was still moderately lucid. Although Special Branch and the local police had learned nothing coherent from Mrs Chafeskin, maybe Michael's persuasive 'Old Madam' might tease a modicum of sense from the poor woman. That she was very much the driving ambition behind Ronathan's career was of particular interest.

It was barely ten o'clock when Phoebe steered the Steamo along Greenwich's Romney Road, squeezed between the 'Royal Hospital School' to the right and the Christopher Wren designed 'Royal Naval College' on the left. The Stanford map took them along the Woolwich Road, past the 'Greenwich Union Workhouse', then turned them right, by 'The Royal Hospital Cemetery'. That name alone would not have inspired confidence for the old patients, thought Michael – while Phoebe mused on the idea that the only official building not aggrandised with the 'Royal' designation was the workhouse.

As you know, the Chafeskin residence was on Ormiston Road, a quaint street a way to the east of Greenwich Park, which all but backed onto Westcombe Park Railway Station. Phoebe drew the Steamo to halt outside the Chafeskin's terraced cottage, which was close enough to the station to hear the steam engines, and see the puked-up puff balls of grey smoke float above the roofs, as they heaved their carriages to and from London.

\*\*\*

In fact, at that moment, two such passengers were aboard the Kent bound train about to arrive at Westcombe Park.

"I discern this a most salubrious suburb of the capital," said Mr Skrill, the slender shrew-faced one, dressed in shabby black with a weather-worn top hat, rubbing the grime from the carriage window, with his cuff.

"Loobius, hnur, hnur, hnur," chuckled Mr Drago, the bigger of the two, whose own view of the area was made easier by licking at the window and rubbing it with the palm of his hand.

Their fellow passengers regretted that at London Bridge they had picked the wrong carriage to travel in. Drago and Skrill were not the kind of people whose gaze you would wish to meet. Especially the oaf. Not that Drago and Skrill were much concerned as they discussed the horror they had been directed to commit.

"His Excellency's communiqué is agreeably specific," said Skrill, holding the scrap of paper.

"Spiffic, hnur, hnur, hnur," agreed Drago.

"The popinjay magician accompanied by his wanton slattern is to be found at this particular address at some time of this morning's a.m., Mr Drago, and His Excellency has graciously granted us the carte blanche to employ the vilest most painful methods at our considerable disposal to dispatch them to the fires of hell. Which I contend shall bring us great pleasure and amusement, Mr Drago. Great pleasure and amusement indeed."

"Musemun, hnur, hnur, hnur."


~18~


The man who opened the front door of the Chafeskin cottage was tall and slender of limb, with thick sandy hair and a sallow face. His tan waistcoat was buttoned, his tie straight, but the sleeves on his white shirt were rolled up to the elbow.

He looked at the two people and his face fell. "Who are you?" he demanded, in a creamy, cultured voice. He looked over their shoulders. "You're not them."

"Which is, in itself, correct, depending on which 'them' you were expecting," said Michael.

He then introduced himself and Phoebe as consultants to Scotland Yard. Both produced their warrant cards as if from nowhere, with a magical flourish.

They explained that they were calling to extend their condolences to Mrs Chafeskin and reassure her that the resources of Her Majesty's Special Branch would be employed to their fullest to ensure an investigation of rigor and ultimate success into her husband's untimely passing. Well, obviously it was Phoebe who expressed it in that way, and not Michael.

All he added was: "That's us neatly wrapped up. Who are you?"

"Dr Skene," the man announced proudly. "Mrs Chafeskin's personal physician. And she is far too distressed to be seen by anyone. Special Branch or otherwise."

A shriek of hilarious laughter came from inside. "Bring her in, bring her in!" More happy laughter.

"She sounds distressed," said Michael. "Dr Skin…"

"It is Skene. I will thank you kindly to go away."

And he closed the door. Quickly, too. Far too fast for Phoebe to employ her don't-try-that-with-me, boot-in-the-door trick.

"How very charming," said Phoebe. Then for good measure called: "I care little for your bedside manner, Doctor."

"Miss Le Breton," whispered Michael, in that thoughtful tone which was entirely fake, accompanied by a mischievous look which was entirely genuine. "Based on what you just said, are you suspecting that man is not a medical person at all, but a money grabbing Lothario, keen to embezzle the grief-stricken widow? Especially with his sleeves rolled up. Because if you are thinking such a thing, I would have to agree."

"Why, Mr Magister, yes, I am thinking such a thing and furthermore rather feel it would be a dereliction of our duty as Scotland Yard consultants not to protect the vulnerable Mrs Chafeskin. We have more than enough suspicion to enter the property uninvited. So…"

Phoebe hoisted the hem of her purple skirt.

"That's a flanged rim," murmured Michael.

"Excuse me?"

He pointed to the round brass handle on the door. "One of the newer door locks on the market, so let's say we give the Picker-Nicker a rest and let me show off a little with this. You ready?"

Michael twirled his black walking cane, gave the silver band below the silver skull a twist counter-clockwise, and hinged it back to reveal a neat circle of interchangeable attachments: a magnet, a tiny circular mirror, a small hook and a nasal hair trimmer. Michael selected the small hook and clicked it into place on the ferule at the base of the stick.

After inviting Phoebe to "Observe", he quietly lifted the brass flap of the letterbox and thrust the stick full length through. A nifty finger twirl of the cane swung it ninety degrees, pointing the hook in the direction of the lock.

The flanged rim lock supports a turning barrel with a handle on either side of the door and a brass buttony-switch thing, as we say in the trade, in the bodywork of the lock. Clicked one way, the deadlock is engaged. Click the buttony-switch thing the other way and the lock is released. An easy, highly secure modern design. Unless, of course, you're the Magister, working blind from the wrong side of the door, but gifted with deft special judgement.

Unsurprisingly, Michael judged the location, hooked onto the buttony-switch thing and with a gentle pull released the lock and withdrew his cane.

"Try that, Miss."

"Show off!" Phoebe whispered, before slowly and silently turning the handle, pushing the door open and slipping inside.

~19~

As you might imagine, neither the dreadful Mr Drago nor the awful Mr Skrill had tickets to travel on the train down from London. In fact, as far as transportation was concerned, tickets were never purchased, in the well-founded belief that having put the wind up the porters and ticket collectors, their permission to travel would never be questioned.

Except this morning.

Messrs Drago and Skrill, having alighted from the train at Westcombe Park, *were* stopped at the gate by a Station Master, having the shocking audacity to demand their tickets. However, when rebuffed with a combined torrent of eloquence and incoherence, the Station Master, a curly-haired, well-made fellow called Ridgehunt from Bawtrey, had the self-preserving good sense to let the grotesque twosome pass through the barrier, "just this once".

"Most gracious and most wise, my man," said Skrill, extending his left leg straight, sweeping his hat off his head and bowing low. "I thank you."

"Hnkew, hnur, hnur, hnur," chuckled Drago.

"Mindful this retribution is sincerely overdue, how now shall we dispense with the peacock illusionist and his Jezebel strumpet, Mr Drago? Which instrument of murder finds favour with you? We could take recourse to the rope, with strangulation being at the same time noble, ancient and most effective. The revolver is the most satisfying, but our lack of possession of such ordnance renders that method null and void. Which requires us to turn, if we may, to weighty instruments with the purpose of inflicting cranial trauma…"

Drago looked puzzled.

"To wit, the smashing in of their godless skulls," explained Skrill.

Drago looked delighted.

"Hnsmash, hnur, hnur, hnur," he chuckled.

~20~

The floor of the narrow hall of the Chafeskin house, with its checkerboard of black and white tiles, was not best suited to stealth, especially in Phoebe's heeled boots. Michael and Phoebe thanked goodness for the masking sound of Dr Skene's mellifluous yakking, coupled with shrieks of female laughter.

The open front parlour door not only spilled daylight into the hall, it also afforded Michael and Phoebe any easy high-low scan of the room. Neither the doctor nor his patient was in plain sight, shielded as they were by the large brown settee which sat in the middle of the room facing the fireplace, and with its back to the door. But from the noises … hello …

The room was a handsome size for a terrace. Taking in the details, Michael noted the tall ceiling, plenty of elbow room, all-glittering chandelier and elegant furniture. The walls papered a symphony of blues: sky blue above the white dado rail, cerulean blue below. Hanging above the mantelpiece, an oval wood-framed mirror. In the recess to the right of the chimney breast hung a wood-framed canvas of the crater-pocked full moon in oils, yellow and grey. To the left, hung a complimentary head and shoulders portrait of Eadie Chafeskin in the same colour scheme, but this was composed in watercolours. Which was a very good choice because one, the subject herself was certainly no oil painting, and two, it gave me the opportunity to make that trite comment.

Light flooded in from the bay window on the right. Opposite stood a dark-wood sideboard with storage cupboards and drawers and a line-up of sepia photographs arranged along the top.

A woman's stockinged foot appeared above the back of the settee, followed by another happy cackle of bereavement – at which point Phoebe felt it appropriate to announce their presence with a polite throaty cough.

They heard the woman gasp. Then the panicked murmur: "She is returned! The banshee! She is returned!" Immediately the whisper became a furious shout. "I will kill her! Kill her with a knife!"

Instantly a wild face popped up over the top of the settee. Terrifying. Snarling. Wisps of hair rat's-tailing down her totally grey face, relieved only by the vivid red encircling her manic eyes. "Be gone, banshee! Are you the banshee?"

"Not necessarily," placated Michael, not a little alarmed.

The woman then ducked from view, whimpering. "Doctor, keep her away, keep her away."

Dr Skene stood, scarlet and rigid with fury. A welcome, measured emotion compared to the extremes they had just witnessed. He was holding a hypodermic, loaded with a cloudy concoction Phoebe figured she recognised.

"What is this outrage? You were told Mrs Chafeskin was far too distressed to see…"

"Oh, Doctor, you were in such a hurry you left the front door completely open," lied Phoebe, while crabbing around the settee. There she found Mrs Eadie Chafeskin, a matron in her forties, wearing a frilly trimmed white blouse and full black skirt, laying huddled and foetal.

She saw Phoebe and yelped: "She's a banshee! Keep her away!"

Dr Skene turned his attention briefly to his patient. "No, Eadie, the banshee will not come near to you." Then looked back at Phoebe. "The warders are on their way. Stand away from her. Stand away!"

And thrust toward Phoebe with the needle.

~21~

"One might resort to the candlestick," continued Skrill, as they walked along. "However, sourcing two such items within the house of death may prove time consuming. The same which applies to the spanner. So it appears to me, Mr Drago, the only practical option remaining is to crack their heads open with lengths of lead pipe. Would such a method bring satisfaction to your high professional standards, Mr Drago?"

"It-im, hnur, hnur, hnur," chuckled Drago, gesturing accordingly.

"Marvellous. Then let us thank the Lord most high for granting us the providence of carrying such items of murderous beauty about our persons," said Skrill, tapping the length of lead pipe he kept up his sleeve. "Now, where is Ormiston Road?"

The two unemployed undertakers stood on the corner of Humber and Halstow Roads, scratching their heads. Every pedestrian they approached for directions had fled.

"Well, this shall not do, Mr Drago, this shall not do. Here are we receiving co-operation most scant from the local populous. Most scandalous, I deem it to be, Mr Drago, most scandalous. Especially when God-fearing fellows such as we have the urgent business of murder to conduct. What is this world coming to?"

*\*\**

Phoebe backed up. Caution. Distance. Room to manoeuvre. "Oh, my days. She is as bad as that…?"

"Dr Skin…" urged Michael.

"Skene," corrected Phoebe, sharply. "Michael, the gentleman's name is Dr Skene…"

"Sorry, Dr Skene, but we really need to speak with Mrs Chafeskin.

"Before she's taken away."

"And ideally before you…"

"Administer more laudanum," said Phoebe.

Eadie was now muddled. And whimpering. Skene was just as confused, flashing his eyes between Michael and Phoebe.

Michael shot a look at Phoebe. "Really? *Laudanum?*" She nodded. "Let me calm Eadie, okay, Doc. Without your happy juice. Just let me give it a go."

"Give it a go…? What does such a thing mean?" demanded the medical man.

"He says these things," Phoebe said with a knowing look. "But you ought to let him try. He is very effective with hysterical women."

"And she is very persuasive," Michael told the doctor.

"I believe I am," Phoebe told the doctor. Who was now sufficiently distracted to allow Phoebe to step in and, with a sincere apology, a grip of his wrist and an easy twist, relieve him of the needle.

## 22

"How dare you!" said the shocked Skene, grabbing at the hypodermic, finding his effort skilfully repelled by Phoebe's single-handed Bartitsu techniques. "This is outrageous! I shall have you hauled before the authorities!"

"We are the authorities," said Phoebe firmly, leaving Michael to swoop round to the front of the settee. On his knees at Eadie Chafeskin's level. The deck of cards was already in his hands, riffling, cutting, waterfalling, then showboating a card shuffle with one hand. Easy and smooth.

"Hello, Eadie. Do I look like the banshee? That is absolutely right, I am nothing you would want to ban and I am definitely not a 'she' – I am Michael." Despite the nonsense he was talking, his voice was calm and soothing. "And with your natural English rose beauty, I think if you were to have a playing card named in your honour, that card would be this one:"

The Queen of Hearts gently rose from the deck, resting halfway up. "And there she stands, in all her majestic beauty. See her? She is the absolute image of you, Eadie."

Almost at once she was enchanted by the tranquil, personal attention and the calming visual distraction of these remarkable cards. And the flattery. Who couldn't be? Even Skene was stunned by his frenetic patient's new found quiescence.

With forefinger and thumb, Michael slipped the Queen of Hearts clear of the deck, and invited Eadie to blow the card a kiss goodbye, with the assurance that her loving gesture would grant the card the power of Astral Psychic Travel. To invisibly fly from Michael's hand to another place entirely.

At first she looked puzzled, but encouraged by the conjuror's warm smile, pursed her lips like a shy child. Kiss blown, Michael vanished the card and presented a now empty palm.

"And look, Eadie. The card has gone. Your loving kiss has flown the Queen of Hearts right to where she belongs, straight to your favourite photograph standing right there on the sideboard. So, Pheebs if you would, please?"

"With pleasure, Magister."

Phoebe laid the syringe on the side table, crossed to the line-up of sepia prints, each photograph sandwiched between a sheet of black cardboard at the back and one of clear glass at the front, all clamped together with four small silver clips. Naturally, Phoebe anticipated the posed portrait of the smiling slender man standing beside a telescope. Ronathan Chafeskin. "Might your favourite photograph be this handsome fellow, I wonder?"

Eadie waved her finger and pointed. "No … the next one."

I know! Her favourite photograph actually turned out to be the one of herself. Posing in a broad-brimmed hat with a peacock feather poking up from the band, and fur stole finery draped about her shoulders. Who would have thought? Even Michael was taken aback by the woman's self-awareness. Not that it mattered for the trick. Phoebe scooped up the picture.

"This lovely lady?"

Eadie nodded eagerly. Her eyes bright.

"And, Eadie, to prove your loving kiss ensured the card took flight, at no time will I come in contact with that photograph," said Michael. "The Goddess of the Aethyr will deliver the photograph straight to your hands." With an elaborate gesture, Phoebe presented the almost infantile woman with her own image. "Your loving kiss, Eadie, blew the Queen of Hearts straight to this beautiful portrait. And if we open the photograph up…"

Michael encouraged her to slide the bottom silver catch free, then shake the whole thing up and down. And, well, you guessed it, the corner of a playing card slipped down between the print and the backing. Eadie pulled the proud corner free, to find she was holding the Queen of Hearts.

Eadie's jaw dropped. A stunned expression grew into a broad beaming smile.

Michael explained that the miracle of the astral flight was all down to the power of Eadie's kiss. And she believed it. Which meant she was now trusting and relaxed enough to answer his questions about her husband. Not that he got the opportunity.

"Pah, do you see, Doctor?" said the widow, now sitting up, lucid and confident. Albeit a little wild in the eyes. She turned to face Michael. Up close. "I knew I possessed this power. I knew it."

Phoebe looked at Michael. What is she talking about – power?

## 23

The two top-hatted vagabonds, disenchanted with the progress of their mission so far, had turned to the power of prayer for salvation, which then almost immediately hove into view.

"Praise be to the Lord most high. Lookee here, Mr Drago. We should intercept this wagon with our usual persuasive sophistication."

So Drago stepped straight into the roadway, waving his arms. The driver of the cart pulled his pony up to a halt to the shrill accompaniment of whinny and skid. The load of dented, silver milk churns rattled and rolled.

"Kindly forgive the intervention as you go about your business, my good man, and the distress caused to your magnificent steed. However, my colleague and I find ourselves cast upon a mission of mercy that demands passage most expedient to Ormiston Road. Might you know the whereabouts of such a street within these fine environs and be willing also to assist us in our quest? By driving us there to?"

"Ormiston, you say?" The driver was a well-covered man, clearly nourished daily by the produce he carried. He pushed back his leather cap. "Ormiston?"

"That is our destination, good sir," said Skrill. "Might you be able to convey us to such a location?"

The driver thought and shrugged. Drago was very disappointed not to have to yank the man from his seat and pummel the directions out of him, because the man said: "Can, if thy wish. It dun't divert me none from my route."

"Oh," said Skrill, hugely surprised. "That is most civil, my man. Come along, Mr Drago."

So the dreadful duo clambered aboard the back of the cart, amid the wobbly churns, struggling to keep their balance and their hats, as the driver lurched his pony on.

Now, you see, the cart had only travelled a distance of fifty yards, basically across the Halstow Road Bridge spanning the South Eastern Greenwich and Woolwich Branch Railway below, when the driver drew the cart to an abrupt halt.

"Ormiston Road," he said, before pointing to the side turning immediately on the right. "Be jus' over there."

The blue and white painted street name on the side of the first cottage confirmed as much.

Mr Skrill said, "Oh," for the second time in fifteen seconds. But quickly covered his surprise by saying, quite naturally, "Thank you most kindly, my man. You have been most obliging."

And with that, he and Drago jumped down from the cart.

~24~

"Eadie, what power do you possess?" Michael asked calmly.

She tapped her temple, eyes still wild, and whispered: "In my head. Oh, in my head, I already knew my Ronathan was destined to become the Astronomer Royal's Chief Assistant. I had no need to consult the banshee. No need!"

"Yes, Eadie, tell me about this banshee."

"It is the woman who speaks with Nostradamus," she said, as if it were common knowledge. "The spirit who predicted my Ronathan would take his rightful role."

"Eadie…" Michael remained calm and gentle. This was important. "When did you consult the banshee woman?"

"Before the Goronwy Dapper man died. Not long. At the séance." Eadie adopted a mocking voice. "*The position of assistant to the Astronomer Royal shall be taken by Dr Ronathan Chafeskin. This I foresee and thus it shall be.'* Pah!"

Then her face hardened. As did her tone. "But Dapper died anyway! Did he not? Pah! I say keep your seances, Cordelia. And your Nostradamus. Pah!"

Then she gasped. Panic filled her eyes. She now gripped Michael. "The banshee! I should have paid her! Paid her the money! She is in two places at once you know." Cordelia pointed wildly. "In the street right around the corner. Then directly opposite. Two places at once! And my Ronathan might not be…"

A torrent of tears dribbled down her cheeks.

"Oh, my days, these mood changes. This lady is not well," thought Phoebe.

With Phoebe's attention drawn to Eadie's growing mental collapse, Dr Skene seized his chance. He dipped to the side table, snatched up the syringe, shouted something like 'that's enough now'. Giving Michael or Phoebe no chance to react, he lurched forward and plunged the needle into the vein on the back of Eadie's hand.

Immediately her eyes rolled.

"Oh, you idiot!" Phoebe heaved the doctor back, hypodermic and all, and dashed him to the floor. Skirt hitched up; she was on him like a badger.

Well, the man bucked and protested, as best as he could with Phoebe straddling his chest.

Not that Eadie Chafeskin took much in the way of notice, as the chill of the drug snaked its way up her arm. Half a syringe-full was proving more than enough.

Michael dispensed with his Charlie Charm act. Instead, he gripped the woman by the shoulders and fixed her with a firm grip. "Eadie, tell us about the séance. Eadie. Don't go to sleep. Tell me. Who is the banshee?"

He heard her slur something like: "The séance. Cordee ... Raven…" and then her eyes rolled again and she was lost in the arms of Morpheus.

"Eadie's doped with sleepy juice," said Michael, rising to his feet.

"Rats! I fear the doctor is much the same way," said Phoebe, fanning Skene's face with that goodbye gift from Nikola Tesla, which made not the slightest difference. She held up the empty hypodermic. "As he hit the floor, I am afraid he rather jabbed himself. A doctor suffering a taste of his own…."

At the same time, Phoebe and Michael became aware of two figures standing in the doorway.

"Well now, here is a sight most welcome, Mr Drago. It appears, in the name of our Lord, that our fortune takes a turn for the better," smiled the slender weasel.

"Behner, hnur, hnur, hnur," chuckled the thick-set oaf.

"I'm guessing you two are not the warders from the asylum," said Michael.

## 25

"Magister, further you could not be, from that fact," smirked Skrill.

"Fackt, hnur, hnur, hnur," chuckled Drago. And there was an overwhelming truth in that sentiment.

"We left the front door open, didn't we," said Michael, out of the side of his mouth.

"I rather think we did," admitted Phoebe, wrinkling her nose. "Do we know you gentlemen?"

Skrill adopted an obsequious, hand-on-heart pose. "Regretfully, M'lady Le Breton, you do not. But you will, I am certain, be cognizant of our master, His Excellency The Black Bishop."

Ah.

"My associate and I, we are but humble emissaries, commissioned to convey His Excellency's displeasure with you both. And with prejudice most extreme."

Drago and Skrill each made the sign of the cross with one hand, while allowing a length of grey lead piping to slide down from inside the sleeves of their grubby coats, and into the other.

"Was it something we said?" asked Michael, swallowing hard. "We can get you complimentary tickets for the show."

"Michael, they are here to murder us," said Phoebe.

Skrill's mouth stretched to form a malevolent grin. "Mr Magister, yes. But certainly not you, dear lady. Well, let us say not at first."

"Hnur, hnur, hnur."

"In the name of the Lord, shall we, Mr Drago?" invited Skrill. "I think we should." That was the cue.

"Ahh! Not the face!" whimpered Michael, cowering, turning and holding his hands to his cheeks.

With a fearsome shriek, Skrill raised his lead cudgel and leapt the settee, aiming to crack open the back of the cowardly magician's skull.

But instead of the expected impact of the Magister head, Skrill felt a thunderous jolt in his stomach. The air exploding from his lungs. The sense of being flung backwards. A concussive shattering. And then nothing.

Drago watched it unfold. In total horror:

Mr Skrill. Leaping into the air. Shouting, "Ay-eee!" His pipe raised to smash the Godless fiend's head.

But instead...

WHUMPH!

He watched his friend take a gloriously timed Magister back kick, full in the belly, with such a force it launched Mr Skrill clean off his feet and...

KERR-RASSH!

...straight through the central pane in the bay window, and out into the front garden, coming to rest in the hedge.

TINKLE...

Drago was all but too shocked to comprehend. Until he did. And snarled like a raging beast.

His hog face contorted, he turned to mete out revenge on the harlot. And was met square in the chest with a searing, agonising blast. Which shot him back off his feet. Into further pain and total darkness.

Michael watched it happen, in wonder.

Drago roaring in fury. Raising his pipe, turning and taking half a step forward, just as Phoebe lunged, jabbing her Tesla fan straight and true at the oaf's barrel chest.

KA-FFZZZT!

A great flash of energy discharged and Drago was flung into reverse, off his feet, through the open door, into the hall and...

SPLEEE-UMP!

...smashing his head straight through the bannisters of the stairs outside. Where he hung like a lifeless doll.

Drago and Skrill.

For all their murderous elaborations, both had been dispatched in less than ten seconds. My, the Black Bishop would not be pleased.

Phoebe blew the smoke from the tip of her fan.

"Tesla'd," said Michael.

## 26

The smashed front window, the shattered bannister rods, the four people unconscious, slumped hither and yon, two of them broken and the other two drugged. Not to mention why the only pair left standing were finely dressed Music Hall magicians claiming to work for Scotland Yard. Yes, it took a good deal of explanation to the local Constabulary. Especially when three tunic'd officials suddenly rolled up in a horse-drawn ambulance from the Stone House Hospital Lunatic Asylum in Dartford.

It could not have been more apt.

But, after twenty minutes of enduring smooth talk, flattery and the detailed inspection of warrant cards, the Greenwich police were really very glad to see the back of Michael and Phoebe. And any further strange stuff to do with the Special Branch.

"I have to say that donkey kick of yours was impressive," said Phoebe, with her feet up on the dashboard, as Michael steered the Steamo west along Woolwich Road. "And might I say extremely courageous. Considering you were cringing with your eyes shut at the time."

"Whimpering, too. You might as well throw in the whimpering."

"Where did you pick up such an effective move?"

"Watching you."

Phoebe raised her eyebrows, flattered. "Well, that was very effective for a first try."

"Actually, I should admit – that wasn't my first donkey kick. In the future, when we were trying to escape, I used that same move on a female robot called Debbi. Aboard the Dodo, forty feet above Hyde Park."

"And it worked that time?"

"Yes, it did. Apart from where she grabbed hold of my opera cape and damn near strangled me."

"Well, the next time that happens, remember to point your heel. It focusses the impact."

"And there may be a next time," said Michael thoughtfully. "Pheebs, did you find it curious that those two Black Bishop dunderheads knew precisely when and where we would be?"

"I did wonder. But how?"

"I'm thinking maybe Skindrick wasn't the only spy in the Special Branch.

***

With Phoebe in charge of directions, honking and complaining about male drivers, Michael chugged the Steamo through that south bank of the river lunchtime bustle, where everyone conspires to step, saunter and steer in your way. It wasn't until she late-called a sharp right turn onto the new and wonderfully gothic Tower Bridge that they finally got the chance to escape the congestion, and review what they had learned at Eadie Chafeskin's.

"Such was her desperation, she consulted a fortune-teller to learn of her husband's future career prospects," said Phoebe. "Eadie struck me as someone who wanted the very best, so it is perfectly natural she would consult the very best fortune-teller in history – who has been dead for three hundred and fifty years – and who just happens to make regular contact with a medium. I must admit, Michael, combining astrology with the society vogue for speaking with the dead really is an inspired fiddle."

"Absolutely. Nostradamus the fortune-teller. Still sees everyone coming," said Michael.

"Remember, Eadie said if she'd paid the banshee woman, Ron would still be alive. Maybe the banshee made Ron pay with his life."

"Bear in mind, Eadie was rather anxious when she told us," said Phoebe. "Almost hysterical."

"But those Starsign Killings show a whole bunch of care and planning, and a weird precise mind to link them all square with fortune-telling. What do we know about the banshee?"

"The name Eadie gave us before she drifted away was 'Cordee Raven'. Or something."

"Our next move is to find this medium. This Cordy the Raven, whoever she is. Maybe take in one of her séances. Question is, unless she advertises in the papers, how do we find her?"

Phoebe remembered the day of the week. Rats, he wouldn't be in Hindhead. Oh, well. Needs must when the Michael drives.

"I know the very person to ask."

## 27

Phoebe led the way through the hall and up the stairs of number twenty-three Montague Place.

"Arthur? Really? He'd know?"

"Michael, Uncle Art is a polymath, who enjoys myriad interests. Magic, of course. Cricket. Golfing. Alpine skiing. Grief, I remember when he started learning the banjo."

"The banjo?"

"Oh, yes…" said Phoebe, in a tone suggesting gratitude for a pastime which turned out to be a passing fad. "What you might not know is for the past six years Uncle Arthur Doyle has been a fully paid-up member of the 'Society for Psychical Research'. Oh, yes. So, there is every chance he will know someone who has heard of Cordee Raven."

Phoebe tapped on the door to the Doyle apartment. And steeled herself.

"This will not begin well," she told Michael.

"Leave it with me."

The door opened. Only a little. Enough for an eye to peer out.

"Good afternoon, Madam. My associate and I are Scotland Yard investigators looking for a criminal author," charmed Michael. "We heard the best could be found right here."

"Mr Magister," said Jean Leckie, brightly. "And Miss Le Breton." Although that last acclamation was not quite as bright, but better than Phoebe expected.

"He says he is working," said the lady of the house. "But he is nothing of the sort. Come through."

They followed Miss Leckie into the main living room, line astern. Phoebe recalled the last time she and Michael were here, Arthur was nursing Father Connor O'Connor back to fitness with so much care and attention that the priest could stand it no more. Michael tried hard to ignore the image of the Montague Mansions Massacre, firmly reminding himself it now never happened.

Jean knocked on the half open study door. "My darling, it is Mr Magister. And Phoebe."

Arthur Doyle awoke with a jolt. He was sitting at his large desk, his back to the small window, looking ethereal in a grey cloud of inspiring tobacco smoke. Beneath that bushy moustache his grin broadened, he laid down his pipe and there followed much embracing and warm words.

The room was small, panelled, shelved with books, mostly his; a creative sanctuary for a world-famous author in which to do nothing but what he does best.

"Apologies, Uncle Art. What have we interrupted?" said Phoebe, tapping the handwritten foolscap pages piled on the green, leather-top surface.

"Ah," said Arthur, pleased to be asked. "A romance. Almost completed. Concerning the preparations of two much-in-love characters for their wedding. I think possibly to be my finest work to date. Mmm. Mmm. Entitled," he showed the handwritten front page "'A Duet, With Occasional Chorus'."

"Trips off the tongue," nodded Michael, trying to sound convinced.

"That it does," agreed ACD. "And as soon the manuscript is complete, I promise to be along to the theatre to witness the baffling 'Diabolical Tanks of Diogenes' of which I hear so much."

"Uncle Art, we would like your advice."

"With an illusion? Splendid," he ejaculated. "I have penned some ideas."

"No."

"Oh."

"With a case."

"Ah."

Arthur's response did not exactly effuse the kind of enthusiasm Phoebe had rather hoped for.

"Uncle Art, I know you are now frustrated with those innumerable and constant offers to return to detective fiction, but the advice we seek is not so much investigative but more intelligence-related. Believe you me, both Michael and I also turned our backs on criminal investigation, until Superintendent Melville's arm-twisting coercion compelled us to become involved in this particular puzzlement."

Michael stood. "Pheebs, Arthur's right. We're wrong to ask. It's not what he does anymore."

Phoebe looked decidedly miffed. "Not even when that case involves two related and rather mysterious deaths? And a possible third? When we believe both to be murder, with their victims linked to their Star Signs, which in itself is very odd considering both men worked as astronomers at the Greenwich Observatory? No, you are quite right, Michael, I can see how none of that would be of any interest to Uncle Art."

"The past is the past," sighed ACD.

"Which is a shame because the strangest part of the case is a séance. Involving the spirit of Nostradamus." Michael figured this was the last bait they had to hook the great man.

It did.

Arthur sat up. "Nostradamus, you say?"

"You know of him?" demanded Phoebe, suddenly excited. "Nostradamus?"

"Please sit."

They did.

Arthur lowered his voice. "Cordelia Ravenport."

Michael and Phoebe shared one of their knowing looks. That was Eadie Chafeskin's 'Cordee Raven'!

Arthur sat back on his desk, puffed a couple of clouds and continued in a soft voice.

"I learned of Miss Ravenport from various colleagues. A medium new to London society but of swiftly growing popularity. She is a lady of a certain age, who channels Nostradamus in a liaison most alarming to behold. Mmm. Mmm. One asks a question pertinent to one's future and its likely outcome. But during the séance the dear lady becomes so utterly consumed by the spirit of the great seer, she loses all control."

"Uncle Art, how do you know such details?"

Arthur leant forward, resting his forearms on the desk.

"I attended one of her gatherings."

~28~

"Mmm. I visited the dear lady. Not two evenings ago. She lives in Tavistock Chambers on Hart Street, not a ten-minute walk from here. In the company of my fellows from the 'Society for Psychical Research'. Our President, Sir William Crookes and Herbert Wells, the novelist, of course, whom you once met."

"Yes," frowned Phoebe.

"He still has the bruises to prove it," said Michael.

ACD flushed, then continued. "All of us be sceptical fellows. But, do you know, I'm bound to say, we were all astonished to witness the spectacle of Miss Ravenport being physically transported. Astral travelling. Mmm. At one moment she is sitting in the chair beside me. In the next she is possessed by Nostradamus and dissolves, to reappears in another chair, on the other side of the table. Once the spirit has communicated his predictions, and departs her body, Miss Ravenport is physically transported to her original seat. Mmm. It is a thing most remarkable."

Michael and Phoebe listened carefully. Noted the details. Then Michael said: "Arthur, when Cordelia moves between chairs, her astral travelling, do the lights go out?"

"As I recall – well, of course, now you say it, the gas lantern suspended above the table, that *flickers*." Arthur began to frown. "Oh dear, dear. You are not about to tell me you suspect skulduggery?"

"It's very clever. Very slick. And from what you say, timed to perfection. You'll see us pull the same gimmick with 'The Diabolical Tanks of Diogenes'."

"We use identical Garrideb masks," said Phoebe.

"Oh dear, dear, dear," whispered Arthur, as the realisation grew. "There are two of them!"

"Most likely identical twins. I am sorry, Uncle Art."

"How could I not realise?"

"As Michael said, they are very slick. Not only when conducting a séance. The wife of the second victim claimed she saw Cordelia in two places at once, outside her house."

"They bring the science into disrepute." ACD thumped the desk with a determined fist. His papers and inkwell jumped; his pen sprayed a line of black blobs across his manuscript. "Phoebe. Michael. They must be exposed. As nothing short of fraudsters and charlatans."

"And a whole bunch worse," said Michael. "But if we're going to get close to nailing it, we need to get to one of their séances."

"Quite so," said Arthur. "I shall arrange another appointment. Immediately."

Not far short of noon the next day, Michael, Phoebe and ACD waited on the steps of the colonnaded portico of St George's Church, Nicholas Hawksmoor's masterwork on Hart Street, Bloomsbury. Nowadays a fine, nicely-to-do district, but at the time of its consecration, a century and a half ago, the building stood in the midst of deprivation. At the top of the spire stands a statue of King George the First, dressed as an ancient Roman, for reasons known to nobody.

Both Phoebe and Michael were dressed this morning in a more understated manner. Almost drab by their usual standards. Not a thread of sass or skin to be seen. Phoebe in black and white, hair in a bun and round spectacles perched at the end of her nose, trying for the look of a young governess. Michael in mismatching shades of brown. Apart from the new boots. High up the calf, decorated with half a dozen buckles. Flamboyance was thought to be a suspicion-causing distraction on this particular gallivant.

Arthur wore his grey tweed three-piece, with the plus-four trousers, looking as if he'd come straight from the eighteenth green of the Royal and Ancient. He had even waxed the tips of his moustache! So sharply, if he gave anyone a kiss on the cheek he would stab their eye out.

"How do you like the boots, Arthur? They're new."

"A little chic-for-your-shabby, would you say, Michael? Mmm?"

"He just cannot help himself," sighed Phoebe, as a black carriage and pair scraped and clattered to a halt outside the church.

Driver Constable Coxhead was at the reins. He saluted, red nose aglow. The door of the carriage opened and Detective Inspector Pym stepped down.

"We're very grateful you volunteered, Walter," said Michael brightly.

"I drew the short straw," came the reply. He doffed his bowler at Phoebe. "Where did you get your outfit, Magister? Gin Alley?"

"The boots are new, Inspector."

"Mr Wilde having a clear out, was he?"

"Touché, Inspector," said Michael.

Pym was very pleased with that. "So, you really believe without firm evidence you can expose these 'twins' as murderers?"

"Walter, in circumstances such as these in particular, and when dealing with ladies in general, we have to place our faith in our secret weapon," said Phoebe.

"Which is, pray tell?"

"My charm," admitted Michael.

Pym called: "Coxhead! Take us back to the Yard!"

"Inspector," purred Phoebe. "Do you really wish to pass over the opportunity to be hailed as the arresting officer of the Starsign Serial Killers?"

Pym frowned. Looked resigned. Then said: "All right. What is the plan?"

Relatively straightforward, in truth. The entire group would pose as relatives of Arthur's seventh and youngest sister – Bryan. I kid you not. That was her name, Bryan Mary Doyle.

Anyway, Arthur, having been so impressed by Cordelia and Nostradamus during the last séance, had convinced his dullard nephew, his lovely niece and her handsome fiancé to seek advice from the seer concerning their individual futures.

"A clever covert ruse, I wager, Inspector. Mmm? Mmm?" said ACD.

"And I bet I know which relative I am supposed to play in this charade," sighed Pym.

"Exactly, Inspector," said Phoebe, slipping her arm through his. "My handsome fiancé."

Michael mugged a gormless smile, pulled his necktie awry. The nephew.

Which was more than enough for Pym to say: "All right. Lead on."

~30~

Cordelia, prim as ever in her black buttoned-to-the-neck dress, welcomed Dr Doyle and his young relatives with her usual smiling, dotty innocence. The greatest surprise for Michael, Phoebe and Pym was the woman's age. Easily in her seventies.

She led the Doyle family party along the dark passageway, up the two steps and into the windowless panelled séance chamber with the gas mantle hanging down over the middle of the black-clothed table, the one with the white astrological symbols.

The air was heady with incense. The gas lamp burned. Its lighting subdued.

Cordelia invited her guests to take their places around the table. Phoebe continued to fuss over Pym, while Michael simply uttered incoherent noises, inspired by the Drago creature which had tried to murder him yesterday morning.

"Not that seat if you do not mind, my dear," Cordelia told Michael.

"Hnur?" responded Michael, at his gormless best, without a trace of the Americas about him.

"It is the favourite chair of Nostradamus."

"Hnur," grunted Michael, to suggest he understood the order.

With everyone now as comfortable as they could be on the hard wooden chairs, Cordelia took her seat between Arthur and Phoebe. Pym sat next to Phoebe, with the empty seat between himself and Michael.

"Now, my dears, before we commence, if you do not mind, I will ask each of you to state your birth signs. Such knowledge helps Nostradamus concentrate his thoughts, you see."

"Virgo," lied Phoebe.

Pym coughed nervously. "I am Aries."

"The ram!" said Phoebe, eagerly.

"Buhll," slurred Michael. "Me, Torress."

"As you know, dear lady," said Arthur. "I am Geminian."

"Oh, that is wonderful, my dears, such an eclectic mix of lovely starsigns." Cordelia's eyes sparkled with enthusiasm. "Now, have your questions prepared and ready to pass on to Nostradamus, my dears."

"We have many questions," said Phoebe.

"Now, a tiny word of caution. Nostradamus can be a little cantankerous and sharp of tongue. He is, after all, three and a half centuries old. And once he enters me, I have no control over anything which might ensue, or what he may say. But his predictions are rarely ill-founded. Is that not the case, Dr Doyle?"

"Dear lady, since my previous visit, my faith in such a noble spirit of The Other Side remains unimpeachable."

Cordelia beamed, then told all gathered there to place their hands upon the black tablecloth and close their eyes. Which they obliged. The gas lamp dimmed, apparently of its own accord.

"Spirit of the great oracle Nostradamus, pray do enter me," incanted the old spinster. "Do not be shy, my dear. Pray do enter me."

None of the guests around the table sat with their eyes terribly firmly closed, squinting at her every move.

"Nostradamus, are you there, dear?" Cordelia asked, meekly. "Come forth, my dear."

Then, like a judge's gavel:

BANG! BANG!

Everyone jumped.

And Cordelia gasped. Her eyes widened. Her body jerked. Head thrown back. Mouth gaping.

The voice like dry leaves in the wind swept into the chamber. "I hear you, banshee! Sss. I hear you well! Sss. And see you clear. Look ye not upon my myssstic wayssss."

Which again was the point where things livened up, with sibilant whispers and violent spasms as Cordelia Ravenport's body was racked with the spirit's possession. The gas lamp spluttered and flickered.

A blink of total darkness.

Then flickering and the growing yellow glow.

Everyone looked to Cordelia's chair. It was empty.

"Good God," jumped Pym.

"Thossse gathered here," hissed the voice of Nostradamus.

Everyone swung their gaze to the other side of the table. To where Cordelia Ravenport now sat. Next to Michael. Wild eyes wide and mouth a-gaping.

Much like Pym's reaction.

"Tell me now. Ssss. What you wisssh to know."

At which point Michael perked up and dispensed with the gormless nephew guise. He leant across and placed his hand on her wrist. "That was incredible. So good. Has to be the best transposition we've ever seen. But it's okay to stop the act now. We know what you're doing. It's over."

The old woman did not flinch. Continued to stare and gape. Oh, she was good.

"Sssilenceeee," demanded the voice of Nostradamus. "Unhand the banshee, guttersnipe!"

BANG! BANG!

"Please," said Phoebe, slightly tetchy. "I promise you, there is no further need for the drum."

"Ssssilence, I sssay," demanded a furious Nostradamus.

"I admit it," said Michael, addressing 'Cordelia' with a winning smile. "This is the best performance Pheebs and I have ever witnessed. And we're sitting right next to you. But you know better than me, you can't kid a kidder."

"Thisss isss ssssacrilege!"

"Okay. Pheebs, would you mind?"

So she stood, pulled back the vacant 'Cordelia' chair to make room, lifted the tablecloth and bent under the table, poking about in the dark with her parasol.

"Oh, for an Obsidian Lamp at a time like…" They all heard the yelp when she struck something.

"Oh. I am so sorry, Miss Ravenport, I imagine it is rather uncomfortable down there. Let me help you to resume your seat."

With scraping and bumping, Cordelia emerged from beneath the table. Still sweetly benign.

Arthur and Pym looked one way, then the other. So it was true. Cordelia Ravenport was sitting at both ends of the table. They *were* twins. Identical. Dressed exactly the same.

"Pheebs, can you manage a drum roll?"

Phoebe pressed a pedal which tightened the cord which forced the hammer to strike the skin of the drum, a simple contraption rigged up to the table's underside.

BANG! BANG! BANG!

Pym had sufficiently recovered his poise to say to the sister closest to himself: "Let me get this straight. You are Miss Cordelia Ravenport?"

"Yes, my dear, I am," said Cordelia Ravenport.

"So, who are you, Cordelia number two?"

The old woman sitting beside Michael maintained her pose and contained her silence until co-operation with the nice, kind gentleman was encouraged by her sister.

"I am Regan. Regan Ravenport," said Regan Ravenport. The voice was much the same, but less agreeable.

"But on the plus side, ladies," said Michael. "I have to give you full credit. That changeover using the traps below the table. That would have taken days of rehearsal to execute with that kind of speed."

"Oh, that is very kind of you to say so, my dear," said Cordelia, bucking up.

Pym piped up. Intrigued by the requirements of how to put the uncanny into practice. "How did you know there were doors beneath the table?"

"I expect it was the two steps up into this room that were the giveaway, my dear?" asked Cordelia.

"Where the floor has been raised, to create a void," said Regan.

Michael nodded. "A very clever gimmick."

"Oh, I am so pleased you approve. Are we not, my dear?"

"We are, my dear," Regan grudgingly agreed.

"And the way my sister lies in total silence before the clients enter?" asked Cordelia, actively soliciting praise!

"So professional. And awaiting her cue to climb up, as you slip down," said Phoebe. "It was a joy to witness."

"Even with the distraction of the fluttering lamp and the sharp blackout, I have to tell you, ladies, as a close-up illusion this is incredible work." Michael was addressing Arthur and Pym in particular when he announced: "We should be honoured, gentlemen, I believe we are sitting in the presence of the best in the world."

Cordelia, and even Regan, glowed with pride.

"You know what is so teasing about you ladies?" said Michael. "Your name. Ravenport. I think that's a mischief masterstroke. Hidden in plain sight."

"Oh, I am so delighted you think so, my dear, oh thank you," blushed Cordelia. "We were tickled with it, were we not my dear?"

"We were, my dear."

Michael revealed to Arthur and Pym the sisters' real identity.

"Cordelia and Regan are related to the famous Davenport Brothers. William and Ira Davenport, from Buffalo, New York. One of the most successful acts in the U.S."

The twins agreed with pride.

Michael explained to Arthur and Pym how The Davenport Brothers ran the spiritualist act in the U.S. "It was a classic. William and Ira were trussed up tight, wrists and ankles, to chairs inside the Spirit Cabinet with a bunch of musical instruments: guitars, trumpets, violins."

Phoebe continued, just to break up the exposition. "Once the cabinet was locked up tight, they summoned supernatural forces and from outside, the audience suddenly heard the instruments being played. Of course, when the doors were unlocked, the brothers were still tied to their chairs. Wonderful!"

"And successful," agreed Michael. "It was only a lucky peek that helped Nevil Maskelyne spot their slip-knot escape technique."

"You worked out the name Ravenport came from Davenport?" wondered Pym.

"It is there if you want to see it," said Phoebe. "Michael felt there was something in the sisters' name and spotted that if you add a couple of legs beneath the letter D you can form an R, and that is how Davenport becomes Ravenport."

"Oh, I say," gasped Arthur Doyle. "That is first class."

"Not wishing to cause offence, my dear, but unlike yourself, my sister and I have worked hard to soften our accent."

"You see, Arthur? Another example of these ladies' brilliance." Michael offered a generous round of applause toward the sisters.

"You are so very kind, my dear," said Cordelia, blushing some more.

Pym shuffled uncomfortably. Unlike the sisters, his patience with this gathering of the Ravenport Admiration League was beginning to wear in the way of thin. "What about the other … business?"

Phoebe took the hint. "Michael, you should lavish the most important praise upon the sisters' most remarkable achievements."

"I need to ask about the locked door mysteries," he said. "I have to say, how you pulled those off is totally incredible. Getting in and out of Mr Dapper's house, then in and out of Mr Chafeskin's observatory, while keeping the doors locked from the inside. Baffling. All we can think is this: you pick the doors, get in, then lock the door again from the inside. You hide and wait until someone breaks the doors down. Then, during the distraction, you can slip out of the open door, into the night with no one the wiser. Now tell me, ladies. Is that even close?"

Cordelia and Regan looked at one another.

"That picture you paint is so beautifully crafted and most ingenious," said Cordelia. "But it is not even close to being correct, is it, my dear?"

"In fact, it could not be more wrong, my dear."

Excellent. Here it comes. The admission.

"But we would never have any need to practise such an escape, my dear," said Cordelia. "Our one illusion concentrates upon the gatherings we hold here. Why would breaking into houses of others hold any purpose for us?"

"Nor do we know of your Mr Dapple or Mr Chafescreen, my dear. We have never heard of such people, my dear."

Oh. Bugger.

That did not go as planned. Michael was so confident he could flatter the Ravenport Sisters into walking straight into an unguarded comment of self-incrimination. And until that moment he was convinced he had. The disappointment sunk into his stomach. Especially when Arthur and Pym looked hopefully across. Come on. What else have you got?

"But you do know the suburb of Greenwich," tried Michael.

"I cannot think we have ever had the rhyme or reason to visit the district," said Cordelia.

"Never once," agreed Regan.

"Ladies," said Phoebe, "Mrs Eadie Chafeskin will confirm, on oath, in a police court, that you both visited her house demanding a fee for the correct outcome of a prediction made by Nostradamus. She will even swear she saw both of you."

"She may well believe she saw us, but all I can say is, she is either mistaken, or making up spiteful tales," said Cordelia.

"And who would wish to take notice of such a mad woman?" said Regan.

Well, that was it. For once, Michael was stumped for something to say. He and Phoebe had played an instinctive gamble. And lost.

Dammit. They should have realised sweet, little old ladies with a penchant for scheming and murder would be too smart to fall for a bit of his Old Madam and slip up.

Phoebe, frustrated and not a little furious, resorted to direct accusation. The Ravenport Sisters murdered Goronwy Dapper and Ronathan Chafeskin.

"Based upon what evidence, my dear?" said Cordelia.

"You have none!" said Regan.

They were right. And the dear, elderly Ravenport sisters were far too shrewd to be seduced into false security by charm and flattery.

Pym stood and announced himself as an Inspector with Special Branch, warrant card and all. Annoyingly, the Ravenport sisters did not seem remotely surprised. "But I can arrest you both for obtaining money under fraudulent pretence."

"Quite so, Inspector," said ACD, really quite sternly.

Pym reached into his coat pockets for the handcuffs.

"We know you manipulative harpies murdered those two gentlemen," snapped Phoebe. "And very likely other poor souls! With every bogus séance you hold you sow the seed of misery. A pox on the pair of you."

Cordelia and Regan did not react. Just sat there. Impassive.

"But all I have to say is, well played, the Davenport Sisters." said Michael. "You beat us."

Michael and Phoebe stood to leave.

Then Regan, with more than a hint of smug: "By the way. Before you depart, do tell us…"

"Who are you?" said Cordelia, with innocent distain.

For Michael and Phoebe, that was the final crushing insult.

"Compared to you two," said Michael. "We're nobodies."

~32~

With Phoebe and Michael gone, Arthur banged the table with his fist. "Do you know, I'm bound to say," he ejaculated, "I am truly disappointed. In the both of you, ladies. This is not simply a flagrant deception and fraud, but you do grave disservice to the psychic sciences and to those decent practitioners who genuinely commune with the spirit world. And those two good and gifted friends of mine out there," Arthur pointed to the door to indicate Michael and Phoebe, "may at least take some comfort in exposing you two charlatans and knowing you shall never practise your psychic fakery ever again. Mmm? Mmm?"

Pym shook both pairs of handcuffs to dangle them loose, and ordered the sisters to present their wrists, which they duly obliged.

It was about then that Arthur and Pym became aware. Of something. Their attention was drawn to the table. And the black cloth, decorated with the astrological symbols. It seemed to stir. Then ripple. Then gently undulate. And for no reason they could see.

Well, Pym had witnessed his share of very odd doings of late, but this? "Dr Doyle…? What is this afoot 'ere…?"

Arthur felt his spine chill. What would Michael and Phoebe do? Look for the gimmick. The trickery. Where were the wires?

FLLURRRR!

The gas lamp flared brightly.

"What devilry is this? Mmm?"

The twins said nothing. Only stood. Their wrists still benignly offered.

"The manacles, Inspector," said Arthur. "And quickly too, I'll warrant."

With handcuffs open and ready to be snap-locked, Pym stepped forward, but was met with resistance. He tried again. It was like pushing against a soft, invisible wall. He tried again and now found himself unable to move.

Then he felt a welter of pain as the 'cuffs were ripped from his fingers and flung across the room, clattering to the floorboards in a far corner.

Before Arthur could react, the force of Nostradamus bled into the room from everywhere.

"No fiend shacklesss the banshees!"

The tablecloth swirled up from the table. Arthur and Pym, both now rooted, unable to speak, could only watch in awe. The white symbols looked to dance hypnotically as the black fabric gently swayed in the air, before swooping about the room like a wraith, curling itself into a roll.

Arthur and Pym suddenly felt themselves lifted from the ground. Could only watch in terror. As the cloth coiled itself like a serpent. And then struck!

~33~

"I truly thought we could lull them, Pheebs," said Michael, bitterly disappointed. "Never underestimate a Davenport. Deception runs through the veins."

Even though he tapped his cane on the carpeted floor, and she pressed the handle of her parasol against her chin in frustration, at least by waiting in the hall outside the apartment, Michael and Phoebe would be able to watch Cordelia and Regan 'cuffed and marched away to some kind of justice.

"Did you notice the Regan sister?" said Phoebe, reaching for some positives. "She claimed she had never heard of Chafeskin, yet somehow knew his wife was too insane to testify. Not an admission of murder … but I thought the explanation of the locked doors was inspired."

"Falls down on the number of days the Sisters would have had to hole up in Dapper's house, with his decomposing body upstairs, before the door was broken down."

The silence was broken by Phoebe asking about the voice of Nostradamus.

"Has to be some kind of incredible ventriloquism. The kind which puts Fred Russell to shame."

More silence. Until Michael said: "Neither of those women complimented my new boots."

"That did not go unnoticed. And what are they doing in there? How long does Walter take to read them their rights?"

\*\*\*

In the séance chamber, Cordelia and Regan stood, pointing and giggling like schoolgirls.

Watching Arthur Doyle and Inspector Pym, suspended in mid-air. Red faced, silently gasping and their legs kicking. The tablecloth roped about both their necks.

\*\*\*

"Mind you, Michael, you were absolutely right about the names," said Phoebe. "Ravenport becoming Davenport."

"I just *knew* there was something. I mean, come on, Regan and Cordelia Ravenport, Davenport, what kind of names are they anyway? It sounds like the kind of switch Oscar pulls with his fancy crowd-pleasers."

"Oh, my days," said Phoebe. A thought hit her so hard she had to grip Michael's arm. "You're quite right. Their names! But not Oscar Wilde, it's Shakespeare! The daughters of King Lear are Cordelia, Regan – and Goneril."

"There is a third twin?"

They looked at one another, inspired. "The voice of Nostradamus!"

~34~

Michael and Phoebe crashed back into the séance room to be confronted by a sight that even they had to blink twice to believe.

The round table, polished dark wood without that black cloth. And Cordelia and Regan. Standing. Giggling like children. Looking up at the choking Arthur Doyle and Inspector Pym. Their hands to the cloth constricting their necks.

"Let them down!" Phoebe screamed at the twins.

Who giggled some more.

Until…

KERRACK!

Phoebe thrust the handle of her parasol straight into the ribby chest of Regan, sending her staggering backwards, where she cracked her head against the wall and fell in a heap.

Michael threw a chair on the table. Under Arthur's legs. Then another. For Pym.

"It's the third sister!" shouted Michael. "She must be controlling this!"

"You find Nostradamus. I have this."

"Really?"

Cordelia looked at her sister, then back at Phoebe, snarled and screamed and charged, hands and fingernails a blur in Phoebe's face. Only to be met with…

ZHONG!

…an upper cut which smacked the feisty twin right under the chin and snapped her head straight back.

"Okay," said Michael, who promptly turned and ran into the passageway.

Phoebe jumped straight onto the table and wrestled Arthur's legs onto the chair.

***

Michael counted three doors along the passageway. All closed. Where was Nostradamus? How was she doing this? And where the hell was she? The first room Michael barged into was the kitchen. Orderly, bright, cool and empty.

Next door, a bedroom. Two single beds. Floral, bright and cool. Michael swept under the beds with his cane, jabbed inside the wardrobe. Nothing.

He heard Phoebe yelling for him to hurry.

The next room. Tried the handle. Locked. But the handle was warm. Very warm. As was the door. A tight fit within the frame. He barged it with his shoulder but was bounced back.

***

In the chamber, now with Pym's legs supported by a chair, Phoebe used a third chair for extra height. Balancing between the two men. Trying to prise her fingers between the tight black ligature round their necks. It was hopeless. She needed both hands on the same knot. Arthur's face was purple. As was Pym's. Dear Lord, who to save?

Her decision was made. Until the end of the cloth snaked around quickly about her own neck and gripped tight.

## ~35~

Fancy lock-picking gizmos were never an option, nor a running shoulder barge at the door. The passage was too narrow for a run up.

Michael turned his back on the door. Two inches above the handle. The weakest spot of the lock. The screw on the keep would give way.

He raised his knee. And stabbed the back of his boot at the door. A donkey kick.

BAKK!

The door nudged. But only just. His knee jarred more. What was it Pheebs said? 'Point your heel'. So he did. With a huge effort.

321

BAAKKK-KRAK!

The screws flew from the jamb and the door flung inwards, hinging back on itself.

DHOOM!

A blanket of heat met him like an open oven. The room was blinding after the dark hall. He blinked against the glare from a dozen wall-mounted gas mantels. Squinted to force his eyes to adjust. And there she was. Goneril. The third twin.

Nostradamus!

Floating in a glass tank, full of clear solution – but just a human head. Hairless skin puckered and grey. The mouth, a black gash. The eyes closed. Its brow furrowed in concentration.

Below the neck, dangled the withered torso of a baby. Its useless limbs swaying in the fluid.

It was utter revulsion at the image that shuddered Michael to a gawping halt.

He saw the head react to the noise of the door. The eyes opened and glared. Milky and repulsive. Lined with red.

Michael snapped himself back to reality. And his purpose: "'Nostradamus'! Let them go! You let them go now or I swear I will…!"

"Sssso sssay you!" The blackened lips mouthed words of sneering contempt, but the voice was all around. "Asss I sssstrangle harder ssstill!" The brow furrowed. Even more intense.

Michael charged toward the tank. His cane thrust forward Phoebe-like, ferrule tip first, aiming straight at the front pane of glass. And struck.

Against what felt like a soft brick wall. He was two inches short.

The heel of his hand on the silver skull top of the cane gnawed with pain as he tried to push. He leaned in with all his weight. The unseen force gave an inch, but that was all.

Nostradamus frowned. Deep concentration. Keeping Michael at bay, and squeezing Phoebe, Arthur and Pym toward their death rattles.

Michael shoved again. His face contorted. His palm in agony.

A desperate thought. A final try. With the cane. He twisted the silver skull. Just enough. The extra length spiked from the end of the ferrule. Three thin inches. Which struck the glass.

KRACK!

A moment of nothing. Then the brittle glass splintered.

Nostradamus flared her eyes open. Looked down as the cracks traced across the pane like a spider's web.

"No…sssss!" gasped the arid voice of Nostradamus, as the glass gave out and the fluid burst from the tank…

Zzzzitzzz – SSHHHPLOSH!

…cascading onto the floorboards and the front of Michael's trousers. The grey head and torso slopped and dropped out to land on his boots – and the force was gone.

Michael looked down. Saw the black mouth on the head gaping and the wasted body flapping like a fish on a quayside. Saw the black dots. Felt the room spin. Then nothing.

***

The next thing he felt was a hand. Tapping his cheek. And a voice he knew. Not the rasping whispers of Nostradamus. This was more a sensuous purr.

"Michael, Michael, wake up."

He wasn't dead. But the face he opened his eye to was angelic. "Pheebs."

"Welcome back," said Phoebe

"Is anyone…?"

"All quite well, considering. Uncle Art and the Inspector are rather sorer about the neck than I am, but we are breathing again and so very grateful.

Phoebe helped Michael rise gently to his soggy feet. They both looked down on 'Nostradamus'.

"Your new friend does not look so chipper," said Phoebe. "But I believe you have that effect on women."

Michael smiled. Then nodded. "I think we did well."

"I rather think we did."

"You know, I've ruined these boots."

"Oh, you annoying man!"

And she hugged him tight.

~36~

Two days later found Michael and Phoebe restored to their colourful finery, a black choker covering the raw weal on her neck. They were sitting with Inspector Pym at the desk of

Superintendent Melville at Scotland Yard. Pym's throat was wrapped in a white bandage.

Melville was pleased to report that Cordelia and Regan Davenport were currently held at Her Majesty's pleasure, awaiting a decision by Sir Augustus Stephenson, the Director of Public Prosecutions and the Treasury Solicitor, as to whether or not the sisters should stand trial for murder.

"Murder? How?" said Michael.

"A search of the sisters' apartment..." gravelled Pym.

"Dear God, Inspector, is that you, or Nostradamus," faked Michael with alarm.

Pym pulled an impatient face. "A search of the sisters' apartment uncovered a Large Velvet Crab housed in a fish tank in the kitchen, with every indication it was the creature employed in the death of Goronwy Dapper."

"And the third twin? The remarkable Goneril, or 'Nostradamus'?" asked Phoebe. "Is her body now subject to all manner of scalpel-led examinations by unseen government scientists in unknown locations?"

"I am not at liberty to say," said Melville, suggesting Phoebe was not far from the truth.

"Maybe being all brain helped her to project that voice and those crazed, supernatural mental powers," said Michael. "Do we know how she did it?"

Melville shook his head. "And perhaps we never shall."

He slid the sealed envelope across the polished desk toward Phoebe, who stopped it with a gloved hand. "From a grateful nation."

"Thank you, kind sir, she said."

"And thank you. Both of you," said Melville, standing to suggest the meeting was over. "Until the next time."

"We'll see," said Michael, opening the door of the office and allowing Phoebe to leave first.

She slipped her arm in his as they walked away from Scotland Yard.

Neither looked back.

## THE END

## ~ ADDENDUM ~

## MICHAEL'S FORGOTTEN MEMORIES IN HIS OWN WORDS.

I thought about paraphrasing, heaven forfend embroidering, Michael's account of his epiphany and of what he meant when he finally woke up in Dr Phunn's sarcophagus and announced he 'remembered it all'. And then blamed me – and Wicko – for not telling him. But once you have read his account of what happened, you may understand our reasons keeping the strange circumstances from him. He would never have believed us anyway.

So instead, I reproduce for you below those restored memories in fuller detail, and written in his own words.

*Let me tell you straight from the off, I don't know if any of this is going to hold your attention because I'm more a showboating talker than a writer, as you're about to see, but the Professor asked me to tell you this first hand, 'now the misty fog has* ~~discrpated, dissipated~~' *he means 'blown away'.*

*Oh. By the way, I should tell you that I'm writing this sitting here, up in my dressing room, waiting for Phoebe to walk out on stage and build up my big introduction after my 'mysterious' three-week absence. And truth be told at the moment I'm still not feeling too clever. But Dr Phunn says dying, and then being dragged right back from death with your burnt lungs and skin patched up with the weirdest medical juju of the nineteenth century, affects different people in different ways. Yeah. As if I'm going to meet anyone else like me to compare patient notes with any time ever.*

*So. What do I mean by 'remembering it all'? I mean remembering everything I forgot right up to when I first* ~~met~~ *saw the Professor and his friend Nikola Tesla. And do you know what? Turns out most of what happened in that time is not that memorable!*

*My childhood? Who cares. Not me. Because now I recall the whole thing I might just as well have kept it forgotten. Apart from borrowing an amateur conjuring book from the orphanage library and Mrs Ward the over-friendly librarian, who always encouraged you to take out more than books! So, let's* pick it up from when I was aged 18 and what happened ~~which~~ that caused me to find myself thrown back 112 years to 1889. Still in New York.

I was 18 and performing a magic act on Broadway. Well, okay, I worked as a street magician on the sidewalk of Broadway picking up dollars here and there before getting moved on.

And I kept that side of things going during the day, even after I landed a job as the featured illusionist in the nightly "Spectacle d'Horreurs", staged in a small theatre off Broadway. Well okay, it was a long way off Broadway. In the Lower East Side.

Anyway, it'll come as no shock to you that there was a woman involved. Mature. Worldly wise. Dark hair. You know me. And I like to think she was taken with my 'weave and faro shuffle' with the card deck that morning on Wall Street. She stopped and got to talking. Saying she was a financial director with time to pass before a lunchtime meeting and I'm guessing you can already see where this is headed. Oh, she was dressed the part and talked as if she knew what she saying, but when she didn't suggest taking a hotel room, but knew the way up to the clock tower of the chapel on Fulton Street, by the station, my alarm bells should have jangled, or at least tinkled. But the day was going pretty well so far and it wasn't yet 10 a.m.

So, anyway, she sneaked us into the clock room, half way up the tower which houses all those important cogs and works, the time-keeping stuff I never gave much of a thought to back then.

Yes, clothes were removed, and shame on me, none of it with any thought of respecting the beautiful building we'd just invaded. Then it hit me! And whatever it was was hard and heavy. I didn't even see her pull out the damned cosh. I think she was out of that clock room before I hit the floorboards.

I remember the dreams I had while I was out. Not pictures as such, but sounds. The commotion. Outside. Somewhere. Everywhere. Incredibly loud sounds. Then this roar and the air being hit by this flash of energy. I remember getting lifted. Snatched away to a place of heat and cold and falling. That terrible constant falling. Then crashing to the floor in a heap. It was that that made me sit straight up. I remember the smell of burning and the cogs smoking. And finding I'd been robbed. Of everything. My wallet, cash, and my clothes! Except for my jacket, which was rolled up under my head like a pillow. So maybe the thieving city woman con-artist wasn't all bad.

Anyway. There I was, in the clock tower of this great old chapel. No cash. No cards. No pants. But knowing I could walk away with my dignity intact. And here's how.

*I wrapped the arms of the jacket around my waist and tied them off in front of me. It was just enough to cover what I needed to cover to go and find one of New York's finest to report my robbery. But then here's where it started getting weird. Well, even more weird.*

*I remember staggering down the stairs as best I could, then sneaking out the rear door and into the little graveyard this chapel has out back. The graveyard was the same. The chapel was the same. But that was it. On Vesey Street to the right, and Fulton to the left, none of the buildings I recognised. And there was no traffic. No sirens. No horns. No shouting. There were horses in the street and carriages. City men in top hats and women with long black skirts and bonnets.*

*So that's the memory I lost. How I came from 2001 back to 1889, and being found by Professor More and Nikola Tesla, in nothing but a jacket, huddled terrified against a gravestone.*

*And after a whole bunch of, well, adventures, mishaps, here we all are, ten years later. 1899. In London. From what I hear. the Professor is planning to tell his side of story. How he and Wicko and the Phunns got here. But that's for his next book.*

*Right now, I better stop. I can hear Pheebs downstairs onstage building up my back-from-the-dead introduction. It's showtime. And, you know what, suddenly I'm feeling better. At least I'm alive. What the heck else can happen?*

*Best wishes – Michael*

*X*

Coming Soon
~THE CONAN DOYLE CURIOSITY~
STEAM, SMOKE & MIRRORS IV

~1~

"Arthur Conan Doyle has disappeared!" gasped H. G. Wells.

Wicko's heart had sunk as soon as he saw the sepia image of the author, fizzing and crackling on the screen of the Spectrascope. And not so much at the news.

"Say that again, Aitch," sighed Wicko impatiently, into the Communication Tube.

Never mind anything of a cliched civility, like 'Hello, Mr Wells, the renowned writer, how nice to see you, would you please mind repeating that urgent statement?"

No. Here at the Metropolitan Theatre of Steam, Smoke and Mirrors, he got: "Say that again, Aitch?"

I suppose Wicko's brusque insouciance stemmed from Herbert George Wells' last visit to the theatre and his misguided incident with Miss Phoebe Le Breton, some goose grease and a rolled-up copy of the Strand Magazine.

You see, in spite of his slender frame, and that nasally high-register voice, and a moustache so hispid it could shame a hairy walrus, and those permanently weary eyes, Wellsy was an absolute demon for the ladies. He was! Dear Lord, he made the antics of Father Connor O'Connor, our holy local specialist in the laying-on-of-hands, seem positively monastic.

"No wonder Herbert's eyes are always weary," Michael had archly observed.

Naturally, on that unfortunate occasion, Phoebe had sent the man politely on his way with a dented ego and matching scrotum and no more was said. That was then, but this was now.

"Wicko, my dear chap, you must believe me," whined Wells. "Arthur Conan Doyle has disappeared. Vanished!"

"Well, he's not in here," huffed Wicko, not even trying to sound as if he cared.

"But as a matter of fact, he is," said Wellsy, who could be given to a patronising pomposity and on this occasion *was* so given.

"As a matter of fact, I am. Mmm? Mmm?" echoed the voice of Arthur Conan Doyle, in that recognisable, gently fading Edinburgh burr.

Hold up. "Arthur? Is that you?"

Wicko adjusted a couple of red valve wheels plumbed into the side of his Stage Door Lobby desk. Half a turn here and there. Just enough to poke the lens on the bellows camera bolted beside the Stage Door outside round to the left and over to the right. Our dwarfish friend even leaned forward for a closer peer at the screen. Very odd. There was Wellsy in his dark suit, wing collar and tie. But where was ACD?

"I haven't got time for messing about, Aitch," said Wicko. "We've just rung down a show and we're all tired."

The second performance had gone well, with a standing ovation, two altercations and three people in the audience fainting clean away.

"Perhaps you will allow me a few precious moments to prove it to you, m' dear Wicko. Mmm? Mmm?" asked the voice of Arthur Conan Doyle.

Then, to Wicko's great indignation, the Stage Door jolted, clicked, hissed, opened and then swung inwards, closely followed by H. G. Wells and nobody else.

"Here, do you mind!" protested Wicko. jumping down out of his seat. "This is a secure backstage area."

"Wicko, you must surely *now* appreciate my presence," said the voice of ACD. "Mindful that Herbert does not know the entry code on the door, what!"

"Well, I do *now*..." smiled Wellsy, having watched the letters M A G I C typed into the keyboard outside.

It was now that Wicko noticed H. G. Wells was clutching a brown paper parcel, tied up with sisal. About eighteen inches square, six inches high, and whatever was wrapped up inside was clearly no effort to carry.

"Yeah. All right, Art," said Wicko, looking cautiously about, up, down, left, right. "I give in. How are you doing this? You can't be hiding in the package."

"It is a splendid ruse, is it not? Mmm? Mmm?" chuckled Arthur.

"Ventriloquism?"

"I have talents many-fold but that is not one of them," said Wellsy, smiling.

"Hidden speaker horn?"

"It has been said, but not on this occasion," said Wellsy, grinning.

Wicko was not so jollified. In fact, he was flummoxed. And beginning to bristle with resentment. So rather than send for Michael and Phoebe, he reached into one of his Stage Door desk drawers, pulled out a Pulsa Pistol and aimed it two-handed, straight at H. G. Wells.

"Arthur!" he called to the unseen figure. "Tell me how you're doing this right now, or I'm shooting Aitch!"

Wellsy twitched, cleared his throat, flicked his eyes to the empty space on his right and said from the corner of his mouth, "I believe now would be the time to tell him, Arthur."

"Tell me what?" said Wicko, adjusting his aim from Wellsy's chest to, well, you can imagine.

Not that it would afford much in the way of protection, but Wellsy lowered the brown parcel anyway to cover the new target.

Silence.

"Arthur!" encouraged Wellsy, now more than a little nervous.

"Yes, yes, very well, mischief over," said Doyle. "You see, Wicko, it really is quite simple. Mmm? Mmm?

I am invisible!"

~2~

"So we see, Arthur," said Michael. "Or in this case…"

"…do *not* see," finished Phoebe.

They were standing on the house-lit stage of the theatre, along with Wicko and myself, all of us looking at H. G. Wells still holding the parcel, and with that pleased-with-himself face on. And no sign of Arthur Conan Doyle.

I asked if either famous author would care to quickly enlighten us. This, after all, presented unhappy memories of our most recent gallivant: the unseen voice of Nostradamus revealed as a grotesque homunculus.

"It began when I received a message from our friend, Sir William Crookes," said Wellsy.

"Yes, it did," said ACD. From over there, somewhere.

"Sir William Crookes, the scientist?" said Phoebe. She turned to Michael. "He invented the Crookes Tube and the Crookes Radiometer."

"That is exactly right, Miss Le Breton," said Wellsy, with a swagger.

"Sir William Crookes. Very smart man," nodded Michael.

"You have no idea, do you?" whispered Phoebe.

"Not a clue," whispered Michael.

Arthur Doyle's voice pitched in again. "Upon receiving the missive, Herbert insisted I join him at Sir William's home to share this most recent discovery."

"It was a cathode tube emission dispenser," said Wellsy, "which, when directed toward a living being, saturates the cells with such properties of transparency as to render the tissue impossible to see."

"An invisibility ray!" said Michael, suddenly interested.

We all tried hard not to gasp. The myth of Plato's 'Ring of Gyges' and subject of Wellsy's best-selling imagination had been made real? Really?

I know Sir William Crookes, he is a good friend of mine. A polymath with a remarkable brain. Particularly fond of physics, investigating the properties of the Aethyr waves in telepathy. But it was his work with spectroscopic light and cathode rays, what he called 'The Fourth State of Matter', which always fascinated me.

Sir William was also the President of the 'Society for Psychical Research' which was how he knew Wellsy and ACD.

"He was proud to announce that my notion of 'The Invisible Man' had been successfully pressed into service," swanked H. G. Wells, to Phoebe in particular.

"To be fair, that is incredible," said Wicko.

"Absolute genius," said Michael.

"And totally irresponsible," snapped Phoebe. "Uncle Art, how could you allow yourself to be irradiated with rays when not having the faintest idea of the consequences or side effects?"

"My dear, Sir William is a responsible scientist. Mmm? Mmm?" said Arthur. "By Jove, he has spent months testing exhaustively. And the effect on the tissues remains for only two hours at most before one's corporeal visibility is restored. The purpose of this demonstration was for you and Michael to consider the possibilities for the show, what!"

"So, Arthur, what's it like?" said Michael, unconvinced. "Does it hurt?"

"Ah, well, no. You see, in this state of invisibility, one's senses remain unimpaired. I can see and hear perfectly well, smell, touch, and of course, with no clothes on, feel the cold."

"So we can see," said Michael.

We all nodded in agreement.

It was only Arthur who had failed to notice that the invisible effect on his tissues was beginning to deteriorate and his nude body was now gently fading back into view.

And even with the best will in the world, I could never say ACD in all his glory was a pleasant sight to behold. Mercifully Wellsy started unwrapping the paper parcel of clothes.

"Quickly, Arthur. I believe you may need these."

*** 

Less than an hour later, Michael had steered our horseless carriage, the Steamotivator to Number Seven, Kensington Park Gardens, the imposing six-storey Queen Anne villa in London's Notting Hill. The home of Sir William and Ellen Crookes and their six children.

It was Sir William who asked Wellsy and ACD, having played their childish prank, to invite us all along to his house. Sir William was keen to personally demonstrate what he called 'natural magic at work'.

His extensively equipped workroom was set in the cellar. In this laboratory many of the great advances in physics of recent times had been made.

The entire house was in darkness, save for the orange light outlining the edges of the drawn curtains at the basement window.

ACD and Wellsy led the way down the stone steps at the front of the house, and as we all filed behind, the door of the basement opened, flooding orange light out into the darkness. The slight figure of Sir William Crookes stood there to welcome us. But standing he was not. More leaning. His hand held to a head wound. From which flowed a steady stream of blood.

Arthur and Phoebe scrambled forward to catch Sir William before he collapsed. Both heard him whisper:

"A man … in a black hood … the Invisibility Ray. It has been taken…"

~TO BE CONTINUED~

# BIBLIOGRAPHY

As ever, I scoured hundreds of sources for factual information with which to support 'The Nostradamus Curiosity' but the following books were particularly helpful.

'Dr. Joe Bell – Model for Sherlock Holmes' by Ely M. Liebow (Popular Press, the University of Wisconsin Press, 2007)

'Dynamite, Treason & Plot – Terrorism in Victorian & Edwardian London' by Simon Webb (The History Press, 2012)

'Horror in Silent Films – a Filmography 1896-1929' by Roy Kinnard (McFarland & Company, 1995)

'Lord Grimthorpe 1815-1905' by Peter Ferriday (John Murray, 1957)

'Regency Slang Revealed – Grose's Dictionary of the Vulgar Tongue & Later Versions – Organised and Indexed' by Louise Allen (2016)

'Stars Who Made The Halls' by S. Theodore Felstead (T. Werner Laurie Ltd., 1946)

'The Cosmical Horror of H.P. Lovecraft – A Pictorial Anthology' edited by Stefano Piselli, Federico de Zigno and Riccardo Morrocchi (Glittering Images)

'The Power of the Mind' edited by Dr. Carl Sargent (Orbis Publilshing, 1986)

'The Science Fiction Book – an Illustrated History' by Franz Rottensteiner (Thames & Hudson, 1975)

'The Triumphs of Big Ben' by John Darwin (Robert Hale, 1986)